TUMBLEDOWN

Visit us at www.boldstrokesbooks.com

By the Author

Snowbound

Desolation Point

Tumbledown

TUMBLEDOWN

by
Cari Hunter

2014

This Trade Paperback Original Is Published By
Bold Strokes Books, Inc.
P.O. Box 249
Valley Falls, NY 12185

First Edition: February 2014

CREDITS
EDITOR: CINDY CRESAP
PRODUCTION DESIGN: SUSAN RAMUNDO
COVER DESIGN BY SHERI (GRAPHICARTIST2020@HOTMAIL.COM)

Acknowledgments

Thanks first and foremost to Rad, for giving this one a chance. To Cindy, for comma-wrangling and for sound advice. To Sheri, for another gorgeous cover. To Kelly (my long-suffering Work Wife), who gets possibly the worst name-check ever and is still giddy about it. To the lovely ladies on the C-Spot forum, for Kitty and Frances, laughs, loot, and knitted goods. To all those who picked up the first two, left feedback, made friends, and gave Boo such a big head. And to Cat, for a splendid, tireless beta, but mainly for her unwavering support and love.

Dedication

For Cat

We make a sensational team

CHAPTER ONE

It was always the first thing Caleb did, before his cup of coffee, before he dressed, before he ate the breakfast that Leah set in front of him. He had told her countless times how expensive the computer had been, as if that fact alone meant his efforts were righteous. The sleek black machine was high spec, and the e-mails were sent into a series of temporary accounts that would be difficult for the feds to track or trace.

Leah placed his coffee on the desk and stood by his side, counting the messages as they arrived: twelve in total. The program began to decrypt the code in which they were written. Five of the messages served only to confirm that their senders would continue their efforts, the latest in facial recognition software and straightforward searches on name variants having found nothing. With sweat dampening the palms of her hands, she watched as Caleb opened each of the remaining seven in sequence. One by one, he compared the photographs or descriptions with the two images stored on his desktop. She knew every inch of the young women's faces by now, and she discerned as quickly as he did that none of the search algorithms had yielded anything useful.

She stepped back as he closed the computer down and ran his hand over the coarse growth of stubble on his chin. The negative outcome was not unexpected, nor would it discourage his efforts, but she could never be certain how he would react in the short term.

"My daddy always preached patience and perseverance," he said, his tone pleasant and conversational.

"Your daddy would be proud of you," she told him. She could feel the sweat cooling on her skin.

He nodded once before picking up his coffee and heading into the bathroom. She waited for the door to close completely and then sat in his chair until the trembling stopped.

The water swirled rapidly down the drain, leaving rust-red clinging to the white porcelain in a vivid tidemark. Sarah gripped the brush and scrubbed at the stubborn stains beneath her fingernails. The skin on her fingertips grew tender from the vigorousness of her efforts, but she continued until only the faintest trace of the color remained. She used a detergent-soaked cloth to wipe the sink clean and dumped the garbage into a cardboard box so it would be easier to burn. When she swiped the steam from the bathroom mirror, she barely recognized the woman looking back at her.

"Holy crap."

The exclamation—and the wolf whistle that followed it—came from the doorway. Sarah grinned, turning slowly to face her partner.

"You like it?" she asked. She fished an empty pack out of the box and read from the back cover. "This month we've gone for *Autumn Brilliance*, which apparently 'adds a touch of mischief to every woman's day with its feisty hints of red and plum.'" She checked the mirror again and frowned. "Personally, all I see is brown."

Alex crossed the small distance between them and let strands of Sarah's hair fall through her fingers before taking hold of one particular length. "This bit looks kinda feisty," she said seriously.

Sarah laughed. "Idiot." The laugh turned into a sigh as she felt Alex's lips touch the side of her neck. "Y'know, it's not true what they say about blondes having more fun."

"No?" Alex breathed the word against Sarah's throat. "That's a relief; I don't remember the last time you were blond." Her hands were already beneath Sarah's tank top and stroking across her chest. "So you feeling mischievous, then?"

"Maybe," Sarah hedged, but she hummed low in her throat as Alex pushed a hand below the waistband of her pants. "Oh shit, *definitely*."

Alex chuckled and Sarah leaned back into the warmth of her body, feeling the starchy scratch of Alex's uniform shirt against her bare arms.

"You're on late," she said. "You have a good day at the office, dear?"

"Not bad." Alex adjusted her grip, all but propping Sarah up as she moved her other hand in slow, lazy circles. "Have to say, though, it just got a hell of a lot better."

Sarah murmured when Alex kissed her forehead, but she didn't wake. Tiptoeing out of the darkened bedroom, Alex heard sharp toenails tap-tapping across the wooden floor of the living room as Tilly—their rescue mutt with lopsided ears and a tail that had been chewed off by some unidentified critter—came to join her.

"Hey, girl." She patted Tilly's side and let her lead the way through the kitchen to the back door. "Five minutes, then you can help me do my checks."

The air that came drafting in when Alex opened the door hadn't been cooled much by the setting of the sun, and it carried with it the scent of pine and of the honeysuckle that Sarah had planted close to the back porch. Tilly headed straight toward the trees and disappeared into the shadows, muffled grunts and the sound of her scrabbling in the dry grasses the only indication of her whereabouts. A thin crescent moon and the soft glow from the kitchen window provided enough light for Alex to negotiate her way down from the porch and across to the hen coop to ensure that the girls were safely secured for the night. An indignant bout of clucking told her that they were all accounted for and unimpressed at being disturbed.

In response to a low call, Tilly trotted back to Alex, and together they returned to the cabin. The bolts installed to the top and bottom of the back door slid easily into place and, with Tilly at her heels, Alex walked around each room, checking that the windows were locked and that nothing had been disturbed.

"Okay, Tilly-bud," she said and then shook her head at herself; the nickname was Sarah's invention, but it seemed to be sticking. "You're in charge." The announcement earned her disdainful looks from Flossie and Bandit, the two cats entwined on the sofa, but they seemed too cozy to hold a real grudge. She left the menagerie to its own devices and crept back into the bedroom.

"All safe and sound?" Sarah asked, her voice thick with sleep.

Alex lay down beside her and inched closer to her warmth. "Snug as a bug in a hug," she confirmed.

"Rug," Sarah corrected her. "Snug as a bug in a rug."

"Like that makes any more sense." Alex spoke through a yawn, and the only response was Sarah's steady breathing. She smiled, tucked the sheets around them both, and closed her eyes.

❖

The high-pitched beep shocked Alex from a dreamless sleep. For a moment, she was completely disoriented, her heart beating so rapidly against her breastbone that it felt like it was quivering in her chest. Her surroundings slowly came into focus: the simple wooden posts of the large bed, the knitted throws cast carelessly toward the end of the mattress, welcome in winter but too thick for the summer heat. They had forgotten to close the drapes, and through the slats on the shutters she could see that it was still dark outside.

"Yours or mine?" Sarah sounded as muddled as Alex felt. Alex heard her slapping against the small table at her side of the bed, and the beeping noise shifted, broadcasting itself with greater intensity as Sarah lifted her pager.

"Oh, whose bloody stupid idea was this?" With a groan, Sarah rolled over and sat up, her movements automatic and clumsy as she reached for the clothes always set out in readiness.

"I think it was your idea," Alex said, flicking a lamp on so that Sarah could see to get dressed. Sarah turned to scowl at her, and Alex choked back a laugh. "Yep, pretty sure it was yours."

Two minutes later, Sarah had made a phone call and was heading into the living room, one sock flapping where she hadn't quite pulled it up enough. Her hands reached automatically to tie her hair back, though it was too short to need that now. Alex followed her out and perched on the arm of the sofa, watching her absently pet Tilly in passing and then pick up her bag.

"Go back to sleep, love," Sarah said, although she must have known that Alex would do nothing of the sort.

"Be safe." Something in Alex's expression or the tone of her voice must have given her away, because Sarah ran back and kissed her gently.

"I will."

The soft touch on Alex's cheek made her want to grab hold of Sarah's hand and force her to stay home, but the contact was only fleeting and she was gone before Alex could say or do anything else.

"Dammit," Alex whispered, listening to the Jeep's tires crunching over the loose stones of the driveway. As if sensing her distress, Flossie inched onto her knee, while Bandit stalked into the kitchen and demanded his breakfast in a series of shrill yowls. Alex shook her head at his increasingly desperate dramatics, trying instead to concentrate on Flossie's purring in the hope that it would soothe her nerves. "I know, I know," she said as Flossie kneaded her thighs and showed no real indication that she was listening. "Sarah's a big girl who can take care of herself." Tilly's ears pricked up at the mention of Sarah's name and she gave a yip.

"Oh, you only take her side because she spoils you rotten," Alex retorted, a little embarrassed to be holding a conversation with a dog. She carefully set Flossie aside and went to make herself a drink.

Alex dipped a chunk of chocolate into her coffee, held it there long enough for it to leave a slight film on the surface of the liquid, and then pulled it out and sucked the melted mess into her mouth. It was a disgusting habit that had always appalled Sarah, but Alex figured it was Sarah's fault for introducing her to Cadbury's chocolate in the first place. There was only a third remaining of the bar she had just sneaked a piece from, and she made a mental note to e-mail Ash—one of Sarah's closest friends—to ask her to send over a selection of candy in time for Sarah's birthday. The thought prompted her to steal a glance at her watch. She told herself she was trying to work out what time it would be for Ash in the UK and absolutely, definitely not checking how long it had been since Sarah phoned with an update. The callout had been to a febrile child who had had a seizure. The mother was distraught, and Sarah was waiting with her until the ambulance arrived. Dispatch had given an ETA of fifty minutes, forty-two and a half minutes ago.

Alex cradled her mug, leaned her head back against the sofa, and stared at the ceiling fan as it slowly rotated. No one knew where she and Sarah were, she reminded herself, something she did so often it had become habitual. The problem was that she never really believed it, no matter how reassuring the updates they received from Mike Castillo, the FBI agent who had taken a personal interest in their well-being, speaking to them at least once a month throughout the two years since she had first met Sarah.

Despite her unease, she found herself smiling at the seeming normality of that phrase, as if they had met in a club, or through a mutual friend or a dull nine-to-five office job. In reality, she had found Sarah terrified and bleeding, hiding in a crevice beneath a rock in the North Cascades as two violent criminals hunted her down. She and Sarah had spent almost a week fighting to stay alive in the wilderness, and they had come out on the other side of that ordeal bruised, battered, and somewhat surprised to find themselves very much in love. For a short while, they had also been five hundred and eighty thousand dollars richer, thanks to money they had been awarded for assisting in the apprehension of an escaped convict and the large-scale disruption of the terrorist group with which he had been operating.

Alex lowered her head, tension giving her an unpleasant ache in the back of her neck. Before she and Sarah had left the hospital, Castillo had given them a warning, and his words always came back to torment her at moments like this: "This group did not go down lightly, and they did not all go down. Do you understand?"

Nicholas Deakin, the late founder of the Church of the Aryan Resistance, had had a tight-knit family and a devoted following. Alex and Sarah had been instrumental in causing his death and primarily responsible for the breakup of his organization. As their statements had also resulted in the incarceration of two of his most trusted lieutenants, Alex had no doubt that she and Sarah were right at the top of the Deakin family shit list.

The coffee had gone cold, but she gulped it regardless, to ease the dryness of her mouth. She knew that, logically, she should feel safer. They had moved to Avery, a tiny town situated deep within Aroostook County, Maine, just over a year ago. It was, as Sarah put it, as far away from the Cascades as they could get without falling off America altogether. Their small log cabin was nestled in thirty acres of forest that sloped gently down toward the shores of Avery Lake, and it took a lot of finding for anyone unfamiliar with the access road. After sticking a pin in a phone directory, they had both changed their surnames to Hayes, and they had repeatedly altered their hairstyles and hair colors.

When in company, Sarah—having the more distinctive accent—took pains to temper it, making it less obviously northern English and more regionally indeterminate, and they were cagey about any personal details they gave to their new friends and colleagues. So far, at least, their precautions appeared to have worked; no one seemed the slightest bit aware of what had happened to them during that October storm.

Alex took her mug into the kitchen. The sky was lighter, with another hot day forecast. She flicked the kettle on and spooned coffee into her mug, making it stronger than usual and adding sugar for good measure. She knew she would need the caffeine; her shift started at seven a.m., and there was no way she was going back to sleep.

"Here you go, sweetie. You don't like that, do you? I'm going to take it off now." Sarah dialed the oxygen cylinder down and lifted the small mask away. Candice Ryman rocked her son gently, her eyes still wide with fear.

"It was so sudden," she said tonelessly. "He was fine going to bed, but he woke me up crying and then he just…and with Grant at work…" She shook her head.

"I know. It must have been horrible for you." Sarah leaned Grant Jr. forward and slipped his pajama top over his head. "Can we get him stripped down to his nappy—" She corrected herself immediately. "Sorry, diaper? It'll help cool him down."

Candice managed a weak smile at Sarah's mistake and cooed at Grant Jr. as he began to move more purposefully. Her own demeanor relaxed as he slowly recovered, and she helped Sarah to undress him.

"I like your accent," she said once he was settled again. "It's quite unusual. You're British, aren't you?"

"Yes, that's right," Sarah said, relieved when Candice nodded vaguely and didn't press for specifics.

"And you live with Officer Hayes now?"

"I do." Although she answered casually, she felt anxiety of a different sort twisting like a knot in her stomach. Avery was a very small town, and she was never sure whether her relationship with Alex would prove to be an issue for its residents. The fact that Alex worked for the local police force and Sarah volunteered as an emergency medical responder certainly hadn't hindered their acceptance into the community, but she was always wary of that initial awkward contact with strangers.

"Margot St. Clare said you were studying to be an EMT."

Sarah rolled her eyes. "And Margot St. Clare would know."

Her comment broke the ice, and Candice gave a surprisingly girlish giggle. Margot St. Clare ran the post office and was a legendary distributor of gossip.

"She's wicked, isn't she?" Candice had lowered her voice as if her postictal son might somehow feed her opinion back to the woman in question. "I thought she was going to explode when she heard about you and Officer Hayes buying the old Gardner place, but I guess she underestimated most folks' inclination to live and let live 'round here."

Sarah nodded, catching hold of a chubby hand as Grant Jr. rediscovered his curiosity and reached out to her. "I think he's feeling a bit brighter," she said. She took the bottle of children's Tylenol from the coffee table and measured out a dose. "Okay, young man. Come on. Down the hatch."

It was a messy business, but the pink goop was eventually swallowed down and showed no sign of being returned with interest. Sarah accepted Candice's offer of peppermint tea and found that she was able to relax slightly. She had only been a first responder for six months. This was the first febrile seizure she had attended, and although the seizure had stopped by the time she arrived, being confronted with a pale, unresponsive infant had been almost as frightening for her as it had undoubtedly been for his mother. The nearest ambulance was based in neighboring Ruby, a good fifty-minute journey away, and that was only if its crew wasn't tied up on another call. Although there was always the option of LifeFlight, she knew from firsthand experience that the chopper needed to be reserved for the direst of emergencies.

"You said yes to honey, right?" Candice's question cut into Sarah's thoughts, and she murmured her confirmation. She would have paid quite a lot of money right then for a proper cup of English tea, the sort that was strong enough to stand the spoon up in, but she took the proffered mug and made space beside herself on the sofa. Candice lifted her son onto her knee and held up a bottle of juice from which he slurped noisily.

"Are you going to the potluck picnic on Saturday?" she asked, unconsciously stroking her son's cheek.

"Um, I'm not sure. Alex mentioned it, but we hadn't decided."

The potluck picnic was an annual event held at the lake where Sarah had recently started up her own swimming classes. The lessons were already popular enough that she was able to meet her half of the household bills, something which her own sense of pride demanded, and which Alex knew better than to argue about. Sarah had inherited a considerable amount of money when her mother died, but it was tied up in investments back in England, and she and Alex had donated most of their FBI reward to the groups and individuals who had helped save their lives. They had kept just enough to fund a year of traveling and to buy their cabin. She knew that most people would think them stupid, but she didn't care; she preferred to be able to sleep at night. If nothing else, going along to the picnic would be a good way to network for new students.

She looked up from staring at the thin green murk in her mug when she realized that Candice was still talking about the picnic. She took a sip of tea to cover for her silence.

"You should go," Candice insisted. "Everyone'll be there, and we have some real good cooks in this town. You could make something English and exotic."

Sarah coughed a little on her mouthful; the terms "English" and "exotic" seemed mutually exclusive when applied to her national cuisine.

"I make a mean lamb hotpot and jam roly-poly," she said, "but they're winter comfort foods. We're not exactly famed for our balmy summer climate." She racked her brain but failed to think of anything remotely suited to hot weather. "Maybe I could do a curry and everyone could just drink plenty of cold beer with it. That combination is practically the national dish."

"Sounds great, I love—" Candice held her hand up in apology as someone knocked on the door. "Excuse me."

Sarah looked expectantly toward the hallway, where she could already hear a familiar voice raised in cheerful greeting. She smiled when Lyssa Mardell poked her head around the door.

"Hallo, hallo," Lyssa said, blithely massacring an English accent. "What brings you out of bed at this ridiculous hour?"

Sarah indicated the toddler now dozing on the sofa cushions. She handed over as much information as she could to Lyssa and her partner and then stepped aside to watch the two paramedics assess Grant Jr.'s vitals.

"He's still a little warm. Breathing and pulse are elevated," Lyssa told Candice when she had finished. "Probably just a viral infection, but with him having the seizure, we'll run him in to Cary."

Somewhat forgotten in Candice's rush to gather things for the trip to the hospital, Sarah stooped to pack her kit back into her response bag. Lyssa crouched beside her and offered her a fresh oxygen mask to replace the one she had used.

"Thanks."

"No problem. You did a really great job here, Sarah."

"I was shitting myself," Sarah admitted quietly.

"Yeah, but"—Lyssa nodded toward Candice—"she didn't suspect a thing, which is half the battle." She patted Sarah on the shoulder. "You get those exam results yet?"

"No, not yet."

"Same time on Friday for study club?"

"That'd be great, if it's no trouble."

They stood together and ushered Candice ahead of them.

"Bake me something chocolaty and it's no trouble at all." Lyssa grinned and opened the rear door of the ambulance. "You get back to bed, hon."

Sarah watched the ambulance as it pulled away and slowly negotiated the uneven track that led out to the main road. Birds were just beginning to chirp in the branches overhead, and she could see the light changing over the distant hills, faint traces of orange eating into the blackness. A yawn caught her unawares. She hefted her bag onto her shoulder and pulled out her cell phone. Her call was answered on the second ring.

"Hey, sweetheart," she said. "Everything's fine. I'm coming home."

CHAPTER TWO

The town of Avery comprised a main street, a tiny schoolhouse, an even tinier station house, and a neat white church that seemed unusually happy to accommodate disparate denominations. The shops and buildings lining Main Street were mostly constructed from local timber, their facades faded but neat, their signage swinging gently in the breeze. A floral competition with the two neighboring towns had seen the locals decorating every conceivable free space with brightly planted ceramic pots, and the warm summer days had made for a spectacular display.

A creek meandered alongside Main Street as it led down to the lake, neatly bisecting the town, so that people described themselves as living in either East Creek or West Creek. In winter, East played West at hockey; in summer there were rival softball and soccer teams. Agriculture was the main source of income for most families, while pretty much everyone else worked shifts at the lumber factory on the back road. By the time they hit their teens, the majority of the local kids were looking to leave, to move to Boston or New York or anywhere with a population numbering more than two thousand eight hundred and three. More often than not, though, they returned to Avery to settle and raise their own children, only appreciating what they'd had once they'd given it up.

Alex waved at Jo and Syd Bair as she drove toward the station house. Jo, heavily pregnant and already looking uncomfortably hot, waved back and then appeared to berate her husband for not paying attention. Through her rearview mirror, Alex saw him raise his hand in a belated greeting. She drove carefully, keeping well below the already cautious speed limit. Three times in the last two weeks, a moose had wandered casually across Main Street and caused minor traffic collisions, escaping on each occasion unscathed and ignorant of the chaos it had wrought. She harbored a sneaking suspicion that Chief Quinn was hatching a grand scheme to shoot it in time for Saturday's potluck spectacular.

When she arrived at the station parking lot, it was empty of civilian vehicles. She parked next to the solitary patrol unit, leaving plenty of room for Quinn to take the prime spot at the entrance. During his thirty-two years on the job, Bill Quinn had built up a capable, loyal workforce, but—as Esther on dispatch so succinctly put it—he had a "real bug up his ass" about his parking spot, and only an idiot would dare try to occupy it. No one had thought to warn Alex about this on her first day, but, not being entirely ignorant of workplace politics, she had parked right out on the edge of the lot. She and Quinn had gotten along just fine ever since.

Working alongside Chief Quinn in the Avery Police Department were two sergeants, four full-time patrol officers, three reserve officers, and two dispatchers. Their only detective was currently off on indefinite sick leave, but with so few cases falling within his remit, the department was coping perfectly well without him. As the local population was so sparse, the Avery PD dealt with all the law enforcement functions arising from the three towns within its jurisdiction. Of the three, Avery was the smallest and seemed a strange choice to house the department, but its location was central to neighboring Ruby and Tawny Ridge, and it was undoubtedly the prettiest, something that Alex suspected was more to the point. Castillo had given her a heads up about the full-time vacancy there, after hearing of Quinn through a mutual friend. Thanks to his behind-the-scenes machinations, what had happened to her and Sarah in the North Cascades had never made it into her official records.

"Good morning." Esther looked up from her Sudoku as Alex walked into the station. "Sarah get home okay?"

Too little sleep and synapses firing solely on caffeine made Alex take far longer than she should have to work out how Esther knew about their predawn wake-up call.

"Oh," she said slowly. "You passed her the emergency." She shook her head at her own ineptitude. "Yes, thank you, she got home a few minutes before I left."

"Lyssa said she did real good."

"Yeah?" Pride made Alex's voice soft. "I'll be sure and tell her."

There was a rustle as Esther sorted through the papers on her desk. "Not much else going down last night. Barrel Charlie is in cell one."

"Great," Alex said through gritted teeth. Barrel Charlie was Ruby's most notorious drunk, so called because of his propensity to howl the lyrics to "Roll Out the Barrel" in the town square at three in the morning. Often belligerent, not to mention doubly incontinent, he was usually transported home by the officers to avoid the stench he left in the cell block. "What did he do this time?"

Esther made a show of reading from the paperwork, even though Alex knew she could have recited the details verbatim. "Sergeant Emerson apprehended him at 2:27 a.m., drunk, incapable, and naked from the waist down."

"Is he still naked from the waist down?"

"No, Sergeant Emerson found him some sweats. Charlie claims that a group of local kids stole his belt, and that when his pants fell down it was easier just to step right on out of them. He had chosen to 'go commando' due to the hot weather."

"And where might Sergeant Emerson be now?"

"Uh." Esther winced. "He clocked off over in Ruby a half hour ago."

"Of course he did," Alex muttered, and Esther gave her a sympathetic look. No matter what Alex did, how hard she worked, or how pleasant she tried to be, Scott Emerson consistently treated her like crap. She had yet to figure out why. Fortunately, they usually worked opposing shifts, which meant she was able to tolerate the snide comments and disdainful looks in the little time they were forced to spend together.

"Tell the chief I'll deal with Charlie as a priority before it gets too warm down there."

"Coffee first?" Esther was already pouring out two mugs.

"Oh God, yes, please." Alex breathed in the rich aroma, half-convinced that that alone would be enough to prepare her for extracting a statement from Charlie's hung over, incoherent ramblings.

"You have a good day now," Esther told her without a trace of irony.

Alex raised her mug in salute and walked slowly toward the cells.

❖

The rough granite of the diving rock was almost within touching distance. Swimming steadily, no more than five yards away from her young pupil, Sarah saw him fix his sights on the rock and set his jaw. She didn't need to say anything to encourage him; they had been working toward this for almost three weeks now, and for a twelve-year-old, he was incredibly motivated. She watched him stretch out, putting all his energy into a final kick and then grinning as he slapped a hand on the rock.

"Holy fucking shit sticks." For a twelve-year-old, he also had an extremely varied and imaginative vocabulary when it came to cussing.

"Bradley!" Well accustomed to teaching adolescents, Sarah struggled to sound outraged. She hid her laughter by diving low, only breaking the surface when she saw the rock loom large in front of her.

"You did brilliantly," she said, treading water as Brad climbed out. He was small for his age, and severe asthma meant that he had spent a significant portion of his childhood in the Cary Medical Center. She hoisted herself up to stand beside him and they both waved at his mother, who was waiting anxiously on the shore. Brad's skinny chest heaved, the skin sucking in between his ribs as he tried to catch his breath.

"Let's have a minute, huh?" Sarah tugged his hand to make him sit down. "Then we can get back."

They sat together, toes dipped into the cool, clear water. Avery Lake was vast, stretching for almost thirty square miles. Here and there small boats bobbed on the water, but mostly it was an uninterrupted expanse of aquamarine that only began to taper in width as it reached the craggy hills at its southernmost edge. Sarah had spent almost a year traveling with Alex and seeing some of the most beautiful places imaginable, but she didn't think she would ever tire of sitting on the diving rock and looking at this view.

"Miss Sarah?" Brad's voice was still breathy, but he appeared to be recovering well.

"What's up? You want to start back?"

"No," he said. "No, not yet. I just…" He shook his head, pretending it was nothing important, but he couldn't seem to look her in the eye. "How did you hurt your leg?" His question was quiet, imbued with the awe of a boy young enough to think all scars were cool.

Sarah leaned back on her hands. She no longer made any attempt to cover up the long scar where her femur had been fixed back together, or the scattered pattern of scarring across her abdomen where internal bleeding and more lately a gunshot wound had been treated. With her surname changed, anyone attempting to Google or research the finer details would be disappointed.

"I was in a car accident a few years ago," she said, and Brad nodded solemnly. "I, uh, it was pretty bad." She took a deep breath, staring out at the blue-green water and waiting for the rush of grief to fade. A drunk driver had plowed into her mum's car, killing her mum and her little sister instantly, but Brad didn't need to know that.

Chilly, damp fingers patted awkwardly against her own.

"That's really shitty," Brad said.

"Yeah. That's what I thought too."

He scrambled up and held his hand out to her, having apparently thought of something he was sure would make her feel better. "Wanna dive in with me?"

She laughed, forcing back the sadness as she took his hand. "Okay. On three. Ready?"

Alex's patrol unit drew up just as Sarah's toes touched the smooth rocks at the shore. Brad was already chasing Tilly through the shallows, and they both looked around when they heard the car engine. Tilly barked excitedly, racing toward Alex, who let out a yelp of her own as thirty-five pounds of wet dog closed in on her.

"Uh oh, are you gonna get arrested, miss?" Brad asked Sarah in a singsong voice.

"I doubt it, but you never know." She winked and steered him over to his mom, who thanked her before wrapping Brad in a thick towel and leading him back to their station wagon.

With Tilly running rings around her, Alex stooped to collect Sarah's towel. They met in the middle of the beach, and she draped the towel around Sarah, using it to pull her close, but the romantic gesture was ruined somewhat when Sarah hesitated, crinkling her nose.

"Alex, what have I told you about rolling around in the drunk tank?"

Alex grimaced. "It's not me. I took a shower at the station. It's the car." It was only then that Sarah noticed all four of the car's doors were wide open. "I'm trying to air it out."

"Barrel Charlie?" With one hand on Alex's elbow, Sarah steered her upwind toward a sheltered spot close to the water.

"Yup."

"Oh dear. Well, never mind. Got time for lunch?"

Alex rustled a paper bag that had been concealed beneath the towel. "I'm all yours for the next hour."

Eyeing the familiar blue and white bag hungrily, Sarah wriggled into her shorts before sitting on the sand and pulling Alex down beside her. "If that's from Barnaby's, I'm all yours forever."

Alex laughed as she handed her a generous greaseproof package. "In which case, it's a good thing you're cute and I kinda like you," she said, unwrapping her own roll.

Despite being some distance from the coast, Barnaby's had fresh Maine seafood delivered to its kitchen every morning. The diner was an Avery institution, its lobster and shrimp rolls selling out as fast as they could be prepared.

Embedding her toes in the warm sand, Sarah took a huge bite of her roll, just as she remembered that she had something vital to tell Alex. Barely able to breathe, let alone speak, she nudged Alex's shoulder to get her attention.

Alex turned slightly and her mouth dropped open when she saw how little was left of Sarah's lunch. "You skip breakfast?" she asked, gesturing at the scant remnants.

Sarah held up a finger in apology as she finished chewing and swallowed. "No, I just worked up an appetite," she said with a grin. She nudged Alex again. "Guess what came in the mail this morning."

Alex gave an exaggerated sigh. "Don't tell me Bandit's been ordering Cat Snax catalogs again."

"Nope, although I wouldn't put it past the thieving little bugger." The envelope was in the pocket of Sarah's shorts, and it took a fair amount of contortion to reach it.

Alex's eyes widened when she saw the postmark. "Oh hell, that was quick." She toyed with the seal as she studied Sarah's face. "I'm guessing from your smile that it's good news."

Sarah nodded, suddenly feeling a little shy. "Yeah, it's good news," she said quietly. She nibbled what remained of her roll as Alex read the letter.

"Holy shit!"

That was all the warning Sarah had before Alex grabbed her in a hug and covered her face in mayo-flavored kisses. The enthusiasm was so heartfelt that Sarah forgot all about her innate awkwardness when it came to accepting praise.

"Did all right, didn't I?"

"You did more than all right." Alex looked aghast. "Ninety-six percent is more than all right. God." She used her thumb to wipe mayo from Sarah's cheek. "Why do you always sell yourself short?"

Sarah chewed thoughtfully as she considered the question. "Maybe it's because I don't want to get my hopes up," she ventured at length. She watched Alex's posture sag as if someone had slapped all the joy out of her, and she immediately regretted having raised the issue.

"I'm sure we'll hear something soon," Alex said.

No matter how settled they were in Avery and how happy they were in their work, the EMT exam that Sarah had just passed would be worthless without a green card. Three days after Maine had legalized marriage for gay couples, she and Alex had gotten married in a small ceremony by the lakeshore. Walt, the man with whom Alex had worked in the Cascades, stood in for their parents and gave them both away, and Ash and Tess had flown over from England to be bridesmaids. The next natural step was applying for Sarah's green card, but her application was still being processed, and she was increasingly nervous about its outcome.

Sarah took hold of Alex's hand and laced their fingers together. "You really think we'll be okay?"

Alex said nothing, but just squeezed Sarah's hand and kissed her on her forehead. It was the only answer Sarah ever needed.

The gate moved stiffly, its weight making the hinges creak and complain until it finally swung wide enough to allow Alex's Chevy Silverado through. It was early evening, but the sun was still warm on her shoulders as she walked across to close the gate and secure it. She breathed in the hot, dusty scent of the desiccated pine needles beneath her boots and the pleasanter, cooler air that filtered through the trees from the lake. There was no sign yet of the thunderstorm forecast on the weather report that morning, but the humidity had seemed to press down during the afternoon, and she knew that eventually something had to break.

She climbed back behind the wheel and restarted the engine, pulling away slowly, with her arm hanging out the cranked-down window and her fingers tapping a tune on the bodywork. She loved her job, loved being back in the uniform, but one of the best things about it was coming home: driving through the forest, listening to birdsong and squirrels quarrelling, and knowing that Sarah would be waiting for her. It was enough to make her smile no matter what her shift had thrown at her.

The cabin came into view as she rounded the final corner of the track. Tilly darted across the back yard, making the hens scatter as they tried to avoid being flattened by her enthusiasm. The chaos was a nightly routine, and as usual, it brought Sarah out onto the back porch. Flour puffed up from her hands when she clapped them, but Tilly ignored her, continuing to make a beeline for Alex. Sarah gave her a helpless wave.

"I've got a pie cooling and Bandit lurking," she called.

Alex nodded her understanding. Bandit would eat anything that didn't eat him first. "I'll feed the girls and see you in there."

"'Kay."

The screen door slapped back into place behind Sarah, and Alex chuckled when she heard a short yelp and a stream of indistinct cursing immediately afterward. The door slammed again, and Bandit slunk onto the porch to begin washing a face stained suspiciously with purple. Alex fetched the tub of feed pellets, becoming a Pied Piper for their six chickens as they followed her across to their trough.

"Here you go," she said, the pellets rattling down against the metal as she scooped out their supper. Leaving them to eat and squabble, she swung her kit bag over her shoulder and allowed Tilly to lead her up onto the porch. Her mouth was watering before she had even opened the door. Whatever Sarah had been baking smelled heavenly.

"What can I do to help?" she said as Sarah turned away from the oven.

"Get changed." Sarah pulled off her apron, revealing a flimsy tank top and a ragged pair of shorts. "You're making me hot just looking at you."

Alex waggled her eyebrows and Sarah grinned as she belatedly recognized her double entendre.

"You haven't got a hope in hell until you've put that uniform in the laundry basket and had a shower," she said. "I know who your first punter was today, remember?"

"Ah." Self-conscious, Alex sniffed at her shirt. "Can you still…?"

Sarah laughed. "No, I can't, but everything's set in here, so go get cleaned up and then we can eat."

As if casting the deciding vote, Alex's stomach gave a sonorous rumble.

"Tea's in ten," Sarah warned her.

Alex saluted crisply. "I'll be ready in five."

"This may possibly"—Alex licked the back of her spoon, reconsidering the rest of her statement— "no, *definitely* be the finest cherry pie I have ever eaten."

"You're very sweet," Sarah said, flicking a piece of crust for Bandit to chase off the edge of the porch, "but you say pretty much the same about everything I bake."

Alex shrugged. "I can't help but be appreciative of your many talents."

"It is a bloody good pie," Sarah conceded, cutting them each another generous slice.

She set aside what little remained and then stretched her legs out in front of her. The wood of the porch was rough but warm against her bare feet. In the distance, occasional streaks of lightning flashed silently down toward the lake, but the storm was still miles away and, far from being threatening, the blue-silver slashes gave a spectacular outline to the clouds massing in the night sky. A thin rain was beginning to mist the grass that she had mown that afternoon, giving the parched surface a much needed soak and making everything smell freshly washed. It was so peaceful that she forgot all about the pie in her bowl and just reveled in the sense of calm.

"And then I asked Quinn if I could go in naked tomorrow and he said that was fine..."

She blinked, suddenly aware that Alex was studying her intently.

"Sorry, what?" She mentally replayed the last thing she remembered hearing. "If you're going into work naked, love, at least remember to wear sunscreen," she said.

Alex let out a bark of laughter. "So you were sort of listening."

"No, sorry. I didn't hear a damn thing apart from that last bit," Sarah admitted. "I was just..." She put her dish down and turned to face Alex properly. "I never thought I'd find this. Did you ever think you'd find this?" The words came out in a bemused rush.

Alex patted the space on the bench between them, and Sarah shuffled closer to nestle into her embrace.

"Honestly?" Alex asked.

Sarah nodded to prompt her to continue.

"I thought I'd stay in LA, end up living in some crappy condo where you can always hear your neighbors fighting or their TV screeching, but I'd tell myself that it wouldn't matter because I was a cop and that was everything I wanted my life to be. At best, I expected a few meaningless relationships, and realistically, I'd probably have hit the bottle sometime in my forties and gone on to drink myself into an early grave."

"Fucking hell, Alex." Sarah shifted, looking up to see whether she was joking.

Alex licked her lips nervously. "I know now that I didn't have anything," she said. "I had the job, but there has to be more than that. Family, or good friends, or if you're really lucky, someone like you."

Sarah wrapped her arms around Alex and felt Alex fumble for her hand and grip it tightly. For the past two years, they had really only had each other for company. Sarah's closest friends were in England, while Alex's friends from LA had fallen out of touch with her long before she moved to Maine. Although both of Alex's brothers had come to the wedding, her parents, living barely four hours away in Boston, hadn't spoken to her since she was released from the hospital in Seattle, and they had refused to acknowledge her relationship with Sarah. Alex rarely mentioned them, and Sarah knew better than to push for reconciliation.

Alex stroked her thumb across the back of Sarah's hand. "If you'd asked me a few years ago whether I could see myself living in the depths of rural Maine, working as a small-town cop and coming home to half a petting zoo and a beautiful wife, I would probably have laughed in your face." She kissed the top of Sarah's head. "I never knew I was looking for this," she said, her voice thick with emotion. "So, no, I never thought I'd find it."

Her palm was warm against Sarah's and she took a deep, shuddering breath. Lightning blazed across the sky and rain began to pelt the ground in fat, heavy drops. Sarah stared at the approaching storm until the rain and her tears blurred into one. She felt Alex move and then a tug on her hand.

"Let's go inside," Alex said.

CHAPTER THREE

Okay, I've beaten this to within an inch of its life. What do I do now?" Alex peered into the bowl as if the mixture itself could provide her with an answer.

On the other side of the kitchen, her hands covered in sticky marinade, Sarah attempted simultaneously to fend off a marauding cat and assess the creamed butter and sugar in Alex's mixing bowl.

"That's good. Should be fine," she said, trying to shift a strand of hair from her eyes by blowing upward. "You whisked your eggs?"

Alex nodded.

"Okay, whack the eggs and flour in together. You're supposed to add them a bit at a time, but it doesn't really matter if you fold them in gently."

"Fold them in gently," Alex repeated. She chewed her bottom lip, looking from the bowl to the remaining ingredients. "I have no clue how to do that," she said, feeling like an idiot. Her family had always employed kitchen staff, and no one had ever taken the time to show her how to cook. She had been learning the basics from Sarah and already had a few simple recipes in her repertoire. This, however, was the first cake she had made, and although the Victoria sandwich in the illustration looked impressive, the process of putting it together was proving a little tricky.

She glanced up from the recipe book when she heard running water. Sarah dried her hands on a towel and came to stand beside her.

"I'm sorry. I promised I'd show you how to bake a cake, and I'm just leaving you to struggle, aren't I?" She sounded apologetic, but she was smiling.

Alex smiled too. Sarah had made her that promise when they had first met. "Well, we are working to a tight deadline," she said.

The potluck picnic wasn't scheduled to start for another three hours, but the kitchen had been a hive of activity since dawn. They had run out of eggs and spent the morning bribing the chickens into laying the extra one needed for the cake. A triumphant squawk from the coop less than twenty minutes ago had signaled success, but now that all the ingredients were in place, Alex wasn't certain her rookie skills were up to the challenge of doing anything with them. She watched Sarah pour the whisked eggs into the bowl.

"Okay, chuck in your flour as well."

Alex did as she was instructed.

"Fabulous. Now grab hold of the spoon like this." Standing behind her, Sarah placed a hand onto Alex's, and together they managed to get a workable grip on the wooden spoon. "You don't want to beat this or you'll knock all the air out of it and we'll end up with a pancake." Her voice was low and amused, the warmth of her body was pressing close, and Alex tried very hard to concentrate on the words and ignore the fact that she was suddenly finding her cake baking lesson incredibly erotic.

"A pancake would be bad," she murmured, feeling that she should say something at some point.

Sarah laughed, her chest shuddering against Alex's back. "A pancake would be as bad as whatever it is you're currently imagining, Alexandra Hayes."

"I am imagining cake," Alex said, a flush heating her cheeks. She had always loathed her given name, but the way Sarah said it made tingles shoot right down her spine.

Sarah rested her chin on Alex's shoulder as she began to work the spoon. "You're a terrible fibber," she said, her fingers not so much guiding now as stroking the ones beneath them.

"And you're making it very difficult for me to concentrate." Alex's protest came out a little higher in pitch than she had intended. "It's gonna be a pancake!"

"No, it's not. You're doing beautifully. Some people cheat and use a food processor for this, but personally," Sarah dropped her voice, speaking confidentially into Alex's ear, "I prefer to get hands on and do it the old-fashioned way."

Alex shivered, despite the kitchen's heat. "You're actually trying to kill me, aren't you?" She felt Sarah's teeth nip at her earlobe. "Oh God, is this finished? It looks finished to me."

"It's fine. It's done. Get it in the tins," Sarah said with unmistakable urgency.

"What about the curry?"

"Simmering." Sarah hurriedly smoothed the top of the cake batter into an even layer. "I'll stick a lid on it so it'll be Bandit-proofed. And these"—she picked up the tins and slid them into the oven—"will take about fifteen minutes."

"Fifteen minutes." Alex checked the clock. "What could we possibly do for the next fifteen minutes?" When she turned around, she found Sarah perched on the kitchen table, her shirt already unbuttoned and pushed low on her shoulders.

"Well, that'll save some time," Alex conceded, using a finger to smooth frosting across Sarah's lips before kissing her. Vanilla and rosewater combined on her tongue. It was delicious, and when they broke apart, they were both wide-eyed and panting. Alex considered the bowl of frosting in her hands.

"Can we make more of this?"

"Yes." Sarah nodded quickly, leaning back on her hands to allow Alex to paint a line of it down her chest. "Jesus, I don't remember cookery classes at school ending like this." She gasped as Alex followed the line with her mouth.

"Then you went to a very boring school," Alex said, and reached for the bowl again.

The sun was so hot, so vivid, that it burned orange beneath Sarah's closed eyelids as she lay back on the blanket. Water dripped down her face from her soaked hair, but she couldn't be bothered to dry herself, letting the midafternoon warmth do the job instead. The music from the small funfair and the gleeful sound of children's laughter seemed to fade into the background, and it was only when something hard and cool poked her in the ribs, startling her, that she realized she had been dozing. She snatched at the offending object and heard Alex yelp.

Opening one eye, she found Alex grinning down at her and a half-gnawed carrot gripped in her fist.

"Can I have my carrot stick back?"

"Definitely not," Sarah said, making a show of crunching into it. "Did you get anything other than rabbit food? I'm starving."

"I'm not surprised, little champ." Alex patted the small trophy Sarah had been presented with after a series of swimming races, and then passed her a plate laden with an assortment of food.

"Wow." Sarah stared at the mass of seafood, salads, cornbread, and barbecued meats. "Sure we got enough here?" She caught the fork Alex threw her and raised her bottle of beer. "Cheers."

"Cheers." Alex took a long drink and rested the cool glass bottle against her forehead. "I would've gotten some of your curry, but there was none left."

Sarah cracked open a freshly steamed crab claw. "I can always make it for tea one night. Maybe in winter, when it's not a million and one degrees in the shade."

"Good call." Alex dropped her voice a notch. "I did manage to snag a piece of our cake though." She winked in such a knowing manner that Sarah almost choked on her crabmeat.

"God, if they only knew," she said, looking around at the families gathered on picnic rugs and the children chasing each other across the beach.

Alex started to laugh. "Margot St. Clare caught me by the barbecue and told me it was one of the best cakes she had ever tasted." Her shoulders were shaking so hard that she had to put her plate down. "She wanted to know what the secret ingredient in the frosting was."

Sarah closed her eyes slowly. "Alex, what did you tell her?"

There was a pause as she waited in agony for Alex to compose herself sufficiently to respond.

"Rosewater," Alex said at last. "What the hell else did you think I was going to say?"

Any retort Sarah might have made was forestalled by a screech of static and a crackling public address announcement.

"Oh, that's my cue." Alex gave her a quick kiss on the cheek and scrambled to her feet. "Wish us luck."

"Break a leg," Sarah called as Alex dashed through the maze of townsfolk and pets and shrieking children.

The Police Department versus Avery All-comers Tug o' War was—according to everyone Sarah had spoken to in the past week—the undisputed highlight of the potluck picnic. Feeling too comfortable to move from her blanket, she stayed where she was, deciding that she had a decent enough view. The rope had just been raised, and the teams were poised to take the strain when Lyssa Mardell waved and trotted across the sand toward her.

"Hey." Lyssa had three bottles of beer in her hands. She offered one to Sarah and set the second bottle in the cooler. "Save this for Alex when she's finished. She'll probably need it as a consolation prize," she said, sitting on the edge of the blanket.

Sarah shuffled over to make a bigger gap for her. "Thanks. You off duty today?"

"Hell, yes. I'm back in on Friday night." Lyssa snagged a piece of chicken from Sarah's plate and looked at her expectantly. "So, you heard yet? You must have heard by now."

Never sure what Lyssa's shift pattern was, Sarah hadn't wanted to risk disturbing her after a night shift by calling her. As a result, she had been sitting on her good news for three days. She smiled, feeling shy all over again. "I got ninety-six percent," she said.

For a second, Lyssa just stared. Then she gave a whoop of delight and threw her arms around Sarah. "That's brilliant! You're brilliant!" She kissed her sloppily on the cheek. "Hey, *I'm* brilliant!"

"You are brilliant," Sarah said. "Couldn't have done it without you." Her arm was still around Lyssa and she hugged her close. "I owe you, massively."

Since meeting Sarah on an emergency call four months ago, Lyssa had been helping to coach her through her EMT course, and the extra tuition, in addition to Sarah's college course in Ruby, had paid dividends.

"Onward and upward." Lyssa clinked her beer against Sarah's.

"Definitely."

They sat side by side, cheering on the teams laboring in the contest. For the first time in five years, the police seemed to have the upper hand, and the handkerchief tied around the center of the rope was inching inexorably in their direction. A minute later, the Avery team capitulated en masse and, without warning, stumbled and fell gracelessly into the shallow water. Sarah clambered to her feet, pulling Lyssa up beside her, and waved at Alex.

As the noise and fuss subsided, Lyssa sat back down, but Sarah turned, suddenly uncomfortable for some reason. A few feet behind her, Margot St. Clare was sitting on a deck chair. She had evidently been watching Sarah and Lyssa for a while, and her face twisted into a scowl of distaste when Sarah caught her eye. It was Sarah who looked away first, back toward the lake, where she saw Alex diving into the water with the rest of her team. Trying to push her unease aside, Sarah retook her place on the blanket, but she could still sense Margot's gaze fixed on her. She cradled the beer that Lyssa gave her but shook her head at the plate of food; she had completely lost her appetite.

"Here, drink this and tell me what's bugging you."

Sarah obediently cradled the mug and sipped from it slowly. The tea was exactly how she liked it: strong, piping hot, milk no sugar. As she drank, Alex reached across and rested a hand on her forehead.

"Not post-picnic heatstroke, then," she murmured.

Sarah looked up at her. "I'm okay."

"Mmhm." Alex sat on the bed. "You're far too quiet and you're not eating." She squeezed Sarah's hand. "If it was just the not talking, I wouldn't be so worried."

Sarah gave her a weak smile. "It's stupid, really. You'll think I'm being stupid."

"Try me."

"Margot St. Clare…" The name was barely past her lips when she was interrupted by Alex's theatrical groan. "See, I told you you'd think I was stupid." She pulled the sheets up to hide her face, so that she heard Alex's apology from beyond a layer of cotton.

"I'm sorry. You can tell me. I won't say a word until you've finished. I promise."

Peeking out, Sarah grimaced and then spoke quickly. "At the picnic, I told Lyssa about my exam, and she hugged and kissed me, and Margot obviously saw it and gave us both a really nasty look." The words sounded completely ridiculous as soon as they were out in the open, and when she saw a muscle at the corner of Alex's jaw begin to twitch, she put her out of her misery by laughing first. "I feel like such a fucking numpty."

"Oh, honey." Alex reached up and tousled her hair. "Margot hates pretty much everyone and everything. I think she once put a hex on Quinn for growing an ungodly moustache."

"She did not."

"Or maybe it was unmanly. Y'know, a bit too 'Village People.' I forget," Alex said. They were still giggling when the phone rang. "Speak of the devil," she muttered when she saw the number on the screen. For a moment, Sarah felt sure it was Margot calling to damn them from afar, but then Alex mouthed "Quinn" and picked up the handset.

"Hello?"

Whatever Quinn told her made her sit up a little straighter. Sarah set her mug down, watching Alex's face for clues, but Alex gave nothing away until she'd ended the call with a crisp, "Yes, sir."

"Dare I ask?" Sarah tried to keep her voice light, but she could hear the tension creep into the question.

Alex's eyes were bright with excitement when she turned around. "That warehouse in Ruby, the one we've had under surveillance?"

Sarah nodded; it was the biggest operation Alex had been involved with since starting with the Avery PD. Meth, cocaine, and prescription drugs were all finding their way into the hands of dealers via a large, nondescript warehouse in one of Ruby's less salubrious districts.

"Quinn's planning a raid on it tomorrow night," Alex said.

"But you're on an early tomorrow." As soon as Sarah spoke, she knew what the phone call had been about. "Oh."

"Yeah." Alex dragged the word out and Sarah saw the conflict flit across her face; she wanted to be involved just as desperately as she didn't want Sarah to worry. "He asked me to swap my shift."

Sarah cupped a hand beneath Alex's chin and raised her head until their eyes met. "You be careful," she said.

Alex nodded. "Will you be okay?"

It took a lot for Sarah not to blink, but she managed it. "I'll be fine."

❖

The trail beneath Sarah's sneakers was carpeted with pine needles and other detritus from the forest surrounding her. The cushioned layer was hard work to run on, but the route was lovely, looping through the land they had bought with the cabin and marking the halfway point of her jog by suddenly leaving the trees and breaking out onto a beautiful mile-long stretch at the side of the lake.

A breeze hit her flushed cheeks as she followed the path to the right and continued along the shoreline. She could feel the sweat cooling on her back, and a slight ache where the old fracture in her ankle had knitted together in imperfect alignment. A series of splashes told her that Tilly had decided to interrupt her own run with a swim, and high in the branches something brightly colored sang as they passed.

Sarah welcomed the myriad distractions; they stopped her from looking at her watch or thinking about how near the sun was to the horizon. She planned to finish her run, have a long bath, and then go to bed. She would not sit up all night, monitoring the hours as they ticked by and waiting for Alex to call; she refused to allow herself to fall into that kind of pattern. Alex was a cop. When they had gotten back from their travels and the job opportunity had arisen, Sarah had actively encouraged her to go back to the force. They both knew and accepted the potential risks that the job entailed, and Avery wasn't exactly a hotbed of violent crime, which made tonight's raid the exception rather than the norm.

Her feet pounding rhythmically against the rough path, Sarah nodded in appreciation at her inner monologue's sensible tone. She whistled for Tilly just as the path hooked back around into the twilight of the forest. The change in light was so abrupt that she had to wait for her vision to adjust before she picked up her pace again. The sweat that had chilled against her skin began to run freely as the breeze disappeared, and she wiped a damp hand across her forehead. She looked ahead into the gloom, the fears she had managed to quell so effectively beginning to inch back into her thoughts. She knew how easy it was to be rational in the daylight, but painful experience had taught her that the hours in the depths of the night were the ones to dread.

Still rubbing her hair dry, Sarah slipped and skidded barefoot across the wooden floor of the bedroom. She launched her towel onto the bed and took hold of her pager, silencing its shrieking with the press of a button and picking up the phone to dial through to dispatch. Sod's law, she thought, as the number slowly connected and all hopes for an early night disappeared. So much for best laid plans.

"Hey, Esther."

"Sarah. Thank goodness." Esther sounded incredibly stressed. Sarah, immediately thinking of the raid, glanced at her watch, even though she was certain that the teams weren't scheduled to move on the warehouse for at least another hour. "It's Jo Bair," Esther continued, putting her mind at rest on that score at least. "She's in labor and bleeding."

Sarah propped the phone between her ear and shoulder and started to get dressed. "ETA on the ambulance?" she asked.

"That's the problem. Frances Stokes had a heart attack not twenty minutes since. The ambulance only just left for Cary."

"Shit." She stopped dead, her keys in her hand. "Esther, I don't—"

"I know," Esther said softly. "I got hold of a midwife in Tawny, but she's a good hour out and all the police resources are tied up with the raid so I can't get her there any quicker. I'm afraid you're it, honey."

Sarah nodded, even though Esther couldn't see her. "Don't say anything to Alex. She's going to have enough on her mind."

"Not a word."

"Thanks, Esther." She picked up her bag. "Give me the address."

The briefing room at the station house was two storage closets that Bill Quinn had long ago knocked through with a sledgehammer and a fair amount of devil-may-care enthusiasm. As such, it was cramped, windowless, and—with ten people crammed inside—verging on airless. Its back wall was dominated by a whiteboard on which Quinn had sketched the layout of the warehouse. A series of scribbles and numbers delineated the tactics he intended to put into play during the raid.

Alex watched the progress of her designated number as blue Sharpie arrows made it sweep from the rear to cut off any fleeing perpetrators and then directed it to search the offices clustered at the left of the building. Scott Emerson and Larry Tobin—one of the reserve officers, who at twenty-eight was becoming increasingly desperate to be employed on a full-time basis—would be the other members of her small team.

While Sarah had been teaching at the lake, Alex had spent the day studying the blueprints of the warehouse, cleaning and checking her service weapon, and reading through the rap sheets of the men whose comings and goings had been logged over the past months. She recognized three of them, having documented their activities in detail during several night shifts tasked to surveillance duty, and the remainder seemed to fall into the same career pattern: minor criminality, then a steady progression toward more violent, riskier schemes that promised bigger payoffs. They reminded her of Nathan Merrick, the ambitious crook whose own bid for glory had seen him link up as a supplier to Nicholas Deakin's hate organization. Merrick's reward had been an ignominious death in a puddle of filth at the side of a small campfire in the Cascades. It was the only time that Alex had ever shot anyone, and he was the only man she had ever killed outright.

"Alex?"

She jumped as a hand touched her arm. People were beginning to leave the small room, but she had no idea at what point the briefing had concluded.

Larry Tobin withdrew his hand with a sheepish grin. "Sorry. I just…" He gestured toward one of the straps on his Kevlar vest. "Little help?"

"Yeah." The word came out hoarsely and she cleared her throat. "Sure, hold still." She adjusted the strap so that the vest sat snugly in position. "Better?"

Tobin struck a few exaggerated poses she vaguely recognized from one of her training manuals, and she wished she could request a change of team. Her own vest was still in her locker; it was another fifty minutes before they were due to leave the station.

"That's great, thanks," he said. "Can't believe I get to be a part of this." His grin stretched almost from ear to ear and he was fairly bouncing on the spot.

She bit back the obvious response, clapped him on the shoulder, and wondered whether Esther was busy. Esther always had a stash of really good coffee, and something told Alex that she was going to need a lot of it.

❖

The Bair house was ablaze with light, as if sending up a desperate signal for someone to come and help its occupants. Sarah grabbed her response bag and the obstetrics pack that Lyssa had managed to sneak out of stores for her three months ago. They had spent an afternoon going through the contents of the pack as Lyssa regaled her with home birth horror stories and anecdotes. Watching Lyssa squeeze a cantaloupe through an inflated water wing had been the sum of her obstetrics training to date.

Her legs were trembling as she got out of the Jeep. Even from the driveway, she could hear Jo Bair screaming in pain. That was not a good sign; she clearly remembered Lyssa making that point. "If you can hear them yelling from the street," Lyssa had said with a huge grin, "get your catching mitt on."

"Fuck," Sarah whispered. She ran up the driveway and pounded on the door. "Fuck, fuck, fuck."

Behind the glass paneling, Syd Bair was fumbling with his keys. He dropped the entire set before trying the wrong key twice. By the time he opened the door, he was close to tears.

"Oh God, where's the ambulance?" He looked over her shoulder, as if willing one to appear. Somewhere off to the right, Jo shouted for him.

"It's not going to be here for a while," Sarah said, somehow managing to keep her voice level. "There's a midwife on her way, but she's coming from Tawny."

"Do you know what you're doing?" he asked.

The question was so pointed that she almost told him the truth.

"I've had training." She deliberately chose not to expand on that, but ushered him ahead of her toward the bedroom. At the door, she caught hold of his sleeve. "I'll need your help, Syd, so you're going to have to stay calm."

He ran a hand through his hair, then nodded once and pushed the door open. "Honey, Sarah's here," he said, kneeling by the side of the bed and taking hold of Jo's hand.

Jo wearily raised her head from the pillows and gave Sarah a little wave.

"Thought first ones were supposed to take forever," she said between heavy breaths.

"Got caught a bit short, did you?" Sarah smiled as Jo rolled her eyes in agreement. She set her bag down and pulled on a pair of gloves, her damp palms making them cling and wrinkle. Even with her lack of experience, one glance at Jo told her that the birth was imminent. The bed was soaked with bloodstained, straw-colored fluid and, as another contraction started, she could see the bulge and retreat of the baby's head.

"Okay," she said. "I think you're having a baby."

Jo nodded wryly. Then she let out a yelp and started to strain.

"What can I do?" Syd asked, his eyes flickering with fear.

Sarah tried to think logically. "Towels. See if we can get Jo onto a dry spot, and we'll keep some warm ones for the baby. Jo, how far apart are your contractions?" She had her answer almost immediately as Jo groaned through the onset of another one. "Okay, so, less than a minute."

She opened the maternity pack, arranging clamps and scissors, a small bulb syringe for suction, and a bowl that Lyssa had said was about as much use for catching a placenta as a blind man with no hands. Syd passed her a multicolored pile of towels, having apparently pulled everything he could find from the bathroom closet.

"Lovely," Sarah said, surprised by how calm she felt. "Right, Jo, let's shuffle you this way a little."

Between the two of them, she and Syd managed to move Jo off the sodden bedding and onto the thickest of the towels.

"How're you doing?" Sarah asked gently, as a contraction faded.

"Bit scared," Jo said. "Not quite how we planned it."

"No?" Sarah held a glass of juice for her to sip from. "Had you fancied a water birth or something?"

Jo gave a harsh laugh. "No, I'd *fancied* an epidural! Oh fuck…" The pain hit her without warning, and she moaned, bearing down until her face turned an alarming shade of red.

"Go, go, go, you're doing great," Syd chanted.

"Squeeze his hand," Sarah said. "He got you into this mess." She licked her dry lips, gauging the progress of the delivery. "Jo, you're crowning. I need you to pant through this one."

"Pant?" Jo sounded incredulous. "I want it out!"

"It's coming out, sweetheart." Sarah fervently hoped that she was remembering correctly. "But I don't want you to tear, so pant, okay?"

Jo was already panting, the pain making her rock back and forward.

"Good, that's brilliant." Sarah watched as the baby's head slowly emerged and then turned. Its eyes were closed, its face swollen and purple beneath the mess of birthing fluids, and Sarah swore quietly when she saw the loop of umbilical cord coiled around its neck.

"Jo." She patted Jo's thigh and tried to keep the urgency out of her voice. "You need to give me a really good push."

Syd had seen the cord too. He looked at Sarah, his mouth opening to ask a question, but she cut him off with a sharp shake of her head as Jo began to bear down again.

"Keep going, keep going," Sarah said. She tried to remove the cord, but there was no slack for her to work with; there was no way she could loosen it until the baby was completely born. Jo was pushing for all she was worth, and she delivered the baby in a rush of blood and black liquid.

"Jesus Christ." She fell back onto the pillows, leaving Sarah with her hands full of a slippery, silent baby.

"Little girl," Syd whispered.

Sarah had the cord freed and cut now, but the baby still wasn't moving. When she placed a hand on the small chest, there was no sign of breathing.

"Why isn't she crying?" Jo had her eyes closed, as if afraid to look.

Sarah rubbed the baby vigorously with a towel, holding her tilted downward to allow her airway to drain clear. A foul green-black fluid trickled from her mouth.

"Come on," Sarah muttered. "Come on."

She could feel a slow pulse at the crook of the baby's elbow. In desperation, she closed her mouth around the baby's nose and mouth and gave five quick breaths. The pulse beneath her fingertips quickened and she breathed for the baby again, watching her chest rise and fall rapidly in response. This time, when Sarah lowered her, her chest continued to move. Then she twitched her fists before letting out a wail that almost made Sarah's knees give way. Jo started to sob uncontrollably and Syd leaned forward, his hands covering his face. The baby's skin color slowly changed from dusky blue to a far healthier pink.

"There you are," Sarah whispered. She lifted the baby onto Jo's naked chest. "Say hello to your mum, little one."

"Is she okay?" Jo systematically counted fingers and toes as the baby's wailing subsided into hiccups and she settled into Jo's warmth.

"I think she'll be fine." Sarah sat shakily on the edge of the bed and clapped Syd on the back, just to make sure he hadn't fainted with his eyes open. He looked up and beamed at her, tears streaming down his cheeks.

"She's beautiful," he said.

Jo was shivering, the speed and intensity of the birth beginning to hit her. She leaned forward with Syd's help and closed her eyes gratefully as Sarah wrapped a thick robe around her.

"Thank you," she murmured. "Thank you so much."

Sarah smiled and stroked her finger along the baby's downy cheek.

"I think you two did most of the hard work," she said.

"Seven pounds, two ounces," the midwife announced, handling the baby as if she were a sack of potatoes instead of a tiny, breakable thing. By the time the midwife had arrived, all that remained for her to do was provide an official birth weight, give the baby a shot of vitamin K, and, for some reason Sarah had yet to figure out, measure the circumference of the baby's head.

More than happy to relinquish control to a professional, Sarah sat on a chair in the corner of the bedroom, drinking hot tea and reveling in the sense of tranquility that had settled over the new family.

"Do you have a name for her?" The midwife passed the baby to Syd, who looked terrified and had to sit on the bed for fear of dropping her.

"Abigail," Jo said.

"That's lovely." The midwife had one of those soothing voices that instantly made Sarah feel sleepy. "The ambulance should be here any time now. Everything's just fine, but I think monitoring Abigail for a day or two in Cary would be safest." As she began to pack away her equipment, Syd stood up.

"Would you mind?" He beckoned Sarah over and handed her the baby. "Would you mind getting a shot of us all?" he asked the midwife.

"No, of course not."

Perching around Jo on the edge of the bed, they formed a makeshift tableau, smiling for the camera.

"Say cheese!" the midwife said, and the baby let out a wail as the flash of the camera startled her.

❖

Sarah unlocked the back door and almost fell into the kitchen. It wasn't even that late, but after the adrenaline rush of the birth had come the inevitable crash, and she barely had the energy to put one foot in front of the other. She had left Jo and Syd at the same time as the midwife, blushing at their profuse thanks and promising to bring Alex around for a visit.

Not wanting to wake up properly, knowing that that would only start her thinking about what Alex might be doing, she washed herself and brushed her teeth with her eyes closed. She left her clothes where they fell and didn't bother with pajamas. She was asleep within seconds.

CHAPTER FOUR

S cott Emerson drove carefully, his every maneuver by the book, as if he were daring Alex to find fault with something. The air conditioner kept the car tolerably cool, but his sideburns were damp and she could smell the sweat that his deodorant and cologne weren't quite able to mask. She said little, leaving Tobin to fill the silence with aimless chatter until he too seemed to succumb to the tension and pushed back into his seat, his expression subdued. Alex wondered why Quinn had partnered her with Emerson, who had never made a secret of his dislike for her. Perhaps that was Quinn's reasoning, though: throw them together in a situation where they would have no choice but to watch each other's back, and force them to come out smiling on the other side. She admired his optimism, but she had a feeling that things wouldn't be quite so straightforward.

As they neared the warehouse district, the streets became noticeably emptier. Sickly orange pools of light from sparse streetlights gave Alex only fleeting glimpses of boarded-up storefronts and kids speeding away from street corners on pushbikes. Ruby was more densely populated than Avery, but it was largely prosperous and the vast majority of its crime seemed to originate from this one quarter mile of industrial lockups and tangled, darkened streets. On occasion, Alex saw small groups of the destitute or desperate congregating around the gaudy neon of cheap liquor stores, but they seemed to sense that the unmarked navy blue sedan had the potential to bring trouble, and they flitted back into the shadows as Emerson drove past.

"Hang a left, then second right," she said.

Emerson grunted in acknowledgment. His name had never appeared on any of the surveillance schedules, and the rear entrance of the warehouse would have been difficult to find even if he had been familiar with the area. He extinguished the headlights as he made the right turn, and then he parked in a well concealed spot behind a large Dumpster. In Alex's earpiece, Quinn tersely announced that he was ten minutes out and that they were all to hold their positions until he gave the word.

A click and a snap made her glance across at Emerson. He had pulled his Glock from its holster and its clip was in his hand. He slid it back into place, but not before she had spotted the slight tremor making his fingers twitch. She quickly looked away, not wanting to make him self-conscious. He was nervous, probably scared, and for the first time she considered how young he was. Although she knew next to nothing about him, she figured he had most likely been a small-town cop for his entire career. Her own heart was pounding double-time, but at least she had a good idea what to expect, having participated in countless armed raids while in LA. That, coupled with what she and Sarah had survived in the mountains, made her surprisingly sanguine about what was to come. Emerson, on the other hand, appeared to be on the verge of throwing up.

The warehouse loomed not thirty feet away, dark and seemingly deserted, but with a solitary white van in the parking lot. Alex nodded toward the vehicle.

"Soon as the shit hits the fan, that's what they'll be trying to reach," she said. "Be a shame if someone had tampered with it."

Emerson ran his tongue across his lips before he answered her. "Be my guest."

She allowed herself a small smile. "Just keep an eye on the warehouse. I get shot in the ass, you and Tobin are all alone out here for another five minutes before Quinn can come save you."

For a second, she thought she caught a flicker of amusement on Emerson's face, but he buried it beneath a scowl and turned his attention to the rear entrance of the warehouse. Alex opened her door soundlessly and dropped to a crouch on the asphalt, her Glock clasped in her hand. She had forgotten how warm the night was; perspiration prickled at her hairline and made her shirt cling to her back. Without giving herself time to hesitate, she ran across the parking lot, aiming for the far side of the van. Its engine was still ticking as it cooled; it hadn't been parked for long.

The first tire let out a painfully loud hiss as she stuck her pocketknife into it. She closed her eyes, counting the seconds, waiting for someone to come find her, but the warehouse door remained firmly sealed as the tire deflated. She had seen too many idiotic criminals careening around city streets on the rim of one blown tire, so she stuck her knife into a second, making sure it was completely ruined before she scurried back to the sedan.

"Done?" Emerson asked curtly.

"Done." She let out a short laugh as Tobin gave a muted whoop from the rear seat.

Emerson was not amused. "Quinn's in position," he said.

"Okay then." Alex's unplanned solo mission had settled her, burning off the excess adrenaline to leave her clearheaded and focused. "Lead the way."

Keeping low, they ran toward the warehouse door as Quinn started a countdown from ten. The earsplitting smashes of the battering ram wielded by the team at the front door were more than enough to cover the noise of Emerson prizing open the back. Alex could hear distant shouts, the thump of booted feet across concrete floors, doors slamming in rapid succession. In stark contrast, the corridor her team entered was quiet and dimly lit. Emerson had taken point, moving steadily toward a left-handed corner around which the offices were located. The air smelled stale: body odor, the chemical stink of an overused toilet, and oily fast food. Behind Alex, Tobin had dropped back, his panting breaths loud in the enclosed space. She slowed her pace to fall into step with him.

"You okay?" she whispered.

The whites of his eyes gleamed in the beam of her flashlight. He nodded, sweat dripping from his nose. When she glanced back toward the corner, Emerson was nowhere to be seen.

"Damn." She activated her radio. "Emerson?"

"Third office," he answered impatiently. "First two are clear. Sounds like Quinn's team has them pinned down." He sounded disappointed, as if he were suddenly spoiling for a fight now that there wasn't going to be one.

"Copy that." Alex turned to Tobin. "Stick with me," she said. "There were only five offices, so we're almost through."

He seemed to relax a little at that, squaring his shoulders and indicating that she should carry on. She led the way around the corner, trying to listen to the reports in her earpiece and simultaneously reconcile the memorized blueprints with the layout of the corridor onto which they had turned. Glass windows and doors, one of each per office, interrupted the continuity of the right-hand wall, while shuttered blinds concealed the rooms' contents from view. The first two offices were close together, the remaining three farther down and a greater distance apart. She had stopped, intending to radio Emerson for his position, when she saw a flash of light behind the blinds of the second window.

"Fuck." Instinct made the hairs stand up on the back of her neck.

With no time to think, she pushed Tobin back toward the corner as the door of the second office was flung open. A man large enough to fill the doorway launched himself into the corridor and slashed out wildly with a knife.

"Police!" Alex yelled. She already had her Glock raised, but a sudden, sharp pain along the length of her forearm made her hand numb and she couldn't prevent the gun's weight from pulling her arm down. She kicked out at the back of the man's knee, causing his leg to buckle. The unexpected pain made him pause, and when he turned toward her, she used her left arm to deliver a backhand that had as much effect as swatting an elephant with a feather. The punch he threw in retaliation smashed into her cheek and slammed her against the wall. Sliding slowly to the floor, she heard the rapid approach of footsteps and Emerson screaming something that ended with "*Now,* motherfucker!"

She saw Tobin creeping back around the corner as the knife clattered onto the concrete, and she allowed her eyes to close, figuring that she had earned the right to just sit still and let the others sort it all out.

"Don't worry, 'm fine," Alex had said on the phone, but her words had slurred together into a drowsy mess and that was the point at which Sarah had really gotten scared.

At three in the morning, the roads were empty. Sarah pushed hard on the gas, creeping beyond the legal speed limit and having to force herself to slow down again. Quinn had called first, the noise of the phone bringing her out of a restless sleep and making her feel sick with panic. Although he tried to explain about the raid, about a man with a knife and why Alex was currently en route to the hospital in Cary, she had been too busy throwing her clothes on to listen to him properly, and she had dropped the receiver as she reached for her pants. When the phone rang for a second time, Alex was on the other end, telling her it was only a little cut and probably wouldn't even need stitches. "Stay in bed," she had insisted, but Sarah was already halfway out the door.

The emergency department was quiet; an elderly couple sitting close together with a shared air of resignation and a disheveled man muttering to himself were the only people waiting on the hard plastic seats. Sarah gave Alex's name at the desk just as she heard someone call her own. When she looked around, she saw Bill Quinn raising his hand, and the clerk buzzed her through.

"She's fine. She's in X-ray," Quinn said. He didn't know Sarah well and seemed keen to preempt any hysterics on her part. With a hand on her arm, he led her through to a small cubicle. Bloodstains on the white tiled floor indicated where Alex's bed had been.

"What the hell happened?" Sarah asked. There wasn't a lot of blood, but the sight of it still made her stomach churn.

"Uh…" He wrapped a hand around the back of his neck and massaged the muscles there. "We're looking into it," he said evasively, which suggested to Sarah that someone had fucked up, royally. "Alex took a knock to the head and she has a cut on her arm. Doc says it's nothing serious."

She nodded, not trusting herself to speak.

"She did good, Sarah."

That made her look up at him. "So it wasn't Alex who fucked up, then?"

The question appeared to catch him off guard, but he was too honest a man to leave it unanswered. "No," he said. "No, it wasn't Alex." He sighed. "You be okay to take her home when they're through with her?"

"Of course." She realized then that he had important tasks he needed to be doing, tasks he was neglecting in order to stay with his officer. "Thanks for looking out for her," she said softly.

He smiled, but his expression remained troubled. "I'll need to debrief her sometime tomorrow. Ask her to give me a call when she's ready."

"I will."

He laid a hand on her shoulder for a moment and then left her sitting alone, staring at the blood on the floor.

Alex's bed was returned without ceremony by an orderly with a sour face and a ridiculous but determined comb-over. He grunted at Sarah and pulled the drapes closed as he departed. She barely noticed him leave; her attention was fixed on Alex, who was lying curled on her side, apparently asleep. Someone had exchanged her uniform for a gown, and blood had started to ooze through the bandage that covered her right forearm from wrist to elbow. The upper half of her face was swollen, with bruises darkening across her cheekbone and beginning to gather purposefully just beneath her eye.

Sarah clamped her mouth shut, trying not to make a noise, trying not to cry, but it was too much like the last time, and tears filled her eyes regardless. Bending low and brushing aside a strand of Alex's hair, she found a patch of skin that wasn't bruised and kissed it gently.

Alex stirred at the touch, a frown crinkling her brow.

"Quinn?" The name came out in a barely coherent mumble.

"Since when has Bill Quinn been giving you kisses?"

The sound of Sarah's voice brought a lazy smile to Alex's lips and she opened her eyes, blinking like a creature emerging from hibernation into bright sunlight. She reached toward Sarah's cheek, wafting the air repeatedly until Sarah took her hand and guided it into place. Her smile broadened into a grin, and Sarah allowed herself to relax slightly as it became apparent that Alex was not so much concussed as drugged up to the eyeballs.

"Told you not to worry," Alex said, tripping over her words and failing utterly in her attempt to sound stern. "And here y'are, all worried and stuff."

"Yeah, yeah." Sarah brushed her fingers across Alex's forehead. "So, dare I ask what the other guy looks like?" It was a standard joke, but Alex didn't seem capable of anything but the most literal interpretation.

"Pretty fuckin' big," she said, her eyes widening as far as the bruising would permit. "Huge." She held her hands apart, trying to give an impression of the man's size, but she couldn't coordinate the movement and ended up looking like an angler who'd caught quite a small fish. "And mean," she added as an afterthought.

Sarah touched the bandage lightly. "What happened here?"

"He cut me with a knife." Alex made the admission with obvious reluctance. She took hold of Sarah's finger and gripped onto it tightly, to Sarah's relief. The wound to her arm was still bleeding through its dressing, but she seemed to have a good range of movement, so any serious damage to the nerves or other underlying structures was unlikely.

"It went a bit numb at first, but it's okay now," she said, as if reading Sarah's mind. She wriggled her fingers when Sarah stroked each of them in turn. "And that tickles."

Sarah shook her head. "I wish you'd learn to bloody duck." She tried to keep her expression serious, but Alex looked so remorseful that she had to smile.

The start of a heartfelt apology was interrupted by a doctor hurrying into the cubicle.

"Officer..."—he checked the paperwork in his hand—"Hayes. Sorry for the delay. A frequent flier of ours decided that tonight would be a good night for self-immolation." Halfway through snapping on a clean pair of gloves, he paused thoughtfully. "Messy business. I absolutely do not recommend it." He rolled a small equipment table toward the bed. "You must be Sarah," he said, seeming to notice her for the first time.

She nodded, assuming that at some point Alex or Quinn had mentioned her name. She moved to the opposite side of the bed, giving him room to tuck a sterile sheet beneath Alex's arm.

"The X-rays were clear, no fractures," he said. "Can you just..." Alex obligingly raised her arm so that he could unwind the bandage. "Thanks. Yes, given the swelling, I expected worse."

The final piece of gauze fell onto the sheet with a wet slap, and he cleaned away the blood to expose the injury. Sarah stepped closer to see the damage and immediately wished she hadn't. The knife wound extended from the underside of Alex's wrist to the middle of her forearm. In the stark light of the cubicle, it gaped and glistened like a sick smile.

"Nasty," the doctor said with considerable understatement. As he started to perform a series of tests to assess circulation and sensation, Sarah watched Alex trying to concentrate even though the pain was making sweat break out on her forehead. When he was finished, he patted the back of Alex's hand.

"That's all fine. You take it easy now while I get everything set up here."

Sarah soaked a handful of paper napkins at the small sink and used them to wipe Alex's face. "Better?"

"Mmm." Alex nodded gratefully.

"Have you home and tucked up in bed in no time."

"Sounds lovely."

The doctor held up a syringe and squirted a small amount of clear liquid from a needle that was anything but small. "Okay, Alex, this is going to sting a little."

His warning made her roll her eyes, and Sarah stifled a giggle; they had both lost count of the number of sutures they had needed in the last three years.

"Hey, at least you're getting an anesthetic," Sarah said drily.

Alex snorted, but composed herself when she noticed the doctor's curious expression.

"Long story, doc," she said, and clamped down on Sarah's hand as he dug in with the needle.

The voice sounded as if it were coming from a long way off. At first, it was patient and cajoling, but became gradually more insistent, with just a hint of amused exasperation. It took another long minute for Alex to work out that the voice belonged to Sarah and that she was trying to persuade her to get out of the Jeep.

Alex opened her eyes and groaned as hot light seemed to pierce her retinas and lodge right at the point where her head was pounding. Drool had stuck her cheek to the warm leather seat, and moving any part of her body made her feel sick. The cardboard bowl on her lap, along with the small pile of them in the footwell and the disgusting taste in her mouth, suggested it had been a very long journey home for Sarah. Alex, however, could barely remember leaving the hospital.

Apparently deciding that she had given Alex enough time to regain her equilibrium, Sarah took hold of Alex's good arm and slung it across her shoulders.

"You've got to help me out here, love. You go all Bambi-legged and we'll both end up on the floor."

"I'm good," Alex muttered with as much indignation as she could muster. "Been walking since I was ten months old."

To prove her point, she swung around out of the passenger seat and managed to stand by clinging on to Sarah and the doorjamb.

"Okay, go," she said urgently. It felt like the world was tilting on its axis, and she was no longer quite so confident in her ability to remain upright. Her feet clomped clumsily as she took a step; someone had put her work boots back on and not tied them tightly enough. Meanwhile, there was a strange draft around her thighs.

"What the fuck?" She looked down at the pink, flowery hospital gown she was still wearing, and brought Sarah to a halt at the foot of the porch steps. "Is my ass hanging out?" she asked, afraid that she already knew the answer.

Sarah took her time, glancing behind Alex to check. "Yes, it is," she finally confirmed. Her eyes glinted with amusement; she wasn't taking Alex's discomfiture at all seriously. "No one's looking. Not even the chickens."

"Did they steal my underwear?"

"Who? The chickens?"

"No, the doctors!"

"Oh. No. No, your underwear is present and correct."

Slightly mollified, Alex allowed Sarah to lead her up the steps. By the time they reached the kitchen, she was so dizzy that she had to grab onto the table for support.

"I think I might throw up," she whispered, shocked by how awful she felt.

"Almost there, hang on," Sarah said and continued to guide her slowly toward the bedroom.

Sarah closed her book and rested both hands on its tattered cover. The instant she moved, pins and needles raced down her left leg and prickled heat into her big toe. She shuffled awkwardly on the chair, uncurling herself and stretching each limb in turn. Something in her spine popped and cracked in protest, but that was nothing new, and it hadn't been loud enough to disturb Alex. She smiled at the soft snores; it wasn't like Alex to sleep flat on her back, but she appeared to be comfortable enough. In the past seven hours, she had managed to sleep through Bandit chasing a frog around the kitchen, three phone calls, and a mass chicken brawl. After the noise of the second phone call provoked no meaningful response, Sarah had decided to switch a small reading lamp on, and Alex hadn't seemed bothered by that either. Every two hours, Sarah carefully shook her awake. She dutifully stated her name and date of birth, told Sarah how tired she looked, and fell back to sleep. According to the doctor, she had a mild concussion; sleep, pain relief, and a responsible caregiver were the only management required.

Running a hand through her hair, Sarah tried hard to stifle a yawn. A quick check of her watch told her she had another forty minutes before she needed to disturb Alex again, so she headed to the kitchen in search of food and caffeine. She fed the animals, slung the local paper on the table to browse through later, and set the kettle to boil. By the time she returned with a tray of toast and tea, Alex was awake and attempting to sit up.

"Oh, hey. Here, let me…" Sarah plumped the pillows and arranged them behind Alex. "How's that?"

Alex didn't answer straight away. She had closed her eyes and seemed to be deciding whether being upright really was an improvement. After a few seconds, she cracked one eye open and relaxed her white-knuckle grip on the sheets.

"That toast smells amazing," she said.

Sarah made a skeptical noise. "How about we see if you can keep water down first?"

"Have I not been doing that?"

"Not as such, no."

"Oh." Alex looked disappointed and then noticed she was lying on a towel. "Oh," she repeated, with greater understanding. "Shit, sorry."

Sarah perched on the mattress. "You look a bit better."

"Feel a bit better." Alex tentatively flexed her bandaged arm and then appeared to remember something vitally important. Her face lit up with a grin. "So what's this I hear about you being some kind of baby-delivering all-round heroine?"

Sarah put her head in her hands. "How the hell did you find out about that?"

"Esther managed to keep it a secret until they got me to the hospital. Then she told Quinn, who told me and the doc and just about anyone else within earshot."

The Avery grapevine was legendary; Sarah should have known that that piece of gossip would spread around the town in a heartbeat.

"It wasn't really a big deal." She laughed as Alex arched a disbelieving eyebrow. "Honestly, I didn't have to do all that much."

"Yeah, well, Syd Bair is telling a different story. He thinks you're amazing."

"The birth was amazing. It gave me goose bumps."

Undeterred, Alex continued her original theme. "Your undisputed amazingness calls for a celebration," she said. She shifted over to make more space in the bed. "Come on, and bring that tray. We can share."

Relief at Alex's recovery made Sarah compliant. She pressed closer, positioning the tray so they could both reach it.

"One piece." She handed Alex the toast. "And you eat it slowly. Then you can take your pain meds."

"I'm very proud of you, and I love you," Alex said, nibbling on a corner.

"You love toast."

"I do also love toast."

In spite of herself, Sarah started to laugh. "Alex, if you're going to wink at me, try doing it with the eye that isn't swollen shut."

The phone rang, cutting off Alex's comeback. Recognizing the number on the caller ID, Sarah passed it straight to her with a muttered "Quinn."

Only privy to one side of the conversation, Sarah watched her slowly put her toast down as Quinn spoke. When she hung up, her face was pale, with no trace of humor left.

"Emerson's been suspended, pending an investigation," she said. "He pretty much admitted to only opening the doors of the first two offices. He told us they were clear, but he hadn't gone inside and searched them properly."

"Jesus." Sarah shook her head. "Where was the guy who assaulted you?"

"Came out of the second office."

"What the fuck was Emerson thinking?" The crockery on the tray rattled as she spoke, and it was only then that she realized she was shaking.

"I'm not sure." Unlike Sarah, who felt ready to throttle Emerson with her bare hands, Alex sounded more bewildered than angry. "He was scared. Maybe that made him sloppy."

"He could have got you killed."

"I know." She was staring blankly into the darkened bedroom.

For a terrifying moment, paranoia gripped Sarah. "Do you think he meant to?"

"No." Alex answered quickly, but when she turned to Sarah, she looked uncertain and very tired. "I don't know," she said.

The admission hung between them, its implications too deep for Sarah to fathom after so little sleep and so much stress. Hand in hand, they sat in silence. It was Alex who eventually spoke.

"Maybe we should call Castillo."

CHAPTER FIVE

A lex eyed the small pink pills with disdain.

"Come on. Down the hatch," Sarah said. Her hand was cool from the water, her touch light against Alex's aching head, and Alex took the first pill just to prolong the moment. It didn't make anything worse so she chased the second down with a gulp of water.

"Oh bugger," Sarah muttered. The advice leaflet from the medication was on the bed, spread out in front of her.

"What? Am I allergic?" Alex might have felt alarmed, had she not been so damn tired.

"No. Well, I don't think so." Sarah studied her, her expression quizzical as she tried to remember. "I thought beetroot was the only thing you were allergic to."

"Those pills were awful pink."

The worry on Sarah's face softened as she smiled. "Unlikely to be beetroot flavored, though." Her finger rested on a section of the leaflet. "It's this warning: 'may cause drowsiness.'"

She must have had a point to make, but Alex couldn't discern it. Blinking at her, she tried not to yawn. "That gonna be a problem?"

"We need to phone Castillo." Sarah sounded as if she were speaking to a child: slow, careful, ensuring that Alex could follow her. "That means I need to know what happened last night, and everything you have on Emerson, because I don't think you're going to be in a fit state to speak to anyone in an official capacity."

Alex nodded in a manner she hoped was serious, but found she had concerns of a far more pressing nature. "Can I have your toast?"

Sarah swore beneath her breath, but passed the spare piece of toast over before taking a notepad and pen from the bedside table.

"Scott Emerson," she said, flipping the pad to a blank page. "Go."

"He doesn't like me," Alex ventured. For some reason, that made her feel incredibly tearful, and chewing the toast was the only thing keeping her bottom lip from quivering. "I don't know why. He gives me all the crappy jobs to do."

Sarah made a "carry on" motion with her hand; she hadn't written anything down yet. "Do you know anything that might help Castillo look into his background?" she said. "His home address? Is he married?"

"He lives out on Pike Road, right up the top end. I think he's single. There was cake in February." Something gave a twinge in Alex's injured wrist and she instantly forgot why her last point had been salient. "There was cake in February." She looked up at Sarah helplessly. "I can't…"

"Think his birthday might be in February?" Sarah asked gently.

"I guess. I don't remember the day, but he's thirty."

The notepad page was half-full of scribbles.

"You're doing fabulously," Sarah assured her. "Does he have any distinguishing marks? Tattoos?"

"Not that I've noticed." Since being held hostage by Deakin's gang of racist thugs, they had done their research. Tattoos were a notable feature of many white supremacist groups, but Emerson would have to have been insane to display any such markings, given his choice of profession. "I've never heard him say anything out of line, either," she said. "He seems like a decent officer, metip, meticul…" She stumbled over the word, her teeth and tongue getting in each other's way.

"Meticulous?"

"Yes. And last night, the look on his face—Sarah, he looked terrible."

Sarah paused in her writing, the pen hovering over the page. "Terrible because you were hurt or terrible because he was in deep shit and you weren't actually dead?" She made no attempt to temper her bitterness, and there was a flush creeping upward from her chest to her neck.

Alex closed her eyes, uncertain exactly what she had seen before her head smacked into the wall, or how to interpret it.

"He tried to stop me from bleeding," she said. She remembered that much, remembered Tobin being useless in the background while

Emerson pressed his bare hands against her wound. But that could have been tactical as well; the wound obviously wasn't going to prove fatal, so he had to be seen to be helping his fallen colleague. Didn't he?

When she opened her eyes, the tray was gone and Sarah was rearranging the pillows behind her.

"Come on. Lie down," Sarah said, and her voice was like a balm, kind and lovely.

"Did you get enough to tell Castillo?"

The pillow was soft beneath Alex's head, urging her deeper into it.

"I got enough." Sarah pulled up the sheets and tucked her in. "I'm going to call him now. You need anything?"

"'M good, thanks."

"I'm right next door," Sarah said, and clicked the room into darkness.

Given the late hour, Sarah was surprised to catch Castillo on his office number. He answered by stating his official title, but he sounded as if he were chewing a mouthful of food. The familiarity of his voice, and the sense of security that it evoked, made her feel calmer.

"You eating a load of bloody rubbish again?" she said in as broad a northern English accent as she could muster. She heard him chuckle in recognition and then slurp something that was probably a milkshake.

"Who are you, my mom? Sorry, *mum*," he countered cheerfully, before his tone became more serious. "Good to hear from you, Sarah. Everything okay up there?"

He already knew the answer to that because he was always the one who phoned them. They were only supposed to initiate contact in the event of a problem.

"Alex got hurt," she said, and all of her preparations, her notes, and her carefully constructed arguments were lost in the aftermath of that short statement.

"Is she all right?" He sounded closer somehow, as if concern were making him speak more directly into the phone.

"She will be." Sarah managed to steady her voice. "Something went wrong on a raid at a warehouse. She got slashed with a knife and ended up with a concussion."

She could hear him breathing, but he didn't interrupt so she continued.

"There's a sergeant she works with. He…We don't know. He screwed up, caused Alex's injuries—"

"And you don't know if he acted intentionally," Castillo finished the thought for her.

"Yeah, it crossed our minds," she said. "He's been really weird with her since she started. He could just be a homophobic prick…" Castillo snorted at that. "But something about it doesn't feel right."

"Yeah, no point being a homophobic prick if your target doesn't know that's why you hate her."

"Exactly." She found herself smiling. "We're so bloody eloquent, darling," she said affecting the clipped tone of a BBC newsreader.

There was a pause, during which he seemed to be blowing bubbles into his milkshake.

"Okay, that's less eloquent, more disgusting," she said.

"Helps me think." She could practically hear him shrugging. "What details do you have on this guy?"

She gave him everything she had gleaned from Alex and extrapolated on the events at the warehouse. He seemed to be typing the information directly onto his computer; keys clacked rapidly as she spoke.

"Two problems with this," he said once she had finished. "One: there's not a lot to go on. Two: once I track this guy down, a thorough background check is going to be tricky. I'll have to disguise the origin and purpose of any file requests, or I'm going to have the Avery PD wondering why the hell I'm investigating one of their men."

She rubbed her eyes with the back of her hand. They felt gritty and swollen with exhaustion. "Can you do it?"

Castillo's answer was laden with caution. "Yes. It'll just take time. We could be talking more than a week before I know anything concrete."

She tried hard to keep the disappointment from her voice. "Any advice for us until then?"

"Keep your heads down." His response was automatic. "If this guy is dangerous and he's suspended from work, he has a whole lot of time on his hands."

"Yeah." That was something she had already considered.

"We are watching them," he said. He didn't need to be any more specific; she knew he meant the remaining members of the Deakin family and those from the Church of the Aryan Resistance who had so far escaped criminal charges. His reassurances would have been more effective, though, had he not already told them the outcome of the FBI's surveillance review meeting three months previously. With no sign of a credible threat, the budget for the surveillance had been reduced in spite of his arguments, leaving it little more than a monthly exercise in checking the criminal records of everyone on the watch list and ensuring they were all still living where they should be.

She rested her head against the receiver for a moment and then forced cheerfulness into her voice.

"Listen, thanks, Mike. It helps just to chat, y'know."

"No problem, honey. I'll check in with you in a week or so. I'm gonna make a start on the paperwork, okay? Tell Alex I said hi."

"I will."

"I'll be in touch."

She didn't want to hang up, but reluctance to put the onus on him made her end the call. The phone gave a tinny beep as she returned it to its charging unit, and she saw Tilly's ears prick up.

"Shh, girl, everything's fine."

Tilly lay back down, taking her at her word. The absolute trust made Sarah smile sadly; she wished she could be so easily convinced.

Lying as still as she could, Sarah listened to Alex mutter unintelligibly in her sleep. A touch on her arm and a few whispered words were all it took to soothe her, and she turned over without waking. Sarah watched the drapes sway in a breeze that didn't reach the bed and wondered whether this was what people meant when they said they were too tired to sleep. She was too hot, too restless, and no matter how hard she tried not to move, something unreachable would itch as soon as she thought about it. The stark red display of the alarm clock told her that over twenty-four hours had passed since she last slept.

Unable to lie motionless any longer, she inched herself out of bed and wandered into the living room. Three sets of glinting eyes tracked her progress, but none of the animals seemed inclined to leave the sofa.

She envied their drowsy, untroubled state. With nowhere comfortable left to sit, she poured herself a glass of water, added ice, and took it out onto the back porch.

She had grown to love the darkness that night in the middle of the forest brought. Above her, there was nothing but a waning moon and the tiny pinpricks of millions of stars. She wrapped a thin blanket around her shoulders, curled up on the bench, and let the coldness of the glass in her hand numb her fingers. Her eyes were growing heavy and her head was beginning to nod when something suddenly flew down from the eaves, its rapid wingbeats so close that she felt them stir her hair. She jumped, making water slosh from the glass. Even when the creature flitted past again and she realized it was a bat, her hand still trembled.

"Jesus," she whispered. She pulled the blanket closer, unsure whether to laugh or cry. "Jesus Christ."

She looked out across the yard, toward the point where the trees thickened and crowded around the edge of the land she and Alex had cultivated. Leaves and undergrowth rustled as creatures stirred, but she couldn't see what was moving out there, and the sound of her heartbeat thumping in her ears quickly obliterated any further noise. Fear made her clumsy; she banged her thigh on the arm of the bench as she stood and turned to go back inside. She shut the porch door behind her, turned the light on in the kitchen, and systematically slid every one of the locks into place. It should have been enough to make her feel safe, but doubt still nagged at the back of her mind. She walked through the living room and stood in front of a painting she and Alex had bought at a market stall in Lhasa. It was a gorgeous, stylized riot of color; they had spent so long trying to arrange for it to be couriered to Ash and Tess in England for safekeeping that they almost missed their train departing. Sarah reached up and removed it from its hook, exposing the safe behind it.

For the first time in months, she entered the four-digit code into the keypad. The lock disengaged with a smooth click and the weight of the safe door swung it open slightly. There were two cases inside, both black and solid with grip handles and individual locks. She slid out the upper case, set it on the table, and unlocked it. The Glock 17 nestled snugly in its molded foam interior, along with two full magazines. She eased the gun from the case and spent several minutes familiarizing herself with its weight and features. Technically, both of the guns belonged to Alex, but soon after they moved to Maine, she had arranged tuition for Sarah at a local shooting range, lessons to which Sarah had agreed with considerable reluctance. Despite the history that she and Alex shared, she was still uneasy having the weapons in the house.

The metal was warm and heavy in her hands, and a memory abruptly assailed her: a sharp recoil that had knocked her onto the floor, the stink of burning and blood, and the sound of a man screaming his hatred at her. She pushed the Glock back into its case and sealed the lock with fumbling fingers. It would make sense to leave the gun out of the safe, to position it somewhere strategic, someplace it would be quick to access, but she couldn't yet bring herself to acknowledge that that might be necessary. Not until they heard something from Castillo.

She lifted the case back into the safe and reset the combination. Her vision spun drunkenly as she turned around, and she felt cold enough to make her teeth chatter. Touching the edges of the furniture for guidance, she made her way back into the bedroom and eased herself between the sheets. Compared to her own skin, Alex's fairly blazed with heat, and she snuggled as close as she dared. As if sensing her need, Alex pushed into the curve of her body. Sarah kissed Alex's shoulder and closed her eyes.

❖

Leah had always dreaded this day. At night, praying to a God she was no longer sure even existed, she had begged him to stop this day from ever arriving. Now, the joy on Caleb's face and the triumph blazing in his eyes served only to confirm her fears: nothing out there was listening to her prayers.

She spilled hot coffee onto her fingers as he grabbed her around the waist and pulled her closer to him. The computer was on, its screen filled with an image of a young woman. Leah bit down on the cut in her lip as she recognized the woman's face.

"Found the little bitches," he said.

The woman in the photograph didn't look like a bitch; she looked happy and proud. The article was from the online edition of a small-town newspaper, and it identified her as Sarah Hayes, a first responder who had helped a local couple to deliver their baby. She had cut and dyed her hair and changed her surname, but she was undoubtedly the same woman whose picture was a permanent fixture on the computer desktop.

"Two for the price of one," Caleb said, clicking the mouse. The browser loaded a second report from the same newspaper. There was no accompanying photograph this time, just a headline that read: "Local cop injured in warehouse raid." He tapped his finger on the screen, smearing greasy sweat across the name in the article.

"What are the fucking odds of that?"

He seemed to be expecting Leah to answer, so she smiled and kissed him, tasting blood as his tongue explored her swollen lip.

"Get the gear ready," he said, spitting her blood onto the floor. "Either they're fucking idiots, or they haven't seen this newspaper yet. And I don't think they're idiots."

She nodded mutely, her eyes still skimming the newspaper article. The injured police officer had been named as Alex Hayes.

❖

The shower kicked in with its usual sputter and clang. Standing outside the small stall, waiting for the water to run clear and heat up, Alex counted slowly to twenty. She let out her breath as she reached her target. If Sarah had been awake, she would have been in the bathroom by now, probably brandishing a roll of Saran Wrap to keep Alex's stitches dry, while simultaneously admonishing her for getting out of bed on her own. All Alex wanted to do was get clean and then eat something more substantial than toast.

She wrapped her arm in a plastic bag and ducked beneath the spray. The warm water made the swollen skin on her face burn at first, but the discomfort eased within a few seconds and she gave a sigh of unalloyed pleasure. She washed herself as thoroughly as she could manage one-handed, but for the most part just allowed the water to sluice away the sweat and dried blood that had been making her skin foul and itchy. When she finally turned the water off and the steam began to clear, her one good eye picked out a small form sitting motionless on the side of the bath. She opened the shower door a crack.

"Before I come out, exactly how much trouble am I in?"

She thought she heard Sarah smother a giggle but couldn't be sure.

"More than you could possibly imagine, missy."

"Well then, I'm staying in."

Sarah came to the shower door and offered her a towel. "Come and get dry, you silly sod."

Alex turned to let Sarah wrap the towel around her. "You looked so peaceful," she said, figuring that a good defense was as effective as any offense.

Sarah was still frowning at her, however. "And you could have fainted, or had a dizzy spell and clocked your head again."

The argument was far too logical to refute. Alex nodded sheepishly, conceding defeat without a fight. She couldn't help but smile at the Saran Wrap propped against the bathtub, though.

"That would have done a better job than your bag," Sarah said.

The knot Alex had tied in the plastic bag had worked loose once the water had slickened it, and she could feel how wet the dressing beneath it was.

"Will you be okay getting dressed?" Sarah asked.

Alex nodded.

"And will you let me change that soggy bandage once you're done?"

Another nod, and Alex pulled the towel tighter around herself. "You mad at me?"

With a sigh, Sarah sat on the closed toilet seat and used the towel to tug Alex toward her. She wrapped her arms around Alex's waist and kissed her bare midriff. "I'm not mad at you," she murmured, "but you've got to let me fuss over you when you're not well."

Alex stroked Sarah's hair back from her face and kissed her forehead. "You can fuss over me any time."

"In which case, will you stop getting yourself clobbered?"

"I will definitely try."

Sarah smiled up at her. "Sweetheart, that's all I ask."

❖

For the second time in less than twenty-four hours, Alex recounted the events of the warehouse raid. This time, however, Bill Quinn was the one asking the questions, and she had skipped her pain meds in order to answer them in full. Scott Emerson had apparently accepted full responsibility for what had happened, asking Quinn to offer an apology on his behalf until he could see Alex in person. Unaware of any potential ulterior motive, Quinn had told her he was willing to chalk up the incident to lack of experience and log it as a training need. Alex was disinclined to argue with that; if Emerson were reinstated, at least she would have a better idea of his whereabouts.

She cradled her sore arm as Quinn finally clicked off the small tape recorder. Her head ached and all she wanted to do was sit out in the sunshine with Sarah.

Quinn drained his coffee cup and pushed his chair away from the table.

"I spoke to the doc at Cary," he said. "He thinks you'll be good as new in a few days."

"The sutures can come out next week," she said, collecting the empty mugs together and setting them in the sink. "You got some paper I can push around till I'm cleared for active duty?"

"Got better than that. There's a two-day course running over in Crystal: forensics and interview techniques. Starts the day after tomorrow, and I already signed you up."

Alex shook her head; Crystal was a three-hour drive away, which would have to mean the course was residential.

"Every force was obliged to send an officer, and you're it." He held up a hand to stop her from arguing. "It's fully catered in a hotel," he added in a tone that implied she should be grateful for the opportunity.

There wasn't anything she could say. How could she explain that she needed to be here with Sarah, when Quinn knew absolutely nothing of what was going on?

"I have to get back over to Ruby," he said. "The evidence logging has been a fucking circus. I'll speak to you in the morning, see how you're doing."

"That's okay," she said. "You don't need to if you're that busy."

"I'll speak to you in the morning," he repeated firmly, heading for the door.

She nodded her acquiescence. As soon as Quinn had started his car, she went back into the kitchen and sat at the table. She pushed the local newspaper aside to make space for her to rest her head on her arms.

"Everything okay?" Sarah came in and took the other seat. She had been working in the yard and her hand was gritty with compost when she laid it on Alex's arm.

"I think Quinn will end Emerson's suspension in the next day or so," Alex mumbled against her sleeve.

"Right," Sarah said slowly, obviously considering the pros and cons. "Would make it easier for you to keep an eye on him."

"Well, that was my theory." Alex sat up straight. "But Quinn's sending me on a two-day residential course starting in Crystal on Thursday. Apparently, he won't take no for an answer." She looked at Sarah, trying to gauge her reaction, but her expression gave nothing away.

"We can't tell him about Emerson," Sarah said at last. "If we're wrong, everything we have here will be ruined, and we probably are wrong. I mean, what are the chances he'd have recognized us? Or waited so long to do anything about it?"

"I know." It was all Alex had been thinking about since waking up that morning. It made so little sense that she had almost phoned Castillo to apologize for wasting his time.

"It's only two days, Alex." Sarah sounded brighter, more confident. "And Lyssa will be round for one of them. I'll be fine."

Alex nodded, not wanting to imply that Sarah was incapable of looking after herself. She of all people knew how far that was from the truth.

"You can sit here and fret," Sarah said, "or you can come and see what I've been doing in the garden." She held out her hand, waiting patiently until Alex sighed and took it.

Soil crumbled against Alex's palm, smearing muck across her fingers. She gripped Sarah's hand regardless, and followed her out into the yard.

CHAPTER SIX

Caleb had spent most of the day on his cell phone or the computer. Dutifully packing duffel bags with clothes and provisions for the trip, Leah had heard snatches of his conversations and the harsh staccato of his fingers on the keyboard. She had seen him do this before: reach out to contacts, pull together support, resources, and research, find a weak link, a way in. She emptied her glass into the sink as the water she had just drunk settled like a rock in her stomach. Not for the first time, she wished he wasn't as good at this as his father had been. He had inherited his father's charisma, too, which meant he had his own followers now, and there was always a weak link out there waiting to be exploited.

She left one bag lying open on the kitchen table, knowing that he would want to pack his own weapons. At some point, while waiting for a call to be returned, he had brought various items from the garage and sorted them into a neat pile. A roll of duct tape, rope, cable ties, and a Taser were now sitting beside the fruit bowl and a half-finished lemon drizzle cake.

Leah had already been sick once that morning; now she felt the familiar roiling start up again. For two years, she had listened to him plot and fantasize, each new idea more elaborate than the last. He had tried to explain how there was a greater ambition at work, how doing this would resurrect the fervor his father had inspired in his followers and reunite the disparate members of the church beneath a new banner. She had listened and nodded, and nursed the bruises he gave her when he saw any hint of doubt. Despite his justifications and his idealistic rhetoric, she knew that what really fueled him was the simplest of motives: revenge.

The rattle of the screen door as he came in startled her; she hadn't heard him go out. He placed a large armored box onto the table and entered a combination on the keypad. As he lifted the lid, the fastidiously cleaned weapons gleamed in the late afternoon sun.

"Got us a contact and a place to stay, baby."

She nodded, certain that she would scream if she opened her mouth. He had already told her that he needed her as part of his cover. While a lone male might raise suspicions or at least get curious people in a small town gossiping, a married couple renting a holiday cottage was unlikely to attract any undue attention.

"Ain't that worth a kiss?" he asked. With one hand, he tugged at her skirt, leaving her no option but to walk toward him. Instead of kissing her, he put his cheek against her abdomen. "Gonna take my boy on an adventure," he said to the twelve-week-old fetus whose gender was as yet unknown.

Leah Deakin placed her hands lovingly on her husband's head. It seemed like the sort of gesture a faithful wife would make. As he pressed his lips to the barely noticeable swell of their first baby, she stared out the window at the yellow, gnarled grass in the yard. This tiny piece of North Carolina was her home. Her family lived less than a mile away, her mom already busy sewing clothes and thinking of names for her first grandchild. Her parents had always given their unquestioning support to Caleb, and to Caleb's father before him. It would only be afterward, when it was too late to intervene, that her mom might consider the repercussions. Leah didn't think her father ever would.

It was so early that even the chickens weren't awake. Alex pushed a forkful of eggs around her plate and scowled at the world in general.

"Try and eat something, love. You've got a long drive."

Sitting in front of her, nursing a mug of tea, Sarah was still wearing pajamas and her hair was tousled with sleep.

"Not really hungry," Alex muttered.

"Just try." Sarah batted her eyelashes winningly, forcing Alex to smile. "For me?"

The eggs were unexpectedly tasty, and once Alex had taken a first bite, she ate the rest with enthusiasm. "You spiked these with something?" she asked during a pause for breath.

Sarah laughed; playing "guess the secret ingredient" was a familiar game. "Bit of cream, ground black pepper, and paprika. Thought it might perk you up a little."

"I am perfectly perked, and I still don't want to go."

"No, I know that. But at least now you're going with a full stomach."

Checking her watch, Alex was surprised how effectively she had managed to procrastinate. She swigged the remainder of her coffee as she stood. "I'm just going to brush my teeth. Meet you outside?"

"Sure." Sarah raised her lips for a kiss as Alex hurried past.

Dumping the pots in the sink to deal with later, Sarah watched sunlight tentatively lick at the edges of the yard, as the tallest of the trees swayed in the breeze. She wondered whether it would be too hot tomorrow for her and Lyssa to study outside. Today she would vacuum, or maybe clean the tiles in the bathroom: anything to take her mind off the fact that she would be alone in the cabin once night drew in. Alex regularly worked night shifts, but that was different somehow. A night shift never dragged her hours away across the county and never left Sarah feeling so vulnerable.

She picked up Alex's bag and carried it out to the Silverado. Tilly followed so closely that Sarah had to weave to avoid stepping on her.

"Neither of us can go with her," she said, crouching to rub Tilly's ears.

"Okay." Alex walked toward them. "I am minty fresh and good to go." She displayed her teeth in an outrageously forced grin, making Sarah laugh.

"Phone me when you get there," Sarah said, wrapping her in a tight hug. "Or before then, and at any point in between."

Alex chuckled. "Be back before you've even missed me."

They both knew it wasn't true. Sarah shook her head hopelessly. "How on earth did we end up so bloody codependent?"

"You fell for my charm, good looks, and skill with a needle and thread." Alex kissed her. "Be safe."

"You too." Sarah pushed her gently toward the truck. "Go on."

She watched Alex turn the truck in a broad circle and give a final wave before driving slowly down the track. When she went back into the bedroom to get dressed, she found a single pink rose on her pillow, with a slip of paper bearing the words: "Miss you already."

❖

It was cooler this far north, the heat tempered by pleasant breezes and lacking the energy-sapping humidity to which Leah was accustomed. They had traveled for almost twenty hours, arriving at the quaintly furnished holiday cottage in the middle of the night. Caleb had left again at first light to meet with his contact, taking the rental car and giving Leah no estimation of when he would be back. She had been alone in the cottage all day.

Looking out from the porch, she could see only thick forest. Huge firs gave the air a moist, fresh scent, but they crowded in on the small clearing, leaving it completely shadowed. The track from the access road was concealed by a tricky curve that night blindness and exhaustion had almost caused Caleb to misjudge when they first arrived. A welcome pack left by the owner of the cottage spoke of its retreat-like nature, which presumably explained why there was no telephone. During lulls in the evening chorus came the distant lapping of waves on the lakeshore, but there was no obvious path through the trees, and Leah was afraid that if she went looking, Caleb would return to find her wandering and ask her why. The irony of her situation was not lost on her; she was free to do as she wished, but unable to go anywhere.

The sun was beginning to set, the sky splashed with glorious tones of orange and pink, but she turned away from it and walked back into the kitchen. Earlier, thinking about the baby, she had forced herself to eat, and she knew Caleb would expect a meal whenever he came in. As she was fixing sandwiches, the back door slammed and he strode into the kitchen, looking confident and excited. She wiped her hands on a towel, waiting to see if he would tell her anything. On the night of their wedding, he had taught her to be wary about asking questions.

He picked up a sandwich and chewed a mouthful deliberately.

"Nice place they got out here," he said. "Their land drops down to the lake. They lock their gate, like that makes a difference."

"He took you out there?" She thought she was safe enough to ask that, since Caleb obviously wanted to boast.

"Just about knocked on the fucking door. I could've done it tonight, but he reckons the other one is out of town till tomorrow, and where's the fun in that?"

She tried to join in the joke, tried to agree with him, but couldn't get anywhere close to pulling it off. She turned to pour him a drink instead. He wanted the women to suffer together, and that was too awful a thing for her to dwell on.

"Only gonna get one shot at this," he said. "We get there in good time and we can follow the bitch right through the front door."

She stared at him, hoping she had misunderstood. "Your contact." She put a hand on the table, aware that she was swaying slightly. "Is he not going to help you?"

His fist twitched, and for a second, she thought he was going to strike her. She flinched involuntarily, the reaction conditioned by years of abuse.

"My contact's a fucking cop," he spat. "This is as far as he goes." He touched her cheek with calloused fingertips. "No, baby. I think we should keep this in the family."

❖

"Oh no, don't, Tilly. Don't eat that. It's got chocolate in it!"

Sarah somehow managed to clap her hands, clear the kitchen of dog and cats, and keep hold of the phone at the same time. In her ear, Alex's laughter was faint and tinny.

"It's not funny," Sarah said, stooping to pick up the other brownies she had dropped. "They're bloody tag teaming me." That just made Alex laugh harder. "I won't save you any if you keep this up."

"Sorry, sorry." Even with the poor signal, Alex managed to sound reasonably contrite. "What time's Lyssa coming over?"

"About an hour. She's bringing her uniform and going straight to work from here."

"Sounds like a plan. I should be on my way home by then."

"Now that really does sound like a plan."

"Yeah?" Alex said. "I thought so too."

Sarah closed her eyes, picturing Alex's face. "You should go," she told her reluctantly. "They'll be out looking for you if you hide in the loo any longer."

The previous day, Alex had called during a lunch break, but today, not wanting to interrupt Sarah's study session, she had sneaked out of one of the group exercises.

"I guess you're right." She sighed directly into the receiver, the transmitted sound deep and mournful.

"I am right. Go on. I'll see you tonight."

"See you tonight. Save me a brownie."

"I already have." Sarah heard Alex cheer and took that as a cue to hang up.

By the time she had cleaned the kitchen, scrubbed brownie mixture from beneath her nails, and gotten her books together, Lyssa's SUV was slowly weaving through the potholes on the driveway. She scooped up the picnic rug and went out to meet her.

"Not too early?" Lyssa shouted from the open window as the SUV shuddered to a halt.

"Nope, right on time." Sarah spread out the blanket and then went to help Lyssa, who was staggering across the grass, her arms laden with books, a bag, and something that looked suspiciously like a severed limb.

"Dare I ask?" Sarah gingerly turned the appendage over. It was an arm: fleshy and realistic, with multitudes of tiny holes scattered along its prominent veins. Someone had taken the time to paint its fingernails bright red.

"Thought we could have a play with IV access, if we get bored," Lyssa said. "I borrowed some stuff from the training room."

"Bloody hell, don't get yourself in trouble."

"Naw, I actually asked this time, now that you're all famous and everything."

Sarah laughed. "Yeah, right. You want a drink?"

"Sure. Something cold. Need any help?"

"I made lunch. Come and carry some out with me?" When she pushed open the screen door, a flash of movement caught her eye. "You little shit!" She chased Bandit away from the quiche, ignoring Lyssa's giggles. As she picked him up to take him outside, he dug his claws into her wrist.

"Ooh, ouch," Lyssa said, holding Sarah's wrist to the light to assess the damage. "Get it rinsed off before you catch cat cooties."

"I don't know why we put up with him." Sarah winced as cold water hit the scratches. "If his little sister didn't think the sun shone out of his arse, I'd take him into the middle of the woods and leave him there."

"You don't mean that."

"No, I don't," she conceded. She passed the quiche to Lyssa and packed the remainder of the picnic into the cooler. "Besides which, he'd only find his way back. He—"

"Hey, hey, you're gonna ruin this!" Lyssa had stopped by the kitchen table. Sarah went to peer over her shoulder to see what had caught her attention and found her flicking pieces of grated cheese from the local newspaper.

"Why hasn't Alex already gotten it framed for you, anyway?" Lyssa asked. "Hell, she even gets a mention on page two."

"Jesus," Sarah whispered. For a second, she couldn't do anything but stare at the front page. Lyssa had unfolded it to display the prominent lead story in all its glory: *First responder saves life of newborn baby.* The color photograph accompanying the feature was the one taken by the midwife, with Sarah in the center of the shot, facing the camera and smiling broadly. Originally folded with the back page uppermost, the newspaper had lain unread on the table for two days, or was it three days now?

"You said Alex gets a mention?" She tried to make her question sound natural, but Lyssa must have detected the quaver in her voice because she turned around.

"Yeah, page two. They covered the raid," she said. "You okay? You're as pale as a ghost."

"Fine, I'm fine." Sarah forced herself to smile, but it felt wrong, as if her lips had just twisted in response to something sour. "Not used to being a celebrity," she said, struggling to think through the possible ramifications. The newspaper had a Web edition, which meant that her image would now be online together with her and Alex's first names. She thought of the vast array of technological equipment found by the FBI during its searches of Nicholas Deakin's compound, and wondered how much of it had remained undiscovered, how much his people had managed to salvage before the raids. Castillo had warned her and Alex explicitly: no Facebook or any of the other social network sites, no images in e-mail attachments, and they should stay off the Internet as much as possible. They had done exactly that, keeping e-mails to a minimum and chatting with Ash and Tess through anonymous accounts, avoiding mention of names or locations or anything else that might identify them. They had done everything he had told them to do; they had been so damn careful. It had been bad enough worrying about Emerson, but now the floodgates might have opened: anyone might have seen this paper.

"Shall I bring it out so you can read it?" Lyssa was still looking curiously at her.

Sarah nodded automatically to cover her lapse, then shook her head. "No, it's okay. You go on out. I'll just be a minute."

She took up the newspaper and waited until she could see Lyssa sitting on the grass with Tilly.

"Come on, Alex, answer your damn phone."

Alex's cell rang out before switching to voice mail.

"It's me. Call me as soon as you get this," Sarah said, and then realized how frightening that must have sounded. "Don't worry," she added hurriedly. "Something came up and I need to talk to you before you set off home. Love you."

She wanted to tell Alex about the paper before she left the hotel, so that she could be vigilant driving home, aware that someone might be out there looking for her, but as Sarah ended the call, she wondered whether she had overreacted. Looking out onto a sun-drenched lawn, she watched Tilly chase a ball for Lyssa, and the terror the photograph had instilled in her began to wane. She would speak to Alex about contacting Castillo, who might be able to tell them the likelihood of anyone tracking them from a single image. Now that she considered it logically, that seemed almost impossible. Feeling calmer, she splashed her face with cold water, picked up the cooler, and went out to join Lyssa. For the time being, at least, she could pretend that everything was normal.

❖

Caleb drove in silence along a narrow strip of deserted road. His contact had shown him a barely used route that weaved between large tracts of forest, affording Leah glimpses of sunlight sparkling on a lake that stretched for miles. Unsure exactly what Caleb was planning, she had left nothing behind at the cottage. He had told her to wipe all of the surfaces, though that was something she would have done anyway. Other people would have arranged to rent the cottage—honeymooning couples or families with children—and she wanted no trace of Caleb or herself to taint their vacation.

The air conditioning was blasting out at full strength, but she could feel herself sweating. Her thin cotton shirt was damp at the back, the material so cold it was making her shiver. In contrast, her cheek was hot and swollen where a fresh bruise throbbed. She didn't remember why he had punched her, only the crack of pain and the smirk on his face. He seemed long ago to have stopped needing a reason.

The turn was difficult to spot, but he obviously knew where he was going. He took a left onto a rough one-lane road, heading away from the sun, leaving the interior of the car dimly lit in hues of green. Huge trees lined the track, so close at times that branches scraped along the car's windows and bodywork. The forest provided a security barrier of sorts, but after approximately a mile and a half, there was also a large metal gate on sturdy concrete posts. It took Caleb less than five minutes to pick its lock. When he set off again, he drove more slowly, his eyes continuously flicking to the right as he searched for something. Leah saw it at the same time he did: a natural gap in the trees that was large enough to pull into and would conceal the car from anyone driving past. Satisfied with his position, he put the car into park and lowered the windows. She could hear nothing but the creak of branches moving in the wind. Breathing in the scent of warm earth, she tried to ignore Caleb as he pulled out a handgun and strapped a Bowie knife onto his belt.

"He figured she'd be back in about four hours," he said, and Leah nodded, her eyes seeking out the clock on the dash. "You're gonna flag her down, say you had an accident." His thumb stroked across the newly marred skin on her cheek. "Sure do look the part."

"What do I do then?" she whispered.

He smiled, baring his teeth. "Then you leave the rest to me."

❖

Sarah put down her cell phone when she heard Lyssa coming out of the bathroom. Alex still hadn't been in touch, but her course was due to finish within the hour, which would fit in conveniently with Lyssa's departure for work.

"Okay, I am outta here," Lyssa said, neatly catching the bag of leftover brownies that Sarah threw her. "I'm guessing these won't see out the shift."

"Well, hopefully they'll help keep you awake." Sarah gave her a hug. "Thanks for coming over."

"Any time." They walked out to Lyssa's SUV. "Keep smilin', sweetie. She'll be home before you know it."

Sarah nodded. "She will. Sorry if I've been a bit off today. I'm not used to her being away," she said, keen to offer a reasonable excuse for her distractedness.

Lyssa smiled, accepting the explanation without question. "Right, I better motor or I'll be late." She turned the key in the ignition and blew Sarah an exaggerated kiss. "That's for Alex."

"I'll be sure to pass it on," Sarah yelled above the rattle of the engine, and Lyssa laughed, narrowly avoiding a hen as she drove away in a cloud of dust and diesel smoke.

Excited by the noise, Tilly chased after the SUV, ignoring Sarah's attempts to call her back. Deciding to leave her to it, Sarah went into the cabin to wait for Alex to call.

Leah heard the vehicle at the same time as Caleb. She looked across at him and saw his uncertainty; the police officer—Alex—wasn't supposed to be home so early, and the vehicle seemed to be approaching from the wrong direction. He quickly recovered his composure, however.

"My contact must have gotten it wrong," he said, and then smiled, apparently making a snap decision. "Hell, if they're both here already it'll make this a whole lot easier." He reached across Leah and opened her door. "Go."

Her body didn't seem capable of moving, but when she hesitated, he placed his gun to the side of her face.

"Go."

She shrank away from him and scrambled out of the car. His door clicked open seconds later, and she could hear the snap of twigs beneath his feet as he followed her at a short distance. Sunlight momentarily dazzled her, and she raised her hand to shield her eyes so that she could pick her way up onto the track. As she did so, an SUV rounded the corner, making steady progress. There was a single figure in the front, a woman wearing shades and a cap pulled down low against the late afternoon sun. Leah felt her heart sink as she saw the woman's uniform shirt and realized that Caleb had been right: she had to be the police officer.

Dust flew up as the SUV slowed; the woman had obviously spotted her. Leah staggered sideways, light-headed with nervousness and despair.

"Hey, are you hurt?"

The hand on Leah's arm made her jump; she hadn't been aware of the SUV stopping or the woman approaching her.

"No." She shook her head, all her thoughts stalling on that one word. "No."

"It's okay, you're okay. I'm a paramedic. Let's get you sitting down."

The woman was walking carefully backward, holding Leah's hands with both of hers and guiding her over to the SUV, and what she had just said took Leah an age to register.

"It's not you." She stopped abruptly, knocking the woman slightly off balance. "It's not you. Oh God." She pulled her arm away, looking frantically around to warn Caleb to stay out of sight, but he was closer than she had expected, his focus intent on the woman as he darted through the trees to a position directly behind her. Taking advantage of the woman's confusion, he lunged forward and looped an arm across her throat, applying enough pressure to make her choke.

"Don't make a sound," he warned her. He held his knife to the corner of her eye, letting her sense the blade. She froze, her mouth open as she panted for breath.

"It's not her," Leah said. "She's a paramedic."

"The fuck?" Holding the woman roughly by her collar, Caleb knocked her cap off and then spun her around so he could look at her face. Seeing the knife lowered, the woman took the opportunity to kick out at him, aiming for his groin and connecting solidly enough to make him yell and stumble backward. She shook her arm free and ran, reaching her SUV before he had recovered sufficiently to sprint after her.

The expression of absolute rage on his face was all too familiar to Leah. He no longer cared whether this was the right woman; she was merely a woman who had dared to fight back. He caught hold of the SUV's door and yanked it open just as she tried to slam the lock down.

Leah's legs finally collapsed beneath her when she heard the woman cry out in pain. The knife in Caleb's hand flashed silver and crimson as he raised it and plunged it down again.

"Jesus, oh Jesus," Leah gasped. A dog barked close by, but the woman had fallen silent. Leah glanced up to see Caleb standing over the woman's unmoving form.

"Get the fuck over here and grab her legs," he said, trying to drag the woman back up into her SUV.

"I can't." Leah held up her bare hands; he was the only one wearing gloves.

"You useless fucking bitch." He was struggling with his burden, but she couldn't help, couldn't do anything but stare at the blade sticking out from the center of the woman's chest. He had stabbed her so violently that the handle had snapped off the knife. Blood covered her white uniform shirt, and her face was gray and slack. Leah willed her to twitch, to wake up and struggle, but she didn't move, didn't even take a breath.

"Caleb, we have to go," Leah said. He gave no indication of having heard her, so she repeated herself more forcefully, pulling at his hand.

He shook her off and heaved again on the woman's body. "No, nothing changes. We can leave her in the SUV. If the cop sees a body, she'll freak. But if she just sees the SUV, she'll stop to check what's wrong."

"Look at her," she insisted, sensing a way to end this before anyone else got hurt. "She's dressed for work. When she doesn't show, they're going to wonder why. If she told anyone she was coming here, this will be the first place they'll look."

He was listening now, trying to figure out the logic, whether they had time to wait for the cop before someone came to ask about the woman he had just murdered. He snarled, slamming a fist against the SUV, and then dropped the woman like discarded trash, leaving her in a heap on the ground. A key fell from her shirt pocket and he knelt to scoop it up.

"Gate key," he said, and Leah nodded, relieved that he wouldn't have to pick the lock again, that they would be able to get out sooner. Not wanting to alert anyone to their presence, he had re-locked the gate behind them when they first arrived.

Her lips moved in a silent prayer and tears stung the raw skin on her cheek as she waited for him to stand. She felt his fingers close around her bicep, and somehow managed to keep up with him as he hauled her back to their car. Curling herself into the hot leather seat, she hid her face in her hands, trying not to breathe in the thick stench of blood that filled the air. He ignored her, concentrating on the track as he drove at a speed far too great to be safe. She closed her eyes, her hands moving instinctively to protect her abdomen, and wondered dully at what point he would kill her too.

❖

Sarah was standing on the porch, waiting for Alex's voice mail to begin its message, when she heard the noise. She ended the call and strained to listen. She had no idea what it had been or where it had come from, only that all the hairs on the back of her neck had prickled in response. Within moments, she heard it again. It was clearer this time, carried along on the strengthening breeze: a terrible prolonged howl that she instantly recognized as canine.

"Shit."

She slid her phone into the back pocket of her shorts and swapped her flip-flops for sneakers. Only a few minutes had passed since Tilly followed Lyssa's SUV down the path, which meant she couldn't have gotten far. Sarah set off at a slow jog, not wanting to miss her, pausing every hundred yards or so to call her name and listen for any indication that she was close by. Ten minutes down the track, she heard barking, constant and distressed.

She increased her pace at once, sprinting toward a sharp corner and almost blundering into Tilly, who met her on the curve and began to leap up at her, still barking wildly.

"Hey, girl. Hey, hush." Sarah put a hand out to her collar, trying to calm her, but she bounded away. Muttering a stream of curses, Sarah followed her.

"What the hell?"

She stopped so suddenly that her feet skidded in the dirt. Just ahead of her, Lyssa's SUV was parked at a slight angle, as if she had braked hard enough to kick out the rear end. The driver's door was ajar and Sarah could see something dark lying beside it. Walking in agitated circles at the side of the SUV, Tilly let out a howl that made Sarah's skin crawl.

"Lyssa?" She meant to shout but managed only a whisper. Then she was running, reaching the SUV in seconds, having already realized what it was that she had seen at the door.

"No, no. Oh fuck, no."

There was so much blood soaking into the dust that she immediately knew Lyssa was dead, even as she knelt in the dirt and turned her onto her back. When she tilted Lyssa's chin to open her airway, she felt a hint of residual warmth beneath her fingers. Abandoning common sense, she pinched Lyssa's nose shut and breathed into her mouth, fighting not to gag on the blood that coated her lips. After two breaths, she went to start chest compressions, but saw for the first time that there was a blade protruding from Lyssa's sternum, right where she needed to position her hands. The metal was so firmly lodged that she couldn't move it, despite her efforts. Instead, she placed her clasped hands close below it and pushed down hard, counting a rhythm in her head, heedless of the razor-sharp edge that carved into her fingers.

Two breaths to thirty compressions; she repeated the cycle continuously, though she could feel her back and arms beginning to cramp. Something cracked beneath the heel of her hand and the next time she gave a breath cool blood flooded into her mouth. Unable to stop herself, she turned her head aside and vomited until her stomach ached. As the spasms relented, she wiped her mouth and bent low to give another breath, but Lyssa's face was now cold to the touch, and when Sarah looked at her eyes she saw that both pupils were blown.

Too distraught to think logically, she closed Lyssa's eyes and crawled away from the SUV. The grass at the edge of the road was cool beneath her sticky hands; she wiped them slowly at first and then with growing urgency, until the grass was flattened and stained. She drew her knees up to her chest and rested her forehead against them. It was only as she shifted her position that she remembered the phone in her pocket. It took her three attempts to dial 911, and when the operator answered her call, she couldn't remember what it was she needed to say.

"Caller, what is your location?" The man's voice was composed and insistent. He stayed on the line, patiently repeating the same question. He didn't dismiss the call as a prank, and she slowly realized that it was because he could hear her crying. She swiped at her face, streaking blood, tears, and mucus along her bare arm.

"The old Gardner place," she said. She coughed, tasting copper and bile, and tried to speak more clearly. "Off Quick Edge Road. Lyssa's been stabbed and I tried to do CPR." She was hyperventilating now, unable to get her breathing under control, and the words spilled from her between snatches of air. When she shook her head, tears splashed into the dirt. "I can't help her. I tried, but she's dead. Please send someone, please." Her voice dissolved into sobs. She heard the man asking her more questions, but in the end, he stopped trying to coax information from her and began to just murmur reassurances. A vague sense of etiquette made her listen for a few seconds before ending the call.

The second number she dialed came easily to her, her fingers automatically seeking out the name from the top of the directory.

Alex answered on the first ring, sounding fraught. "Sarah, are you okay? I only just got your message. I've been trying to call."

Sarah's teeth were chattering so hard she could barely speak.

"Lyssa's dead," she whispered. "Please come home."

CHAPTER SEVEN

The blare of the horn warned Alex to pay attention. She over-corrected her steering, swerving away from the oncoming truck, and felt the tires vibrate as she hit the rumble strip marking the shoulder of the freeway.

"Fuck," she muttered, blinking against the glare of the truck's headlights. She would be no use to Sarah if she wiped herself off the road.

More than an hour had passed since she had spoken to Sarah. Using hands-free, Alex had kept her on the line, trying to get her to piece together what had happened and, when that failed, just trying to prevent her from falling completely apart. Little of what Sarah told her had been coherent. After only a few minutes, Alex had heard sirens in the background, and moments later Larry Tobin—his voice taut with stress—had assured her that he was taking care of Sarah and then disconnected the call. She had been averaging seventy-five miles an hour ever since.

She had locked the doors of the Silverado and kept a keen eye on her rearview mirror for anyone attempting to tail her. Her holster dug into her hip, reminding her that her Glock was within easy reach. She drew comfort from its presence. Sarah hadn't been in a fit state to tell her much about what had happened, but she had repeatedly begged Alex to be careful.

❖

The first police officer to arrive had told Sarah that his name was Tobin and then wrapped his jacket around her shoulders. He looked at the body only briefly before giving the area around it a wide berth and coming to sit beside Sarah on the ground.

"Paramedics and more officers are on the way," he told her. "Are you hurt?"

She shook her head, shying away from his flashlight. At some point, unnoticed by her, dusk must have fallen.

"Okay, that's good," he said. "Do you know what happened to Lyssa?"

She shook her head again and the motion caused his jacket to slip from her shoulders. When she raised a hand to adjust it, he caught hold of her wrist.

"How did you get these?"

He aimed his flashlight at her wrist and she stared at the wounds blankly; she had forgotten they were even there. His finger touched one of the deeper slashes, the discomfort making her stiffen and then attempt to pull away.

"I had to do CPR," she said, shuddering at the memory. "The blade was in the way."

He studied her face just long enough to make her feel uncomfortable, before releasing her hand. The wail of approaching sirens interrupted whatever else he might have asked, and he stood to guide the vehicles away from the immediate crime scene. Several of the responding officers activated auxiliary lighting on the patrol units, and the brightness of the halogen beams brought everything back into horrifying clarity. One of the paramedics approached Lyssa's SUV and immediately lurched away again out of the light. Sarah heard him retching violently and clamped her mouth shut as her own stomach threatened to rebel once more.

After a few minutes, his colleague walked across to her.

"Hey." He looked pale and there was sweat trickling down from his temples. "Officer Tobin told me you have some cuts to your hands."

She nodded but glanced back toward the SUV, where Bill Quinn was shaking his head, his expression halfway between astounded and furious.

"I'm fine," she whispered. "Is Lyssa—?" Her voice broke on the name.

"I'm afraid there was nothing we could do for her." The paramedic offered her his hand. "C'mon, honey, you need to let me check you over."

She allowed him to help her stand and then clutched at him as a combination of stress and gravity threatened to put her back on the ground. He sat her on the gurney and swapped Tobin's jacket for a thick blanket. She didn't make a sound when he began to clean the lacerations with a saline-soaked swab.

"Some of these will need sutures," he said, frowning at the crisscross pattern of wounds that continued to bleed sluggishly as he wiped them. "Keep pressure here for a minute." He positioned her fingers to hold a wad of gauze and left her alone in the ambulance. She leaned back against the pillow, wondering where Alex was and watching the paramedic confer rapidly with Quinn. When he returned, Quinn came with him.

"Hi, Sarah." Quinn crouched down beside the gurney and smiled at her. "Tim here says you're going to be just fine. Now, we'll need a statement from you, and we need to do a couple of things down at the station. If you're feeling up to that, we'll take you straight over there now."

It wasn't really phrased as a question, but she murmured her consent regardless.

"I've spoken to Alex," he continued. "She's going to meet us there."

Relief hit her so hard that she had to hang on to the sides of the gurney for support.

"Okay," she said, unable to process anything except that final detail. "Okay, I'll come with you."

"Can you just...?" The CSI moved Sarah's arm a fraction and readied her camera. "Stay real still now."

Sarah did as she asked, staring at the blood trickling onto the scale-marker that the woman had set by her arm. "I think it needs stitches," she said, but the woman didn't appear to be listening to her. "The paramedic told me it needed stitches."

The coverall Sarah had been given to wear rustled as the CSI brought her other arm forward. Quinn had requested her blood-spattered clothing and asked for permission to document her injuries. He had also given her forms to sign to allow the collection of a DNA sample and fingerprints: to rule her out of the inquiry, he had assured her. The entire process seemed to have taken hours; she sat numb and compliant with exhaustion, watching herself bleed onto the metal table.

"Okay, Sarah, I'm all done. I'll let Sergeant Emerson know you're ready to give your statement."

Sarah's pulse rate sped up at the unexpected mention of Emerson's name, and she realized that Quinn must have reinstated him while Alex was away. She still had no idea whether she could trust him—for all she knew he could just have murdered Lyssa—which meant she certainly didn't want to be interviewed by him. Her head started to ache and she closed her eyes miserably; there was no way she could request a different officer without causing herself even more problems.

She folded her arms across her chest, wishing she had never agreed to come to the station. She wanted a shower to clean away the streaks of Lyssa's blood, and she wanted something to make her sleep and keep her from having nightmares, but more than anything else she wanted Alex, who wouldn't talk to her like a victim while treating her like a suspect.

"Sarah?"

She looked around to see a dark-haired man standing in the doorway with a steaming mug in one hand and a glass of water in the other.

"I wasn't sure if you wanted water or coffee, so I brought one of each." He set the drinks in front of her. "Go ahead, I'm good with either."

She took the water as he sat, and found that it settled her stomach somewhat. He let her take a few sips before introducing himself.

"I'm Sergeant Emerson." He clicked two buttons on a small tape recorder. "I need to ask you some questions about what happened this evening, if that's okay?"

She nodded and he prompted her to speak for the benefit of the tape.

"Yes, that's okay," she said.

"I want to make it clear that you are not under arrest and that you can ask for the interview to be terminated at any point." He spoke slowly, as if to ensure that she understood her rights, but his friendly nature set alarm bells ringing.

"I understand," she said. She couldn't decide which would make matters worse: walking out of the interview and requesting legal counsel, or providing a statement to prove she had nothing to hide.

He cut into her confusion by asking his first question. "Can you tell me why Lyssa Mardell was at your house today?"

He unfastened the top button of his shirt, making Sarah aware how warm the small room was. Despite the water, her throat was parched, and she had to swallow twice before answering.

"She was there to help me study for my EMT course. She came round for lunch."

"Was this a regular date?"

His choice of phrasing gave Sarah pause and she worded her response cautiously. "It was a regular arrangement, yes."

"Ongoing for how long?"

"For about four months now. I met her on a call and we got talking afterward."

"You volunteer as a first responder?" He made a note, swirling his pen to leave an asterisk beside the detail.

"Yes, that's right."

There was a smart rap on the door. Emerson announced that he was pausing the interview, and he stopped the tape as Quinn entered the room. Quinn took a seat just behind him, motioning as he did so that Emerson should restart the tape.

Emerson's initial questions were basic, covering the time leading up to Lyssa's death, and Sarah tried to answer them as thoroughly as possible.

"So you heard your dog barking?" he said. He had filled three pages with notes, even though the tape and a video camera were recording everything.

"I heard her howling," she corrected him. "I was trying to call Alex and I heard Tilly howling."

"Why were you calling Alex?"

She licked her lips uneasily. She couldn't tell them the real reason, not without speaking to Alex and Castillo first. "To ask what time she would be home," she said, but she couldn't make the lie convincing, and she saw Emerson write something in capitals and underline it.

"We might need to look at your cell phone," he told her.

She nodded helplessly.

"What happened after you heard your dog?"

"I followed the noise down the track and found Lyssa's SUV." She reached for the glass of water and her hand shook as she sipped from it. "I knew something was wrong. I could see her collapsed at the side of the door. I started to run."

"Did you move her at all?"

"No," she said, but then faltered, struggling to recall exactly what she had done. "I turned her onto her back. I knew she was dead, but I had to do some—"

"How did you know she was dead?"

"I just did," she whispered. Tears filled her eyes. "But she was still warm when I touched her."

"Where exactly did you touch her?"

"I tilted her chin." She used her sleeve to wipe her eyes, but more tears trickled free.

"You didn't check for a pulse?" Emerson placed two fingers on his own carotid to demonstrate.

She shook her head. "No, I could see she wasn't breathing, so I started CPR."

"Explain how you did that."

Behind Emerson, Quinn leaned forward in his seat.

"I gave her two breaths and then I…" Her voice trailed off and she clenched her fists at her own stupidity. "I tried to move the knife."

"You tried to move the knife?" Emerson repeated carefully, as if afraid that anyone transcribing the tape might overlook the significance of the admission.

"Yes," Sarah said. "To do CPR, but it was stuck." For a second, she thought she might be sick again, and something in her expression must have worried Emerson because she dimly heard him urge her to take a deep breath.

"Okay to continue now?"

She swallowed the last of her water and nodded.

"Good. Did you manage to perform CPR?"

"Yes, but not very well. There wasn't much room and the blade was in the way."

"How did you cut your hands?" It seemed like a stupid question, but she knew that he needed her to spell it out.

"On the blade as I did chest compressions."

"And how long did you perform CPR for?"

"I don't know."

"You didn't think to call for help?"

"I wasn't thinking of much," she said, trying to keep her tone civil. "I'd just found my friend stabbed to death."

"So, do I have this right?" Quinn's interjection startled her; it was the first time he had spoken. "You found Lyssa Mardell with the remains of a knife lodged in her chest, you attempted to resuscitate her despite being aware that it would be futile and despite the knife cutting your hands to ribbons, and you only phoned for help after all this had occurred?"

"Yes," she replied calmly, refusing to allow him to provoke her.

"Yes, what?" he snapped.

"Yes," she said, sitting up straighter. "You have it exactly right."

Any reply he might have made was interrupted by someone hammering on the door. Through the reinforced glass window, Sarah could clearly hear Alex shouting and someone attempting to placate her. Emerson turned to Quinn for guidance and then stated that he was stopping the tape. The door flew open seconds later.

"Oh God." All the anger had vanished from Alex's voice. She knelt by Sarah's side, taking Sarah's hands in her own. That touch, and seeing Alex safe, almost destroyed the shred of composure Sarah was clinging to and she had to bite through her lip to stop herself from crying.

"It's okay, sweetheart, you're okay." Alex ran a finger between the oozing lacerations, her face aghast. "Jesus Christ, Quinn, what the hell were you thinking?"

"I was thinking that your wife is the only witness in the murder of a young paramedic," he said, not sounding in the least repentant.

"You were so eager to question her that you just left her to bleed?"

Emerson had the grace to look ashamed, but Quinn held Alex's gaze and said nothing.

"Is she under arrest?"

"No," Emerson replied quickly.

"Okay." Sarah heard Alex take a breath and suspected she was counting to ten. "I'm going to take her to the hospital. Then I'm going to take her home."

"Your home is a potential crime scene, Alex," Quinn warned her, but then added in a softer tone, "Don't make this any harder than it needs to be."

Sarah felt the tension in the set of Alex's body and gave her hand as tight a squeeze as she could. "Leave them to it," she said quietly. "I can't face going back there tonight." She didn't want to say that it wasn't safe for them to go home, that someone obviously knew where they lived. The fact that Alex chose not to argue indicated she had read between the lines.

Sarah looked across at Quinn. "The chooks, the cats, and Tilly will need feeding."

For the first time since he had entered the room, Quinn smiled at her. Remembering the way he had spoken to her not minutes ago, she didn't smile back.

"I'll pass word to an officer," he said. "You go on with Alex now. We can finish this tomorrow."

She stood and Alex put an arm around her, subtly ensuring that she stayed up.

"Let me know where you'll be spending the night," Quinn told them as a parting salvo.

Alex led her from the room without replying, and Sarah suspected it was only out of deference to her that she didn't slam the door in Quinn's face.

The motel on the outskirts of Cary was small but clean and, unlike the first that Alex inquired at, didn't display a rate for renting by the hour. On the way to the hospital she had phoned the only hotel in Avery, to be told—upon giving her name—that there were no vacancies. She had hung up without comment, but she saw Sarah peer into the hotel parking lot as they passed. There were only three vehicles in it, and one of those belonged to the owner.

She unlocked their motel room and steered Sarah to sit on the bed. "I'm going to get my bag but I'll be right back," she said. Sarah, half-stupefied with painkillers, murmured what sounded like agreement.

The small overnight bag Alex had taken on her course didn't hold much in the way of clean clothes, but it was better than nothing. She clicked the lock on her key fob and then paused with her hand on the truck door. The parking lot was dark and deserted, with no visible closed-circuit cameras. Crouching out of sight of the motel's concrete balcony, she finally allowed herself to give in to the fear and sorrow she had kept bottled up while she took care of Sarah. She wept silently, covering her face and rocking with the force necessary to smother her sobs.

She knew everything now. While they were waiting at the hospital, Sarah had told her about the photograph in the newspaper and the repeated efforts she had made to contact Alex and warn her. Then, in stilted sentences, she had described what she found when she followed Tilly down the track.

"I didn't kill her. I didn't do it," she had insisted, desperate to reassure one of the few people who would never have believed it possible in the first place.

The doctor who eventually stitched and dressed her wounds had offered her counseling and given her a pamphlet aimed at patients with a tendency to self-harm. Neither she nor Alex had attempted to explain how the injuries had actually occurred.

Using a bottle of water from her bag, Alex rinsed her face clean and dried it on a spare T-shirt. She had been out of the room for less than five minutes, but when she returned she found Sarah asleep, still wearing the scrubs the hospital had given her. Her face creased in distress as Alex covered her with a blanket, but she quickly relaxed when Alex smoothed a hand through her hair.

Too wired to sleep, Alex made a cup of coffee in the small kitchenette and carried it across to the table by the window. Adjusting her familiar routine slightly, she double-checked the locks on the door and tilted the window blind so she could see out across the parking lot. She took her Glock from its holster and placed it on the table next to her mug, and then unlocked the screen on her cell phone.

Castillo answered her call in a voice gruff with sleep. "Hello?"

"Mike, it's Alex. Sorry to wake you."

She heard him smack his lips and empathized with the confusion that came from being pulled suddenly from a deep sleep.

"Hey, Alex," he said. Then, as if a switch had been flicked, his tone altered completely. "What's wrong?"

"Everything," she said, unable to keep the quaver from her voice. "Everything's wrong."

"Start at the beginning."

He was quiet when she had finished. She sipped her lukewarm coffee, listening to him type on his computer.

"Okay," he said, and the clicking of keys stopped. "I've sent an urgent e-mail to all the surveillance teams we still have working the Deakin case and asked them to check in ASAP. The way things are organizationally, though, that could take a few days." He sighed. "This is a fucking mess, Alex."

"I know."

"From what you've said, they're going to be looking at Sarah very hard for the murder."

She pushed away her coffee. "I think they already are." She shook her head. "I don't know what to do," she whispered, and the admission made her bow her head with shame.

"My advice would be to come clean with Quinn about everything. Pass on my details for corroboration and see if we can get him to start thinking along other lines of inquiry. He should be putting protection in place for you both, and he won't be doing that if he's stuck on Sarah as his prime suspect."

"Okay." That had been top of her priorities for the morning, but having Castillo confirm her plan made her feel better about it.

"Alex." He sounded her name like a warning. "You could lose your job over this. Quinn will probably see it as a vote of no confidence in him that you didn't disclose what happened in the Cascades."

She had already considered that. She hadn't trusted Quinn enough to tell him her history—hell, she hadn't even told him her real name. She had always thought of him as an honorable man, but after what he had just done to Sarah, she was no longer quite so sure.

"I don't care what happens to me, if it keeps Sarah safe," she said.

"Just be prepared for the fallout." Castillo sounded as sickened as she felt; he had tried so hard to manufacture a normal life for them. "Try and get some sleep now, and I'll be in touch as soon as I have anything. I submitted a request for a background check on Emerson, too. Should hear back from that in the next forty-eight hours or so."

"Thank you." Somehow, the words seemed inadequate. She pushed back in her seat, calmer now that she had a strategy to work to. "I'll call Quinn first thing."

"Good."

She heard a musical chime as he closed down his computer.

"So much for staying under the radar, huh?" he said.

"Yeah." She gave a humorless laugh. "Bit fucking late for that."

It was past midnight when Caleb stopped the car in front of the rental cottage. He had driven slowly, obeying the letter of the law, not wanting to be pulled over for an infraction while covered in blood and with the handle of a murder weapon in the trunk. Rain pelted down on Leah as she opened the car door. She tipped her face toward the sky, relishing the feel of the cool water against her heated skin. Caleb strode past her with two duffel bags, and she followed him into the kitchen, where he stripped naked and handed her his filthy clothes. Then he dug into the side pocket of one of the bags and set the knife handle on top of the pile.

"Burn them. Go a ways into the trees," he said. "Then come back and clean this shit up." He nodded at the blood and dirt his clothing had left on the floor. "We're leaving again in an hour."

His clothes were sodden with blood; by the time she had carried them to a clear spot in the forest, she had to add her own soiled shirt to the small bonfire she constructed. The rain and damp undergrowth made it difficult to keep the fire lit, but the newspapers she had found beneath the kitchen sink eventually caught, and a smell like rancid meat rose up from the flames.

The task took longer than she intended. Glad to leave the stench behind, she hurried back to the cottage as another heavy downpour began to beat on the trees. Far from being angry, though, Caleb smiled at her as she entered the kitchen. He had his cell phone in his hand.

"Take a shower, baby," he said, oblivious to the way she tensed at the endearment. "News I just heard, we don't need to rush."

She had no idea what he was talking about, but he didn't seem inclined to go into detail, so she remained silent.

"Soon as you're good, we're moving to a new place in Ruby." He took her face in both hands and kissed her. "My man reckons we should stick around, see how all this plays out."

The offer of a shower apparently forgotten, he pushed her urgently toward the bedroom. The door shut behind them with a soft snick of metal. She stood as motionless as a statue in the middle of the room and waited for him to tell her what he wanted.

Chapter Eight

Sarah had ordered pancakes, just to stop Alex from worrying about her, but the smell of maple syrup and buttermilk batter was too much for her to stomach. She toyed with a small piece and then dropped her fork, pushing the plate away.

"Here, try this instead," Alex said, swapping the pancakes for her own dish of plain oatmeal. She smiled when Sarah took a tentative taste. "When I was a kid, whenever I felt like crap, our cook would make oatmeal. She told us it had restorative qualities."

Sarah raised a skeptical eyebrow but ate another mouthful anyway. The diner was full of early morning bustle and smells: bacon sizzling on the griddle, people in suits impatiently reeling off orders for coffee that sounded as complex as neurosurgery, and the constant ping of the cash register. It seemed surreal to her that life was continuing all around her, as if the man who wanted two eggs over easy with a side of hash browns should somehow take a moment to acknowledge that a brutal murder had happened just hours before.

The spoon slipped from her bandaged fingers and she made no move to pick it up.

"Did Lyssa have a family?" she asked quietly. "I don't think she ever mentioned her family."

Alex retrieved the spoon for her and carefully closed her fingers around it. "I think she has a sister, somewhere on the West Coast." She sipped her coffee, obviously trying to recollect. "San Diego, maybe? I remember her telling me that they didn't really keep in touch."

"She still had the brownies in the fucking car," Sarah said. "She took some leftovers for her shift and they were right there on the passenger seat, and I keep thinking, what if she'd set off earlier or stayed later or we'd picked another day…" She was beginning to sob, her voice struggling to break through as her chest heaved with grief. "It must have been us he wanted, Alex. It had nothing to do with her."

A woman at the adjacent table tutted loudly as Alex gathered Sarah into her arms and kissed her hands and then her face.

"Quinn will find whoever did this," Alex told her.

Sarah shook her head. "He's not even looking for anyone," she said. "He thinks it was me."

The ring of Alex's cell phone cut off the discussion, but she looked defeated and Sarah knew that she hadn't been about to disagree.

Alex's expression hardened as she saw the caller ID. She had left a message with Esther asking Quinn to contact her as a matter of urgency. For him to be returning her call at seven a.m. indicated how eager he was to hear what she had to say. Sarah watched her face as she listened to him speak. A stranger might have found her difficult to read, but Sarah knew her better than she had ever known anyone, and she could tell that Alex was furious.

"Eight thirty," Alex said. "We'll be there." She disconnected the call and took a long drink of water.

"Tell me," Sarah said as Alex set down her empty glass.

Alex shook her head, and for a moment, Sarah thought she was going to cry. Even in the Cascades, when things had been at their worst, she couldn't remember Alex ever seeming so lost.

"Tell me," she repeated softly.

"Judge Buchanan granted a search warrant for our house."

"On what grounds?"

"Your prints are on the blade, and Quinn is taking issue with the timeline you provided. He and Buchanan are old hunting buddies, so he wouldn't need anything more than that. He has officers over there now, said he was letting me know as a courtesy." Alex ground out the last word, but then terror seemed to overwhelm her anger and she took a ragged breath.

"What else?" Sarah prompted.

"He'll speak to us both at eight thirty, but he advised you to find a lawyer."

"Does that mean he's going to arrest me?"

"No," Alex said, her voice flat and bleak. "No, not yet."

❖

Bill Quinn slowly turned the small card in his fingers. He hadn't said anything for over a minute, and the interview room was so quiet that the buzz of a fly flitting around the overhead light was almost unbearably loud. Alex's mouth was dry from having spoken with little interruption for nearly an hour, but she didn't dare reach for her glass of water. Beside her, Sarah sat motionless, while Scott Emerson sat behind Quinn with his head tilted slightly. At some point, as Alex explained what had happened to her and Sarah in the Cascades, he had stopped taking notes and simply listened, his eyes bright with interest.

When Quinn finally cleared his throat and laid the card face down in front of him, everyone seemed to sit up straighter. "So, it's Alex Pascal, is it?" he said.

Determined that her response not come out as a weak rasp, Alex took a sip of water before answering. "Yes, sir."

"This Agent Castillo"—he tapped the card she had given him, which listed Castillo's official FBI contact details—"been a busy boy, hasn't he?"

"He's helped us a lot." She couldn't keep the edge from her voice; she felt Sarah nudge her thigh, reminding her to keep Quinn on their side. "He's a good man, sir."

"I'm sure he is." His tone directly contradicted his assertion. "And between the three of you, you've decided that one of these white supremacist types, bearing a grudge, managed to locate you via an image from a local newspaper?" He paused, making a show of looking at Sarah and then at Alex for confirmation. "This person then accessed your property and, for whatever reason, murdered Lyssa Mardell?"

Alex didn't grace his question with an answer. It was all too apparent that he considered the theory ludicrous. "Sir, will you at least speak to Agent Castillo? He's expecting you to call. We can get this cleared up right now." Panic was bringing her to the verge of begging. Common sense told her that in order to exhaust all lines of inquiry and build a case against Sarah, Quinn would have to investigate what Alex had just told him, would have to contact Castillo at some point, but it seemed he was going to make her sweat while he took his own sweet time about it.

He folded the card and pushed it into his shirt pocket.

"You join my team under a false name, with an FBI agent working in the background to purge details from your record," he said, his voice dangerously quiet. "And now, when your wife's up to her neck in shit, you suddenly decide you can trust me?"

"No, it wasn't like that," she said, realizing that it appeared exactly like that. "Chief, please, at least consider the possibility—"

He stood, effectively ending the discussion. "The search team has just finished at your house," he said. "I suggest you remain on medical leave and take Sarah home. Beyond that, I wouldn't be making any plans."

He left the room, and seconds later, his voice could be plainly heard through the open door, greeting Margot St. Clare and thanking her for taking the time to drop by. Alex rubbed her face with her hands, wondering what the hell had just happened. She jumped when Sarah touched her shoulder.

"We should go," Sarah said.

Emerson stood as they did, reaching the door just before them. He pushed it closed, blocking their exit. "Half the town is suddenly remembering Lyssa Mardell kissing Sarah at that picnic," he said quickly. "Get a lawyer, a decent one."

Alex stared at him, dumbfounded, trying to figure out what his angle was. He shrugged uneasily and gestured toward the discolored skin beneath her eye.

"Figured I owe you one," he said. "You got another card for your FBI agent?"

She didn't have one, but she scribbled Castillo's number on a scrap of paper Emerson gave her. When she was done, he tucked the paper back into the middle of his notepad.

"I'll do my best, but Quinn's under a lot of pressure to move fast on this."

"Meaning he'll stick with the easy option," she said, and heard Sarah's sharp intake of breath. Emerson must have heard it too, because he shifted uncomfortably.

"It's looking like that," he conceded. "The ADA seems confident enough. She was going to request a detective to come in from Prescott County, but she doesn't think that's necessary now." He put a hand on the door. "I have to get back out there. Leave by the side exit. There's a news crew out front."

He left before Alex could thank him. Feeling more confused than ever, she watched him stride down the corridor.

"I don't get it," Sarah said. "Is he a bad guy, or not?"

"I have no fucking clue anymore." Alex let out a desperate laugh. "Let's just go home."

❖

Newly clean of dust after the rain, Main Street was bright with sunshine. Outside most of the shops, small clusters of townsfolk were deep in earnest conversation. Several of them stopped to gesticulate excitedly as Alex drove past, and the expressions of distaste, and in some cases outright hostility, were impossible to mistake.

"Do we need anything from the store?" she said, trying to pretend it was a regular Saturday.

"No," Sarah replied absently, looking out the side window at Robbie Duggan as he spat in their direction. Robbie was seventeen and had an impressive rap sheet for petty larceny. Alex had arrested him three times in one record-breaking month. "Maybe milk." Sarah fixed her gaze forward. "I can't remember. It doesn't matter."

There was no way Alex was letting her drink her tea black. That really would be the final insult. She pulled into a gap in front of the store.

"Sit tight. Any problems, hit the horn."

Sarah managed a thin smile. "My hero."

The store was dim and cool, smelling pleasantly of fresh fruit and baking bread. It doubled as a general and hardware store, selling everything from household essentials to DIY goods and animal feed. What it didn't stock, its owner could usually procure. Everyone in town went there for their basic groceries and to catch up on the local gossip, and everyone standing in its aisles or at its counters turned to stare as Alex picked up a basket. She walked across to the dairy fridge and selected her milk. Then, too stubborn to be hounded out, she chose a loaf of bread and asked for pastrami at the deli counter. The young assistant blushed to the roots of her hair and accidentally dropped her gum into a dish of olives as she weighed the order. No one else spoke to Alex. As she waited at the cash register for longer than was customary, she picked up a copy of the local newspaper.

Lyssa's murder was splashed across the front page, accompanied by a picture of her wearing her uniform and an ear-to-ear grin that made Alex want to scream at the senselessness of everything that had happened. A breathless editorial was crammed with hyperbole but little in the way of verifiable facts. When Alex reached a quote from an anonymous source who cited a sordid lesbian affair as a possible motive, she threw the paper down and wiped her hands as if they were soiled.

Jenny—the store's owner—hurried out from the back room, the stink of cigarettes still clinging to her hair. She stopped short upon seeing Alex, but then smiled and took her basket from her.

"You look so tired, dear," she said, and the warmth in her voice brought a lump to Alex's throat. "How's Sarah holding up?"

"She's doing okay." Alex handed over a ten-dollar bill as Jenny rang up the total.

"Such a terrible thing. That girl of yours has nothing but sweet in her. You tell her from me to hang in there, okay? It'll come right in the end."

"Thank you. I'll tell her. I promise."

She carried the bag out into the late morning heat and waved as Sarah smiled and waggled three bandaged fingers at her.

"Thought you'd got lost," Sarah said as Alex opened the door.

"Lost, or tarred and feathered?"

"That too," she admitted. She shivered, and Alex saw there were goose bumps covering her arms, but she seemed to relax a little as Alex started the engine and reversed out onto the street.

"Jenny says you're to 'hang in there,'" Alex told her.

"I'm trying." She turned toward Alex, her face pale and drawn. "Please don't let me fall."

There were still several police officers searching the woods along the track to the cabin, but Lyssa's body and her SUV had been removed. Tobin was the only one to raise a hand as Alex drove past; the other officers and volunteers turned their backs or averted their gaze.

"I guess the longer they're out here, the safer we are," she said.

Sarah nodded distractedly, trying not to focus on the crime scene tape or the markers indicating the tire indentations where Lyssa had stopped her SUV. It occurred to her that they were the only such markers she had seen.

"Why haven't they found evidence of another vehicle?" she said. "Whoever killed Lyssa must have driven down the track."

"Did Tobin drive right up to you last night?"

Sarah grimaced, seeing the relevance of the question: that the mere act of responding to her 911 call had made Tobin contaminate the scene. "He kept everyone else back a little, but he drove pretty close." She heard the tires splash through a waterlogged pothole. "And then it rained."

"Yeah." Alex drummed her fingers on the steering wheel. "Unless they initially parked off-road somewhere to wait. But if so, how did they get Lyssa to stop? The easiest way to do that would be to block the track with their car."

"Risky if the first person to come along wasn't one of us…" Sarah's voice trailed into nothing. She took a shaky breath. "So, I guess that's what happened."

"Yeah, I guess." Alex sounded as if something still nagged at her, but her face brightened when they turned the final corner and saw Tilly trying to chew through her leash in her efforts to reach them. Someone had fastened the leash to a tree, and Tilly wasn't at all happy about it. Alex parked and went straight over to release her.

Still standing at the side of the Silverado, Sarah stared at the cabin. Outwardly, nothing had changed. The cats were asleep on the bench, the chickens were roaming freely around the lawn, and the cans she had rinsed out ready for recycling lay undisturbed by the back door. It was only when she started to look for what wasn't there that she began to notice differences. The picnic blanket was missing from the lawn, along with the cooler and the utensils she and Lyssa had used for lunch. The door to the small shed where they kept garden tools was ajar, and she tried to damp down a mounting sense of dread as she watched Alex jog across to it. She knew exactly what Alex would be checking for, and was unsurprised when she came back out empty-handed.

"Son of a bitch." Alex shook her head as Sarah walked across to her. "They took Walt's box."

"They'll have to give it back to you," Sarah said, deliberately not mentioning the real reason behind Alex's reaction. The hand-carved wooden box had been a leaving gift from Walt, and Alex had barely used the Bowie knife it contained, preferring to keep it in pristine condition. Now it could be used to prove that Sarah was in possession of the type of weapon used in Lyssa's murder.

"Come on." Sarah held out her hand. "I'll make a brew." The reversion to her natural accent made Alex react with mock horror. Sarah shrugged. "Fuck 'em," she said. "If our cover's blown, then I'm done talking like a bloody southerner."

Alex pulled her into a hug. "That's my girl."

Inside the cabin, the signs of disturbance were far more blatant. Furniture sat at strange angles and drawers were half-open, their contents messily rearranged. When Sarah reached the bedroom, the sight that greeted her made her waver at the threshold.

"Can they do that?" she whispered.

The bed had been stripped bare, the sheets and pillowcases presumably taken to examine for DNA evidence. The insinuation made her light-headed. She slid down the doorjamb to sit heavily on the floor.

"Put your head between your knees," Alex murmured, rubbing Sarah's back.

Despite everything, Sarah smiled, remembering another time, another place where Alex had given her exactly the same advice. She leaned back into Alex's body and felt Alex's breath on her cheek.

"Come a long way since then," Alex said, and Sarah could tell she was smiling too. She gently tilted Sarah's face and kissed her. "I'll find some fresh linen. You go put the kettle on."

Sarah nodded her agreement, but she was painfully aware that they were on borrowed time, that sooner or later Quinn would be knocking on the door. Alex must have shared the sense of inevitability because she tightened her hold.

"Or we could just stay here a little while longer," she said, and kissed Sarah again.

Sarah brewed a pot of tea and made sandwiches from the pastrami. Having remade the bed, Alex met her in the kitchen and they took their lunch out onto the back porch. Neither explicitly stated that the cabin didn't feel like their own anymore, but Sarah had an almost unbearable urge to disinfect everything it contained, while Alex had looked relieved at the suggestion they eat outside.

Once Sarah was sitting on the bench in the fresh air, Bandit's attempts to steal a tidbit and Tilly's watchful presence at their side helped her relax slightly. She finished her sandwich and bit into an apple. Alex was nursing her tea, her gaze intermittently flicking toward the driveway as if she expected Quinn to come storming up at any moment. The last time he visited the property he had had to phone ahead so they could unlock the gate, but Sarah didn't think he would be quite so courteous this time. She took a final bite of her apple and threw the core onto the grass for the chickens to fight over.

"Alex?"

Alex blinked and turned to her expectantly; whatever she had been thinking about, she evidently welcomed the interruption.

Sarah faltered, reconsidering what she was about to ask, but Alex noticed her hesitancy and set down her mug. "Go ahead," she said.

Despite the words, there was a wariness to her tone that made Sarah shift uneasily.

"Sweetheart, just ask me," Alex said.

Sarah nodded, still reluctant to raise the issue but torn by her genuine desire to know. "What happens when you arrest someone?" she said.

For a second, Alex just stared at her. Then, apparently reaching a decision, she leaned forward until her elbows were on her knees, and interlaced her fingers. From there she could no longer see Sarah, which seemed to be enough to allow her to speak.

"To make a planned arrest, we need enough evidence to determine probable cause, and then we usually need a warrant. That's something a judge like Buchanan has to issue. Once we have that, we go to the suspect's address with whatever backup Quinn deems necessary. Whether we knock or break down the door depends on the suspect."

"I would hope we'd get a knock," Sarah murmured, but she saw Alex tense. She reached out to rest a hand in the small of Alex's back.

"Someone will read you your rights," Alex said, showing no awareness of having switched pronouns, "and then..." She gave a half-shake of her head. "And then they'll probably handcuff you and take you to the station to be processed."

"Processed," Sarah repeated numbly.

"Fingerprints, mug shot, formal interview with the assistant district attorney—that's the State prosecutor. It'll be similar to last night, only no one will pretend to be your friend, and you can have a lawyer to advise you."

"I already told them everything that happened. They obviously don't believe me, so am I best just to say nothing?"

Alex leaned back and opened her hands. "I don't know. Sometimes silence can be seen as incriminating in itself, but then you can't be tripped up that way."

"If I don't answer, they'll assume I'm guilty." In a no-win situation, that seemed worse to Sarah than having the police twist her words to suit their own ends.

"If they've arrested you," Alex said quietly, "then they already think you're guilty."

"Yeah, I suppose you're right," Sarah conceded. She felt weirdly detached, like an observer watching the proceedings but not really connecting with them. She knew that if she let down her guard and allowed herself to become emotionally involved, she would lose the ability to cope with what was happening to them both. "How long can they keep me, or detain me, or whatever? I'll get bail, won't I?"

For a moment, Alex didn't answer.

"Oh shit," Sarah said, the reason for Alex's reticence suddenly becoming clear to her.

When Alex did speak, her words sounded strangled. "In Maine, murder is considered a non-bailable offense."

Sarah turned her head sharply, not quite able to believe what she was hearing. "And that's it? They just lock me up? What the fuck happened to innocent until proven guilty?" A small, sensible part of herself said that she should have expected this, that someone accused of stabbing a young woman to death would not be allowed to walk free until the date of the trial. If she had been a member of Lyssa's family and not the one who had been falsely accused, she would undoubtedly have approved of the state's hard-line stance.

"There have been cases, *rare* cases," Alex emphasized, obviously not wanting to raise false hopes, "where a judge at the Superior Court has used his discretion to grant bail. I'm not an expert, but I think your lawyer would have to challenge the evidence in a special hearing and either convince the judge that there are exceptional circumstances in your case or argue that the indictment was wrong, that there isn't enough evidence to warrant a murder charge."

Sarah didn't know much about the American justice system, but she could guess that if it was anything like the process in England such an appeal wouldn't happen overnight. "So whatever the fuck they decide, I'll be in jail for weeks for something I haven't done," she said. It seemed so much safer to hide behind anger than give in to the terror, but she tried to control her temper, aware that Alex was the wrong target.

"None of that is going to happen," Alex told her, though her tone held little assurance. "We'll find some way to stop it all before then."

Sarah couldn't imagine how stressful it must have been for Alex to have kept this knowledge bottled up in an effort to protect her. She felt like she had scraped the surface off a fresh wound and then rubbed salt into it just for spite. She laid her hand on top of Alex's. "Hope for the best but prepare for the worst, then?"

Alex nodded mutely.

"Okay, so we better get started and find me a bloody good lawyer." Sarah tried to sound positive, but the facade slipped as she put a hand into her pocket for her cell phone and remembered that Quinn had taken it at the meeting that morning. When she thought of strangers searching through her photographs or personal messages, it made her want to smash something hard and heavy, preferably on Quinn's head.

"We can use my phone." Alex was watching her carefully. "If you're gonna break something, make sure it's something we don't need, okay?"

Shielding her eyes from the sun, Sarah looked at her. "Am I really that easy to read?"

"You do tend to wear your heart on your sleeve," Alex said. "It's one of the things I love most about you."

"Maybe you should write me a character reference."

"Naw, I'd only make the judge blush. Stay out here if you want. I have a couple of people to try before I resort to Google."

"Okay."

As the screen door closed, Sarah slipped off her sneakers and walked onto the lawn. The sun was slowly evaporating the downpour of the previous night and the grass was still damp beneath her feet. She sat on it regardless, hugging Tilly close when she pushed into her arms.

"Look after Alex, you hear me?" she said, feeling the words catch in her throat. "She's going to need you, so no more playing silly buggers with the chickens or chasing Bandit around."

Tilly snuffled Sarah's hair and gave her face a lick; while she hadn't understood a word Sarah said, she seemed to have picked up on the seriousness of her tone. They sat together on the grass, watching the chickens scrap over the apple core. It was as effective a distraction as any.

❖

Sarah shut down the Internet browser on Alex's cell phone and watched her and Tilly making their way back toward the cabin. The light had altered in the time they had been gone, the shadows lengthening and wisps of cloud flushing a rosy pink as the sun dipped below the trees. The first time Alex had set out, Sarah had gone with her, only to find the search teams still busy on the track, making it impossible for them to do anything but return to the cabin. Even with dusk encroaching, Alex had insisted on going again to see if the search had finished, and Sarah, aware how agonizing waiting and inactivity were for her, hadn't tried to stop her.

Sarah had used the half hour to soak in a hot bath, indulging in such luxuries while she still could. Although Alex had refused to speak any further about the likelihood of her being arrested and denied bail, Sarah was forcing herself to come to terms with it. It was only as she shaved her legs that she had realized she was getting prepared, that she didn't know whether prison showers came with shaving gel and razors. Suddenly sick with fear, she had made herself focus on the lines she was leaving in the white foam, trying to make them even and neat. Engrossing herself in the task had been just about enough to stop her from getting out of the tub and barring the bathroom door.

"Hey." She waved from the porch bench as Alex came within earshot. "Any luck?"

Alex made a "so-so" gesture. "They've packed up and gone for the night but left some of their gear behind, so I guess they're not quite done yet. Hopefully, they'll finish up tomorrow."

"Come sit with me?"

Alex nodded, her tread tired and heavy on the steps.

"Actually, I've got a better idea," Sarah said, standing and holding out her hand. "Come to bed with me."

❖

Sarah was wearing Alex's favorite nightshirt: white and pale blue stripes with buttons all the way down to where it ended mid-thigh. She sat cross-legged on the bed as Alex painstakingly unfastened each button and opened the material wide. Alex, in contrast, hadn't bothered to wear anything. She pulled Sarah onto her lap, reveling in the sensation of their bare skin pressing together as Sarah leaned in and kissed her. She gently touched her tongue to Sarah's as her hands stroked across Sarah's face, her eyebrows, the curve of her cheekbones, before finally stilling to cup her jaw.

Deepening their kiss, she felt Sarah dip her hand between their bodies. There was a slight roughness from the dressing on one of Sarah's fingers and then nothing but soft skin as Sarah entered her. She traced her hands across Sarah's breasts, making her moan and shift with impatience.

"Please," Sarah whispered, "please." She hummed contentedly when Alex eased her fingers inside her and they fell into a rhythm that was so familiar it made them both smile.

Alex closed her eyes, desperately trying to commit everything to memory.

"Alex," Sarah said. "Look at me, sweetheart."

Alex did as she asked.

"I promise you won't forget this," Sarah told her, holding her gaze steadily. She raised her free hand to brush her fingers against Alex's cheek. "Whatever happens, love, we'll be okay."

CHAPTER NINE

Y our man Emerson is so clean he squeaks."
Even through the crackles on the phone line, there was no mistaking the defeat in Castillo's voice, as if he had expected Emerson to have so many skeletons in his closet that it would leave Quinn no option but to consider him a viable suspect and consequently shift the focus away from Sarah.

Having allowed herself to entertain the same hope, Alex took the news like a physical blow, rocking back in her chair. "Shit," she muttered. Then, unable to stop herself, "What the fuck do we do now?"

"My hands are tied here," Castillo said. "I'm still waiting on word from the surveillance teams, and I have no jurisdiction in Avery. If I start requesting forensic reports and case files, I'm only going to get Quinn pissed at me, and I don't think he likes me much as it is."

"He spoke to you?"

"Briefly, yesterday. I sent him all the declassified intel I have on the Cascades and the wider investigation into Nicholas Deakin, but I got the impression he considers his case against Sarah solid enough to make any other potential leads a pretty low priority."

"It's all circumstantial," Alex said. Her phone beeped once, indicating a call waiting, but she didn't recognize the number on the screen so she ignored it. "Everything he has on her, it's bullshit."

"I know, but when your town is baying for blood and there's a media circus demanding action, circumstantial is going to be sufficient for a warrant."

"And then what?" Alex snapped.

"And then you stop feeling sorry for yourself and start acting like a cop."

"Ouch." His rebuke stung, but in a strange way, she appreciated his bluntness.

"Yeah." He dragged the word out as if remorseful, but he didn't apologize. "Look, the only thing that flagged up on Emerson is his ownership of a second property. It's a small apartment in Ruby. Might just be a rental, but on a cop's salary it's a little odd."

She reached for a pen. "Be worth checking. You got the address?" She scribbled down the details, recognizing the area as quiet and well heeled, bordering the river on the western outskirts of town.

"Once the pressure is off of Quinn," Castillo continued, "that'll be the time he'll start looking at alternatives, if he has any doubts at all that he can secure a conviction against Sarah."

"I'd like to think he has doubts. But he's stubborn and proud, not to mention mad at me, so at the moment he'd be happy to just lock her up and throw away the key."

"How is she?" Castillo asked.

Alex swapped the phone to her other ear and opened the study door a crack. She could hear Sarah in the kitchen, whisking something while cooing at one of the cats. "She's braver than I am. She's been baking all morning. She won't say anything, but she's making sure I have meals for when she's not here." Her voice cracked and she hurriedly wiped her eyes in case Sarah came in and saw her crying. "I fucking hate this," she whispered.

The sound of tires spinning hard and fast over the gravel on the driveway drowned out his reply. She stood and pried open a slat on the blinds, even though she didn't want to look, even though she knew what would be out there. It was too soon. The search party had been back in the woods at daybreak and still not completed their work, and she hadn't had the chance to do anything with Castillo's information yet.

She heard Sarah shout for her before her eyes could focus in the sun's glare; all she saw was blurry shadows opening and then slamming white doors on white cars. Someone had left their strobes on, blinking an urgent blue and red alert, and she wondered whom exactly the idiot was trying to warn: the chickens?

"Jesus Christ, I have to go," she said, suddenly remembering Castillo on the other end of the phone. "Quinn's here."

She hung up as the banging started. It wasn't a polite knock, more a demand to comply.

"Alex?" Sarah was in the living room, out of sight of the porch door. She looked pale, but when Alex got closer, she realized there was flour smeared all over Sarah's face, and she couldn't help but smile.

"C'mere," she said, and used her sleeve to wipe the flour away.

"I made you a fruit cake," Sarah told her.

"Yeah?" Unsure whether to laugh or sob, Alex opted for the former, and then jumped as someone loudly commanded that they open the door.

She kissed Sarah's forehead, took her hand, and walked with her into the kitchen. The room smelled of rich casserole and something flavored with basil, with an underlying sweetness from the cake. Taking deep breaths, she forced her leaden fingers to work the locks. As soon as the door swung open, Quinn stepped across the threshold and put his hand on Sarah's upper arm, firmly separating her from Alex and telling her that she was under arrest for the murder of Lyssa Mardell. Three other officers crowded onto the porch, scaring the cats, who scurried beneath the bench. One of the officers held Tilly's collar as she barked furiously.

"You have the right to remain silent." The officer reciting the Miranda worked most of his patrols in Ruby, and at a barbecue the previous summer he had taught Alex the best way to grill a moose burger. Now he couldn't look her in the eye. "You have the right to talk to an attorney and have him present with you while you are being questioned."

Quinn was still gripping Sarah's arm, and he used it to turn her so that she faced Alex. He cuffed her hands behind her, making her flinch as the metal dug into her bandaged wrists. She cut off Alex's protest with a sharp shake of her head.

"Do you understand these rights as I have given them to you?"

"Yes," she said, her voice clear and remarkably calm. "I understand."

Quinn jerked her arm and she allowed him to march her over to the first car. She didn't try to say good-bye to Alex; she seemed determined not to give Quinn the satisfaction of making a scene. He pushed her into the rear seat and shut the door.

Struggling to keep Tilly quiet, Alex watched Sarah lean forward as she tried to find a comfortable position in the handcuffs. Then Sarah looked across at her. There were no dramatic signals or mouthed declarations, just the loose stones grinding beneath the tires and Sarah's gaze holding Alex's until the car turned and took her away.

❖

Someone had tipped off the press, who in turn had tipped off everyone in the vicinity of Main Street. Both patrol cars were forced to approach the police station at a crawl, inching through the gathered townsfolk as camera bulbs flashed and people jostled for a better viewpoint.

Sarah shrank back in her seat, pressing her sore wrists against the warm leather, but there was no way for her to avoid the prying eyes and pointing fingers. Emerson's presence in the station parking lot and the three officers in the convoy seemed to be Quinn's only concessions to crowd control. When the cars stopped, the officers spread themselves thinly along the sidewalk, trying to persuade people to remain within their ineffective cordon, while Emerson opened Sarah's door and reached in to guide her out.

"Keep your head down," he warned her, but she was shaking so hard she could barely walk, and her awkward progress made it impossible to avoid seeing the faces around her.

She recognized many of them, having spoken to them on the street or taught their children at the lake. It was difficult now to reconcile those amiable encounters with the seething mob surrounding her. A hand was suddenly raised, a dark object clutched in its fist, and Emerson reacted quickly, turning his back to shelter her as the rock hurtled toward them. It landed harmlessly on the sidewalk, shattering into smaller fragments. Someone cheered the effort regardless of its failure, while several others whooped and yelled for him to try again. As if that had been their cue, more officers streamed out of the station to surround Sarah.

"Better late than never," Emerson spat to no one in particular, all but running with Sarah to cover the remaining few yards. She heard a sequence of locks click as the doors were secured behind them. He stopped at the front desk and turned to her. "You okay?"

Something in his tone made her answer honestly. "No. Not really."

Before he could respond, an officer strode across to them, carrying a thick file of paperwork. "Quinn wants her processed ASAP," he said without preamble.

Emerson narrowed his eyes. "Where's he at?"

"He stayed outside to give a statement to the press. He wants me to take her to booking." The officer brandished the paperwork to prove his claim, as if he were afraid Emerson would rob him of the opportunity to play his part in such a major case. He had already closed a hand around Sarah's cuffs.

Emerson outranked him, but he stepped back, deferring to Quinn's order. "I'll send Esther to chaperone," he said curtly, already reaching for the phone on the desk.

Without waiting to hear the outcome of the call, the officer steered Sarah beyond a sign marked "Authorized Personnel Only." The corridor he took her into was empty, but he kept a tight hold on her until he needed both hands to swipe his keycard and enter a code on a security pad. The door in front of them opened automatically and strip lighting flickered on as he pushed her forward. It illuminated a dirty white floor and three evenly spaced security doors of thick metal. Each door had a small hinged viewing hatch cut into the metal and each was slightly ajar. Despite taking shallow breaths, Sarah couldn't shut out the stink of vomit and badly drained toilets.

The sharp, rhythmic tap of heels against the tiles announced Esther's entrance. The officer acknowledged her approach with a grunt and a scowl. "Don't get in the way," he said.

"Wouldn't dream of it." She wasn't looking at him; her attention was entirely focused on Sarah. Although they had never met in person, Esther always seemed to be on dispatch whenever Sarah had a callout, and it had become something of a running joke. Her expression was pained as she walked closer.

"Does she really need the cuffs?" she said.

The officer's cheeks flushed, and Sarah suspected he would have left them on if Esther hadn't mentioned them.

"Turn around," he told Sarah.

She did as instructed. There was a rattle of keys and then the metal fell away from her wrists, allowing her to bring her arms stiffly forward.

Esther frowned at the fresh blood seeping through the dressings. "Do you want me to call a doctor?" she asked Sarah.

"No, thank you," Sarah said, profoundly grateful for her concern. "I'm fine."

Impatient to reassert his authority over the proceedings, the officer positioned her with her arms outstretched at her sides and began a thorough search. As he worked his hands around her body, she stared straight ahead, trying not to think of the last men who had done this to her, trying not to think of anything at all. By the time he had finished, she was sweating and swallowing convulsively against the bile rising in her throat. He ignored her, scribbling notes onto his paperwork. There wasn't much to document; she had emptied her pockets when she had gotten dressed that morning.

Another DNA swab from her mouth was added to her file. Then, even though her fingertips still bore the ink-stain from the prints taken on the night of Lyssa's murder, the officer repeated that process too, seemingly determined to place a tick into every box. On his order, she removed the laces from her sneakers and took off her single piece of jewelry: her wedding ring. It was the first time she had been without it since the day of the ceremony. He sealed it in a plastic bag and tossed it into a tray on the desk.

"Move over here."

She followed him across to a blank wall, where she was made to hold a board showing her name and a number as he took a series of photographs. When he was satisfied with the quality of his shots, he told Esther she could return to her desk. With the processing completed, she had no grounds to argue; she left the room, touching Sarah's arm as she went.

Sarah watched the door shut, her pulse pounding against her breastbone. She noticed there was no light flashing on the camera above her head, and wondered who had turned it off and when.

The officer was also watching the door. He waited until the locks reset and then used Sarah's collar to drag her across to the closest wall. Pressing her face up against it, his knee digging into her buttocks, he refastened the cuffs around her wrists and ratcheted them down tightly. Aware that any show of resistance on her part would only give him the excuse he was looking for, she held herself rigid as he spoke directly in her ear.

"Lyssa Mardell was a good friend of mine." His voice was low, the threat unmistakable. "You deserve everything you get, you vicious little queer."

His hand still on her collar, he hauled her to the first cell and shoved her inside so forcefully that she collided with the breezeblock wall opposite. Despite having the wind knocked out of her, she turned as quickly as she could, knowing she was too vulnerable with her back to him. He stared at her for a long moment, his fists clenching and unclenching, before he seemed to regain control of his temper, spat at her feet, and walked out of the cell. A key ground in the lock, the viewing hatch slammed shut, and she listened to his footsteps fade.

As soon as there was silence, her legs buckled beneath her. She slumped where he had left her, against the rough wall.

"Fucking hell," she whispered, irrationally relieved to be locked alone inside a tiny cell.

She stayed on the floor until her various aches settled to a tolerable level. Then she pushed to her knees, using the wall to help her stand. Turning in a slow circle, she took stock of her surroundings—not that there was much to take stock of, the cell being barely eight feet square. Devoid of natural daylight, it relied on a harsh overhead light that cut into every corner. The length of one wall was dominated by a solid raised slab, on which a rubber mattress had been thrown, and a small metal toilet with a discolored rim was bolted onto the adjacent wall. Someone had obviously tried to remove the stains and smears littering the paintwork, but it had been a halfhearted effort, and the heat trapped in the tiny space intensified the foul smell.

Sitting as close to the edge of the mattress as she could, Sarah tried to find a position that would relieve the strain on her bound arms. She groaned as she felt sweat begin to trickle down her chest and her back. She felt thirsty but sick to her stomach, and she was already missing Alex terribly. When she closed her eyes, the light was still bright, the silhouette of the toilet lingering on her retina. She kept her eyes closed, letting the image melt away, and wondered how long it would be before someone came for her.

Alcohol was strong on Caleb's breath as he gripped Leah around her waist and pulled her to sit on his knee. Holding her in place with one arm, he used his free hand to increase the volume on the television set, drowning out the music playing in the apartment below theirs.

"What goes around comes around, bitch," he said, throwing the remote down and picking up his beer. Leah froze, assuming at first that he was speaking to her, but he was watching the screen intently, his grin widening to reveal his teeth.

She recognized both of the young women in the news report. The upper left corner of the screen held an image of the paramedic Caleb had murdered. It was a stock photograph, the same one used in the newspapers piled up on the table. The remainder of the screen was dominated by footage of Sarah Kent being paraded in front of the cameras by the police. With the media unaware that she had once used a different name, the scrolling banner touted the arrest of "Sarah Hayes" and made no mention of any other suspects being sought in connection with the murder. That Caleb had known this all along was so obvious that Leah felt ashamed for not having figured it out before. Since the night of the murder, his contact must have kept him informed as to what the police were doing and who their main suspect was, which explained why he had been confident enough to stay in the area. Not only had he killed an innocent woman, he was now sitting gloating as another was wrongly accused of the crime.

He raised his bottle to salute Sarah as someone in the crowd threw a missile at her, and then he pulled Leah down into a kiss. His mouth was sticky against hers. "Just the cop left now," he said. "An eye for an eye. So I guess she gets to pay for my daddy."

His beer slipped from his fingers, spilling foam onto the carpet.

"I'll get you another," she said quickly, trying to prevent a violent reaction, but his eyes were already half-lidded and he didn't stir when she slid from his knee. She left a fresh bottle beside him and went to sit by the window.

Gazing at the perfect blue sky, she tried to block the television images from her thoughts: two lives ruined, and he was already plotting to ruin a third. A sudden surge of nausea made her mouth water. She opened a pack of saltines and ate one to ease the sickness that plagued her all day. She was never sure if it was caused by the baby or Caleb. Clean air drifted through the open window from the river below; she looked out onto the wide, constant flow of water. On the riverbank, a child threw bread for the geese and clapped his hands in delight when they ate it greedily. She traced her fingers across her abdomen, her imagination springing to life, giving her a glimpse of what could be possible for her and her baby. In that single moment, she felt a burst of happiness. Then, as if a switch had been flicked, it was gone.

❖

Alex had started out sitting on the sofa and ended up perched on the edge of the coffee table, as close to the television screen as she could get and still focus. The local cable channel had interrupted its regular schedule of soaps and crappy game shows to air a special bulletin featuring Sarah's arrest. For almost two hours, Alex had watched an unvarying loop of footage showing Emerson leading Sarah into the police station.

Shards of glass in the far corner of the room picked up the colors on the screen and reflected them back at Alex. The anger that had made her smash the bowl against the wall had slowly dissipated, taking with it the shock and hatred and leaving her only a bitter grief. As a police officer, she had always considered perp walks to be a necessary evil, something that her superiors clamored for and that she tried not to think about too deeply. Watching Sarah undergo the ritual humiliation, knowing that she was innocent and yet presumed guilty by everyone there, forced Alex to see the process in an entirely new light. That Quinn had arranged it, or at the very least approved it, hurt her more than she would ever have expected.

As the commercials began, she stabbed a finger on the mute button and picked up her phone, but found there were no voice mails or e-mails from Castillo. Intent on doing something, *anything* that might help, she collected her keys, fastened her Glock onto her belt, and went into the kitchen. Emerson would still be at the station, which meant she had time to get to Ruby and find his apartment, maybe even ask a few questions if any of the neighbors proved cooperative.

About to unlock the back door, she hesitated, looking at the answer machine. Sarah would have the right to three phone calls. As Alex had already arranged a lawyer for her, she would undoubtedly use those privileges to call home. Uncertainty seized Alex; she knew there were numerous places out on the road where she would lose her cell phone signal. The possibility of missing a call from Sarah made her decision an easy one, and she threw her keys down so hard that they skidded along the countertop. Leaving them where they landed, she clicked the switch on the kettle.

When the coffee was ready, she carried her mug and a slice of fruitcake through into the living room, setting them on the table next to her cell phone and the house phone. She turned the television back on but left it silent; it wasn't telling her anything she didn't already know.

As soon as she was settled, Flossie sat on her knee and began to purr, oblivious to her agitation. Biting the skin at the side of her fingernail, Alex watched Emerson shield Sarah from the crowd and tried her best to figure out why the hell he would bother to do that if it was his scheming that had put her there in the first place.

❖

The scratch of a key in the lock made Sarah jolt her head up. She wanted to move, to push herself into the farthest corner until she knew who was coming through the door, but her body refused to obey her commands quickly enough. For all Quinn's reported haste, he had left her in the cell for what felt like hours, and the pain from her restrained wrists had not only exhausted her but rendered her unable to focus on anything else. If he had intended to break her down prior to interrogation, he had done a good job.

Annoyed by her passivity, she forced herself to sit up properly, ignoring the spasms that ran like electric shocks into her numbed fingers. The door opened slowly, and the officer who had processed her stepped over the threshold, holding a bottle of water in one hand and a set of keys in the other. Reminding herself that she had survived far worse, she remained perfectly still as he sat right beside her, invading her personal space. That she didn't cower or otherwise react seemed to disconcert him; he pushed back so that his thigh was no longer touching hers, but then, as if punishing her for his own lapse, he took hold of her handcuffs and casually lifted them.

"Oh God, don't…" She tried to twist away but he caught hold of her hair.

"You listening to me?" he hissed, raising the cuffs another inch.

Too breathless to answer, she nodded.

"I'm going to take these off now, and you're going to play nice, drink your water, and not breathe a fucking word about them to anyone. Y'know why?" He gave her head a shake, mocking her inability to speak. "Because a good buddy of mine is working the night shift down here, and he knows how to turn that little camera off too."

He let go of her and she bowed her head, breathing through her mouth until the pain became bearable and she no longer felt faint. By the time her vision cleared, he had taken the cuffs off, but her arms were deadened and useless and she couldn't lift her hands. He held the bottle of water to her lips, tipping it too high. It was evident from his haste that he was working to a deadline. She struggled to swallow quickly enough and water spilled onto her shirt, making him grin. She didn't care. The cell was stifling and the water gloriously cold; he could've emptied the bottle over her head and she would have smiled and thanked him for his trouble. She licked her lips, savoring the last droplets as he screwed the lid back on. She felt better, calmer, now that she knew Quinn was unaware of what his subordinate had done to her. She could cope with one man's vendetta; a conspiracy involving Avery's entire police force had been a far more terrifying prospect.

The officer was scrutinizing her, obviously reluctant to take her anywhere until she had recovered enough to avoid rousing suspicion. She made him wait as she massaged her wrists and rotated her aching shoulders. When he checked his watch for the third time, his forehead already running with sweat, she finally relented. Placing her hands back in her lap, she waited for his next instruction.

"Your lawyer is here to see you," he said, surreptitiously dabbing at the dampness on his upper lip. "Play nice, remember?" He yanked her up by her arm, grinding his fingers into her bicep.

"I remember." She forced the words out.

He took her out of the cell and past the desk, walking her beneath the camera whose light was now blinking reassuringly. He held open the door of a small washroom and pushed her inside.

"Two minutes," he told her. "Clean yourself the fuck up."

Bridget Reagan shook Sarah's hand firmly.

"Call me 'Bridie,'" she said, by way of introduction. She was a small woman with an unassuming demeanor, but when she caught sight of the bloodied bandages around Sarah's wrists, her eyebrows arched almost to her hairline.

"Are they treating you okay?" Her tone implied she already knew the answer.

"I'm fine." Sarah tucked her hands beneath the table. There had been a fresh bar of soap in the washroom, but the officer hadn't thought to bring clean dressings to cover up the evidence of his abuse.

"Mmhm." Bridie fixed her with a look. "Let me know the instant you're not 'fine.' I understand that you don't want to rock the boat right now, but letting them hurt you is not an option, okay?"

"Okay." Sarah nodded but said nothing further, the officer's threat still fresh in her mind.

Bridie sighed but chose not to push the issue. She opened the file in front of her and uncapped a pen. "I already met with Alex, who gave me a rundown. I just need to go over the salient points before Quinn and the ADA get their hooks into you. Oh, and"—she held up a finger as if to excuse her absentmindedness and pulled a small foil-wrapped package from her briefcase—"Alex sends her love."

Sarah couldn't stop herself from smiling as she unwrapped the purple foil. Within it were three squares of Cadbury's chocolate. She broke them apart and offered one to Bridie.

"No, thank you, but you go ahead. It took me long enough to get it approved by Quinn. Strangely, he couldn't confirm that you'd been given anything at all to eat since your arrest."

Sarah bit at the edge of a piece, nibbling daintily in deference to Bridie. When she heard Bridie chuckle, she gave in and put the entire chunk in her mouth.

"I'll give you a moment, shall I?" Bridie asked.

Sarah spoke around the melting chocolate. "I'm good. Go ahead."

Bridie nodded, her pen poised at the top of a fresh sheet of paper. "So…tell me exactly what happened on the day that Lyssa Mardell was murdered."

CHAPTER TEN

Quinn pressed the button on the tape recorder and then stated the names of those present in the interview room, the date, and the exact time. It was later than Sarah had thought, which explained the pain just above her right eye. Hours of stress and dehydration had given her a pounding headache, but Bridie's request for medication had been denied. With Sarah's arraignment scheduled for the following afternoon, Quinn had refused to postpone the interview, and Sarah, wanting to expedite the inevitable appeals process, had stopped Bridie from objecting.

Sitting beside Quinn, Emerson looked long and hard at Sarah's wrists before meeting her gaze. Unable to tell whether his concern was disingenuous, she kept her expression blank, leaving him to draw his own conclusions. She had been in the cell for six hours; if he had been so worried about her, why hadn't he checked on her during that time?

A swish of paper diverted her attention to the woman sitting to Quinn's right. On starting the tape recorder, he had identified her as Assistant District Attorney Linda Kryger, and he didn't waste time introducing her formally to Sarah. Most of Sarah's legal knowledge had been gleaned from television shows where ADAs struggled altruistically for the good of society while private legal practice raked in all the money. Kryger, however, with her expensive tailored suit and beautifully manicured nails, didn't appear to be laboring on the breadline.

She had taken a series of glossy photographs from a folder and now placed them in front of Sarah one by one, lining them up in a sequential horror show. Transfixed, Sarah stared at the images: a detailed shot of Lyssa's eyes wide open and lifeless; Lyssa's blood-soaked body splayed on the ground; Lyssa's body washed and naked on the slab, with two stab wounds marring the pale skin of her torso. Sarah drew that final image closer and traced a finger over the second wound.

"He stabbed her twice?" she whispered. No one had told her that. She shuddered at the violence implicit in the photograph. The abdominal wound was a wide, thick line just below Lyssa's navel, obviously deep and, given its proximity to the aortic artery, probably fatal. It explained the massive blood loss evident when Sarah had attempted resuscitation. She had never thought to look for other wounds, and she found herself fervently hoping that Lyssa had died or lost consciousness before she had had time to understand what was happening.

Instead of answering Sarah's question, Quinn tossed another set of photographs on top of those already laid out. "Explain how you got these injuries, Sarah."

The images were close-up shots of her own hands, the slash marks and lacerations too numerous to count. She glanced at Bridie for guidance, getting a short nod in return. In their earlier meeting, Bridie had advised her not to go into unnecessary detail and to answer as succinctly as she could.

"The blade was in the way as I did CPR. I cut myself on it."

"And this one?" Kryger asked, with a pleasant lilt to her voice. She took her pen and separated the photographs, revealing one that Sarah hadn't noticed. Using two fingers on its margins, Sarah turned it slightly, her heart sinking as she saw its focus. She had no recollection of the photograph having been taken, but the CSI must have zoomed in on the marks while she was documenting the knife wounds.

"Bandit, my cat, he scratched me that afternoon," she said, knowing how implausible it sounded. The three angry raised welts across her wrist looked exactly like those made by fingernails.

Quinn folded his arms, pushed his chair away from the table, and gave her a self-satisfied, condescending smile. "Did you know Lyssa Mardell was gay?"

"No," she replied mildly. She was surprised he hadn't mentioned this before.

"You didn't know?" His tone made no secret of his incredulity. "All those cozy little afternoon sessions and she never confided in you? Not once?"

"No," she repeated. "Lyssa wasn't gay; she was bi."

"By what?" For a moment, his own ignorance made him falter.

"Bisexual," she said quietly, trying not to bait him. "She slept with men and women." Technically, Lyssa had always described herself as a "try-sexual," as in, she'd try anything once, but that was none of Quinn's business.

"Were you sleeping with her?" he snapped, clearly embarrassed by his mistake.

"No, I wasn't sleeping with her."

He ignored that, warming to his theme. "We have testimony from a number of witnesses claiming you and she were real familiar with each other as soon as Alex's back was turned."

He paused, but Sarah refused to dignify his statement with a response. She wasn't certain she could have kept it civil.

He took one of the photographs and studied it as if giving due consideration to what she had told him. It was a transparent ploy; he was building up to something.

"Don't you think this CPR story is a little too convenient?" he asked at length, looking at Kryger, who nodded confirmation to his entirely rhetorical question. "It *conveniently* explains away your injuries, injuries that are consistent with defensive wounds. It *conveniently* explains why your fingerprints are all over the blade of the knife." He put the photograph down and tilted his head at her. "Shall I tell you what I think?"

He was going to do so no matter how she reacted, so she said nothing. He pulled his chair close to the table again.

"I think you and Lyssa were involved," he said, his deep voice unpleasantly intimate. "You met with her frequently, and at first it was probably only to study, but one thing led to another, as it often does." He made it sound so reasonable, just something that had happened, something for which no one was to blame. "That afternoon, you take advantage of Alex being away, phoning her at frequent intervals to ensure that you and Lyssa won't be interrupted unexpectedly. You spend the day with Lyssa. Afterward, she showers and gets ready to leave for work. Maybe you're already arguing, maybe she wants to tell Alex and you don't, maybe she's making threats, but you're still arguing when you go down to the gate with her, and you need to shut her up."

Sarah shook her head, half in denial, half in confusion, but he gave her no opportunity to interrupt.

"You already have the knife on you, but Lyssa manages to get ahold of it. There's a struggle, during which you sustain your injuries, but you get the knife back and lash out with it." He closed his fist around an imaginary weapon, driving it upward to mimic the abdominal wound and then stabbing down in an arc onto the table. "The handle breaks off, but the blade is stuck. You try to free it, leaving your prints on the metal, but then you start to panic. So you step away and think. You're medically trained; you know how this should go. You concoct a story about finding Lyssa and attempting to revive her, and I have to admit it's a good one." He nodded in exaggerated admiration, before his expression darkened again. "It's also complete and utter horseshit. Your delay in phoning for help gave you the opportunity to get rid of the blade's handle, time to get your story straight. Meanwhile, Lyssa is bleeding out. Did you walk away from her while you hid the evidence, Sarah? Did you leave her to die while you tried to save your own hide?"

"No," she said vehemently. "No, it didn't happen like that. You've got it wrong."

"How?" he asked. "How have I gotten it wrong?"

"Lyssa had her own key."

Uncertainty flitted across his face. "What?"

"For the gate." She put a hand to her aching head. It had taken her far too long to identify the fundamental flaw in his theory. "We had one cut for her. Jenny's store on Main Street might still have an invoice."

Quinn and Kryger ignored this latter point, but she saw Emerson jot down a note.

"There was no key found on Lyssa's person or in her SUV," Kryger said.

That, unfortunately, made perfect sense to Sarah. "Then whoever killed her took it to let himself out."

"Then how did he let himself *in*?" Kryger retorted. "Officer Tobin had to cut the padlock when he arrived. It showed no sign of having been tampered with prior to that."

"I don't know," Sarah admitted. "The killer must have picked the lock in the first place. Then I suppose he took Lyssa's key with him because it made it easier for him to escape."

"So we're back to that." Kryger gave a long-suffering sigh. "Your mystery assailant, who leaves no trace of himself or his vehicle, kills the wrong woman, and disappears into the night."

"Have you even explored that as a possibility?" The contempt in Bridie's tone was withering. "It seems to me you have a lot of unsubstantiated supposition, backed up by testimony gleaned from every homophobe in town. What you are lacking is anything for which my client cannot provide a logical explanation. Do you really think she's capable of stabbing a young woman so violently that the medical examiner has to cut the blade free from the victim's sternum?"

Kryger gave Quinn a thin smile, as if Bridie had given them the ideal opening for their trump card. The photographs he threw down this time spun repeatedly before coming to rest at odd angles. For a moment, Sarah couldn't work out what she was seeing. Then she shoved her chair back with a gasp, trying to get as far away from them as she could. Bridie picked them up and looked at each of them in turn before laying them facedown on the table.

"I think your client is capable of quite a lot of things," Kryger said. "She shot a man and left him to die. I think a jury would be very interested to hear all about that."

Sarah barely heard Quinn state the time and stop the tape recorder. Nicholas Deakin's river-battered corpse had loomed large in one of the photographs. In the other, Tanner, the man she had shot in a desperate bid to save herself and Alex, lay unconscious in a hospital bed, his leg in traction and a ventilator breathing for him.

"Her arraignment is scheduled for three thirty tomorrow," Quinn reminded Bridie as he stood. "We'll see you there."

Uncertain what was supposed to happen next, Sarah sat and watched Quinn politely gesture Kryger in front of him as they left the room. She could hear Bridie's pen still scratching urgently across her notepad.

Emerson's voice broke the tension. "Do you want something to eat?" Like Bridie, he looked troubled.

"No." The thought of food tied Sarah's stomach into a knot. She was coming to realize for the first time how likely it was that a jury would convict her of the murder; how easily, given the evidence as Quinn had just presented it, any regular person—let alone one with ingrained prejudices—would be persuaded of her guilt. She would never be able to go home, never be with Alex again. The room seemed to tilt and she had to put her head into her hands to steady herself.

"It'll be okay, Sarah." Bridie's voice sounded distant and uncertain.

Looking up, Sarah gave her a wan smile. "Thanks," she said, not wanting her to feel responsible.

Emerson's chair scuffed the floor as he stood. "I should get you back to your cell."

"I'll see you in the morning, to prepare for the arraignment," Bridie told her. "Try not to worry."

Sarah knew she meant well, but the reassurance rang hollow. There was only one thing on her mind as she looked at Bridie and Emerson in turn.

"When do I get to make a phone call?"

The call was snatched up on the first ring.

"Hello?"

Even suffused with anxiety, Alex's voice brought a smile to Sarah's lips.

"Hey, it's me," was all she could think to say. She heard Alex laugh brokenly and knew she was crying, even as tears dripped off her own nose and splattered against the dirty plastic of the phone. For the first few seconds, all they did was listen to each other breathe.

"How you doin'?" Alex asked finally.

"I'm okay. Better now."

"Yeah, yeah, me too." Another pause as Alex blew her nose. When she spoke again, she sounded stronger, more composed. "How did it go with Quinn?"

"Not too well." Sarah rubbed her eyes with the back of her hand, knowing Alex would be able to tell if she lied and needing her to have an idea of what was coming. "Alex—"

"*Don't.* Don't say it. Don't even fucking *think* it, Sarah."

"I have to. We both have to." Her voice caught. "And I need to know you'll be all right, that you won't do anything stupid."

"I'm not going to let you go to jail," Alex countered. "We'll find something that proves it couldn't have been you."

Sarah shook her head. "Whoever did this is still out there. He knows where we live. You need to be getting yourself to someplace safe, not worrying about me."

Her words prompted a lengthy silence, broken only when Alex started to laugh despairingly. "Well, aren't we just a pair of self-sacrificing idiots?" she said, and Sarah could practically see the derisive roll of her eyes.

"We do have a distinct tendency." The photographs of Deakin and Tanner had once again brought the Cascades and everything she and Alex had had to do to survive there to the forefront of her thoughts. She reminded herself that, in times of crisis, food was a reliable subject on which to fall back. "Are you eating okay? Did you have something for your tea?"

"Cake," Alex said. "I think, given the circumstances, cake is acceptable as a meal."

"Yeah." Sarah smiled. "Should've baked a fucking file into it." From the corner of her eye, she saw Emerson tap his watch. "I think I have to go," she said. "My arraignment is at three thirty tomorrow."

"I'll be there."

Something in Alex's voice destroyed Sarah's ability to be brave. "I miss you," she whispered.

"I miss you too." Alex sounded as if she was walking the same tightrope Sarah had just lost her grip on.

"I'll see you tomorrow." Unable to bear a protracted good-bye, Sarah hung up the phone. She stared blankly at the receiver until Emerson came across to the desk. Then, without saying a word, she followed him back to her cell.

The guard on the night shift made it easy for Sarah to gauge the passing time. At what she guessed were hourly intervals, his boots would clomp across the tiled floor. Then he would open the observation hatch in the cell door, usually whistling or humming tunelessly as he did so. As soon as he was satisfied that she was behaving herself, he would slam the hatch so hard that the metal door shook, making the noise reverberate around the cell. He never opened the door, never stepped across the threshold, or threatened her with violence. He just left the light glaring overhead and ensured that once an hour she was startled from what little sleep she had managed to snatch.

As the metal rang for the seventh time, she pushed herself up to lean against the wall, in the hope that it might lessen his enthusiasm with the hatch. It didn't, and she heard his cackle of laughter when he noted the success of his efforts. She drew her knees to her chest, pressed her eyes against her knees to try to block out the light, and started to count down the hour.

As the first hints of light began to creep between the shutters and the birds welcomed the dawn with enthusiasm, Alex gave up trying to sleep, abandoning the bed to Tilly and the cats. She had woken frequently in the night, only managing an hour here and there as nightmares tormented her and every little noise made her reach for the Glock on her bedside table. At two o'clock, Tilly had inched her way onto Sarah's side of the bed, and Alex—hating the emptiness there—had let her stay. The cats, sensing an easy mark, had joined them shortly afterward.

Alex showered quickly and threw on the clothes closest to hand. She collected a flashlight and Sarah's camera, clipped her Glock to her belt, and whistled for Tilly.

"Stay close, girl," she said, and Tilly, somewhat less boisterous since Lyssa's death, obediently walked to heel.

It was quiet and cool outside, but the cloudless, pale blue sky promised another day of unrelenting heat. Alex tried not to think about Sarah being held in a cellblock where fixing the air conditioning was always way down on the station priorities and fixing the drains didn't even make the list.

She walked slowly, noting the tire impressions left on the driveway by the patrol units the previous day and snapping a photograph of a particularly clear example for potential use as a comparison. The more she thought about it, the less convincing she found her initial theory that Lyssa had been forced to stop by a vehicle blocking the path. Alex was pretty sure that she or Sarah had been the intended victims, not Lyssa, but Lyssa had at least been driving away from the house and might at a fleeting glimpse have been mistaken for one of them. If the murderer had jumped to the wrong conclusion and stopped her at gunpoint, he might have killed her in a panic when he realized she would be able to identify him. But what if the first person down the track had happened to be a deliveryman? The killer would have had to wait somewhere to watch him go by.

Alex kept walking, scouring the edges of the track for anything the fingertip searches might have missed and shining her flashlight into the denser patches of undergrowth. Tilly sidled closer to her as they neared the site of the murder. They were completely alone; there was no one guarding the area, and she wondered whether the search had finally been called off.

"S'okay, we're okay," she murmured, as much to reassure herself as Tilly.

All the CSI markers had been removed, furthering her suspicion that the police wouldn't be returning, but still it was obvious where Lyssa's body had lain. Four holes remained where a forensics tent had been staked, and the ground between them bore a deep black stain. Alex imagined Sarah kneeling in the blood, trying to help, knowing it was useless but refusing to let Lyssa go without doing everything possible to save her. The price Sarah was now paying for that made Alex want to punch her fist into the trunk of the nearest tree.

She knelt to comfort Tilly, giving them both a minute to settle. The area of forest surrounding her was largely unfamiliar; she and Sarah usually walked or jogged toward the lake instead and only crossed this stretch by car. The track wasn't easy for drivers to negotiate, forcing them to focus straight ahead, so when she set off again she started to pay attention to what lay on either side.

Ten minutes later, she reached the gate.

"Shit."

She had been working on the assumption that Lyssa's assailant had driven beyond the gate. She had no idea what his original plans had entailed—she was pointedly trying not to contemplate that—but he would surely have known that leaving in his own vehicle would be less dangerous than stealing one of theirs. They lived in a small town; the wrong face behind the wheel of a familiar car would have drawn attention. Now, having seen no place he could have concealed a vehicle, she wondered if he had risked parking on the public road and continuing on foot, perhaps planning to use one of their cars to return quickly to his.

It took her another fruitless hour to reach the access road. Shielding her eyes from the glare of the sun, she surveyed the deserted stretch of pothole-strewn asphalt and acknowledged the impossibility of the task she had set herself. The perpetrator could have approached from either direction and he could have parked anywhere. Completely disheartened, she turned around and began to retrace her steps.

Instead of unlocking the gate when she reached it, she chased Tilly through the trees until they were past the barrier and back onto the path. The quick burst of exercise brightened her spirits and she threw a stick for Tilly to fetch, wondering whether she would have time to drive out to Emerson's apartment before Sarah's arraignment. It was only as she stooped to wrestle the stick from Tilly's mouth that she noticed the gap in the trees. Just large enough to drive through, the opening was well concealed by a line of saplings and half-grown spruce that rendered it undetectable from the direction of the house, but it was more apparent now that she was heading back. Anyone driving at low speed and keeping a lookout for just such a hiding place might have spotted it.

"Tilly, sit." Alex didn't want anything to disturb the area or distract her. She lowered her hand, adding emphasis to the command, and Tilly immediately obeyed. "Good girl, stay."

Her pulse quickening, Alex walked off the track and down a slight incline, keeping to the margins to avoid trampling on any possible evidence. The early morning sunshine was barely penetrating the thick canopy overhead. She panned her flashlight across the ground, picking out nothing but leaf litter, pine needles, and fallen cones. Unwilling to admit defeat, she walked farther, and found a small clearing surrounded by trees sturdy enough to prevent any vehicle's progress. She shone her light around the area. It was perfect: close enough to the track that the killer would hear anything approaching, but concealed enough to provide him with complete cover. She focused her flashlight downward, crouched low, and put her hand to the layer of debris covering the forest floor.

"What the hell?"

She pulled her hand back and looked around, staring first at the natural patterns where leaves had blown and drifted and then at the quite unnatural pattern she had just found. Someone had tried hard—

too hard—to make the ground appear undisturbed. The area had a swept-over, churned look to it, old leaves commingling with new, and partly rotted cones lying above fresh ones. Angling her light, she took a series of photographs before carefully beginning to excavate the layer. It was deep; whoever had done this had taken their time. Sweat began to darken her tank top as she tried to fit that fact into a possible sequence of events. Her fingers touched a hard ridge and she started to dig more frantically, scrabbling and cursing at the muck that fell back into the hole. She knew it was the tread of a car tire even before it was fully exposed. Someone had kicked at it, obliterating large sections, but at some stage they must have realized that that wouldn't be enough and covered it with debris instead.

Exertion and anger blurred Alex's first attempt to photograph it. She forced herself to breathe slowly and take several more pictures. When she was satisfied, she stood back a little way and waited for the logical part of her brain to kick the emotional part into touch. Instinct and training told her that the killer probably hadn't covered the treads immediately. No one involved in such a frenzy of violence was likely to be thinking rationally enough to stop and rake leaf mold over evidence, especially if he knew he had murdered the wrong person. He would flee and regroup, work out a strategy. Then—and this time Alex did slam her fist into a tree—he would return at the earliest opportunity to conceal the tracks.

"Jesus fucking Christ."

The urge to drive straight over to the station, slap the photographs in Quinn's face, and demand he send CSI techs out to cast the treads was so potent that she had to dig her heels into the dirt to keep herself stationary. Quinn had been out here. Emerson had been out here. Half the fucking police force had been out here, not to mention a number of civilians. If it was someone on the force who had had the wherewithal to tamper with evidence and perhaps steer other search members from the area, whom could she trust with what she had just discovered? In a worst-case scenario, if Quinn were involved, it would be simple for him to spin everything around and insist that she had made the tracks herself. No one was with her to corroborate her find, and his good buddy Judge Buchanan certainly wouldn't take much convincing of her complicity. She knew she hadn't found enough to change anything.

She picked up her flashlight and walked back to where Tilly lay. "Hey, Tilly-bud."

She scratched behind Tilly's ears and then signaled her to heel. Sarah's arraignment wasn't for another four hours, which would give Alex time to collect the pup tent from the shed and pitch it over the tracks to preserve them for as long as it took her to sort this mess out. She would also upload the photographs and send them to Castillo. In case something happened to her, she wanted someone external to the investigation to have copies. As far as she was concerned, the Avery PD was tainted. For now at least, she and Sarah were on their own.

CHAPTER ELEVEN

Leah was already frying bacon in the skillet when Caleb walked into the kitchen. She poured him fresh coffee and set the mug by his place at the table. Scratching the back of his head absently, he sat and drank. His hair was still wet from the shower, he hadn't bothered to fasten his shirt yet, and the White Pride tattoos covering his chest stood out starkly against his pale skin. Last night, she had run her hands across his torso, tracing the lines and symbols as he told her again what each stood for, as if she could ever forget. Afterward, he had slept soundly while she lay awake for hours, listening to the rasp of his breathing and planning what she would say to him in the morning. She thought she had it worked out now. Whether he would listen to her, though, was another matter entirely.

She piled bacon and pancakes onto his plate and sat across from him, sipping peppermint tea as he shoveled food into his mouth. He frowned at her as the smell of mint cut through the reek of grease, but he didn't comment. She had already told him that too much caffeine was bad for the baby. She waited until he had finished half his plateful and then she pushed her cup to one side.

"Honey, I've been thinking," she said, and watched the way his chewing slowed as he smirked.

"Have you now?" He swallowed and chased the food down with coffee. "About what?"

"Alex Pascal." She shook her head, correcting herself quickly. "The cop."

He never used their names; it was always "the cop," "the bitch," "those fucking dykes." He didn't dehumanize them to make it easier for him to hurt them; he did it because he didn't consider them human in the first place.

"Yeah, so what about her?" He picked up a rasher of bacon and bit at the end. Just as Leah had hoped, his favorite breakfast and plentiful coffee had made him willing to humor her.

"If you go after her too soon, if you hurt her, the police will suspect that it wasn't her girlfriend who killed that paramedic. They'll start looking for someone else." She took a shaky breath. "They'll start looking for you."

He scoffed but hesitated nonetheless, suggesting he might be giving her warning due consideration.

"Patience and perseverance, baby," she said, reminding him of the mantra he had inherited from his father.

"Bitch has her bail decided this afternoon," he said. "She's not getting out, so I guess we'll just wait and see where they send her." Leah could feel the rough skin on his hands as he took hold of hers. "My guy says we can stay here as long as we like, so I'm not going to rush into anything."

"That's good," she told him, hoping she had managed to buy Alex some time. Over his shoulder, she could see the river, a soothing endless flow of green water. She was still staring at it when she felt his hands begin to raise the hem of her dress.

Castillo had agreed with Alex: the tire tread evidence wouldn't be compelling enough by itself, especially if Quinn was somehow involved in its concealment and could subsequently influence the judge.

"Do you think Quinn's likely to be the culprit?" Castillo asked.

Alex thought of his single-minded pursuit of Sarah, the perp walk, his grandstanding for the cameras, his haste to secure an indictment, and the smoothed-over ground she had found that morning.

"I don't know," she said. In the months she had worked for him, he had never been anything but fair to her, and his reaction to her revelations about the Cascades had certainly seemed genuine enough. "I don't know what to think anymore."

"I guess not." Castillo cleared his throat. "I'm looking at getting someone out to you, but there's resistance higher up; budget cuts, reluctance to wade into a local matter."

"I'm okay, Mike."

"Yeah, you're always okay." There was wry humor in his voice. "But a little extra muscle never hurt anyone—well, not unless the assholes deserved it."

This time she laughed with him.

"I'll get these images blown up, see if they're good enough to provide us with any identifying details—cuts or nicks," he continued. "I have a few friends who can keep it on the QT. Won't be as accurate as a cast, of course, but it has to be better than nothing."

"I appreciate that," she said. It was already midday and she had another phone call to make yet.

Never one for a long farewell, he wished her luck with the arraignment and hung up. Without giving herself a chance to change her mind, she hit the speed dial again, closing her eyes as a familiar voice answered.

"Alex, what the fuck is going on over there?" Sarah's best friend had never been known for mincing her words.

"Hi, Ash," Alex said. "You better sit down for this."

Standing in front of the grimy mirror, Sarah tugged her shirt straight and drew its sleeves down. It was the smartest item of clothing she owned, and Alex had undoubtedly been hoping it would make a good impression at the arraignment when she chose it. Sarah was just grateful its sleeves were long enough to hide the stained dressings covering her arms.

Not wanting to use the greasy brush her guard had supplied, she ran her fingers through her hair until she bore less of a resemblance to an unkempt hedgehog. She couldn't do anything about her cracked lips or the dark shadows beneath her eyes, however, and as she wiped more steam from the mirror, she noticed a bruise on her left cheekbone where she had hit the cell wall the day before.

"Crap," she whispered. She didn't have a hope in hell of Alex failing to spot that.

Taking a moment to calm her nerves, she folded her tattered towel into a neat square and placed it on the sink. No one had knocked on the door to hurry her yet, but having spent almost twenty-four hours in confinement at the mercy of someone else's schedule, she was keen to reclaim some small sense of autonomy, so she left the bathroom without waiting to be summoned.

The officer on the dayshift was standing in the corridor. Unlike his colleagues, he had shown no interest in making her life difficult, and though his manner hadn't quite extended to friendliness, he had at least been civil to her. He mumbled an apology as he took his handcuffs from his belt. Feeling guilty for making him uncomfortable, she turned around and held her wrists in position behind her back. He seemed relieved that she showed no intention of resisting or playing on his sympathies, and to her surprise, he moved her hands to her front and secured them there.

"Come on, then," he said, allowing her to walk independently toward a security door she had never been through.

The first glimpse of daylight as the door swung open made her shrink back, every muscle in her body tensing as if to ward off a blow, but the exit merely led into a high-walled yard where a single police unit was waiting for her. That Quinn could have brought her into the station by this route the previous day made her more sad than angry. She knew that Alex had always respected him, and she suspected that, although he undoubtedly had his own reasons for his actions, Alex would be holding herself responsible.

A police officer climbed from the driver's seat and nodded at Sarah. He opened the rear door and made sure she didn't bump her head as she got into the car.

"Shouldn't take us long to get over there," he said, looking back at her through the reinforced partition.

She nodded; she knew roughly where the courthouse was in Ruby, but she had never had any reason to pay it a visit. The gates opened automatically when he drove toward them, and Sarah's guard raised a hand in farewell.

As the driver accelerated, Sarah turned in the seat to watch the familiar streets and buildings pass by. The car followed the path of the river through town and then turned left onto the lakeside road. She stared at the water until her eyes unfocused and the finer details blurred, knowing that she would never be able to go back there. She had fallen in love with Avery at first sight, but it didn't feel like home anymore. She didn't think it ever would.

❖

Keeping her head bowed, Alex pushed through the throng of reporters on the courthouse steps. A few of them recognized her; she heard the rapid-fire click of cameras and raised voices asking for comment, but no one pursued her beyond the two uniformed officers standing sentry at the doors, and Bridie had already ensured that Sarah would be brought in via the rear entrance. The press weren't going to get their pound of flesh today.

Bridie met Alex in the atrium. Her handshake was warm and firm, though her palm was slightly damp. She had a reputation as an experienced and canny defense lawyer, often a thorn in the side of the Aroostook County police departments, but Alex wondered exactly how many murder cases she had been involved with. At such short notice, Alex hadn't had the opportunity to research the lawyer's résumé as thoroughly as she would have liked.

"How is she?" she asked as Bridie guided her away from the central thoroughfare. Once they were safely ensconced in a small alcove, Bridie took care in propping her briefcase on the floor, as if giving herself time to decide how much Alex needed to know.

"She didn't sleep well," she said, evidently concluding that subterfuge was not in anyone's best interests. "And she's nervous, of course, but she did say thanks for the shirt."

Alex smiled. Sarah didn't have many options when it came to formal attire. "Will I be able to see her? Beforehand, I mean, not just from across the courtroom?"

"I doubt that, Alex. It's not common procedure."

"But not unheard of?"

She whipped her head around as Quinn's familiar baritone voice filtered through the indistinct conversation of the people milling in the atrium. Standing beneath a huge oil painting of some long-dead dignitary, he was deep in animated discussion with Linda Kryger. Alex winced when she recognized the ADA. Kryger was tenacious, quick-witted, and hugely experienced. More worryingly for Sarah, she had a real knack for winning judges and juries over to her "hang 'em high" philosophy.

"I'll be right back," Alex said, heading across to Quinn at a near jog, preempting Bridie's inevitable attempt to stop her. Both Quinn and Kryger watched her approach, neither appearing particularly receptive.

"Sir," Alex said with a nod. "Ms. Kryger."

Kryger didn't deign to return her greeting, leaving the onus on Quinn to speak.

"What do you want, Alex?" he said, making her feel like a recalcitrant schoolchild hauled in front of the principal. It took a great effort of will not to shuffle her feet, but since she wasn't going to beg and Quinn had never had time for what he commonly referred to as "ass-kissers," she answered him honestly.

"I want to see Sarah."

She wouldn't have thought it possible, but Kryger's perfectly glossed, thin little lips became even narrower. Quinn, however, seemed to give Alex credit for being forthright.

"She's down in the holding cells," he said, which at least wasn't an outright refusal.

She held his gaze. "I know, sir. I'm just asking for a few minutes, that's all."

Kryger's lips twitched upward in a sneer, but Quinn's expression softened slightly. He looked at his wristwatch and then gestured to someone behind Alex. She turned to see Tobin hurrying over.

"Escort her down to the holding cells," Quinn instructed him. "She gets five minutes with Hayes, no more."

"Thank you, sir," Alex said, but there was something in the way he looked at her that made her shiver. Not wanting to give Kryger time to change Quinn's mind, she quickly fell in step with Tobin as he strode toward a double set of glass doors. For the first time, she noticed the subtle change in his uniform that identified him as a full-time officer.

"Congratulations," she remarked drily.

He grasped her meaning and had the grace to look flustered. "Yeah, uh, thanks." He covered his unease by signing them both through the initial security checkpoint. "Quinn said I did good responding to the Mardell shout and managing the scene, so...Uh, it's this way."

She allowed him to let the subject drop. She accepted that she would never be able to work for Quinn again, and since Tobin had been sidelined for years, she couldn't begrudge his taking her job.

At the entrance to the holding cells, a security guard waved an electronic wand around Alex and then gave her a thorough pat down. He issued her with a temporary visitor's pass, and led her and Tobin down to Sarah's cell. Like a teenager on a surreal first date, Alex waited tense with apprehension as he unlocked the third door on a row of four. He stepped aside to allow her into the cell.

Sarah was sitting on the edge of a small cot. For a second, her eyes stayed fixed on the guard, and Alex noticed the way her hands gripped the mattress. Her mouth dropped open in confusion when she realized Alex was there; she scrambled to her feet but then hesitated, as if unsure whether she was allowed to touch her.

Alex had no such doubts. She closed the gap between them, gathered Sarah into her arms, and held her tightly.

"Oh God." Sarah breathed the words against Alex's neck, her fists clutching at Alex's shirt. "How?"

"Quinn's given us five minutes," Alex told her, noticing that Tobin had stepped a little farther toward the doorway and turned his back slightly. Keeping hold of Sarah's hands, she guided her to sit back down and then crouched in front of her. "Let me look at you."

Sarah closed her eyes as Alex stroked her hair away from her forehead. "Do I look as knackered as I feel?" she asked.

"You look beautiful," Alex said, meaning every word.

Sarah opened one eye and peeked at her. "Fibber."

Alex let her fingertips linger on the small but livid bruise that flared across the arc of Sarah's cheekbone. "Who did this?" she whispered. "Emerson?"

"No." Sarah reached for her hand. "No, he's been okay with me." She sighed, obviously aware Alex would continue to press if she didn't answer. "One of the guards was a friend of Lyssa's. He got a little rough, but I'm fine. Honestly."

"Did Quinn let it happen? Did he know about it?"

"No." Sarah sounded certain of that. "He still doesn't know. Please don't say anything."

The strain in her voice was enough to make Alex acquiesce. Later, when all this was over, she would find out the bastard's name, but not now, not in the two minutes they had left. She sat on the mattress and tucked her arm around Sarah.

"Tilly and the rest of the gang miss you."

"Even Bandit?"

"Naw, Bandit's having too much fun sleeping on your pillow."

Sarah chuckled. "Get where water wouldn't, that little sod."

"Yeah." Alex smiled again, but her throat tightened with longing. She just wanted to take Sarah home where they could sit together on the porch and Sarah could throw weird English insults at the cats and laugh when Alex requested a translation. She felt Sarah's lips brush against her cheek to press a soft kiss there.

Then reality crashed in as Tobin coughed self-consciously and the guard entered the cell.

❖

The courtroom wasn't only small, but it seemed to have been designed specifically with intimidation in mind. Standing in front of Judge Buchanan's ornate, raised pedestal, Sarah felt suitably intimidated. Before speaking to confirm her name, she looked for Alex, who was sitting in the public gallery, and Alex's nod of encouragement enabled her to keep her voice steady. The gallery was packed with spectators, many of whom Sarah recognized, but the seats closest to Alex remained empty in a non-too-subtle attempt to ostracize her.

Buchanan stared at Sarah for a long time, as if he had placed a private wager on how quickly she would crack beneath his scrutiny. She hoped he hadn't wagered much, because he bore more than a passing resemblance to her favorite and much missed granddad, which made it easy to maintain eye contact with him. It was Buchanan who finally looked away. He made a show of placing his glasses on the end of his nose before reading out the details of the charge.

"How do you plead?"

"Not guilty, sir," she said clearly, before adding a hasty, "Your Honor." Her knees were shaking, but she didn't think she was allowed to sit yet. The cuffs around her wrists rattled as she held on to the wooden railing in front of her. At her side, Bridie began to argue that the circumstances surrounding the crime were exceptional enough for bail to be granted, citing Sarah's lack of criminal record, her volunteer work for the community, and—despite the charge—the lack of any substantive evidence against her. Sarah watched Buchanan intently, but his expression gave nothing away. Conversely, Alex was an open book, leaning forward with her hands twisting anxiously on the barrier.

A touch on Sarah's arm signaled that Bridie had finished speaking. Sarah gratefully sat back down as Kryger took center stage and, as good performers often do, commanded the attention of her audience by pausing to brush a non-existent piece of lint from her jacket. Then she introduced herself and requested that, in accordance with state law, bail be denied.

"On what grounds?" Buchanan asked. He had the beginnings of a sly smile on his lips, and Sarah suspected that he was merely toying with the defense team for his own and the public's entertainment, that the decision to refuse bail was a foregone conclusion, but he was choosing to continue the charade regardless.

"On the grounds that Sarah Hayes, also known as Sarah Kent, presents a serious flight risk, Your Honor," Kryger said. Buchanan made a rolling gesture with his hand, urging her to continue. She nodded graciously. "Hayes is a foreign national, temporarily a resident in this country, who has already altered her identity once in the last two years. An FBI agent organized her change of name and the documentation necessary for her to live under this assumed identity."

"The reason being?"

"Hayes would claim it was for her own protection, but I would suggest that it is the citizens of America who require protection from Sarah Hayes. Your Honor, may I approach?" She held aloft a file and walked across to hand it to Buchanan, stating the evidence log number as she did so. He slid out two photographs and took time to study each of them closely.

"As you can see, just two years ago this woman was already displaying a dangerous propensity for violence," she said. "She now stands accused of murdering a young paramedic." She opened her hands, intimating that the link was simple. "Who's to say that as soon as Hayes is released on bail, this helpful federal agent or Hayes' own police officer wife won't take it upon themselves to arrange another change of identity and spirit her out of the country?"

"Your Honor, that is prejudicial, not to mention slanderous!" Bridie had to raise her voice to cut across the murmurs spreading among the spectators.

About fucking time, Sarah thought, but Bridie was immediately overruled and sat back in her seat.

"I'd never do that," Sarah told her in an urgent undertone. "Alex and Castillo would never do that." She felt Bridie pat her hand to quiet her. She looked toward Alex, hoping to find a vote of confidence there, but Alex's face was ghostly pale and she appeared to be on the verge of tears.

"Shit," Sarah whispered, what little hope she might have had now completely extinguished. "Shit."

In the public gallery, Alex opened her mouth to speak and shut it again, terrified of making things worse. Below her, she saw Sarah's posture drop as Kryger summarized her reasoning in a manner that suggested there were some present in the courtroom who might be baffled by her razor-sharp logic. In direct contrast to the defense team, Quinn was sitting bolt upright, obviously relishing the proceedings. He had known, Alex realized, when he granted her time with Sarah, he had known how this would go. He had given her those five minutes to say good-bye.

Buchanan told Sarah to stand, and she grasped the rail to keep herself motionless as he outlined his decision. He took less than a minute to side with the prosecution, overruling Bridie again and detailing Sarah's transfer to the closest county jail with suitable capacity until the date of her trial.

As Bridie publicly noted her intention to file for a Harnish bail proceeding, Sarah swayed a little but then seemed to collect herself, turning away from Buchanan toward Alex.

"I'll be okay." Sarah shaped the words soundlessly, a single insistent shake of her head forcing Alex to see sense and refrain from launching an impromptu appeal of her own.

A guard took hold of Sarah's arm and began to escort her from the court.

"Jesus, just stop a minute," Alex gasped. It was all happening too quickly; she pushed forward, trying to keep up with Sarah as she was led away. By the time Alex had shoved her way to the end of her row, the locks on the security doors at the rear of the court were already reengaging, the lights switching from green to red.

"Fucking hell," she whispered. She heard Bridie call her name, but she didn't want to be consoled, didn't want to hear a sensible, apologetic explanation of what they could do next. She pulled her keys from her jacket pocket and ran out of the court.

CHAPTER TWELVE

The logging truck in front of Alex had maxed out at thirty-five, the gradual incline sapping its speed. Its driver was obviously in no rush, and although Alex repeatedly maneuvered wide to make herself visible in his mirrors, he ignored every opportunity to let her pass. She knew the road well but was too impatient to wait for a safe spot, and she overtook him only yards before a hairpin bend. He blasted his disapproval as she accelerated out of the curve. She would have flipped him the bird, had she not needed both hands to wrestle the steering back under control. As she hit the straight stretch that dropped down toward the lumberyard, her cell phone rang, Castillo's number flashing up again. They had been playing phone tag for the last hour: four missed calls by the time she had gotten out of court. She hit hands free, not trusting herself to multitask.

"Mike?" Her voice was already brittle, her breathing heavy and irregular as she tried to keep herself together.

"Alex, you driving?" Castillo wasn't stupid; he would have heard by now what had happened to Sarah.

"Yeah."

"Well, stop. Pull the fuck over before you get yourself killed."

"You know what they did." She didn't stop but she did slow down, half-blinded by tears. "She'll be on her own in there, Mike."

"I know, honey. I'm already working on it. Where are you?"

"West Ruby."

"You're going to check out Emerson's place." He wasn't asking, but she grunted an affirmative anyway.

"I can't just sit on my ass and do nothing," she said. "I have to get her home."

"We're still looking at the treads," he told her, and she was grateful he didn't try to talk her out of whatever she was planning. "Alex, there's something else."

She raised her eyes skyward; there was always something else, and from the hesitancy in his voice, she knew it wasn't anything good.

"The team monitoring Caleb Deakin lost him about five days back. There was some kind of power outage down in North Carolina, things got a little confused, and he slipped through the gap."

"Fucking hell. He's the eldest son, isn't he?" she said, already attempting the math. Five days—how many had it been since Lyssa's murder?

"Yes, he's Nicholas Deakin's eldest son." She heard Castillo swallow as if his mouth was dry. "And yes," he said, apparently now a mind reader, "the dates check out."

"Shit."

"Yeah, shit."

"No idea where he is?" she asked, more out of hope than anything else.

"No, but I have a good idea where he's been."

She braked sharply for a stop light, the river tumbling by on her right-hand side. "Jesus, if he screwed up his mission first time out, he could still be here," she said, beginning to grasp the implications of that and of what she had just driven across Ruby to do.

"Alex, you armed?"

"Yes."

"Good," Castillo said emphatically. "I'll send a photo to your cell, so at least you know who you're looking out for."

"Okay, thanks." The light flicked to green and she crossed the intersection. A small playground marked the boundary between the shops and offices of downtown West Ruby and a pleasant tree-lined residential area. She dropped her speed, straining to read the street names as she passed them.

"Mike, I have to go. I think I'm close."

"No problem. That photo should be there when you hang up."

"Appreciate it."

"Keep safe."

A tone sounded as he ended the call, followed by the beep of an incoming message. She pulled onto a side street, made a U-turn to leave herself facing in the right direction, and parked just short of the junction to open the image. A thud behind the car sent her hand lurching toward her gun, but then she heard the high-pitched laughter of children, and in her rearview mirror, two boys chased a bright red ball across the road. She kept an eye on them as she unlocked the screen on her phone, trying not to look at the SMS message until she felt ready.

"Fuck this," she muttered, and tapped on the link.

Taken 2010. Assault. Victim refused to press charges, Castillo had written beneath the image.

Caleb Deakin must have guessed the outcome of his arrest because he was smirking in his mug shot. There was little to distinguish him from every other thug Alex had marched off the streets: the same aggressive stance, his mean blue eyes challenging the camera with an "I don't give a fuck" attitude. His resemblance to his father was unmistakable, while a small swastika tattooed above his left ear confirmed his affiliation with his father's politics.

Alex studied the image until each detail was ingrained in her memory. She noted the scar beneath his right eye, and the black ink of larger, unidentifiable tattoos just visible through the torn material of his shirt. The measurements on the wall behind him showed him to be of average height. She tried to visualize him with hair, then with facial hair. He would know the police had his photograph on file and was likely to have altered his appearance. Once she was certain she would be able to identify him on the street, she closed the message and restarted the engine. She checked her map to plot the remainder of her route. Emerson's apartment was less than a half mile away.

Her foot hovered over the gas pedal, but she didn't push it down. Her thoughts were racing too haphazardly to allow her to focus on driving, every theory she had formed suddenly thrown through another loop. She leaned forward and rested her head against the steering wheel, then closed her eyes and tried to concentrate on what she had just learned. Caleb Deakin's disappearance seemed far too timely for him not to have been involved in Lyssa's murder. Had the photograph of Sarah in the newspaper prompted him to act? Or had he already been aware of their location and stepped in personally when Emerson failed to get rid of Alex during the warehouse raid? If he and Emerson had been working together since the raid, that would explain the ease with which someone had covered up the incriminating tire tracks, and why Deakin hadn't recognized Lyssa as the wrong target. Alex had been assuming that Lyssa's murderer was someone local, but now the idea that it was Deakin in collaboration with such a person seemed much more plausible. Emerson might well be one of Deakin's lieutenants, and she knew for sure that he had a place where Deakin could lay low.

That was enough to give her a renewed sense of purpose, and she pulled out of the side street. The traffic had built up, as rush hour brought hot, harried office workers onto the streets. It would be a good time to check out the apartment complex, almost guaranteeing her at least some residents to talk to as they arrived home. They might not open their front doors to her, but catching them in the parking lot would give them less opportunity to avoid her. She watched cars pass her, their drivers shouting into cell phones or gesticulating at the car in front, and she wondered whether any of them would want to trade places with Sarah.

The last woman herded onto the van had stopped screaming abuse at the guards and fallen silent. She twitched now and then, the shackles at her wrists and ankles jangling in time to her erratic movements. Perspiration gave her face a sickly, glassy look; Sarah wondered what the woman was withdrawing from and how the side effects would be managed in a county jail. Thinking about that stopped her from thinking about anything else: Alex, or home, or the overcrowding at the Aroostook jail that was now forcing her and women from several other areas to be transferred to a far larger facility in Prescott. She knew that the raid on the warehouse in Ruby had resulted in prisoners being sent as far away as Kennebec, and was thankful that Prescott would only be a three-hour drive for Alex, when she was allowed to visit.

The van slowed and then stopped, its engine idling. The stomach of the woman on Sarah's right rumbled in the lull, the sound loud in the confines of the secure compartment.

"Man, I am fucking hungry," she said, somewhat unnecessarily.

The woman next to her snorted. "You're always fucking hungry, Kitty."

"So hungry, I could eat your mama," Kitty answered, not missing a beat.

Her friend laughed raucously, the noise of her movements making the silent woman moan and paw at her face.

"How about you, darlin'?"

It took Sarah a moment to realize Kitty's friend was addressing her.

"I'm sorry." She shook her head, unsure whether she was being asked about the woman's mother or her own appetite, and not having a clue how to respond either way.

Kitty seemed to take pity on her. "I think Alma here is asking what you're in for."

"Oh." Sarah looked down at her hands. "Second-degree murder."

Alma whistled, showing her ruined teeth. "Holy fuck."

"That young paramedic," Kitty said. "I thought I'd seen your face before. You've been all over the news."

Alma nodded sagely. "That orange suit makes her look smaller."

"Lesbian love triangle. That's what Tilda Travers on WACN said."

"And she's never wrong."

"I didn't do it," Sarah told them, but they spoke over her, too excited by their close encounter with a notorious criminal to care whether she was guilty. She looked at her hands again. The cuffs were tight enough to make her fingers white. "I didn't do it," she whispered.

The unimaginatively named Riverview Apartments occupied a prime location, overlooking parkland and a gentle curve in the Little Silver River. Each apartment in the three-story building had large glazed doors leading out onto a private balcony. As Alex drove along the access road, she could already see a number of residents taking advantage of the late evening sun by dining outside. The building had two wings with separate secure entrances. She pulled into a parking space just beyond the second door, where a stone plaque built into the wall read "Fifteen–Thirty." According to Castillo, Emerson owned apartment 27.

She studied the pale gray building, counting along the rows and trying to guess which of the balconies belonged to Emerson. His car wasn't in the lot, and he certainly wasn't enjoying a beer in the sunshine like several of his neighbors. Not that she had expected him to be; she already knew that he didn't live here. What she didn't know was whom he leased his apartment to. With her eyes concealed behind dark shades, she scrutinized the various faces, occasionally glancing at the image of Caleb Deakin for comparison. She couldn't see anyone remotely resembling him, and she sagged back in her seat, discouraged. She sat up again, though, when a sleek black convertible pulled into the space next to hers. A smartly dressed woman stepped out, her heels tapping against the asphalt as she strode across the lot. Alex hurried after her, ensuring that they arrived at the entrance together.

"Hey, thanks." Alex smiled as the woman politely held the door open for her. Once inside the lobby, she took her time studying the floor directory and watched as the woman walked to a bank of mailboxes and unlocked box twenty-five.

"I guess you won't know if Scott's around," Alex said, pretending to hesitate at the elevator.

"I'm sorry, who?"

"Scott Emerson. He lives at twenty-seven." She went over to the mailboxes, intending to indicate Emerson's name, but there was a blank tag in the "27" slot. "I should've called first, but I wanted to surprise him."

The woman frowned at her. "I don't think the guy in twenty-seven is called Scott."

"No?" Alex switched her target, feigning confusion. "You sure? He's about a foot taller than me, blue eyes, tattoos. Oh, and he has a scar just beneath his eye, here." She traced a line under her right eye, gauging the woman's reaction, but nothing like recognition showed on her face.

"I'm sorry. I think you must have the wrong address."

"Damn. I was sure I'd written it down right. Maybe I should just try the buzzer, see who answers."

"You could," the woman said, still frowning, "but that really doesn't sound like him. I think the guy in twenty-seven is called Rob."

"Definitely not Scott, then," Alex said lightly, not wanting to make her suspicious.

"No, definitely not Scott." The woman clutched her mail to her chest. "The door opens automatically from this side," she said, leaving no doubt as to what she thought Alex should do.

"Sure. Thanks."

Alex waited until the sound of the woman's heels faded on the stairs, leaving her alone in the lobby. A quick look outside told her that no one was approaching the entrance. She took out her pocketknife and used it to lever the uppermost piece of mail from the over-full box that should have belonged to Emerson. The thick white envelope had a New York postmark and the addressee was a Mr. R. Hollis. She scribbled the name on her hand and slid the envelope back into the box just as the entrance door swung open again. An Asian man hustled past her without making eye contact or stopping to check his mailbox. Unwilling to risk lingering any further, she caught hold of the door and walked back out into the lot.

The heat immediately closed around her, making her clothes cling to her skin and the air catch like cotton in her throat. She looked up to find the sky boiling with thunderclouds; the first drops of rain began to splatter on the asphalt as she jogged across to the Silverado. She climbed inside and shook water from her hair, watching the storm obliterate her view of the apartment entrance. It felt deliberate, as if something out there was sabotaging everything she tried to do, forcing her to take two steps backward for each one forward. The thought was absurd but it still made her feel wretched. Realistically, she didn't think she would get any further information about the apartment. Emerson probably was leasing it out, but now that she'd seen the complex she knew that someone like Caleb Deakin would stand out a mile there and she doubted he was the current occupant. Even so, she didn't want to leave, didn't want to have to tell Sarah that she had given up because it rained, and because she was heartsick, and hungry, and needed to pee. She started the engine and flicked on the wipers, increasing their speed until she could see clearly enough to monitor the building. Chewing on a piece of gum salvaged from the fluff in her pocket, she put her feet up on the dash and settled down to wait.

Lyssa had been murdered, Sarah reminded herself. Lyssa was dead because of something Sarah had done. It wasn't perhaps the most logical of arguments but, as she waited naked and shivering in the small communal washroom, she wondered whether she was just getting what she deserved.

She tried to ignore the catcalls and whistles from the three women already searched and sent to the showers. They couldn't see her—Officer Kendall, the female guard in charge of their intake, had made sure of that—but they knew exactly what was happening, having just been through the process.

"Now the other one, honey."

Staring at the white tiles covering the washroom walls, Sarah followed Kendall's instructions. The steam from the water smelled harsh and chemical, the shampoo obviously designed not only to clean but also to disinfect and delouse. She blinked as it brought tears to her eyes and then she staggered back when Kendall touched her shoulder.

"We're all done. You can get a shower." She handed Sarah a plastic wallet containing basic toiletries. "You're a remand prisoner, so you can wear your own clothes…" Her instructions trailed away; Sarah was already shaking her head. "Don't want to stand out, huh?"

"Not especially." Sarah took the neatly folded pile of beige uniform from her. "Thanks."

"Soon as you're through, I'm gonna ask the doc to take a look at you."

"I'm okay." She pushed her wrists beneath the clothing, but the bandages had been removed for the search and Kendall had already seen the swollen and seeping collection of wounds.

"Sure you are." Kendall gestured for Sarah to move ahead of her into the shower stall. "But I'll feel happier when the doc tells me that."

She closed the door to Sarah's stall and rapped on the other doors to hurry the women along. Sarah hugged her arms across her breasts and inched beneath the spray as it slowly warmed. She squeezed pungent green gel from the shampoo bottle and winced when it ran into the raw slices on her arms. She washed quickly, not knowing the jail's routine and not wanting anyone to come in and see her.

The prison uniform—beige sweatpants, white T-shirt, and beige shirt—wasn't going to win any prizes for style, but it was comfortable enough. The women she had traveled in with were obviously seasoned offenders, who had entered the jail wearing several layers of underwear. Having been allowed to keep the spare sets, they had mocked Sarah for her ignorance of the trick. She made a mental note to ask Alex for supplies. She might be able to tolerate prison-issue clothing, but prison-issue underwear was something else entirely.

"All set?" Kendall nodded at her. "Doc's ready for you, c'mon."

They walked side by side into a large cellblock. At regular intervals, single doors were set into the corridor, each with a narrow central viewing window. Through the reinforced glass panels, Sarah caught glimpses of the inmates, some on their bunks reading or writing, a few already asleep or lying with their eyes open as if waiting for something to take them away. It was the first time she had gotten a proper look at the jail's interior. The van had delivered them directly into a secure, shuttered loading bay, and from there Kendall had taken them straight into the washroom, a relatively quiet area. Here in the main residential section of the jail, noise echoed off the high walls: screams and shouts, the clang of metal on metal, yelled conversations. A door marked "Rec Room" was ajar, and beyond it several voices were raised, arguing about which television channel to watch. From her research on Alex's phone, Sarah knew that most of the women here would be serving sentences of less than two years, but she also knew that that didn't make them any less dangerous. With such short sentences, there was no "good-time credit," and the lack of early release for good behavior meant there was little incentive for offenders to behave.

At the end of the block, a guard behind a protective Lucite screen buzzed Kendall and Sarah through the connecting door. He nodded to Kendall and looked Sarah up and down before returning his attention to his bank of monitors. The brightly lit area beyond the door was silent, and its strong medicinal odor started to make Sarah's nose itch. She sneezed as Kendall stopped and knocked at the infirmary. The smell became even more pronounced as Sarah stepped over the threshold, but it still wasn't enough to mask an underlying reek of feces.

"Sarah Hayes for you, doc," Kendall said through a grimace. "The one I called about."

The doctor had his back to them as he scrubbed his hands at the sink. "How the fuck do they know to put sugar in it?" he asked.

"Huh?"

"Kelly Harrison, about an hour since. Two women pinned her down while another poured boiling sugar water over her back." When he turned to face them, his expression was more puzzled than saddened. "How the fuck do they know that sugar makes burns so much worse?

Google? Wiki-fucking-pedia?" He shook his head. "She shit herself, hence the smell."

Sarah had spent hours chatting to Lyssa and other medics, so she wasn't shocked by his lack of sentimentality. He looked to be in his late fifties, with thin graying hair and tired lines creasing his face. When he noticed her attention, he gave her a tight smile and reached for a clean pair of gloves.

"Not sure the Avery PD has been doing my new prisoner any favors," Kendall said by way of introduction.

"No, I think you might be right there." The doctor ushered Sarah to the examination bed, flicked on the overhead light, and took both of her hands in his. He turned them over carefully and pressed his finger against the most tender laceration. "That one needs reopening and cleaning out. Couple need new sutures." He pulled a sterile pack from one of the drawers. "Course of antibiotics, clean dressings, and a few days away from overly zealous police officers should do the trick."

His manner was brusque but non-judgmental, and he waited for Sarah to nod her consent before injecting local anesthetic around the wounds. Resting her head against the back of the bed, she ignored the drug's vicious sting and allowed her eyes to close as the doctor worked. For the first time since her arrest, she felt safe.

CHAPTER THIRTEEN

The sandwich consisted of stale, tasteless white bread enclosing something that might have been bologna. Sitting in the dark, trying not to disturb the woman sleeping on the bunk below, Sarah persevered with her first mouthful but couldn't face a second.

It had been after "lights out" by the time the doctor released her. Despite Bridie's assurance that remand prisoners were kept segregated from the jail's general population, Sarah had been escorted to a shared cell in the main block. Kendall had made a non-committal reference to a transfer once a single cell became available, before locking her in for the night.

The metal frame of the bunk bed swayed and creaked as Sarah's cellmate turned over. Sarah froze, halfway through placing the sandwich back in its packaging, but any noise she might have made was drowned out by a door slamming somewhere down the corridor and a high-pitched yelling that drew progressively closer. A fist or a boot suddenly collided with her cell door, startling her into knocking the plastic pack over the side of the bed. She held her breath as it dropped onto the tiles. For a second, she thought she had gotten away with it, but then she heard a yawn and a low, drowsy voice.

"If you're through with that, can I have it?"

Peering toward the floor, Sarah could just distinguish a pale hand reaching for the sandwich. "Sorry I woke you," she whispered.

The woman managed to laugh and chew at the same time. "Reckon Lou-Anne had more to do with that. That girl's been like clockwork, every night for a week now. She's comin' off crack," she added, as if that was explanation enough.

"Where will they take her? The infirmary?" Sarah had long contemplated what her first prisoner-to-prisoner encounter would be, but this scenario—a hushed conversation over a midnight snack—had never featured.

"Naw, probably down to solitary. Let her bounce off the walls there and sweat it out." Plastic crinkled as the woman took the second half of the sandwich. "No one told me I was gettin' a fish. You done your time in the tank, then?"

The woman's lips smacked together wetly as Sarah tried to decipher what she had just been asked. Prison dialect was as mysterious to her as her own slang was to Alex. She smiled, imagining getting home and holding a conversation in fluent jail-speak just when Alex thought she had all her colloquialisms figured out.

"I don't know what the tank is," she admitted. "I don't think I went there."

The woman chuckled. "Oh, you're definitely a fish," she said without malice. "That just means brand new in here, honey."

"Right." Sarah vaguely remembered hearing the term on a television show. "And the tank?"

"Fish should go in the fish tank. Stay there for a few weeks to get used to how things are. Get a cell and work duties assigned."

"They put me straight in here. I think the jail might be full."

"Probably. Had three of us to a cell not a month back."

"Bloody hell, how'd they manage that?" Now that Sarah's vision had adjusted to the dim light, she could see the cell more clearly. It was barely eight feet by six, with a small desk, one chair, and a metal toilet-sink combined unit that seemed intended as much for humiliation as practicality.

"Coulda been worse," the woman said, sounding remarkably sanguine. "Coulda ended up with Lou-Anne." Her hand tapped on the underside of Sarah's bed. "I'm Camille."

Sarah wiped the sweat off her own palm before shaking hands. "Sarah."

"Got six months left before I get back to my babies," Camille said as she settled back on the bed. "You?"

"I don't know." A shadow fell across the window in the door, then an anonymous face peered in, and Sarah closed her eyes tightly, like a child tormented by the monsters in the closet. "I'm on remand."

Camille snorted once. "Be here longer than me, then," she said, and within seconds began to snore.

When Sarah opened her eyes minutes later, nothing had changed. The cell was still bathed in a thin, bluish light, the door remained locked, her wrists still throbbed, and the toilet smelled fetid and unpleasantly sweet. The thought of being trapped here for six hours, let alone six months, made her want to claw her fingernails into the wall, just to see if she could break through to the other side and fresh air.

The shadow passed slowly by the window again. She turned her back to it and curled herself into a ball. She didn't know which was worse, the night stretching out in front of her or the prospect of the day that would follow.

❖

The kitchen table was strewn with sheets of paper. In trying to get organized, Alex seemed merely to have created more chaos. She rummaged through the printouts and hand-scribbled notes, looking for her "to do" list.

"Of all the places to park your furry little butt," she said, lifting Bandit from the table and dumping him on the floor. Her list was warm when she retrieved it. "Go earn your keep. Catch a mouse or something."

Sensing her foul mood, Bandit slunk out the cat flap. Alex returned to her seat just as the printer finished churning out a PDF document she had found online. She sorted the pages into order, scribbled "Harnish" on the top in red pen, and added them to the small pile bearing the same heading. Bridie would no doubt be doing similar research with far better resources at her disposal, but Alex, having no in-depth understanding of the bail appeal process, wanted some idea of what they might be up against.

She had spoken to Bridie the previous night, finding out which jail Sarah had been transferred to and the earliest date she would be allowed visitors. As a new prisoner, still within the admission and orientation period, she would have to wait five days before anyone other than her legal counsel could see her.

Alex glanced at her salvaged list and tapped the mouse pad on her laptop, waking it from power save. Tobin had returned the computer and a bagful of bedding earlier that morning. She had unlocked the door to find him attempting to peel off the sticky residue of an evidence label. After mumbling an apology and asking her to sign a receipt, he almost tripped over Flossie in his haste to leave. The bedding had gone straight into the garbage, but the laptop had been a godsend; buying a replacement was now crossed off the top of her list.

Her cell rang as she was typing "motels and hotels, Avery, Aroostook County" into a search engine.

"Hey, Mike." She clicked enter as she spoke.

"Morning." He sounded tired; Alex guessed he had been awake as late as she had.

"There are five R. Hollises living in Avery, Ruby, or Tawny Ridge," he said, cutting right to the chase. "Three of those are female, one owns a bakery out in Tawny where he lives with his wife and kids, and the fifth is seven years old."

"Great." She tapped her pen on her teeth. "So who's the Mr. R. Hollis getting his mail delivered to Emerson's apartment?"

"That would be the million dollar question."

She bit the pen top until it cracked. "Think we might be going in the wrong direction here? Every turn we take with Emerson, we slam into a brick wall."

"It's possible." Castillo sighed. "Hate to follow bad news with shit news, but the tire images didn't show a real lot of anything."

"Wow, and here was I thinking they might have a name, number, and license plate carved into them." She knew Castillo was absolutely not the villain, but she couldn't keep the sarcasm from her voice.

There was a short silence.

"You get any sleep, Alex?" he asked finally.

"No." She ran her hands over her face. "No, not really. You?"

"Here and there."

"It's driving me fucking crazy. Trying to get it straight in my head. It's like the worst game of Clue, only with no one holding that little wallet with all the answers in it." She heard him grunt in agreement. "I think Caleb Deakin killed Lyssa," she continued, absently scribbling "CD – L" on a blank sheet of paper. "But those tire tracks must have been concealed by someone on the search teams, so I still think there's a local involved. Maybe before heading out here Deakin found someone sympathetic to his cause, someone who could later volunteer for the search without seeming out of place."

"Sounds plausible enough," Castillo said. "Sleep deprivation must agree with you."

"This is probably my manic phase. Next up is crash and burn, followed shortly afterward by rocking in a darkened room."

"You're doing fine."

"I just want to keep going until I've tried everything. I'm starting to look into places nearby that Deakin could have stayed at. If he's not at Emerson's apartment, he might have rented somewhere else around here. Motel, hotel, trailer park."

"Holiday home," Castillo added.

She nodded, scribbling another note on her list. "Of course, he could just have slept in his damn car. You know more about the family than I do. Is he the type to turn tail and run straight back to North Carolina?"

"No, he's not."

"And he's probably going to have contacts within the prison system."

"I'm running background on as many of the staff and inmates at Prescott as I can, but—"

"I know," Alex interrupted, not wanting him to have to state the obvious. "Budget cuts, jurisdiction, your stack of official ongoing cases that aren't related to this entirely unofficial ongoing case."

"Damn, Alex, you sound just like my boss, but that wasn't what I was going to say." The faint trace of humor that had been in his voice vanished. "Deakin isn't a threat just to Sarah. You need to move. You're far too vulnerable out there on your own."

"Are you trying to scare me?" she asked, unwilling to admit that he was right.

"Yes. You should be scared."

She looked out the window, watching the chickens wandering about on the grass and Tilly snoozing with her head on her paws. Beyond the grass, the forest loomed into her peripheral vision, and beyond that, she had no way of knowing what was out there.

"Maybe when I start my research I'll find somewhere suitable to move to." It was the only concession she was willing to give at that moment. "Somewhere pet and chicken friendly."

"Jesus, Alex, get a friend to feed the fucking chickens."

"You offering?" She waited for the penny to drop, waited for him to realize that they didn't have any real friends left. It didn't take him long.

"Shit."

"Don't worry about it," she said. "I'll sort something out, I promise."

"I'm going to hold you to that." A phone rang on his side of the line. He swore indistinctly and the ringing stopped; she suspected he had flicked it through to voice mail. "I spoke to Quinn again and e-mailed him Caleb Deakin's record," he continued. "He didn't seem very interested, even when I pointed out the relevance of the dates, but I got him to promise that his officers would receive copies of the information."

"Thank you. And I'm sorry for being a bitch."

"I think you're allowed a lapse here and there, given the circumstances."

"Still, I am sorry."

She heard another man's voice in the background and Castillo's low reply, before he came back to the phone. "I have a meeting in five," he told her. "Let me know if you find anything."

"I will."

She hung up and wiggled her finger on the mouse pad again. A list of rental properties in Avery filled the screen. Deciding to start systematically before broadening the search, she dialed the number for Avery's sole hotel. If it was anything like the last time, she didn't expect them to be at all receptive to her inquiries and was pretty sure they would inform Quinn, but she wasn't about to let that deter her.

The narrow window level with Sarah's bunk looked out onto a concrete yard that was surrounded by a double chain link fence topped with rolls of barbed wire. Bird excrement covered the sill, but no birds came to perch there while she watched, and even when the sky grew lighter, she could hear nothing but the varying degrees of Camille's snoring and a woman muttering endlessly in the adjoining cell.

Camille, adjusted to the jail's routine, woke up three minutes before the process of unlocking the cells began. She shook her head as she studied Sarah's face. "You'll get used to it," she said.

She looked younger than Sarah had expected, but she had badly healed scars on her arms that appeared to be the result of self-inflicted wounds and the veins standing out against her pale skin were blown and pitted. She tilted her head when she saw the bandages covering Sarah's wrists, evidently supposing that she and Sarah had something in common.

Sarah, weary of trying to tell people what had actually happened, said nothing.

"Washroom first, so take your kit." Camille indicated the plastic wallet containing Sarah's allocation of toiletries. "Then breakfast. I usually shower after dinner, when it's less crowded."

Sarah nodded her agreement. The babble of voices in the corridor was increasing as the cells were opened sequentially and the inmates shouted greetings to each other, but it took another twenty minutes for her door to be released. Keeping close to Camille, she waited for her turn to use the toilet, doing her best to ignore the curious looks and murmurs of recognition or speculation from the other women. By the time a cubicle came free, she was so nervous that she kicked the door shut and knelt over the toilet bowl, retching, but she had eaten little the day before and her dry heaves amounted to nothing. At the sink, she splashed cold water on her face and brushed her teeth with thin, gritty toothpaste.

"Don't swallow the water or you really will puke," Camille said, and shrugged in apology as Sarah hurriedly spat out her mouthful.

The crowd in the washroom had thinned, leaving the last woman in the shower humming cheerfully to herself in relative privacy. Sarah followed Camille to a dining area that appeared to have been modeled on a school cafeteria, except that it lacked the motivational posters and metal cutlery, and every piece of furniture was bolted to the floor. Waiting in line with her compartmentalized tray, she looked around at the tables of women, some eating in silence, others chatting and laughing. Many appeared perfectly at home in their surroundings, while the guards seemed to favor a tactic of minimal intervention, remaining in the background as inmates served their fellow inmates and everyone cleaned up after themselves.

Several women on different tables tried to wave Camille and Sarah over to empty seats. Camille grinned. "Fish are always the most popular girls in the room," she said, before noticing Sarah's bewilderment and explaining, "Newbies never feel like eating nothing. They'll all be hoping you'll share."

"Oh, right." The strong smell of institutional cooking certainly did little for Sarah's appetite, nor did a breakfast offering of white bread, peanut butter and jelly, grits, and a plastic cup of milk.

"Make sure you get something in trade." Camille led them over to a table with two spare seats. "Or they'll take your food even when you are hungry."

Within five minutes of sitting down, Sarah had swapped her bread and the peanut butter and jelly for the promise of paper and a pen. She had also inadvertently revealed that most people in England wouldn't be able to identify a bowl of grits in a breakfast cereal lineup.

"You don't have grits in England?" One of the women appeared genuinely horrified by the thought.

"No, we don't," Sarah said. "People tend to stick with porridge. Would you like mine?" she added, feeling the urge to make amends for the transgression.

The woman eagerly scooped the grits onto her tray, took a forkful, and spoke with her mouth full. "Patsy in the kitchen today?" She craned her head toward the serving hatch. "She never puts enough fuckin' salt in."

"Quit bitchin'," Camille said. "If they were that bad, you wouldn't be eating Sarah's." Her intervention was enough to mollify the woman, who resumed eating in silence.

Sarah sipped her milk, hoping it might ease the cramping in her stomach. The shutter on the hatch clattered into place, which the women seemed to take as a signal to finish their meals.

"What happens now?" she asked.

"Lock up and cleaning," Camille told her, pointing out where to stack the empty trays.

"And then?" It was only eight a.m.; she couldn't imagine the cell would take very long to clean.

The look she received in response, however, implied she had asked a particularly stupid question.

"Then we have lunch," Camille said.

Choking and sobbing, Leah dragged herself up from the floor using the frame of a kitchen chair. She made it onto her knees before a sharp pain in her abdomen forced her to crouch back on all fours.

"Oh God, help me," she whispered, blood dripping from her mouth to paint patterns on the tiles.

In the next room, Caleb lowered the volume on the television, now that he no longer needed it to conceal the sound of his blows. His cell phone rang and he must have knocked something over as he grabbed for it; Leah heard a thud as the object landed on the carpet.

"She's in Prescott County," he said. Then, almost yelling, "No, not Penobscot, Prescott, you dumb fuck."

Leah wiped her chin with her palm. Then, still gripping the chair, she pulled herself to her feet. Caleb's laptop lay in front of her on the kitchen table. Although its screen was dark, whatever he had seen on there had gotten him so enraged that he hadn't taken the time to close it down, and it sat as if waiting for further instructions, its cooling fan whirring patiently.

She rinsed her mouth at the sink and found a clean cloth to press against the tattered cut on the inside of her cheek. She could hear Caleb next door, still preoccupied on the phone. She touched the mouse pad with one finger, telling herself that was all she would do; if it didn't work, she would leave it alone.

A color mug shot of Caleb instantly filled the screen. Beneath the image, several lines of text listed his date of birth, his employment record, and his home address—including the date he had last been seen there. There was no mention of his being married. Perhaps whoever had been watching him hadn't been watching him very closely, or perhaps they just didn't think Leah was significant. The short message in the e-mail made the blood in her mouth and the ache in her belly easier to bear, though: "Received from FBI. Sent out to all the police officers in the district."

She stared at the photograph until the screen dimmed and then darkened. There was a sudden, rapid approach of footsteps in the stairwell, and Caleb paused his telephone conversation mid-sentence. She turned hopefully toward the front door, but there was no knock, no battering ram to splinter the wood and force a way in. A woman shouted for her children to stop running about, and shortly afterward everything fell quiet.

As Leah hobbled into the bathroom, Caleb started talking into the phone again, his voice now wary and hushed. Let him see how it feels to be hunted, she thought, dipping a handful of tissue between her legs to check if she was bleeding. The tissue was clean when she pulled it away. She sat heavily on the edge of the bathtub, offering up silent thanks and adding her own whispered prayer onto the end.

"Oh God, please let somebody find us."

❖

"No, thank you. No, it's fine. You don't need to do that."

With the phone clamped between her ear and shoulder, Alex taped the top of the cardboard box shut and wrote "Food" on it in marker pen. Realizing that the woman on the other end of the line wasn't going to relent, and too polite to just hang up on her, she reeled off an e-mail address she had long ago deleted so that the woman could attempt to send her a holiday home rental brochure.

"Thanks. Yes, I will. Good-bye." She struck the address off her list and caught the phone as it dropped. That particular scruffy-looking cottage had been standing empty since January, which explained its owner's desperate sales pitch. After five days of making phone calls, chasing down answering machine messages, and fielding e-mails, Alex had only eight of the seventy-nine local holiday homes left to contact. She was also preparing to move into one of them.

As she set the box of food by the back door, she heard a rustling from under the porch. Even though the noise was familiar and she was sure of its cause, she took up her Glock, unlocked the door, and peered out to check.

"Tilly, they're not under there, sweetie."

She waited for Tilly to crawl out from beneath the cabin and threw her a chew treat to distract her from her search for the chickens. They had already been collected by Esther, who owned a plot of land big enough to accommodate them and who was one of the few people Alex could think to ask for help. The small lakeside cottage Alex had arranged to rent in Tawny did allow pets, but she thought that six chickens, in addition to two cats and a dog, might be stretching the definition somewhat.

A sharp scratch to a fingertip made her aware how vigorously she was drumming her hands against the porch railing. She dug out the splinter, stuck her finger in her mouth, and checked her watch: ten a.m. Although sorely tempted to get in the Silverado and head straight out to Prescott, she forced herself to wait another half hour. That would still leave ample time to find the jail and pass through the security procedures. She had been on the verge of dozing off the previous night when Bridie phoned to confirm her place on the visitor list and to tell her that the allotted time for surnames A–L was two till three p.m. It would be the first time Alex had seen Sarah since the arraignment.

Every time they spoke on the phone, Sarah would say, "I'm okay, don't worry," and Alex would agree and promise not to worry, and then spend half the night reneging on that promise and the other half thinking about what else she could do to help Sarah when it was finally light enough to give up on sleep. Sarah's priorities were slightly simpler: "spare knickers" had been her main request, along with a few dollars for her commissary card. Alex might not be able to guarantee her any progress on her case, but she would at least be able to supply her with some decent underwear.

Twenty-five minutes.

Alex decided to take a shower before selecting an outfit that wouldn't fall foul of the jail's dress code. As it mainly focused on the prohibition of "see-through tops, low-cut blouses, miniskirts, halter tops, and gang colors," she didn't foresee much of a problem. While Tilly resumed her hunt for the missing chickens, Alex relocked the back door and tried to remember which box she had packed all the toiletries in.

Sitting cross-legged on her bunk, Sarah reread the paragraph of impenetrable legalese, then gave up and closed the book. She had been trying to concentrate on the text for the last fifty minutes, but nothing was sinking in and her notes made little sense. There was still another hour to go before visiting and—unlike many of her fellow inmates—she had yet to perfect the art of whiling away the time.

The block was calm, for the most part, and she had the cell to herself, as most of the women congregated in the rec room or lingered over lunch. In the last five days, she had concluded that jail was an awful lot of loneliness, boredom, and petty routine, broken up by an occasional outburst of violence and the serving of barely edible food. The majority of the convicted women passed their sentences watching television, volunteering for work and study programs, or dozing in their cells. The remand prisoners, meanwhile, were given unrestricted access to the jail's small legal library, and those literate enough were encouraged to research their own cases.

Every inch of the thin pad of paper she had bargained for on the first day was now covered in scribbled notes, with the exception of the single sheet on which she intended to write a letter to Alex. She had started the letter three times in as many days, each time shredding the first lines until the paper was barely a third of its original size and looked like a rat had nibbled on it. What she wanted to say was so simple: "I miss you, I love you, and I hope you're okay," but it always made her cry, which inevitably smeared the ink or stained the paper. Alex would never believe what Sarah said on the phone if she sent a letter that looked as if it had been used to blow her nose. She shook her head wryly. She didn't have a hope in hell of Alex believing her anyway, so she might as well just write the damn thing. *Later*, she promised herself, and swapped the legal tome for a copy of *Pride and Prejudice*. She had always intended to catch up on the classics one day, and now seemed as good an opportunity as any.

Prescott County Jail was a new redbrick building, housing a facility that had outgrown its original position adjacent to the County Courthouse and been relocated to a patch of waste ground on the outskirts of town. The guard at the gate directed Alex to park in a small underground lot and follow the signs to the visiting center.

"First time here?" he asked, and gave her a set of instructions without waiting for her to answer.

She skimmed through the salient points, before leaving everything in the Silverado except her keys and driver's license, which she handed obediently to one of the guards in the lobby. She watched a child in front of her stand stock-still for a pat down search and then assume the correct position for the guard to pass an electronic wand over him. He couldn't have been more than six years old. When the guard had finished, the child grinned at his guardian and skipped through the arch of the final metal detector. Following his lead, Alex submitted to the various search procedures without uttering a word and nodded her thanks to the guard.

"Second door on the left," he told her as he made a note of her driver's license number. "You're authorized for a contact visit."

She nodded again and tried not to show any emotion. That meant she and Sarah were allowed a brief hug and kiss at the start and the end of the visit. Handholding was permissible, too, so long as their hands remained visible on the table throughout. The intimation that she should be grateful for that much opportunity to touch Sarah made her feel ill.

A long line had formed outside the visiting room, and the door opened as Alex tagged herself onto the end. The adults filed in, holding children who chattered and tugged to go faster. All the women sitting waiting at the tables were dressed identically—bright red tabards over beige shirts—and it took Alex a few disorienting seconds to spot Sarah, seated in a far corner, beyond the main locus of noise and activity. She stood as Alex approached, a smile brightening her face even as tears filled her eyes.

"Hey." The familiar greeting came out in a rush of breath and she stepped forward to bury herself in Alex's arms. She felt thin and her face was pale, but when they kissed, her lips were soft and her hands clasped Alex's firmly.

"Not sure beige is really your color, sweetheart," Alex told her as they took seats opposite each other.

"No? You should see me in Prison Transport Orange. It sets off my eyes a treat."

Alex edged a finger beneath the cuff of Sarah's sleeve, tracing the ridge of one of the concealed lacerations. "How you doing? Really?"

"Really?" Sarah held her gaze. "Good moments and bad moments, and then some truly horrible moments. But I'm mostly okay." She caught hold of Alex's wandering finger. "Those are healing fine. The antibiotics kicked in at last."

"Are you eating properly, then?"

In their phone conversations, Sarah had repeatedly mentioned that the antibiotics had reduced her appetite, as if she wanted an excuse for any weight loss Alex might notice.

"Better than I was." She lowered her eyes. "But I ran out of toothpaste and soap a couple of days back, so..." She shrugged, as if the inference was clear. When Alex finally figured it out, her naivety made her want to kick herself.

"You traded your meals." She shook her head, distraught. "Why didn't you ask Bridie for money? You know she wouldn't mind. She'd just add it to the fee." As soon as the words left her, she regretted them; Sarah had had every ounce of her dignity stolen from her, and Alex was sitting there encouraging her to beg for pennies. "I'm so sorry," she said. "Fuck, just, ugh. Are you allowed to slap me?"

"No," Sarah said, but she was smiling. "I think that would probably be frowned on, even in a contact visit."

"I brought all your stuff, and money for your card, so no more skipping meals, okay?"

Sarah's smile widened. "You mean I finally get to wear my own kecks?"

"Is that prison slang or northern English slang?"

Sarah winked. "Just testing. It's northern for knickers, or 'panties' to you. Believe me when I tell you that prison knickers are nobody's friend."

"Scratchy?"

"Oh, that's just the start of it. Scratchy, available in any color so long as it's beige, and amusingly ill-fitting. The pair I have on come up to my armpits."

Alex rocked back in her chair and laughed. "God, I fucking miss you."

"I bet I miss you more." Sarah shook her head and changed the subject. "How're the rabble?"

"The remaining three are slightly confused by your absence and the absence of the chickens, but they're managing."

"Bandit behaving?"

"Hell, no."

"You moving tomorrow?"

"Yeah, rental starts at ten. I put the new address and number in with your things."

"Lovely. So…" Sarah awkwardly tapped the nail of Alex's index finger, obviously reluctant to say what was on her mind.

"Still working on it," Alex said. "I have eight properties left to contact and about ten more that owe me a response. Caleb Deakin's photo is out there and Castillo is busy running background on the people in here. Have you had any—?"

"No," Sarah said. "No, everyone's been okay so far. I'm trying to keep my head down and eyes open and stay out of trouble."

"Sounds like a plan."

"I'm reading *Pride and Prejudice*."

"Yeah? You know, I always meant to read that."

Sarah squeezed her hand. "No, you didn't."

"No, I didn't," Alex admitted.

"Well, I'm quite enjoying it. I think I might have a slight crush on Lizzy, but it's probably just petticoat envy."

Alex found herself staring at Sarah as she continued to talk about the book. Her eyes were lively with enthusiasm, and every so often her hands jerked; she would have been gesturing with them, were she not so determinedly keeping hold of Alex's.

All too soon the officer at the door called a five-minute warning and the mood in the room shifted, voices becoming more hushed and urgent and someone away to the right beginning to weep inconsolably.

"Is there anything else you need?" Alex asked. From where she sat, she could see the guards as they propped the doors open and then stood waiting, on the lookout for potential flashpoints.

"No, I don't think so." Sarah looked around as well, and her cheeks lost a little of their color. "Shit. I'd say time flies, but in here it really doesn't. You're coming back on Wednesday evening, aren't…?" She faltered, as if remembering the distance and disruption involved. "I mean, only if you want to."

Alex used their joined hands to pull Sarah to her feet. Around them, chairs scraped across the floor and infants wailed as some unspoken signal told people it was time to leave.

"Of course I'm coming back." Alex wrapped Sarah in her arms, breathing in the unfamiliar scents of cheap soap and medicinal shampoo, and something beneath those scents that was still unmistakably Sarah. "I love you," she said, kissing her as tenderly as she dared.

"I love you too." Sarah looked at the floor. "Go."

Alex did as she asked, hesitating only when she reached the door. For a few moments, she watched Sarah helping another inmate pile the chairs together, her head still bowed. When people began to grumble at Alex for blocking the exit, she turned and kept walking; she didn't look back again.

CHAPTER FOURTEEN

The sun was setting as Alex secured the gate on the access road. All around her, shadows lengthened, crowding in on her and combining with the eerie noises of nocturnal creatures to give the forest a horror movie atmosphere. As she set off again, the half-light made it difficult for her eyes to adjust, forcing her to creep along for fear of driving straight off the track. It was one stress too many on a day that had already pushed her to her limit. With no quick resolution to Sarah's case in sight, the thought of making that six-hour round trip twice a week was already making Alex consider switching her choice of rental property to one closer to the jail. Her back hurt from the drive and she was tired, lonely, and completely demoralized. During the last hour of the journey, she had kept herself alert by planning her evening, deciding on nothing more elaborate than beer and junk food. She was sure that just this once, Sarah would understand.

A hot shower left her feeling human again. She fed the animals before piling a tray with chips, Oreos, and the coldest beers she could find and taking her "dinner" out onto the porch. She unclipped her holster, leaving her Glock within easy reach, and propped her feet up on the porch rail. One long drink drained half of her first beer. The alcohol hit her empty stomach, and within minutes, she felt herself beginning to relax. Try as she might, she couldn't figure out how to dunk an Oreo in her bottle of beer; she chewed one of the cookies and washed it down with what remained instead. The taste wasn't altogether unpleasant, so she cracked the top off a second bottle and recreated the process in the interest of empirical culinary inquiry.

Her hand was buried deep in the bag of chips, her third beer just foaming at the top, when she spotted the man on the path.

"Fuck. *Fuck*." She wiped her greasy fingers on her pants and took up the Glock. She wasn't drunk, but nor was she entirely sober, and her knees banged against the deck as she ducked low and pushed off the bench. In the kitchen, Tilly had started to bark, but the door was too far behind Alex for her to reach back and open it, and she didn't want to take her eyes off the man.

Through the gaps in the wooden surround, she could clearly observe his approach. He was slim and of average height. In one arm, he cradled something that didn't look like a weapon—if anything, it looked like a paper grocery bag. His progress became more tentative as he drew nearer, but he stayed on the path, making no attempt to conceal himself. Four more steps, and the mellow glow from the porch light caught his face. Alex stood, panting against a head rush, and took aim with the Glock.

"Stop right there."

He halted immediately and began to raise his hands. She jogged down the steps, the gun unwavering in her grip.

"Don't move, Emerson. I fucking mean it."

"I'm not armed," he said.

"How'd you get through the gate? You got Lyssa's key?"

"No." His eyes widened at the implication. "No, I left the car at the gate, then climbed over and walked."

"What's in the bag?" She was closer now, close enough to hear the clink of glass as he shifted its weight.

"Uh, it's beer."

"Beer?"

"Yeah, my pop always said, 'If you're gonna sneak up on an armed woman in the middle of nowhere, better take beer, son.'"

Ignoring this attempt to defuse the standoff, she kept the gun pointed at his chest. "Put the bag on the ground and turn around."

He did as instructed. Then he lifted his arms without being asked and allowed her to pat him down. The bag, she found, really did contain a six-pack of beer.

"What the fuck?" She was so confused, and so tired of this cloak-and-dagger bullshit.

"Rob called me this afternoon," he said. As she gaped at him, he picked up the bag and held it in both hands as if to prove he wasn't a threat; he couldn't hurt her with his hands full. "Told me a woman fitting your description had been around at the apartment asking questions. I figured it might save time if I explained a few things. I'm sure you have more important stuff to do than chase after me."

She realized that her mouth was still hanging open and snapped her teeth together. Her shoulders sagged and she lowered the gun. "It's been a really long day," she said.

"Yeah. I can't even imagine." There was a quiet kindness to his voice and he sounded absolutely sincere. It was enough to shatter what little remained of her resistance.

"Want something to go with that beer?" she asked.

"I guess."

"Give me a minute."

Tilly, curious as ever and smelling turkey, followed at Alex's heels when she came back out with a plate of sandwiches. There was a small, folded photograph lying in the space Emerson had left for her on the bench. He watched her closely as she picked it up. She had holstered the Glock, but it was still visible and within reach, and Tilly was by no means a small dog; she supposed he had a right to feel nervous. It was only when she unfolded the image that she realized he was nervous for an entirely different reason.

"Oh!" she said, unable to mask her surprise. She hadn't seen that coming at all. "I guess this is Rob, then." The man was blond and handsome, with a smile that showed pristine white teeth. Emerson was the second figure in the photograph. He was holding Rob's hand and smiling just as broadly.

"We met in New York, four years ago." He took the photograph back and tucked it into his wallet. "Rob lives there. He's an architect. We keep the apartment for when he visits." Emerson could barely look at her. "He's never been to Avery."

"Damn." She gave a quiet whistle. "This the reason you've been such a shit with me?"

"I thought you'd know, that you'd take one look at me and just know. Isn't that how it works?" He leaned forward, holding his head in his hands. "I figured the best way to stop that from happening was to treat you like crap and hope you'd either leave or decide I was a homophobic fuck who wasn't worth your time."

"You couldn't trust me enough to confide in me?"

"I haven't been able to trust anyone enough for that." His response was fierce and immediate, a kneejerk defense, but then he opened his hands in apology. "It'd kill my parents, and probably end my career, at least here."

"That's not true, not the career part, anyway."

He gave her a sardonic look. "You saw what happened to Sarah, what's happened to you both since. There aren't any pitchfork-wielding mobs around here, and everyone's real nice on the surface, but the second they have an excuse…" He didn't need to elaborate; Alex was already nodding in agreement, and they both knew there was no way she would say a word about what he had just told her. "I've lived here all my life, and it's my home, at least while my mom and pop are alive," he said. "I'm sorry I've treated you like crap, but I just couldn't take the risk."

"No need to have worried on that score. Apparently, my gaydar's completely fucked up."

He smiled weakly and put a hand into his pocket, making her tense until she realized he was merely taking out a sheet of paper, which he passed to her. It was a Xerox of a crumpled and faded order docket. She recognized Sarah's signature in the bottom corner.

"What am I looking at?"

"Quinn's big theory hinges on Sarah accompanying Lyssa to unlock the gate, which places her at the murder scene," he said. "Sarah told Quinn that Lyssa had her own key, that you'd gotten one cut at the general store." He gulped his beer and held onto the bottle, his fingers worrying at the label. "Took Jenny a while to find the record, but she managed it. She also remembered Sarah explaining that the key was for Lyssa, said Sarah had been excited about Lyssa helping her to study."

"Jesus," Alex said, seeing a glimmer of hope for the first time in days. "You don't believe Sarah's guilty, do you?"

"No, I don't."

Alex didn't mention that she had only just crossed him off her own list of suspects, but he had probably worked that out. "Have you shared this with Quinn?"

"No. It's enough to poke a hole in the case but not enough to blow it wide open, and he's too busy having lunch with the mayor to put any serious effort into tracking down other suspects, like Caleb Deakin for example. Quinn's a fucking embarrassment."

"He's a fucking liability," she said.

They both leaned back on the bench and finished their drinks in silence. Emerson held his hand out to Tilly, who approached him warily and then allowed him to pet her.

"I tried to warn you, y'know." He scratched behind Tilly's ears, unwittingly choosing the best way to make a friend of her. "The day Sarah was arrested. I called, but I got your voice mail."

"I was talking to Agent Castillo," she said, remembering that she had a missed call. Following up on it had understandably slipped her mind.

"I knew Quinn had set her up for a perp walk and didn't want her going into it blind. He kept me busy running errands all the rest of that day, so I couldn't get down to the cells to check on her." When he turned to Alex, he looked sickened. "I did my best to look out for her."

"I know you did." Desperate for an ally, especially one within the Avery PD, she came to a sudden decision. By the time she finished telling him about the tire treads and her suspicion that someone in the town—possibly even in the police force—was involved in framing Sarah for Lyssa's murder, he was beet red with anger. She uncapped another beer and set it in front of him.

He took a long drink. "You're not safe out here on your own," he told her.

"I'm leaving in the morning. I found a rental."

"Good." He didn't push her for details. "What else are you doing?"

"Looking into places Deakin may have stayed at. I can't prove it yet, but I'm sure it was him. And I don't think he's slunk back to North Carolina; the surveillance teams certainly haven't seen him since the murder. I think he's still in the area somewhere."

"But not at my apartment." Emerson raised an eyebrow.

"No, not at your apartment," she conceded.

"If there's anything I can do—"

"I'm sure there will be." She patted her pockets, found her cell, and opened the call register. The missed call was still logged. "This your number?"

"Yeah, that's it."

"There is one thing," she said, her brain beginning to kick back into gear. "I need a list of the people who volunteered to search our woods. Whoever covered those tracks covered them quickly, so they must have been out here on the first day. It's unlikely Deakin would have risked coming back here to do it himself. Having those names would narrow things down a little."

"I'll see what I can find." Emerson stood and ruffled the fur on Tilly's neck. "I'm working tomorrow, but call me whenever, okay?"

"Sure. Thanks." She stood with him. It was dark beyond the reach of the porch lights, the sun having set completely. "You want a ride back to your car?"

For a moment, he seemed uncertain, as if some innate pride stopped him from admitting that walking alone down the unlit track was a foreboding prospect.

"Be no fucking use to me if you snap your ankle," she said, making it easy for him.

He laughed, something she had rarely heard him do.

"Yeah, a ride would be good. Thanks."

The sneakers were thin-soled and cheaply made, and Sarah would almost certainly give herself shin splints by trying to jog in them, but by the seventh day of her incarceration, she was willing to take the risk. A daily half hour of push-ups and sit-ups in a cell just wasn't enough exercise for someone accustomed to a regular routine of running and swimming. When she asked Kendall about jogging laps around the outside recreational space, the guard had shrugged and found her the pair of sneakers.

Camille chuckled as she watched Sarah fasten her laces. "You know how hot it is out there, girl?"

"It does look quite warm," Sarah said. The block had basic air conditioning, but today the heat was breaking through, making their current lock-down a sticky and uncomfortable one. They had finished their cleaning tasks and then taken turns to hold their faces beneath the cold tap.

"You're crazy. You're gonna miss—"

Whatever television show Camille was about to extol the virtues of was lost beneath the bang of their cell door slamming open onto the wall.

"Jesus, fuck," she said, sitting bolt upright on her bunk.

"Both of you get over there now." The guard, whose frame almost filled the doorway, grabbed Camille's arm when she didn't move fast enough. Already on her feet, Sarah was quicker to obey and stood where he indicated with her heels pressed flush against the wall. He wasn't one of the regulars on the block; she thought she might have seen him once or twice, but couldn't be sure.

"Aw, man." Camille threw up her hands; unlike Sarah, she'd obviously worked out what was going on. "You couldn't have tossed it before we finished cleaning it?"

He grinned but there was no humor in it. "I guess not."

Sarah put her hand on Camille's wrist, preventing any further protest. They watched in silence as he threw their bedding onto the floor and upended their mattresses, then shook out their clothing and leafed through the pages of the books they had stacked on the desk. He ran his fingers beneath the bed and window frames and along the underside of the desk. Camille had accrued more personal possessions than Sarah, and she stood seething as he rooted through them.

"Fucking asshole," she muttered.

Sarah tightened her fingers as his head snapped up.

"What the fuck you just say?"

"Nothin'." Camille directed her denial to the floor.

He turned to Sarah. "What the fuck did she just say?"

Sarah felt the cool of the concrete propping her up; it was the only thing keeping her on her feet. "I didn't hear her say anything," she told him, damned no matter what answer she gave.

He stared at her until the sound of approaching footsteps made him look toward the door. "Get this shit cleaned up." He made a point of grinding his boots into their bedding as he left the cell.

"Bloody hellfire." Sarah crouched down, relief beginning to make her feel shaky. "Who was he?"

"Fuck if I know. They rotate the shifts every few weeks, stop folks from getting too friendly."

"I doubt that's ever been much of an issue for him." She started to collect Camille's various keepsakes. "These all look okay," she said, arranging them back on the desk.

"Thanks, honey." About to refold a blanket, Camille hesitated. "Hey, maybe you're bad for my karma."

"How do you mean?"

"Well…" She counted slowly on her fingers. "I've been in here six months and eighteen days, and that's the first time I ever had my cell tossed."

A slight tremor in Sarah's hand made her knock one of the ornaments onto its side. "The first time ever?"

"Yeah, they don't do it much in here, not unless you got a bad habit and they think you're hiding shit."

"Right."

A new guard breaking with jail procedure and targeting their cell was far too coincidental for Sarah's peace of mind. She started to remake her bed, turning the sheet so that the boot prints were against the mattress. Every little noise from the corridor made her jump and look toward the door. She thumped her misshapen pillow, taking her frustration out on its lumps.

So much for keeping her head down and staying out of trouble.

❖

From deep within his carrier, strapped onto the rear seat of the Silverado, Bandit let out a pitiful wail.

"One hour, little guy, that's all. Then you get a whole new house to explore." Alex managed to keep her voice cheerful, but she felt as miserable as Bandit sounded. She and Sarah had loved this cabin. They had fixed up the rooms one by one and spent countless hours working on the yard, every little alteration putting their mark on the place and making it their home. She could barely believe how quickly and how completely their life here had been destroyed.

She started the engine, the noise prompting loud complaints from both cats, and turned the truck away from the cabin. She hadn't packed everything—the rental cottage was furnished—but she knew the only time she would come back here would be to collect the rest of their belongings.

"We'll find somewhere else, somewhere safe," she said, trying to distract herself as she approached the spot where Lyssa had died.

She caught sight of the fresh earth she had piled over the bloodstains and of the roses she had cut to lay in remembrance, and a familiar self-reproach overwhelmed her. Lyssa was the one whose life had truly been destroyed. No matter how bad things were for Alex and

Sarah, at least they were alive and could try to pick up the pieces once all this was over, something Lyssa would never get a chance to do. Alex had never been religious, had never believed in a god or higher being, so she had no one to pray to for Lyssa's sake. She murmured a quiet good-bye as she unlocked the gate, but there was no closure in it and it didn't make her feel any better.

The rest of the journey was uneventful, interrupted only by a quick break for Tilly. As Alex drove along the back road that circled Tawny Ridge, she could hear distant church bells ringing out to announce Sunday worship. The town center would be lively with people traveling to church or meeting for breakfast, but hers was the only car using that particular route and no one saw her pass. She had packed enough provisions for her first few days and intended to drive out to the busier, more anonymous stores in Ruby when she needed to restock. The owner of the cottage she had chosen lived in Kennebec, while the cottage itself was in an isolated lakeside spot on the very outskirts of the town. She wasn't moving to Tawny to settle or make friends; she planned to stay only until she had exhausted every possible avenue in her investigation, and then to leave the area for good. In a best-case scenario, no one would even know she had been there.

The cottage had a private access road, like their cabin's, except that there was nothing to stop anyone from driving straight up it. At first, Alex had considered renting an apartment in a large public block, where security would come from having people around instead of attempting to hide away. Ultimately, though, the idea of seclusion, privacy, and somewhere for the animals to roam had won out. Only time would tell if she had made the right choice.

She pulled up on the driveway and climbed out of the truck, grateful to stretch her legs. "Rustic" had been the word used to describe the cottage in the e-mail, and it did have a certain rough-around-the-edges charm, with a deck that needed painting and window frames that had seen better days. As promised, the key to the front door was waiting for her beneath a yard ornament. She let herself in and stood blinking against the dim light of the kitchen until she found the cord for the window blinds. The sunlight revealed rooms furnished in a simple, practical style, designed to meet the needs of outdoorsy visitors and their pets. What it sacrificed in terms of esthetic appeal, it made up for in comfort. It felt like a home away from home, and right then that was exactly what she needed.

It took her three hours to unpack, with Bandit's increasingly inventive escape attempts at least making the task entertaining. In the aftermath of her visit to Sarah and of Emerson's unannounced visit, she had forgotten to check the messages on the answering machine at the cabin. She plugged it in and hit play just as Bandit made a beeline for the only window she had opened.

"You little bastard." She ran across the living room into the kitchen and grabbed hold of him, using one hand to support his weight and the other to pry his claws from the wooden frame. He purred and butted his head beneath her chin, seeming to realize he was in trouble and attempting damage limitation. "Where you gonna go if you get out? You'll get lost and never find your way back...Hmm." She paused to consider that as a paw hit her on the nose. "Maybe I should just open the door for you, huh?"

A woman's voice filtered through from the next room, reminding Alex that she had started the answering machine. With Bandit still in her arms, she went back to listen.

"...and it's strange, because I took them a welcome basket around, like I do for all my honeymooning couples, and they weren't there. He booked the cottage for three weeks, but there was no sign of them. If you're interested in a lease, I can do you a reduced rate for this next week because I don't think they'll be coming back."

As the woman began to recite her contact details, Alex dropped Bandit on the sofa and scrabbled for a pen, swearing when she couldn't find one. The message had ended and gone on to the next by the time she remembered which drawer she had stored them in. She played the tape back, skipping through three people confirming that their homes were currently occupied by vacationing families before she recognized the woman's bemused voice. Alex had only stretched the truth slightly when she contacted the local landlords, telling them she was a police officer investigating a recent murder and asking whether they had received any unusual inquiries about their properties, perhaps a single male requesting a family-sized home or renting for a period beyond what would be considered normal. Of all the responses she had received, this was the only one that hinted at something out of the ordinary.

The woman answered her phone just as Alex was about to hang up. "Oh yes, I remember you, Officer," she said. "I hope you had a good think about my offer."

"It was very kind of you, ma'am, but I'm afraid, being in the middle of such a serious case—"

"Of course, of course. That was a terrible thing, but I thought you'd charged somebody already." Her voice dropped to a stage whisper. "She was a lesbian, a *British* lesbian. They can have her back, as far as I'm concerned."

Alex closed her eyes and counted to five. She hadn't specified which case she was supposed to be working on, but only one murder had taken place in the area recently and the woman had made the obvious connection.

"The gentleman who rented your property, did you speak to him at all?" she asked, once she was sure she could speak without snapping the woman's head off.

"No, it was all arranged through the e-mail."

"Would it be possible for you to send me copies of the correspondence?"

"Well…" The woman hesitated a moment. "Yes, I don't see why not."

"Thank you. And when you went over with the basket, was there any indication that someone had stayed there? Perhaps something had been moved or used?"

"The key had been moved," the woman answered with certainty. "He left the cottage very clean, but someone had definitely been there. There were towels unfolded and the bed had been slept in."

Alex felt her pulse begin to thud at her temples as she thought of the potential for DNA evidence on the sheets or towels. If she found something to prove that Deakin had been in the area when Lyssa was murdered, it might at least throw enough doubt on the charge against Sarah to get her freed on bail.

"And you're sure no one has rented the property since?"

"No, his lease continues for another week yet," the woman confirmed, before giving Alex the opening she so badly needed. "You can go on up there and have a look around if you think it would help at all. I leave the front door key below the first porch step."

"Thank you very much," Alex said, hardly believing her good fortune. "Could you give me the address? I guess it won't hurt to go there and take a look."

CHAPTER FIFTEEN

S arah settled the phone back into its cradle but stayed where she was in the small privacy booth. She didn't want to have to explain to Camille, who was next in line, exactly why she was smiling, given that her calls to Alex more often ended in her curling up on her bunk and staring out the window.

She had known the instant she heard Alex's voice that something had happened. Despite Alex's obvious eagerness to explain about Emerson, the conversation had been restricted to guarded terms, as they were unsure whether anyone else would be listening in. There was clearly a lot more Alex wanted to say, but Sarah understood enough to know that she had a useful ally now, and that he and Alex were planning to investigate a lead first thing in the morning. While Alex's optimism had been unmistakable, Sarah found herself smiling for a different reason: Alex was no longer working alone, and being able to trust Emerson would make her a hell of a lot safer.

An impatient rap on the booth reminded Sarah that Camille was still waiting.

"I'm really sorry," she said as she stepped out.

Camille's demeanor softened. "If I miss *The Amazing Race,* you're cleaning the toilet tomorrow."

"Okay, deal."

They shook on it and Camille ducked into the booth, leaving Sarah to trudge back to their cell. It had taken her a week to decide that the evenings were the worst part of prison routine. Dinner was always served at four o'clock, as if the structure of the day would crumble were it not punctuated by food at four-hourly intervals. The regular breaks in the monotony seemed to suit the majority of the inmates, but for her the early evening meal signaled the end of any opportunity to go beyond the confines of the building, to step outside into fresh air, to exercise, or simply to feel the sun on her face. The only options after dinner were a six-by-eight cell or a rec room screening an endless stream of reality television shows. She would sit and wish the hours away, and she came to hate the sense of waste, the nagging realization that these were days she would never get back. That things could get even worse, should she be found guilty and transferred to a state prison, was something she tried not to think about.

Not wanting to sit alone until lights out, she collected the copy of *Pride and Prejudice* and took it to the rec room, where for once there seemed to be a consensus as to which show to watch. The room was crowded, with one of the tables occupied by an arts and craft group while a larger group played card games at another. She chose a seat away from the flickering of the television and began to read. Ten minutes later, she turned the page for the first time. It was almost impossible to shut out the canned laughter blaring from the sitcom, the commentary of one of the more enthusiastic watchers, and the simmering, barely contained argument as the outcome of a card game was questioned.

This latter undertone of muted dissent made her glance uneasily across the room. It never took much of a spark to light the touch paper among the inmates, and she recognized a couple of the women in the card group as volatile troublemakers. The commentator in front of the television continued to share her random observations, but those around her were beginning to turn in their seats, shunning the screen for the promise of live entertainment.

Kendall was one of the two guards on duty. She moved forward, obviously hoping to diffuse the tension, but the threat of intervention provoked an immediate escalation, and the first punch had been thrown before she had gotten anywhere close to the table. It left its victim sprawled bleeding and unconscious on the floor. Screams of outrage and yells of encouragement drowned out Kendall's urgent radio request for reinforcements, as the expanding melee gave the various factions on the block an excuse to settle scores.

"Jesus." Sarah scrambled to her feet, her eyes fixed on the insensible woman. Dorea was sweet natured, shy, and barely five feet tall, with the skeletal figure of a chronic drug user, and she lay almost hidden amid the crush of brawling inmates. Sarah was close to the door, and would have had an easy route back to her cell, but instead she ran headlong into the fray.

The first fist to hit her hadn't been aimed at her. It glanced off her shoulder, making her stagger backward, and the woman who had thrown it held up her hands as if to say sorry.

"S'okay," Sarah gasped. There was no point trying to interfere; she stepped aside to allow the woman a clearer range for her next effort.

A clatter of booted feet announced the arrival of more guards as Sarah shook off another clumsy punch and dropped to her knees beside Dorea. Several of the inmates veered away from the fight, creating enough space for her to grab hold of Dorea's shirt and begin pulling her toward the rear of the room. She hadn't taken more than a couple of steps when an unexpected crack of pain across her lower back made her lurch forward.

"Shit." She twisted away, landing unsteadily on one knee and just managing to avoid crushing Dorea.

"Fucking stay down!"

Recognizing the guard's coarse voice, she crouched low, trying to protect herself and Dorea from the baton he was wielding. He was the same man who had tossed her cell earlier. She gritted her teeth as he lashed out at her again, the blow landing higher on her back this time. Beneath her, Dorea's breathing was guttural and labored. Risking more punishment, Sarah applied a jaw thrust to support her airway.

The room was quieter now, an uneasy peace punctuated by moans of pain and an occasional curse or wild burst of laughter. The guard with the baton tried to wrench Sarah to her feet, but Kendall stopped him.

"She wasn't involved, Barrett. Get a fucking hold on Macy instead."

For a second, Sarah caught a glimpse of the loathing in his eyes, but he thought better of ignoring Kendall's instruction and strode away across the room, leaving them alone.

Kendall looked down at Sarah. "Doc's on his way," she said.

"Thanks." Sarah used her sleeve to wipe away the blood streaming from Dorea's nose, before resuming the jaw thrust. She tensed involuntarily as she heard the approach of uneven footsteps, but they belonged only to an elderly inmate wearing one sock and one shoe, who stopped short of Sarah and shook her head.

"You don't want to be doing that," she said, indicating the blood on Sarah's clothing. "Dorea has more letters after her name than my goddamn lawyer."

Another woman—her eye well on the way to swelling shut— hooted with derision at Sarah's bewildered expression. "HIV, Hep B, Hep C." She ticked them off on her fingers as she chanted.

"Right." Sarah didn't move, she just stared at the women until they were disconcerted enough to walk away. Her attention was drawn back to Dorea as she stirred and opened her eyes.

"Hey, stay still for me, okay?" Avoiding a bruise, Sarah touched Dorea's cheek. "The doc's coming to help you."

Dorea managed to roll her eyes at the prospect before the gesture developed a worrying authenticity and she lost consciousness again.

The next shoes to appear in Sarah's line of vision belonged to the doctor and a nurse. She gave the doctor as comprehensive a handover as she could, which prompted him to raise an eyebrow at her.

"You a medic?" he asked as he secured a hard collar around Dorea's neck.

"Not really." Sarah shuffled over, and together they logrolled Dorea onto a long board. "I volunteered as a first responder. I was studying to be an EMT." Unlike the doctor, she used the past tense; all of that seemed like several lifetimes ago.

The doctor's expression subtly altered as he made some sort of connection. It was something she had seen countless people do in the past week, as they remembered why her face was so familiar. She looked away from him, closing her hands around the bottom of the board to help lift it onto a waiting gurney, and discouraging him from asking anything else. Something in her back pulled as she stood, preventing her from straightening fully. The doctor didn't notice, but Kendall, standing close by to prevent any further violence against Dorea, touched Sarah's arm.

"You need to join the line for treatment?"

"No." Supporting her back with both hands, Sarah managed to get herself upright. "No, I'm okay, thanks." She looked around but couldn't see Barrett anywhere; he was probably escorting the instigators to the infirmary or to solitary. All she wanted to do was get back to her cell.

Not for the first time, being locked away from vindictive guards seemed the safest option.

"Get a shower," Kendall said. "Your clothing will have to be incinerated."

"Okay."

"I'll find you a fresh set." Kendall turned to leave but then hesitated, indicating the blood on Sarah's clothing. "Why would you do that? I don't..." She shook her head. "I don't know that I understand you, Hayes."

"I haven't even had a fucking trial yet. You ever think I might be innocent?" Sarah had snapped out the retort before she could think through the consequences.

Kendall took a breath to reply but then shook her head as if unwilling or unable to be drawn in on the subject. "I need to finish up here. Let me know if you change your mind about seeing the doc," she said and walked away, leaving Sarah alone.

Sarah peeled off her shirt and balled it up. There was nowhere she could dispose of it, and the rest of her clothing was equally contaminated. The sweet smell of the blood, reminiscent of that night with Lyssa, turned her stomach. She ached all over, and an unbearable surge of homesickness made her sway enough to need the wall for support. For a minute, she indulged herself in her misery. Then she carefully cleaned her face with the sleeve of her T-shirt, pushed herself from the wall, and made her way to the shower block.

The weather-beaten post marked a long-forgotten track down to Avery Lake. Alex tapped the piece of paper in her hand as Emerson drove past the turn.

"Okay, that's the sign we were supposed to look out for." She reread the directions and then paraphrased for him. "Another quarter-mile or so, there's a bend, and the access road's immediately after that on the right."

Emerson nodded, his eyes fixed straight ahead. Curving away from Avery and little used, the road they were traveling on was in a poor state of repair; on more than one occasion he had had to slow to a crawl to negotiate sections almost reclaimed by the surrounding forest. Despite its feeling of remoteness, they were only an hour from town, and Alex couldn't help but wonder at the gall of Caleb Deakin, if he really had been the one who rented this cottage. That he would do anything so brazen only emphasized how hell-bent he must be on getting his revenge. It also made her dread to think what he might do next.

"Here! Shit, sorry."

Emerson braked and then skidded into the turn, cursing, and she slapped both hands on the dash to stop herself from flying forward. As soon as the car was under control, he looked askance at her.

"Some copilot you are," he muttered, though there was no sting in his tone.

"Hey, it was right where I said it would be." She leaned back in her seat, rubbing at the burn where the seatbelt had caught her shoulder. The access road was narrow and the forest pressed in on the car. It reminded her of the woods around her own cabin, but there was something untamed about it, as if the place wasn't meant to be easily found.

"Hell of a place to hide," she said, nervous excitement making her foot tap against the floor. The cottage was marketed as a retreat: no phone, no Wi-Fi, no neighbors, nothing but acres of wilderness and water.

Emerson didn't answer, but she could see the white of his knuckles on the wheel, and his speed was increasing incrementally as he picked up on her agitation. He stopped the car the instant they caught their first glimpse of the cottage.

"Tire treads." It was the only explanation he needed to give. Although the cottage's owner had driven up here recently, there might still be other treads, which could be compared to those Alex had preserved beneath her pup tent.

Standing by the trunk, they pulled on the CSI coveralls, booties, and gloves that Emerson had "borrowed" from the station. To the casual observer it might have seemed like overkill, but Alex didn't care how ridiculous it appeared. She would do exactly the same at every property on her list, if it might help get Sarah safely back home.

"Set?" Emerson asked.

"Yep." She waited patiently, already soaked with sweat, as he adjusted her hood. Then she led him to the porch. The key was beneath the first step, just as the owner had promised. Alex took two attempts to fit it into the lock, her jittery hands belying her semblance of composure. The kitchen she walked into was immaculate, the fixtures and fittings gleaming in the sunlight that came through the slatted blind.

"You smell that?" She stepped farther into the room, allowing Emerson to shut the door. Without the breeze, the chemical odor was even more apparent.

"Bleach," he said, turning full circle on the spot. The tiles shone beneath his covered boots. "And lots of it."

"They never get everything up, though, do they?" Crouching on the floor, she ran her fingers over the grout between the tiles. "They watch *CSI* and think they know enough to get away with murder, but there's always something they fuck up on."

Emerson went into the next room. "Bed's been slept in," he called. "The bathroom's clean, but you can see which towels have been used. I shook one out into the bath, found more hair than my pop has on his head." He came back to stand in the kitchen doorway, frustration written all over his face. "What exactly are we doing here, Alex? Quinn's not going to authorize forensics on the basis of a hunch about a couple who skipped out on their honeymoon."

"I know that. Don't you think I fucking know that?" She didn't know what she'd expected to find: a smoking gun waiting for her in the first room, with a sign saying "Caleb Deakin was here"?

"Bag the hairs," she told him. She wasn't just going to roll over and concede defeat. "Maybe Castillo can get them through his lab under a dummy case number. We'll top-to-bottom every room, and then..." She looked at Emerson as she faltered, willing him to support her, not to advise her simply to give up and let him take her home.

"Then we check outside." He spoke slowly, as if thinking the logic through. "If Deakin came here after killing Lyssa, there'd be things he'd need to destroy: bloodstained clothing, gear—"

"The knife handle."

"Definitely that. So, bury or burn?"

She followed his gaze out the window. They had driven through at least a mile of forest to get to the cottage. "Jesus, be like looking for a needle in a haystack," she said.

"Yeah." He shrugged and plucked a pack of evidence bags from his bag. "Better get started, then."

❖

Alex took the can of soda Emerson offered her and held the cool metal to her forehead. A fingertip search of the cottage had kept her on her hands and knees on the kitchen floor for the past hour, and had yielded nothing. One thing Emerson hadn't been able to procure in time was the luminol necessary to detect microscopic traces of blood. In any case, it wasn't something they were trained to use, and she suspected the owner of the cottage might take issue with their spraying chemicals all over its interior without a search warrant.

"Here, take a look at this and tell me if I'm going crazy." Alex didn't have the energy to get up; she just leaned over and opened the cabinet beneath the sink.

Emerson came to sit beside her, looking as exhausted as she felt. "You tell me what you think you've found and I'll tell you if I think you're crazy."

"Right." Alex winced. "There are four newspapers missing."

"You're crazy."

"No, no, hear me out. This stack is in date order, one local newspaper per week. The owner must collect her own; she's apparently quite OCD about it. I bet she brings them when she cleans after each rental. This particular rental started two weeks back, but the dates don't add up. There are four missing."

"Alex—"

She cut off his protest, though she knew that what she was suggesting was pretty farfetched. "No sign of a fire in the living room hearth."

He was still shaking his head. "Maybe the owner wasn't done reading the latest issues. If she did bring them, they could've been used for anything: barbecue, protecting gifts to take home…"

"You think Caleb Deakin got the grill out while he was here and then went shopping for souvenirs?"

"*If* he was here."

She took a long drink of soda, in the hope that its caffeine and sugar would mask the aching in her joints. "I think he was here," she said, unable to face the alternative. "I think he was here after he killed Lyssa, and he burned whatever he needed to get rid of."

❖

Common sense told Alex she should stop. She hadn't eaten all day, she hadn't drunk enough to combat the searing heat, and they were beginning to lose the light. Using a compass, starting with the land to the front of the cottage and measuring it in paces, they had worked out a rough grid for each of them to cover. Four hours later, she was only about a third of the way through her patch. Much of the undergrowth was too thick to walk through, snaring her feet and forcing her to retrace her steps, or blocking her route completely. She had found no signs of a recent fire, or any disturbed earth indicative of a burial site; it was doubtful that anyone would have been stupid enough to venture into this terrain, no matter what they needed to hide.

The last time she had fallen, a branch had gouged an ugly rent across the center of her palm, and something in the streak of muck and blood had started to itch. She stopped walking to find and pull out the offending fragment of pine needle. The superficial wound hurt far more than it should have, and she realized just how beaten down she was, her euphoria and hope replaced by an all too familiar despair in just a few hours. Sarah had never voiced any real expectations to her, had never pushed or cajoled or pestered to hear what Alex was doing to help her. Every ounce of pressure was coming from Alex herself, and she could feel herself buckling beneath it.

"Alex!"

Her head shot up.

"Alex!"

Emerson's yell was faint, coming from somewhere ahead of her and off to the left. It was followed shortly afterward by a triumphant whoop.

She set off at a run, hurdling obstacles she had just dragged herself around and somehow managing to stay on her feet. He shouted again when he heard her crashing toward him, warning her to slow down, to give whatever he had found a wide berth. She stumbled to the edge of a clearing, only just preventing her momentum from carrying her any farther.

"I think we might have gotten the little bastard," Emerson said, from where he knelt peering into the remnants of a fire pit. "Whoever started this did a decent job, but they didn't stick around to see it through." He looked up at her. "Remember the rain the night Lyssa died?"

She nodded mutely, staring at the prematurely extinguished fire. She could pick out different elements in it now: khaki-green material, another cloth incongruously patterned with pale blue flowers, and something Emerson was indicating with a long stick.

"Jesus Christ," she whispered, and a rush of relief promptly forced her onto the ground. She cradled her torn hand to her breast, too stunned to feel embarrassed by her reaction. Emerson's stick was pointing at a carved piece of wood. Although it was blackened with soot at one end, the fire barely seemed to have touched it and its shape was unmistakable: it was the snapped-off handle of a Bowie knife.

After waiting over a week for something to happen, and then waiting several more hours for Buchanan to sign off on a search warrant, Alex found things suddenly moving too fast for her. She sat on the trunk of a fallen tree, an uneaten sandwich in her hand, and watched the CSI techs photograph, catalogue, bag, and label evidence from the fire. White light blazed down on them as they worked, the generator for the lamps rumbling in the background. Casts were being taken of the two sets of tire treads directly outside the cottage, and the specialist technician was set to go over to Alex's cabin to cast the ones under the pup tent.

A second team was processing the cottage, trying to find hair, fibers, or other DNA samples to link the debris from the fire with whomever had stayed there. Until this link was proven, it would be simple for Quinn to accuse Alex of planting evidence, even if Emerson acted as a witness to refute such a claim. Quinn hadn't yet dared even to intimate this, but neither was he rushing to get the charges against Sarah dismissed. It was small wonder Alex had no appetite; the one bite she had taken from her sandwich had almost come right back up on her boots.

Quinn, subtly shadowed by Emerson, was supervising up at the cottage. He had arrived in convoy with the CSI techs and, barely even making eye contact with Alex, had demanded she provide a full account of her unauthorized investigation. She had drawn a breath to speak and been cut off by his raised hand and a curt: "Not here, back at the station." Then he had stalked away, forcing her to wait for his summons.

A CSI walked past with bulging evidence bags in her arms. Alex gave up on her sandwich and leaned forward to try to gain a better view. Several items of clothing had already been salvaged from the fire pit, one of which—the flowered material—was the remains of a woman's shirt, and all of which bore stains that a Kastle-Meyer test had identified as blood. For the last hour, ever since a sympathetic tech shared the preliminary findings, Alex had been torturing herself trying to think of a local woman who might have collaborated with Deakin. When Emerson had collected Alex to bring her out here, he had given her the list of names she had asked for. Twelve people had helped to search her and Sarah's land the day after Lyssa had died, and three of them were women. That Alex hadn't even considered the possibility of a female accomplice made her feel like handing in her badge and gun before Quinn got around to demanding them from her.

"So fucking stupid," she muttered, not for the first time, her fingers picking furiously at the bark on which she was sitting. She knew she was overreacting; it wasn't as if she had questioned every man in town, ruling out all the women as suspects, but still she felt like an idiot. Her phone rang, earning a reprieve for the shredded remains of her fingernails. Castillo had promised to call back within the hour for another update.

"Hey," she said.

"Hey, Sherlock." Castillo's droll response was enough to make her smile. "Caleb Deakin's married."

And just like that, everything turned on its head again. She was conscious of her mouth flapping soundlessly. "Why wasn't that mentioned on the bulletin?" she eventually managed to ask.

"Administrative SNAFU by the boys in North Carolina. It's real hot down there this time of year, so they figure they're allowed to let things slide a little. They apologized, if that helps any."

"Not really."

"No, I guess not. I'm looking at a picture of her now. Leah Deakin, twenty-four years old, which puts ten years between them. Needless to say, she's not at home. Been a regular patient at the local ER for the past three years or so. Seems to have gotten real clumsy since she married into the Deakin family."

"Poor kid." Alex's response was instinctive.

"A poor kid who may have been complicit in Lyssa's murder," Castillo reminded her.

"Yeah." She scrubbed at her grimy face. "When are you coming up here to straighten all this crap out?" The Deakins, their Church, and the events in the Cascades were all originally Castillo's case. If a direct connection could be established between Caleb Deakin and Lyssa's murder, no one would be able to prevent Castillo's involvement in the investigation.

"Just waiting on clearance. Bosses are dragging their heels a little. They'd prefer to wait for the forensics to come back, but they're also worried they'll be associated with what looks like a cataclysmic fuckup on the part of the Avery PD, so I don't think they'll leave it that long."

"Gotta love that as a motivating factor." She stood and paced away from the glare of the lights, too tense to sit still any longer. "No mention of finding Lyssa's killer or clearing Sarah, just a bunch of suits trying to avoid being left with egg on their faces."

"You know how this shit works, Alex."

"I hate it." Above her, the sky was paler, hues of blue and lilac bleeding into the edges of the black. She had no idea how long it had been since she last slept. "I fucking hate how this shit works."

"Looking on the bright side, I did get the go-ahead to request that Quinn split the forensics. We're getting a batch of samples couriered down here, and the lab's agreed to put a rush on them."

"Oh, thank fuck for that." She put her hand out, feeling the abrasion on her palm catch against a tree. The pain helped to keep her upright.

"You okay over there?" Castillo had raised his voice, making the concern in it more apparent.

"I'm okay."

"Figured that might reduce the risk of Quinn 'losing' any of the samples."

"That possibility had crossed my mind," she admitted. "And the labs here have been known to take weeks."

"Ours will be four days, max."

"That's great, Mike. Really, I don't...Thank you."

"You're welcome, honey."

She raised her head as the first hint of sunlight caught the tops of the trees. "What do I tell Sarah?"

He answered without hesitation. "Tell her we'll have her home soon."

CHAPTER SIXTEEN

The trailer rocked if its occupants walked from room to room too quickly, and its walls were paper-thin. Sitting as still as she could on the bathroom floor, Leah pressed her ear to the partition and strained to hear the conversation between Caleb and his contact.

She hadn't seen the man arrive. His abrupt knock had sounded on the door as she was trying to scrub out the stains on the shower stall. She had smiled, lowering her head to her hands in thankfulness, but only one man had crossed the threshold, and he had made no attempt to arrest Caleb. Instead, the kitchen door had slammed hard enough to make her cling to the stall, and seconds later, Caleb had yelled something unintelligible. The other man was talking now, his tone a tremulous mixture of placation and tension. She knew what it was like, standing in front of Caleb as he raged, but she felt no sympathy for his victim; she only hoped he would bear the brunt of Caleb's temper so that she wouldn't have to.

The police had found the cottage. That in itself was bad enough, but they had also found the fire she had started and then left unattended. Bloodstained clothing and the knife handle had been pulled from the ashes. She understood little about forensics, but she supposed that if the handle was intact then Caleb's fingerprints would probably be on it. He had worn gloves to stab the woman, but Leah remembered that when he had given her the handle to destroy he had done so with his bare hands. He must have remembered that, too, because he was pacing, the floor reverberating beneath his tread.

"How long before she's out?" he asked.

"If it was up to our labs, two to three weeks, but the feds have gotten involved." The man hesitated as if wary of Caleb's reaction. "I heard Quinn say four days."

"Then what?"

"Then the charges will be dismissed and the feds'll probably take her and Alex into protective custody while they look for you."

A flicker of movement caught Leah's attention, and she leaned her head against the wall to watch a roach scurry into the damp corner behind the sink. She hated this trailer. They had been here for five days, after moving at a moment's notice in the middle of the night. She didn't know exactly where they were, only that they hadn't traveled far enough to have crossed the state line. Like the apartment by the river, the trailer belonged to a relative of Caleb's contact, except that this relative had lived here until she died and she hadn't been house-proud.

"Jesus, Caleb. I don't think I can do that." The raw fear in the man's voice made the flesh on Leah's bare arms ripple with goose bumps. She tucked herself close to the wall again, wondering what she had missed.

"I think you can," Caleb said. His voice was level and reasonable and made Leah want to curl up into a ball.

The man was starting to panic, obviously sensing a trap. "They'll find out; they'll find out and I'll lose my fucking job. God, they'll lock me up as an accessory. I can't go to prison. They'd tear me apart in there."

"You won't go to prison. I won't let that happen. You gotta trust me here."

Leah shook her head, but she already knew the man was lost. Either he helped of his own volition or Caleb would resort to violence or blackmail.

"I trust you," the man said. "I trust you."

Even though she couldn't see Caleb, she could picture his smile, and any remaining hope that he might decide to give up and run was finally snuffed out.

"They'll never see it coming," he told the man. There were two distinct hisses as he opened bottles of beer. Glass clinked against glass, the sound incongruous, as if they were friends sharing a drink at a backyard barbecue. The way Caleb laughed made her shiver.

"Be like taking candy from a baby," he said.

❖

Alex pushed the sheets of paper aside, folded her arms on the table, and laid her head on them. She was so worn out that the interview room spun every time she moved, while the cover sheet she had just completed for her statement contained more corrections of simple spelling errors than useful information. She had seen Quinn utilize this tactic before, most recently with Sarah: if your suspects were disoriented from exhaustion or terror or grief, they were far more likely to make mistakes or confessions during interrogation. Quinn's only problem was that Alex—unlike Sarah—understood exactly how the game was played, and, though her coversheet might be shoddy, the statement itself was not only cogent but airtight. It would also make uncomfortable reading for him and for ADA Kryger, whom Alex had seen lurking at the front desk as she was brought into the station, but she was long past caring about Quinn's sensibilities, and she had never cared about Kryger's.

The familiar sounds of the shift handover faded out as she drifted into a light sleep. She heard a door open and the approach of footsteps, and for a long, surreal moment, she thought she was still dreaming, until she raised her head to see Quinn and Kryger in front of her. In no hurry to assume an air of composure, she smacked her dry lips together and grimaced at the sticky patch of drool on her forearm. Kryger's moue of distaste was well worth the crick Alex could feel at the back of her neck.

"Emerson dotted all his i's and crossed all his t's for you?" Ignoring Kryger, she directed the question at Quinn. They had kept her separate from Emerson throughout the search of the cottage, and then driven them straight to the station for questioning.

"He's already gone home," Quinn said.

The lack of subterfuge and the profound weariness in his voice took Alex aback. She collected the pages of her statement together and held them out to him, studying him obliquely as he stepped closer. He looked haggard, as if the night had aged him twenty years. Despite everything he had done and all the chances he had missed to make amends, she couldn't help but feel a little sorry for him.

He tucked her statement into the bulging case file he had brought with him. "Esther just got off her shift. She offered to drive you home," he said, and held up a hand as Kryger drew a breath to protest. "Alex can come back in when she's gotten some sleep," he told her.

He turned back to Alex, effectively ending Kryger's contribution to the conversation. "Agent Castillo acknowledged receipt of the samples a half-hour ago. They'll be in the lab by now."

With an effort, she kept her expression neutral. "Thank you, sir."

He opened the file again and passed her a plastic evidence bag. "Sergeant Emerson said you would recognize this."

She squinted at it. "Yes, sir, I know what this is." It was the original order docket for Lyssa's gate key, well thumbed and tattered but still legible. She passed it back to him, wondering what point he was trying to make. The answer came when he exchanged the docket for a Polaroid.

"A tech found this key in the pocket of one of the shirts he dug out of the fire."

Dizziness hit her again and she dropped the photograph onto the table. The small gate key stood out prominently in the center of the image, a splash of silver on a jet-black background.

"Do you need one for comparison?" she asked, once she was certain she could speak without embarrassing herself.

"Later," Quinn said. He did not explain his reasons for showing her the photo, but she knew the locked gate had formed the crux of his theory against Sarah. She suspected this was as close to an admission of error as he could make at this stage, something he confirmed when he spoke again.

"Two of the guys we arrested at the warehouse made bail yesterday, freeing up a cell in Ruby. I'm going to request that Sarah be transferred back across here, make things a little easier for you both."

Torn between wanting to thank him and slap him, Alex merely picked up the photograph and handed it back. She dared not look again at Kryger, whose face had been reddening throughout the exchange, and who now appeared to be on the verge of dragging Quinn bodily from the room before he made any more concessions. The ADA rarely found herself on the losing side and was not about to admit defeat prematurely on this case.

Alex didn't have the energy to care. Four days, she thought, four days for the forensics to come back, and in the meantime, Sarah would be closer for her to visit. She stood and straightened her rumpled clothing, determined not to walk through the station looking like a suspect.

"Can I go home now, sir?"

"Can you be back here by four?"

She checked the time. He was giving her nine hours to sleep, feed herself and the animals, and phone Sarah. "Sure," she said.

He nodded, suddenly more his familiar, authoritative self. "Good. Let's not keep Esther waiting any longer, then."

❖

"Exercise is good for back pain."

Sarah mouthed the mantra as she jogged toward the scorched area of grass she used as a lap marker and forced herself to continue past it for the fourth time. Her prison-issue sneakers hit the ground flat and hard, making pain jolt through the twin areas of bruising where Barrett had hit her. The muscles in her back seemed to have seized up overnight. After struggling to get out of her bunk that morning, she had limped down to the shower block, where a rare blast of hot water had alleviated some of the discomfort. She suspected Camille had subsequently had a quiet word with Kendall, because two Advil had been issued to her at breakfast and Kendall had waited, hands on hips, until she gave in and swallowed them.

She could see Kendall now, standing by the ruined grass, watching Sarah steadily close the gap between them. It was too hot and she was too sore to go any faster, but Kendall seemed content to let her finish in her own time.

"You're keeping everyone busy today, Hayes," Kendall said as Sarah stooped low, gasping for air.

"I am?" She straightened cautiously and used the bottom of her T-shirt to dry her face. "Did I do something wrong?"

"Apparently not," Kendall said so quietly that Sarah barely caught the words. She hadn't managed to discern their meaning before Kendall spoke again. "Your lawyer's arranged a meeting with you at three this afternoon, the administrator is dealing with a request to transfer you back across to Ruby, and your partner is on the phone."

Sarah pulled her T-shirt back down. "What the hell is going on?"

The expression on Kendall's face suggested she knew more than she was saying. "Don't look so worried," she said. "Come and take your phone call. I think you're better hearing this from Alex."

❖

By the time Kendall had escorted her into a private air-conditioned office and indicated the phone with its red call waiting light flashing, Sarah was almost in tears. Despite Kendall's reassurance, the abrupt break from jail protocol, together with the unfamiliar surroundings and unexpected disruption, had convinced her that something terrible had occurred, and that Kendall was doing her utmost to soften the blow. Sarah snatched up the receiver, spoke before Kendall had pressed the button to connect the call, and had to start over again.

"Hello? Alex?"

"Hey, it's me."

Sarah sat down suddenly, tipping the chair back so hard that Kendall had to put a hand out to right it. "Bloody hell, are you okay?"

"I'm fine. Did they not tell you that?"

"They haven't told me much of anything, just that Bridie's coming in and that I might be transferred and that you were on the phone and—"

"Sarah," Alex cut across her rambling, "take a breath."

"I'm breathing just fine." She gripped the edge of the desk. "Actually, I feel a bit squiffy," she conceded, and heard Alex chuckle.

"You're sitting down, right?"

"Do I need to be sitting down for this?" she asked, scared once again.

"Might not be a bad idea." Alex hesitated, obviously nervous, before continuing in a rush. "Emerson and I found where Caleb Deakin stayed. Sarah, I think we have enough to get you out of there."

Sarah closed her eyes as lights danced in them. "What did you find?"

"Clothing from that night and the knife handle that they hadn't quite managed to burn. Comparable tire treads, hair, semen on the bed sheets, and prints throughout the cottage. The labs are working on it all now, and Quinn's going to get you moved back up here in the meantime."

"Will I get bail, then?"

"You won't need bail." Alex spoke more slowly, ensuring that Sarah understood. "Once the lab work is back, it should be enough to make them drop the charge against you."

"Really?"

"Cross my heart." There was such certainty in Alex's answer that Sarah finally allowed herself to believe what had happened.

"I'll be able to come home." She said it aloud, just to make absolutely sure.

"You'll be able to come home," Alex said. "Sweetheart, I've already put the kettle on for you."

It was stuffy in the bedroom, but Alex pulled the blankets up to her chin and shivered until the sheets warmed up. She felt as if she'd worked a winter night shift: chilled to the bone and trying too hard to wind down into sleep. The cottage was silent, the animals all taking her lead and dozing with her on various parts of the bed. She had drawn thick drapes against the sunlight and foregone coffee for hours, and still her brain refused to let her rest.

Quinn would have read her statement by now. She wondered whether he had been shocked by her allegation that a local was aiding Caleb Deakin, or whether he had already drawn that conclusion himself. His demeanor earlier had been that of a man facing up to a potentially career-ending mistake, not that of one complicit in the crime. So if Quinn wasn't involved, who was?

She kicked the blankets lower, making Tilly snuffle, which in turn startled Flossie. They both settled again before she did. Staring at the ceiling, she tried to picture each of the individuals on Emerson's list of search volunteers, mentally cataloging them into "possible," "maybe," "unlikely," and "don't be stupid." She would need to speak to Quinn about bringing each of them in for questioning...

An unexpected yawn interrupted her thoughts and made her jaw ache. She rubbed her chin and turned over, seeking a cool spot on the pillow. *Castillo* would need to speak to Quinn, she corrected herself. In terms of the investigation, her involvement was probably over. After Sarah's release, the FBI would no doubt assume control of the case. They would have the resources and manpower necessary to end this, and she and Sarah could hide somewhere safe until Deakin and his accomplice were in custody.

She closed her eyes, her head sinking into the soft down of the pillow. Her hands curled into fists, her fingernails nipping at the flesh of her palm, because she was missing something obvious and she needed to wake up and work the answer out. One of the cats curled up in the crook of her legs. She reached a hand out to stroke its head, and the satisfied hum of purring was the last thing she knew.

❖

Caleb's cell rang as Leah lifted the cornbread from the oven. She pressed a finger to the top of the bread, testing its readiness, careful not to show that she was listening in on the call. Caleb didn't bother leaving the kitchen, so she was able to watch his expression alter by degrees: irritation changing to interest, before segueing into a barely-contained excitement.

"Fucking perfect. No, if you're sure that'll work, use it." He walked to the window and peered out onto the dirt road and mounds of putrid trash. "You'll need to do it quick before anyone realizes it's missing."

Leah turned the bread out onto a cooling rack. It smelled like Sunday afternoons at home, stolen time with her mom while the men watched the game.

"Yeah, yeah, I know it." Caleb's voice broke through her reverie. He paced across the kitchen, his eagerness making the trailer sway and undulate. "Be dark by then. That won't hurt none."

She looked at the clock on the oven, calculating the remaining hours of daylight: only five. The rising steam made her face damp and hot as she wiped the counter and tried to glean more details of Caleb's plan. He had already used his free hand to hoist his duffel bag onto the table and was checking its contents, making the odd noise of agreement as he listened to his contact. The one-sided conversation made it impossible for her to work out what was going to happen, but it was obviously imminent.

"Naw, man, you won't need luck." Weapons clacked together as he stacked them side by side. "Let me know when it's done." He ended the call, slapped a magazine into a 9 mm pistol, and screwed a silencer onto its muzzle.

"Pack everything." He grinned at her. "We got places to go, baby."

❖

"You'll miss the Kool-Aid." Camille spoke through a mouthful of candy.

Sarah threw a Milk Dud at her head. "I won't miss the bloody Kool-Aid," she said. The drink accompanied every meal at the jail and it was always grape flavor. It tasted like disinfectant combined with evil. "If I never drink the stuff again, it'll be too soon."

She hadn't told a soul about the developments in her case or her likely transfer, but the cellblock rumor mill was alive with gossip, and Camille had found out all the details. She had bought Sarah the box of Milk Duds to celebrate and was now busily eating her way through them.

"Be home with your girl before you know it." Camille's voice was muffled by caramel, but the thought made Sarah smile.

"Thanks, Camille. I won't miss the Kool-Aid, but I'll miss you."

"You be sure and write me, then."

"I will, I promise." Sarah shook the candy box, heard the lone rattle of the last Milk Dud, and offered it to Camille. "You'll probably be stuck with me for a few days yet, anyway."

"Maybe, or they'll maybe get you back across to Ruby in time for visiting tomorrow."

"That'd be nice." A flutter outside the window caught her eye as a scruffy-looking bird perched on the ledge and began to preen. "Hey, Albert's back." She ducked her head to the bunk below. "I think he lost a few more feathers, poor little bugger." She made space for Camille to climb alongside her.

The bird cocked its head when Camille touched the glass, but it stayed where it was.

"I'll keep you updated on his progress," Camille said. She pressed her hands to the mattress as if evaluating what little spring it possessed. "I might move up here when you're gone. Even that view's better than my solid brick wall."

Sarah pointed to the far corner of the yard where a hint of pink was just beginning to color the concrete. "Best view on the block, this," she said seriously. "Look, it even comes with its own sunset."

CHAPTER SEVENTEEN

Showing uncharacteristic chivalry, Caleb offered his hand to Leah to help her negotiate the rusted metal steps leading down from the trailer. As she stepped onto the ground, he tipped his cap at her.

"How do I look?"

He had left the car engine running and the headlights cast enough light for her to see him wink. "You look good," she said, and touched her fingers to his cheek when he kissed her.

In truth, she barely recognized him. His hair was long and straggly beneath his cap and he hadn't shaved since the murder. She hated it, not because it made him unattractive—he had never been particularly handsome—but because the change in his appearance meant he was less likely to be identified and apprehended. He revved the engine, prompting her to take her seat in the car. She wanted to ask where they were heading and what he was going to do, but she didn't dare risk ruining his good mood. Even more than that, she was afraid to learn the answer.

From dinner until lights-out, the cell doors were unlocked, leaving the inmates free to move around the block, but Sarah and Camille had both chosen to remain on their bunks.

"Wonder if they'll have a copy of this in the Ruby jail." Sarah waggled *Pride and Prejudice* over the side of the bed so that Camille could see it. She heard her shift and then tap the cover with her finger.

"Honey, you'll be able to go into a store and buy your own copy, once you're a free woman."

"Yeah." Sarah hugged the book to her chest, relishing the thought. She had taken so many basic rights for granted until they were stripped away from her. "That would be lovely."

Her mattress bounced as Camille poked it with her foot.

"Let me know if there's a happy ending, 'kay?"

"Be nice if the girl got a girl for a change," Sarah said, "but I think Mr. Darcy would be quite bitter about that."

Camille laughed and the mattress jumped again. Neither of them reacted to the door opening, but Sarah pushed herself up quickly as Barrett stepped into the cell.

"You're to come with me, Hayes," he said. She didn't move, didn't immediately obey him, so he walked over to the bunk and took hold of her arm. "Now." He pulled at her, emphasizing the command, and she shook herself away so that she could climb down from the bed. She didn't want to go anywhere with him, but it wasn't as if she had any say in the matter.

"Where you takin' her?" Camille demanded.

"None of your fucking business." His fingers twisted around Sarah's bicep with bruising force.

"You want me to find Kendall?" Camille asked her.

"No." Whatever the hell was going on, she didn't want Camille involved. "No, I'll be all right." Barrett propelled her into the corridor, and she only kept her balance by grabbing at one of the other cell doors. "Jesus!"

No one tried to stop him as he marched her down the block. Three inmates and another guard all looked the other way or moved aside to allow them to pass. He took her through a security checkpoint into a wing that she didn't recognize and that appeared deserted. As they tripped a sensor, the overhead lights flicked on but then faded out just as efficiently to leave the corridor behind them dim and shadowed. There were no signs of occupancy in any of the adjoining offices. All their doors were shut, and the end of the corridor was invisible in the gloom. She might be able to run, but where to? She looked up, searching for the cameras that tracked and monitored every corner of the jail. They were there, blinking as they detected motion, but still she knew Barrett could do whatever he wanted to her before anyone could intervene. If he was loyal to Deakin's cause, he was unlikely to be deterred by the consequences.

She stopped suddenly and jerked her arm from his grip. "Where are we going?" she asked, hating the way her voice shook.

For the briefest of moments, she thought he was going to answer, but he barely managed a snarl of anger before both his hands were back on her, spinning her around and shoving her against the wall. Without easing up, he shifted one forearm to press across her throat.

"Ask me again," he said. "Ask me again, I fucking dare you."

She shook her head and he moved his arm a fraction, allowing her to answer.

"No," she gasped.

"No, what?" He inched his body nearer still, lifting his knee to nudge her thigh as his harsh breath grazed her cheek.

Closing her eyes, she lowered her head in apparent deference and then did the only thing she could think of: she kneed him hard in the groin, feeling the crunch of ligaments and softer tissue smashing back against his pelvic bone. He released her instantly, staggering backward and holding himself between the legs.

"No, you fucking arsehole, I won't ask you again," she muttered, too breathless to make herself heard above his shrieking as she ran back the way he had brought her. She knew there would be hell to pay for what she had just done, no matter how satisfying it had been. She had gotten barely twenty yards away when a buzzer sounded at the end of the corridor. A door flew open and Kendall sprinted toward her.

"Hayes, you okay?" She turned Sarah roughly into the light. Then, having reassured herself that her prisoner was relatively unscathed, she went over to Barrett and pulled him upright. "You think the cameras wouldn't catch that, you piece of shit?"

He seemed on the verge of hitting her, his face flushed with pain and fury, but he backed down when two more guards came through the door.

"Three strikes and you're out," Kendall told him. "And I'm guessing that's gonna count as your third."

Standing well beyond his reach, Sarah rubbed her bruised throat and tried to make sense of the exchange. The guards frog-marched Barrett away, leaving her alone with Kendall.

"You sure you're okay?" Kendall asked.

"Yes." Sarah was too shaken to hide her impatience. "What the hell is going on?"

"Your transfer has been authorized." Kendall gestured for Sarah to walk with her. "Barrett was supposed to bring you over to collect your possessions and prepare you for shipping out."

"But he took a detour."

"Yeah, you could say that." She sighed, evidently uncertain how much she could divulge. "Look, this is confidential, but seeing as you're leaving us anyway and he targeted you, I guess you have a right to know. He has a couple of ongoing charges for brutality and two unproven claims of sexual assault against him. We've been keeping a close eye on him since he picked up duties on this wing."

Sarah wasn't sure exactly what her face did in response to that disclosure, but it made Kendall stop walking and ask her again if she was okay.

"I'm fine, and I think I owe you a thank-you," she said. Barrett might have had no connection to Deakin, but he had brought her down that corridor for a reason. She didn't want to consider what might have happened had Kendall not been alerted.

"Let's just get you ready to go." Kendall seemed uncomfortable accepting gratitude, but she smiled and unlocked a connecting door. "This is where he should've taken you."

The area they passed into was well lit, with plenty of inmates hanging around, chatting, or wandering between cells. At the end of the block, Kendall entered a small storeroom and came out holding a bright orange jumpsuit.

"Get changed into this. Then we'll collect your gear, and you and I get to take a ride to Ruby."

Sarah followed her to the washroom. "You driving?" she asked.

"No, not sure who is. I'll be spending the entire trip handcuffed to you."

"Oh, aren't you the lucky one?" Despite that prospect, and her close call with Barrett, Sarah was delighted that something was finally happening. She accepted the garish jumpsuit without complaint and took it into the nearest cubicle.

❖

Nothing much had changed at the station in the weeks Alex had been on sick leave; the coffee certainly hadn't improved. She set her mug down on the desk and pulled the case file toward her. Quinn had gone to find sandwiches, leaving her alone in the interview room and providing her with too good an opportunity to pass up. The file was thick but well organized, broken down chronologically and by department: forensics, statements and interviews, autopsy reports, scene photography. Caleb Deakin had a section all to himself, but it was wafer-thin compared to the one marked *Sarah Hayes*.

Alex took Emerson's list from her back pocket and placed it beside the file. Twelve names. She had been working on them through the afternoon, whittling them down using the tried and trusted methodology of Motive, Means, and Opportunity. Which of them was best placed to assist Caleb Deakin? Which of them had something to gain? She couldn't ascribe motive to anyone, and only four had had both the means and opportunity. Those names were now highlighted with red pen and arrows and each of them was an experienced police officer.

"Damn it," she muttered.

Not wanting to antagonize Quinn, she pushed the list back into her pocket before he could return. She went to flick through the file again, but her hand stilled at one of the initial statements. The handwriting was a familiar, lazy scrawl, intermittently illegible despite the number of warnings that had been issued about it. It was the account of the first officer on scene, the first to find Lyssa's body and to raise suspicions about Sarah's injuries. His account was methodical, if somewhat unsophisticated, and it had been enough to earn him a promotion from the reserves.

A small, gnawing sense of unease began to grow stronger as Alex compared the scene time given in the report to the time of the 911 call log. A nine-minute response wasn't unheard of, but with so few officers on patrol, it was highly unusual, especially for a call from a cabin twenty minutes out of town at the end of a tortuous dirt track. Unless…

"Shit."

She was at the door within seconds. She yanked it open and jogged across the empty office to the dispatch desk, where she crouched low so that no one would see her in passing.

"Esther, I need a really big favor."

"I'm allergic to cats, honey."

"What?" Alex shook her head in sudden comprehension. "Oh, no, not more pet-sitting. No, I need to know what Larry Tobin's patrol route was on the night of Lyssa's death."

"Officer Tobin?" Esther frowned, obviously perturbed.

"Yes. He was first on scene. It's really important, Esther. Please."

She heard footsteps and turned to see Quinn opening the door of the interview room. Esther watched too, waiting until he had entered the room before she typed a rapid sequence into her computer.

"East River. There'd been a spate of minor thefts on Coppice Hill, so we'd doubled patrols there." The frown lines creasing Esther's face deepened as she noticed the discrepancy. "Hmm, that's odd."

"Yeah," Alex said. "I thought so too."

She closed her eyes and focused on working through her half-formed suspicion. East River was the opposite side of town, which should have tripled Tobin's response time. Reaching the scene in nine minutes would have been impossible for him, unless he had already known about the murder and—assuming that Lyssa's body would lie undiscovered for hours—had been en route to cover Deakin's tracks for him when Sarah phoned 911.

Alex pushed back onto her feet, using the desk for leverage. As she did so, Quinn came out of the interview room, but he barely even glanced at her as he strode to his office.

"Is Tobin on duty tonight?" she asked Esther.

"Yes. He was on the afternoon shift, but he volunteered to pull a double, so he's staying through the twilight."

"Running solo or partnered?"

Esther checked the roster. "Solo. Quinn's trying to partner him up, but no one's interested."

"I need to speak to Quinn about bringing him in." She wasn't looking forward to that conversation at all. Throughout the first three hours of her interview, Quinn had been reluctant to accept the concept of a local accomplice; she didn't like to think how he would react to the news that one of his officers might be the culprit.

"You really think Officer Tobin is involved?" Esther sounded troubled, as if she had drawn the same conclusion but hoped Alex might talk her out of it.

"Yes, I think so." It felt good to say it aloud, the disparate pieces finally making a cohesive whole. "Will you let me know if he gets on the radio?"

Esther nodded. "Are you going to tell Chief Quinn?"

"I have to." Through the frosted glass of his office window, Alex could see him talking on the phone, which at least gave her time to rehearse what she needed to say. "Wish me luck."

Esther rearranged her headset as a red button began to flash on her display. "Good luck," she whispered. She hit the button and spoke into the headset with well-practiced authority. "Nine one one. What is your emergency?"

❖

As Kendall approached with a set of cuffs, Sarah set down the plastic bag containing her own clothing and offered her wrists. The metal bracelets clicked into place one notch at a time.

"They okay?" Kendall asked, fitting a third cuff around her own wrist to leave herself linked to Sarah by a short length of chain.

"Yep, they're fine." Sarah stooped to collect her bag. "Bit last-minute this, isn't it?" she said, once she'd managed to coordinate walking in step with Kendall.

Kendall shrugged. "I guess someone decided that getting you transferred ought to happen sooner rather than later. Chief Quinn sent an officer across with the finalized paperwork, and the administrator here isn't going to argue about it, not when it means one less out-of-area prisoner he has to accommodate and feed."

"Never really thought of it like that."

"I'm sure you've had other things on your mind," Kendall said, with a hint of contrition in her voice. "Let's just get you one step closer, huh?"

One step closer to what, she chose not to specify, but she returned Sarah's smile as she swiped a card down a keypad. They entered a large loading bay with automated shuttered doors at either end to facilitate a strict one-way system. An Avery PD patrol unit was the only vehicle parked. Its driver got out as they approached.

"Hey, Sarah." The officer nodded at her. "Ready to go?"

"Yep," she said. She recognized him but was struggling to remember his name.

He went to open the car door and then hesitated, seeming to realize belatedly why Kendall was there. "I'm sure I can get her over to Ruby without any problems," he said. He pointed to the restraints. "Is an armed guard really necessary?"

"It's procedure, especially as you're in a regular patrol car with no prisoner cage," Kendall said, not bothering to hide her annoyance that he had even raised the issue.

"Right." His Adam's apple bobbed as he swallowed. "Right, okay." He ushered them into the rear seat and then sat tapping his fingers on the wheel, watching the shutters rise and craning his neck to spot the exit light flicking to green. The instant it did so, he accelerated away, the wheels skidding on the diesel-slick asphalt, the jolt flinging his passengers sideways in their seat.

"Bloody male drivers," Sarah muttered, sitting up again. She remembered the officer's name now; she was surprised it had taken her so long, when he had been the first to help her on the night Lyssa died. It was Tobin, Officer Larry Tobin.

The coffee tasted burned and bitter, but it was the only liquid Alex had to remedy the dryness of her mouth. Quinn had finally ended his phone call, and although she still had no real idea how to broach the subject, she knew she had to tell him about Tobin. He opened his office door just as she was about to knock on it and seemed startled to find her standing there.

"Damn, Alex. Sorry, I…" His eyes flicked to his watch. "I got caught up in something there and lost track a little. You want me to head out and grab us both a burger, then we can finish up?"

"No." The harshness of her tone made them both flinch. She tried again. "No, sir, I need to speak to you about something else."

He regarded her warily. "What?"

"Officer Tobin, sir."

"Officer Tobin?" He almost did a double take. "What about him?"

There was no easy way to tell him, and she had never been fond of procrastination. "I think he's the one helping Caleb Deakin," she said, watching Quinn's expression. He didn't protest, so she took it as permission to continue, explaining about the discrepancies in the response times and about her theory that Tobin had been the one to cover Deakin's tracks. The delay in speaking to Quinn had given her the opportunity to think everything through, and she was certain now that she had identified the right man.

"Tobin is perfectly placed to access inside information." She started to pace as she spoke. "If Deakin knew from the start that he wasn't being considered seriously as a suspect, it would have given him the confidence to stay in the area. He's been able to wait, knowing that whatever happens, Tobin will be able to give him a heads-up in advance." She stopped pacing as she noticed all the color draining from Quinn's face.

"Shit," he muttered. He pushed past her and strode over to Esther's desk. "Get Tobin on the radio now," he told her. "Call him up as a routine voice check. Tell him we're having problems with the transmissions again."

"Yes, sir."

Alex stared at Quinn; he wasn't putting up a fight, wasn't defending his officer. What the fuck was going on?

"I checked my desk, and I checked the file in case someone had put it in there, but I couldn't find it," he said, more to himself than to Alex. He swiped at the sweat on his forehead.

"Couldn't find what?" Alex had to force herself to ask the question.

He remained silent as Esther put out the first call.

"Couldn't find what?" Alex fought the urge to grasp him by the shoulders and shake a response out of him.

"Buchanan authorized my request for Sarah's transfer," he said. "It came through late this afternoon, so I was going to wait till morning to send someone over for her. I was sure I'd left the paperwork on my desk, but it's...I had to call Buchanan up just now to ask for another copy of it."

"Oh, Jesus fucking Christ." Alex looked at Quinn and then at Esther, willing them to tell her that she was wrong, that Tobin had been contacted and was obediently making his way back to the station.

"He's not answering," Esther said, her timing inadvertently cruel.

Quinn pushed her aside and repeated the hail, ordering Tobin to respond. Alex shook her head as static whistled back through the speaker.

"Call the jail," she said, but no one seemed to be listening to her. Quinn hit the mike again, and she tore the handset away from him and slammed it onto the desk. "He's not there. He's going for Sarah!" She was shouting now, panic overwhelming her. "Call the fucking jail!"

Feedback from the abandoned mike screeched as Esther keyed in a phone number. She hit a button, cutting off the radio connection, her fingers working automatically even as she started to hyperventilate. "Sir?" She handed her headset to Quinn. "You're through to the Prescott administrator."

He spoke into the set with remarkable calm, but his posture gave everything away.

"When?" Alex choked the word out, feeling as if her world were tumbling down around her.

"Within the last half hour," he said. "He can't have gotten far. There's an APB going out countywide."

"He's taking her to Deakin."

"I don't..."

Realizing that Quinn was floundering, Alex ignored him and spoke to Esther. "You have Agent Castillo's number?"

Esther nodded, already scrolling through a directory. Alex declined the headset and picked up the phone instead. Castillo answered the call with his usual haste.

"Chief Quinn?" Castillo evidently utilized caller ID.

"Mike, it's me."

"Alex? You okay?"

"They've taken Sarah." She was sobbing now, her chest heaving as she tried to draw enough breath to speak. "Please, you have to help her."

She heard him swear, then something crash to the floor as he banged into it. "I'm on my way to get clearance," he told her. "Stop crying. Start from the beginning."

Chapter Eighteen

Sarah was staring out the car window, watching dark, rolling fields and the occasional brightly lit house go by, when Kendall flicked off her seatbelt and leaned forward.

"Hey," she said to Tobin, raising her voice above the engine noise and the rumbling of tires on pockmarked asphalt. "Hey, you missed the turn for the freeway."

Tobin nodded, his eyes fixed directly ahead. A van passed them at high speed and Sarah noticed the pallor of his face in the flare of its headlights.

"Yeah, yeah." He nodded again. "There was a pileup eastbound when I drove up here; lanes closed, rubberneckers. It was a mess." He seemed to relax the more he spoke. "That's what made me so late. Thought it might be quicker to come this way."

Kendall settled back, evidently satisfied. "Take a left onto Union in a couple of miles or so. If you keep going down here, all you'll find is dust and dirt."

"Yes, ma'am." He used the rearview mirror to watch Kendall fasten her seatbelt before returning his attention to the road.

From her position, Sarah could see the odometer ticking over the distance as he drove. Though presumably unfamiliar with the route Kendall had suggested, he made no attempt to slow or look for the turn; if anything, he was accelerating. Outside, all she could see now was blackness. Unease began to creep into the pit of her stomach. She closed her eyes, unable to shut out the rapid thump of her heart or stop the cold prickle of goose bumps. She told herself that she was being paranoid, that Kendall was armed and that Tobin was a naïve young officer whom Alex had often castigated for making simple mistakes. Feeling somewhat better, she opened her eyes again just as he reached forward surreptitiously to switch off his radio and sped past Kendall's turn. Kendall didn't seem to notice the radio falling into silence, but she saw him disregard her directions and drew breath to protest.

"Don't," Sarah whispered, grabbing hold of Kendall's arm and squeezing it hard enough to force her attention away from Tobin. "Don't say anything."

Kendall shook herself loose from Sarah's grip, but at least she did so in silence, as if waiting for Sarah's explanation. Tobin gave no sign of having heard the altercation, the unlit road demanding his full attention.

Sarah put her mouth close to Kendall's ear. "We have to get out of here," she said.

Kendall stared in confusion. It was clear she had no idea why Sarah was making such a ridiculous suggestion. They were both rocked back in their seats as Tobin failed to slow sufficiently for a hairpin bend, and the car skidded on loose stones as he overcorrected. The roar of the rear tires as they spun gave Sarah enough cover to speak.

"He's not taking me to Ruby." If she was wrong about that, she would gladly suffer the consequences. God, she hoped she was wrong about it. "Use your gun. Make him stop the car."

Kendall shook her head, denial and refusal combined in that one gesture, but she glanced out the window and there was conflict in her eyes when she looked back. "I don't…"

"*Please.*"

Tobin had accelerated again, hitting a straight section at sixty and pushing up well beyond the speed limit. If she had still harbored any doubts, Kendall could have asked him to slow down, could have demanded that he stop and explain his actions. Instead, she undid her seatbelt and used her thumb to disengage the snap mechanism on her holster. She drew her pistol slowly, and then raised her arm to aim the weapon at Tobin.

The same instant, he slammed on the brakes and sent her flying headfirst into the back of his seat. She fell back limp, blood pouring from a split in her forehead, her gun lost somewhere in the footwell. Sarah moved to shield her as the car came to a complete stop. Tobin got out and flung open Sarah's door, his gun already in his hand.

"You stupid bitches." He glared down at them. "You think I wouldn't hear any of that?"

He had been waiting, Sarah realized, biding his time until Kendall made herself vulnerable by removing her seatbelt.

"Did Alex tell you I was a fucking moron, huh?" He lifted Sarah's chin with the muzzle of his gun, forcing her to meet his eyes. "Did she?"

"No."

"You're a fucking liar," he said, nothing remaining of his small-town good ol' boy persona as he dug the gun in hard enough to make her wince.

"Please." She swallowed, feeling her throat work against the metal. "Please let Kendall go. You don't need her."

"Got it all worked out, have you?" he asked, a casual lilt to his tone. "You know who I got waiting for you, then?"

"Yes."

He hooted with laughter, the motion of his hand making the gun bob up and down. "Yeah, I'd be fucking scared too. So, what d'ya think I should do with your friend here? Kill her or let Deakin deal with her?"

Behind Sarah, Kendall stirred as if in response to this casual discussion of her fate.

"Leave her here," Sarah said, trying to keep the rising panic from her voice. She didn't think Tobin would kill Kendall, but Deakin almost certainly would. "He doesn't need to know she was ever with us. Just leave her here and let someone find her. Please, Tobin." She saw the subtle shift in his expression as she begged; he had probably never wielded so much power as he did right then. "Please, she's got no part in this."

He nodded once and stepped back. "Get her out of there."

Still uncertain what he had decided, Sarah coaxed Kendall from the car. Kendall dropped to her knees, half-dazed, with blood running freely into her eyes, the handcuffs forcing Sarah down beside her.

"I'm sorry," she whispered, as Sarah tried to prop her up.

"Shh, easy. You're going to be fine," Sarah said, but her voice faltered on the promise and she took hold of Kendall's hand instead. Tobin came to stand in front of them and touched his gun to Kendall's forehead. The tremor that ran through her was so hard that Sarah felt it, while an acrid smell told her that Kendall had lost control of her bladder.

Tobin waited for a few seconds longer before tapping Kendall's forehead with the gun. "Get out the keys to the cuffs."

Kendall stared at him blankly for a moment, his demand taking time to register, then fumbled in her pocket and drew out a set of keys.

"Unlock both sets."

Kendall's movements were uncoordinated, but the cuffs finally fell away. She knelt motionless, waiting for instruction.

"Cuff Sarah's hands behind her. No tricks, do it good and tight, and hurry it up. I'm on a fucking schedule here."

She darted a glance at Sarah, as if seeking her permission. Sarah nodded, turning with her hands held ready. Having recovered her nerve somewhat, Kendall managed to refasten the cuffs without further problems. Tobin used one hand to check her efforts and nodded his approval.

"You." He pointed the gun at Sarah. "Move a muscle and I'll shoot her, okay?"

"Okay," Sarah said. At that point, she would probably have agreed to anything if it meant keeping Kendall alive. Kneeling on the sharp stones, her fingers already growing numb, she watched Tobin drag Kendall across to a tree not far from the road, where he threw her down, circled her arms around the trunk, and bound her wrists with his own set of cuffs. Leaving her clumsily attempting to sit up, he jogged back to Sarah.

"Someone might spot her if she's lucky," he said. His shrug told her he didn't give a damn either way.

Sarah lowered her head. "Thank you." She struggled for her footing as he pulled her up.

"Don't be thanking me," he told her. He marched her back to the car and shoved her into the front seat. "You just behave yourself, or I'll come back this way, and if the coyotes haven't gotten to her I'll finish her off myself."

He secured Sarah's seatbelt and reholstered his gun. As he maneuvered the car back onto the road, the brake lights briefly illuminated the white of Kendall's shirt before cutting out to leave her indistinguishable. The road stretched ahead, a pitch-black expanse unbroken by any oncoming traffic. Sarah tried not to think how long it might be before someone found Kendall, or what Alex would do when she worked out what had happened. She turned her face away from

Tobin, determined not to let him see how frightened she was. *At least let this be an end to it.* It was the only consolation left to her. *End it with me and keep Alex safe.*

❖

"Were you there when he killed Lyssa?" Sarah's quiet question broke a silence that had lasted for the thirty miles since Tobin abandoned Kendall. In all that time, they had passed no other vehicles and the only sign of civilization had been a single light flickering on a closed gas station. She knew they were getting closer to their destination; Tobin was sweating profusely and a nervous tic made him check the clock on the dash every few seconds. She wasn't trying to antagonize him or bond with him; she just wanted to understand how all this had happened.

"I didn't kill her," he said, as if that made his participation in Deakin's retribution honorable.

"No." Thirty miles had given her a lot of time to think. "No, but you were already helping Deakin by then, and that night you were on your way to our cabin to cover his tracks for him."

Tobin slapped his hands on the steering wheel, a mock round of applause. "Clever girl."

"Not clever enough to work out why you'd do this."

"Duty called and I answered." He puffed out his chest as he spoke and sat up taller in his seat. His gullibility made her want to shake him.

"What did he promise you? Money? A high-profile role in his organization? Half a dozen virgins?"

He scoffed as if the suggestions were preposterous, but she suspected she had hit a nerve. She decided that now that she had gotten Kendall out of harm's way, she would rather take her chances with Tobin than let him hand her over to Deakin, so she pushed a little harder.

"He's going to kill me," she said. "You know that, don't you?"

"He hasn't told me what he's going to do."

She kicked her feet against the floor of the car, frustration overcoming her self-control. "So what? Ignorance is bliss and that makes everything all right? When they catch you, they won't just charge you with kidnapping; they'll charge you as an accessory to murder."

"They won't catch me," Tobin said with the blind certainty of a zealot. "He's going to get me out of the country."

"I think he's going to be slightly too preoccupied with me to waste time smuggling you across the border."

That gave him pause; he looked almost hurt by the notion. "He made me a promise."

Sarah took a breath and went for broke. "Then you really are as fucking stupid as Alex always said."

She had hoped he would lose control, perhaps stop the car and drag her out, giving her an opportunity to fight or run, but he merely gripped the back of her neck and slammed her forward into the dash. The blow made white noise scream in her ears, and it was only dimly that she heard herself groan and Tobin spit out a curse. Something warm and thick trickled down her face, running into her mouth and making her gag. She felt Tobin righting her again, but she couldn't hold herself steady and she sagged against the window. Blood splattered onto the glass when she coughed. Too weary to resist anymore, and all out of chances, she mouthed a heartfelt apology to Alex and let her eyes close.

Sarah wasn't sure what had forced her awake: the change in the car's speed or the knocking of her head against its window as it rattled down a bumpy track. One minute she had been dreaming of home, and the next she was trying to breathe through a nose clogged with blood without letting Tobin know that she was conscious. She kept her eyes shut, listening to him humming tunelessly as he brought the car to a stop. Seconds later, he got out, and she took the chance to peek through the window.

"Oh God," she whispered.

He had left the road and parked in a small picnic area with nothing but forest surrounding it. She could see the lights of another vehicle with a man perched on its hood; as she watched, he strode across to meet Tobin halfway. They shook hands and turned back toward her. In desperation, she considered trying to open her door, but before she could move, it was thrown open and the man crouched down to fill the gap.

Caleb Deakin looked so much like his father that she began to tremble. Tilting his head to one side, he trained a flashlight across her body as if appraising goods he had ordered. She shied away from the glare, her legs uselessly scrabbling to propel her out of his reach, but it was only when he tried to take hold of her that she broke through her panic. She bit at his hand and then kicked out with both feet, catching him hard in the chest and knocking him aside.

Cursing, he grabbed at the door to break his fall, but she had already scrambled past him and out onto the parking lot. As Tobin began to shout, she sprinted for the cover of the trees, her lungs burning, her legs unsteady and already threatening to fail her. Someone gave chase, closing in fast, but then the pounding footsteps stopped, and for a fleeting, surreal moment, she thought he had given up on her. Then dirt and rocks spat up by her feet and she bucked sideways, recognizing the cause as gunfire but not having heard the shots. A second salvo of muted pops followed, and she felt shards of debris slice through the thin cotton of her pants, stinging her legs. She pushed harder, reaching a path of loose stones and grass, the trees less than ten yards ahead of her now. A car engine fired up, and the beams of its headlights moved in a slow circle, stopping as soon as they were trained on her. The orange of her jumpsuit glowed bright, making her a stark target.

Another shot. She heard Tobin, some distance behind, give a playful whistle as it missed. Terrified, she tried to weave from side to side, but water rushed close by and rocks hemmed her in, forcing her straight ahead. She sobbed for breath, knowing she wasn't going to make it and waiting for the bullet that would cut her down. It came within seconds, a shock of heat and pain that made her right leg crumple beneath her and sent her pitching forward. Unable to break her fall, she landed heavily, her body and then her head smacking into the ground.

Someone approached her and a booted foot tipped her onto her side. She looked up into the barrel of a silenced gun.

"Where the fuck did you think you were going?"

Deakin clearly didn't expect an answer, and he punctuated his question by kicking her in the abdomen. It drove the breath from her, leaving her gasping. He was about to deliver a second blow when a woman's voice made him turn sharply.

"Caleb, Caleb, *please*. You don't want to kill her here, do you? Please let me see to her."

The woman sounded young and tremulous, as if she was taking a great risk by intervening. Deakin didn't reply, but he must have relented because he stalked away and left the woman to kneel by Sarah's side. Careful hands touched her face, wiping at the gravel and blood.

"You're okay," the woman whispered. She was as unconvincing a liar as Sarah had ever been. "You're going to be okay."

Sarah didn't have the strength to argue. She felt the woman wrap something around the wound in her leg, and welcomed the renewed surge of agony that finally took her under.

Bare-shouldered and shivering in the cool night air, Leah waited for Sarah's eyes to roll back before she tightened her shirt around the bullet wound Caleb had inflicted. Sarah whimpered, her hands stretching and flexing against the cuffs but unable to reach the source of her discomfort. Her leg was broken, Leah could tell. Even without any first aid training, she had no difficulty identifying the place where the bullet had snapped the bones. Sarah's pants were already soaked through with blood, and the thin cloth binding the entrance and exit wounds felt heavy and wet beneath Leah's fingers. She pressed harder, murmuring to try to calm Sarah when she kicked out in response.

Her attention focused on stopping the blood loss, Leah startled as Caleb's contact suddenly raised his voice.

"You think your people won't find out?" he yelled at Caleb. "I'll tell every fucking one of them that you can't be trusted. That you make promises that you can't keep!"

She looked across to where they were standing, clearly lit by the cars. The police officer's face was scarlet with fury and he used both hands to slam into Caleb's chest, forcing him onto the back foot.

"Shit, Deakin. Do you know what I risked for you?" His tone had altered, sounding more saddened than enraged. He stepped back from Caleb and buried his face in his hands. In the light of the headlights, Caleb smiled, regarding him with obvious pity.

"You knew what you were getting into, Tobin. You should just take your money. This was never about you. It was about what she"—Caleb jerked his chin toward Sarah—"and that other dyke did to my father. If you weren't so day-old fucking stupid, you'd have figured that out by now."

Tobin went deathly still, his hands falling by his sides. "I'm not stupid," he said, the challenge in his voice unmistakable. From where she knelt, Leah saw the fingers on his right hand twitch. "You think I don't know enough to ruin you? Believe me, Deakin, if I go down for this you're coming with me."

She counted silently, knowing Caleb too well to believe that that would be the end of it, that he would let Tobin get into his car and drive away. She had only gotten to three when Caleb took a step back, opened his arms as if to intimate that Tobin was free to leave, and then snapped his hands back together and shot him point-blank through the forehead. She looked away as the body fell, but she couldn't shut out the thud of it hitting the ground. Her hands clenched involuntarily, forcing a thin cry from Sarah.

"I'm so sorry," Leah whispered, helpless to do anything more than delay Sarah's inevitable death. She relaxed her hold a little. The bleeding seemed to have stopped, but there was still too much blood on her hands, her shirt, and the ground beneath Sarah.

She squinted as the light she had been working by disappeared. When she looked up, she saw Caleb pushing the patrol car down a small embankment, saplings splintering and cracking beneath its weight. He had moved Tobin's body, presumably concealing it in the car, but neither was likely to remain hidden for long in a picnic spot popular with day-trippers. Tobin had chosen the perfect meeting place—remote, deserted through the night, yet providing easy access to the coastal routes—never suspecting that it would become the scene of his murder.

Apparently satisfied with his efforts, Caleb ran toward Leah, his eyes wild with exertion and adrenaline. "She still alive?" he called as he approached.

"Yes, but…" Leah's voice trailed off as he dragged Sarah up and hauled her over his shoulder. He set off at a jog, her limp form jostling against his back. Leah followed him to where his car was waiting with the trunk already open. He hoisted Sarah into it, cut off a strip of duct tape, and used it to gag her. Leah recoiled on her behalf, but Sarah barely reacted to his touch or to the pain his rough handling must have caused her. Her hair was soaked with sweat and Leah had never seen anyone so pale. Caleb casually tossed the roll of tape into the trunk and slammed it shut.

"Move," he told Leah. "We've wasted enough fucking time here."

She fastened her seatbelt as he yanked the car into drive. He tore back up the access road and took a left at the junction. "How far d'ya think we'll get?" he asked, a grin splitting his face.

"I don't know, baby." She answered by rote, unable to stop thinking about the young woman with the shattered leg who lay bound and unconscious not three feet behind her.

Caleb laughed. "Can't remember when I last saw the ocean."

"No." Leah had never seen it, and she hated him even more for making this her first time.

The road widened, still empty of traffic and descending gradually. With a whoop of triumph, Caleb lowered his window and stuck his head out, making a show of breathing deeply. Fresh, salty air rushed into the car, and as they rounded a bend, Leah could hear the sound of waves crashing onto rocks. They passed a signpost for Northport and he flipped it the bird, his speed increasing recklessly, almost as if he wanted someone to spot him and start off the chase.

"Reckon we can at least get out of this shithole state," he said, and hammered down on the gas.

Chapter Nineteen

A lex, honey—"
"Don't." Alex cut off Esther's entreaty. "Please don't even say it."

Kneeling beside her, Esther took hold of her hand. "Only an idiot would tell you to go home, but when they find Sarah—and they will find her—she's really going to need you. So, what I was going to suggest is that you find a quiet corner and get some sleep."

Alex gave a wry laugh and looked around the open plan office. Unfamiliar faces occupied each of the four desks: FBI agents from the local field office, who had utilized the space to set up their own equipment. Working with the Avery and Prescott police departments, they were coordinating the search for Tobin and interviewing anyone who had been involved in the initial case. There had been none of the traditional posturing upon their arrival. Quinn—still looking heartsick—had immediately ceded command of the investigation and was now en route with Emerson to liaise with the Prescott police. Alex's request to join them had been vetoed on the grounds of her own safety. An agent had already interviewed her at length and seemed to have taken on the responsibility of keeping her updated, at least until Castillo arrived. Every so often he would come to her with a progress report, but he was obviously running out of ways to tell her that they hadn't found anything yet.

Tobin had used the paperwork he stole from Quinn's desk to collect Sarah, along with her jail escort, Emily Kendall, at approximately 7:45 p.m. No one had noted his direction of travel, and his car hadn't been spotted since. It seemed probable that he had arranged to hand Sarah over to Deakin but, with Deakin's vehicle still unknown, an APB could only be issued for the stolen patrol unit. Having confirmed with the jail that Kendall wouldn't have been carrying a cell phone while on duty, the agents were working with the telecom company to try to track Tobin's cell. Alex drew little solace from the fact that Kendall had been armed; if Kendall and Sarah had managed to escape, surely they would have contacted the police or the jail by now. Prescott County Jail was almost one hundred and eighty miles south of Avery, and Alex was feeling the distance keenly. Wherever Tobin had taken Sarah, it was unlikely to have been back up to Aroostook County.

"How long till your Agent Castillo gets here?"

The question made Alex blink slowly; she suspected it was not the first time that Esther had asked it. She checked her wristwatch, trying to quell the familiar rising panic as she thought of how much time had already passed.

"Two, maybe three hours," she said.

Esther tugged gently on her hand. "Come with me, then."

The small room Esther led her to contained a sofa, a low table, a stack of tattered paperbacks, and a kettle.

"Back when I started working here, there were no other women on the force." Esther patted the lumps out of a cushion and laid it at one end of the sofa. "Quinn gave me this room for my rest breaks and he's let me keep it ever since." She steered Alex to the sofa. "Give me the key to your new place and I'll get my youngest to go over there, feed that menagerie of yours."

Alex fished in her pocket and handed the key over. "Thanks, Esther."

"Sleep. I'll come and get you the second anything happens."

"Promise?"

"Of course I will."

The light clicked off as Esther closed the door. Alex got up and switched it back on; she didn't think for a second that she would go to sleep, and there were far too many monsters in the dark.

A firm touch on Alex's shoulder woke her just before the nightmare could. Finding herself in unfamiliar surroundings, she covered her face with her hands, unsure whether she was really awake. The skin there was sticky with sweat and dried tears, and the feel of it made everything that had happened come rushing back.

"Shit." She bolted upright on the sofa, to find Mike Castillo standing over her. As soon as she moved, he eliminated the height difference by dropping into a crouch.

"Hey," she said, battening down the urge to launch herself into his arms. "When did you get here?"

He looked exactly as she remembered, except that stress had pinched new lines into his face, and the smile he gave her didn't come close to reaching his eyes.

"Couple of hours ago. Esther peeked in and found you sleeping. Didn't seem enough of an occasion to wake you."

"But now?" Dread made the question stick in her throat.

"We've located the patrol unit and found Tobin."

She stood too quickly and had to put a hand out to the wall. "Has he said anything about Sarah? Where was he? Are they bringing him in?"

"He's dead, Alex."

Don't use euphemisms, police officers were always told. Don't say, "He's passed on," or, "He's gone," because people in such situations need to be spoken to in direct terms. Castillo's bluntness worked as effectively as a plunge into icy water, shaking off any remnants of sleep still clinging to her.

"Did you find Sarah?"

"No. There was no sign of her or Kendall. Tobin had been executed and dumped in the trunk of the car. Telecoms finally came through on his cell, and two officers found the body at a picnic area."

"Where?"

"Off Highway One, on the outskirts of Belfast. We've altered the search parameters since then, but the initial exam of the body put the TOD at around nine p.m., which is almost four hours ago."

"Meaning Deakin could be in New Hampshire by now."

"Yeah." Castillo used one hand to massage the back of his neck, his expression pained.

"I'm glad you're here," Alex said.

He nodded, but then shook his head. "I'm so fucking sorry for all of this."

"Not your fault, Mike."

An urgent knock on the door prevented him from replying. The door opened at once, the agent beyond it too impatient to wait for permission.

"Sir," he said, but then hesitated when he saw Alex. "Aw, hell."

"What is it?" Castillo prompted. It would have been futile to try to continue the conversation in private when Alex had heard the start of it.

"Uh…" The agent cleared his throat. "Tobin's patrol car had a video camera. He had it switched on during the meet."

"Jesus Christ," Alex said. "Do you have the recording?"

"Yes. The agents on scene uploaded it onto the system." He couldn't look her in the eye. "Ma'am, you probably don't want to see it."

The walls in the room suddenly seemed to shift, the lines of the paintwork crossing at impossible angles. She felt Castillo put his arm around her, and she held on to him just to stay on her feet. He asked the question that she couldn't.

"Is Sarah dead?"

"No, sir, but—"

"Thank you," Castillo said curtly. "We'll be with you in a minute."

The agent was sensible enough to close the door behind him. For a long moment, there was silence.

"I don't know if I can do this," Alex admitted.

"Then don't."

"I think I have to."

"Yeah, I thought you might say that."

"It can't be worse than what I'm imagining, can it?" Just saying that aloud was enough to make her shudder.

He tightened his arm around her. The fact that he didn't reply was no comfort at all.

"She runs and then Deakin shoots her," the agent had warned Alex, evidently unwilling to let her watch the footage unprepared. After showing her and Castillo into Quinn's office and explaining how to work the media player, he had left them alone. Before she could change her mind, Alex leaned forward and pressed *Play*, making Castillo snap his teeth on whatever he was about to say.

The camera, a standard feature on the district's patrol cars, had been mounted on the center of the dash. Tobin had started recording as he approached the picnic area, and the first minute of footage showed nothing but murky shapes while he negotiated a rough track. The car slowed, then stopped, and he could be seen shaking hands with Caleb Deakin in the beam of the headlights.

"Deakin's gotten himself a new look," Castillo muttered. He tapped the screen with his pen, indicating the two men. "Guess Tobin brought him in front of the camera on purpose; he wanted Deakin to be identifiable."

Alex nodded. "Gives him leverage later, blackmail or a plea bargain if he gets caught." The men moved out of shot, and she wiped her sweaty hands on her pants, anticipating what was to come and trying to guess what was happening as the camera continued to point into the empty parking lot. Thirty-three seconds passed on the counter at the bottom right of the screen. Unable to keep still, she folded her arms, then changed her mind and sat on her hands. She was breathing too fast, her lungs working hard to keep up with the pace of her heart.

The camera shook as it suddenly spun around, the car turning to the left until its headlights pinpointed a small, staggering figure. The first bullet flew wide, a cloud of dust marking its place, and Alex watched with horror as Sarah tried to evade whoever was shooting at her. She had had no chance. Hindered by her bound hands and visibly unsteady on her feet, she stumbled along a path that kept her right in the firing line. Deakin stepped obliquely into view. Seconds later, a perfectly aimed shot threw her headlong, a burst of gray mist exploding from her right leg. She landed badly and lay unmoving as Deakin marched toward her.

"I can't…" Alex pushed her chair back, not looking away quickly enough to miss Deakin kicking out at Sarah.

Castillo moved to stop the player, but then wavered, his hand poised above the escape key.

"Alex."

Something in his tone made her look up again. On the screen, a woman tried to clean Sarah's face and then used her own shirt to bind Sarah's leg.

"She's too young to be Kendall," Castillo said. "She must be Leah Deakin."

As they watched, the woman continued to tend to Sarah, applying pressure to the gunshot wound. Distracted by something, she looked across the parking lot, the lighting catching her perfectly for the camera to render the terror and misery in her expression.

"Jesus." Alex scrubbed her face with the back of her hand, a faint optimism beginning to temper her grief. The stranger on the screen leaned down and spoke to Sarah again, and Alex drew comfort from the knowledge that Sarah had had an advocate, that she hadn't been alone. "That's good, isn't it?" she said, like a child desperate for reassurance. "That Sarah has someone looking out for her?"

The recording lapsed into a mess of gray-white static. Castillo left it running and put his arm around her. "Yeah, that's good," he said, his answer as simplistic as her question. "That's good."

❖

Staring straight ahead until the lights of the convenience store merged into one fluorescent mass, Alex took a sip of her coffee and heard Castillo cough as he tasted his own.

"Put hairs on your chest, that will," she told him, stealing one of Sarah's favorite idioms.

"Got enough of those already." He managed a tired smile. "You better watch out though, the guy poured them both from the same pot."

She laughed against the lip of the Styrofoam, relieved just to be out of the station. Sitting on the sidelines and watching the investigation proceed without being able to help had been driving her crazy. When Castillo announced that he was taking her with him to meet with the Belfast PD, she had almost kissed him.

"What time do you think the rental agencies will open?" she asked as he pulled out of the parking lot.

"I'm not sure. Some of the larger ones will probably be twenty-four seven. Local ones, not so much."

A keen-eyed tech analyzing the patrol car footage had managed to glean a partial plate and the model of the car Deakin had been driving. It wasn't the one registered in his name, so every rental agency in North Carolina would be getting an early morning phone call. If none of those provided any useful information, the net would be systematically widened.

"Just gotta keep chipping away at it," Castillo said. "Local and national news are running Deakin's mug shot and the stills from the video. Someone somewhere will recognize him or Leah, and offering a reward turns everyone into good citizens."

"It also brings out the crazies."

"Inevitable side effect," he said. "But they do tend to stand out in a crowd, and the officers on the phone lines should be experienced enough to spot them."

"I think Emerson's going to be supervising that. He called me just before we left, to say he was on his way back in."

"Sorry I missed him. He sounds like one of the good guys." Castillo took a right, following the interstate toward Bangor. The beacon on his car let him cover the distance a lot more quickly than Alex had when she visited Sarah at the jail.

"He is," she murmured belatedly, trying to push the memory of that visit out of her head; it was the last time she had seen Sarah. "You'd like him," she added, to cover her lapse. She had told Castillo that Emerson was in the clear soon after his unexpected revelations about his personal life. The more sensitive details she had held back, confident that Castillo wouldn't figure them out.

"Maybe when this is all over…" He slowed for a stoplight, checked that the road was clear, and then tore through it. He was about to finish his sentence when his cell rang. He glanced at Alex and put it through to hands-free. "Agent Castillo," he said.

"Sir, this is Agent Somers, out working with the Belfast PD. I know you're on your way over here, but Emily Kendall—the prison officer—has been found on a roadside near Eddington. They've taken her to Eastern Maine Med in Bangor. Figured you might want to swing by there first."

"Thank you." Castillo nodded his encouragement at Alex as she began to reset the GPS. "What's her condition?"

"Head injury, mild case of exposure, but she's conscious and able to speak, sir."

"That's great." He checked the route on the GPS. "We're about fifty minutes out. Thanks for the heads up."

"Happy to help, sir," Somers said, sounding like he meant it. "I'm going to the hospital myself, so I'll see you there."

"Tobin must've dumped her before he met with Deakin. That's why she wasn't on the video footage," Alex said as the dial tone sounded. "Eddington is about forty miles from Belfast, where they found his body."

"Ah." Castillo frowned. "If he didn't want to kill her, why not just leave her to Deakin?"

"Maybe someone convinced him there was a third way."

He looked at her, and she guessed he had been thinking along the same lines. "Sarah can be quite persuasive," he said, with considerable understatement. "Did I ever tell you what she had me do so she could sit with you at the hospital the other year?"

She shook her head, feeling tears well up again. "No, you didn't," she eventually managed.

He fished a napkin from his pocket. "Here, dry your eyes and no crying. It's a nice story." He broke into a smile. "Y'know, I think it's that accent of hers," he said. "It lets her get away with anything."

Sarah awoke to pain and darkness. She had been fading in and out for a while, all too willing to succumb to shock if it would bring her respite from the sickening way the broken bones in her leg shifted when the car hit a pothole, or turned, or made any kind of movement however small. This time she remembered where she was, remembered not to make any more futile attempts to wrestle her wrists free or to scream against the tape sealing her lips. Instead, she positioned her good leg to support her bad one, and then lay as still as possible.

Her eyes adjusted to the dim light, bringing into focus the outline of the trunk and its only other contents, a roll of duct tape. As far as she could see or feel, the trunk had no lever to open it from the inside. There was no conveniently discarded key for her handcuffs, nor anything she could use to pry them loose, and the injury to her leg prevented her from bringing her hands forward.

She lowered her head to the rough upholstery. She didn't know why she was even thinking about getting free; she couldn't exactly run, and even if she tried, Deakin would only bloody well shoot her in her other leg. For some reason, the absurdity of that image made her smile, then laugh, and then cry slightly hysterically. Deakin was going to kill her, that seemed incontrovertible, but the fact that he hadn't killed her outright meant he probably intended to use her to get to Alex. The realization sobered her and she squeezed her eyes shut against a thought that came unbidden: the trunk stank of blood, her own blood. It was difficult to estimate how much she had already lost, but it was enough to quicken her pulse and breathing, and make her teeth chatter despite the warmth of the enclosed space. It would be quite simple for her to tug loose the dressing the woman had applied and then aggravate the wound so that she bled out...

The car bumped over a rut and she let out a mumbled stream of every curse she knew, straining her wrists against the cuffs until she couldn't tell which part of her hurt the worst. It seemed like fair punishment for even contemplating taking the easy way out and leaving Alex to pick up the pieces. However much she wanted to give in right at that moment, she knew she couldn't do that to Alex, not when there was still a chance, albeit a slim one, that someone would find her before Deakin could finish whatever he had planned. With that in mind, she decided to simplify her goals. Escape was impossible, as was overpowering her captors, which left her with only one realistic aim: to stay alive for as long as she could.

CHAPTER TWENTY

With dawn still only a hint on the horizon, the gas station had been empty of customers, while its bored-looking cashier had barely spared Caleb a glance as he pulled up at the pump. Leah had heard Sarah start to kick against the trunk as soon as the car had been stationary for longer than at the average traffic signal. Through the rearview mirror, Leah had watched Caleb open the trunk and say something. Sarah hadn't made a sound since.

Leah jumped as Caleb rapped on the window with his keys. He didn't speak, merely motioning her to go with him. She obeyed without question, scrambling from the car on travel-stiff legs and following him across to the store. As he turned and waited impatiently for her to catch up with him, she wondered what he thought she might do if he left her alone with Sarah. She had no car keys, no phone, no weapon, and there was no one around to help them. It came as no surprise, though, to see how little he trusted her.

The cashier beckoned them to enter the store, clicking open the lock on the door as they approached. He mumbled a greeting and returned his attention to his cell phone. At the side of the counter, a hand-scrawled notice warned potential thieves that they were being recorded, but Leah couldn't spot the camera. For a small, between-towns store, it was reasonably well stocked. She heard a rustle as Caleb chose a selection of snacks and took them to the counter. Cautiously, she set her own purchases alongside his. He glared at her but said nothing, evidently unwilling to give the cashier any cause to remember them.

"All together?" the cashier asked.

"Yeah, yeah, all together." Keeping his head down and his cap pulled low, Caleb took the paper bag as soon as the total flashed up. He paid in cash, pocketed the change, and turned away.

"Have a nice day." The cashier didn't sound as if he cared either way, but when Leah smiled warmly at him he smiled back, caught out by her geniality.

Once they were out of earshot, Caleb thrust the bag at Leah. "What the fuck kind of game are you playing?"

She shook her head. "I don't know what you mean. What game?"

"Getting me to buy this shit, like it'll make a fucking difference in the end."

Relief that he had missed her exchange with the cashier almost left her tongue-tied. "I'm just trying to help," she mumbled, directing her defense at her feet, her eyes cast down as her mom had taught her.

He didn't bother to answer. By the time she had stowed her bag, he was already flicking through the radio stations, searching for news reports. The bulletins were dominated by Sarah's kidnapping, Tobin's murder, and the statewide manhunt currently underway. A generous reward was now being offered for any information leading to Caleb's arrest. He whistled when he heard the amount, but seemed to be taking more notice than before of the few other vehicles on the road, and sweat was beginning to bead on his upper lip.

"Might not make it back home, baby," he said, as if that had ever been likely. He took a long drink from a can of heavily caffeinated soda and looked at her with bloodshot eyes. He wetted his lips with a tongue tinged artificially pink. "Might have to dig in somewhere and see what happens when we rattle the cage some." He grinned and threw the map into her lap. "Find us a quiet place to stop. I need to make a few phone calls."

❖

The corridors of Eastern Maine Medical Center were in nighttime mode: their lighting dimmed, the few voices within them hushed. The squeak of a gurney as paramedics steered it toward an elevator seemed almost apologetic as it violated the stillness.

Emily Kendall had been admitted to a room on the second floor. Grateful to stretch their legs, Alex and Castillo took the stairs. They didn't need to ask for directions when they exited the stairwell; only one of the rooms had a uniformed officer seated outside it. He carefully examined Castillo's ID and then held the door open for them.

In keeping with the rest of the hospital, the room they stepped into was peaceful and softly lit. The woman in the bed appeared to be asleep, but there was a man at her side holding her hand. He beckoned them forward and stood as they approached.

"James Kendall." He offered his hand. "I'm Emily's husband. The officer said you would be coming to speak to her. She dozed off about ten minutes ago, though. Pain meds," he added, by way of explanation.

Disturbed by the activity, Emily Kendall opened her eyes. She looked to be in her late forties and, judging by the naked fear in her expression, she was deeply traumatized. A large dressing covered her forehead, and both her wrists were heavily wrapped. Even without knowing officially what had happened to her, Alex had no difficulty making an educated guess. James Kendall was just about to introduce them when Emily spoke.

"Did they find Sarah?"

Castillo took a step closer to the bed. "No, ma'am. Not yet."

She nodded, but her bottom lip quivered as she looked at Alex. It was obvious that she knew who Alex was. "I wasn't quick enough," she said. She touched her forehead, wincing as she did so. "Sarah tried to tell me, but I didn't believe her at first, and then…" The tears started to fall in earnest and her words became progressively more muffled as she wept. "She saved my life and I just let him take her. I'm so sorry." She began to rock back and forth in the bed, and her husband gathered her into his arms.

Alex looked away, pride in Sarah's actions blunted by a sick sense of irony. For months after the Cascades, Sarah had blamed herself for having been unable to prevent the murder of a prison guard. Fate now seemed to have come full circle; Alex fervently wished that it would just fuck off and leave them alone. She heard Castillo asking Kendall a series of simple questions and the scratching of his pen across his notepad, but Kendall didn't know anything that could be of use to them, and her eyelids were already drooping again. She was the only guard Sarah had ever mentioned by name, the one who had ensured Sarah received medical care upon her arrival at the jail and found her a pair of sneakers to jog in. When Alex went to the bedside, Kendall held out her hand.

"She shouldn't ever have been in there," she said, her voice little more than a whisper.

"No, she shouldn't," Alex said, and felt Kendall's fingers tighten. "But I'm glad you were there with her." She couldn't think of anything else to say, but she saw some of the tension ease from Kendall's face.

"We'll leave you to get some rest, Officer Kendall," Castillo said.

At this quiet prompt, Alex placed Kendall's hand back on the bed and followed Castillo from the room. As he nodded at the officer still on duty outside the door, his cell buzzed.

"Agent Somers has been delayed," he said, reading the message. "He's asked that we meet him at the police station in Concord."

"Concord?" Alex caught hold of his arm. "Concord, New Hampshire?"

He nodded. "He's following a lead. He's not given me the details, but Deakin seems to have crossed the state line."

They took the stairs two at a time, almost running along the corridors and back to the car. When Castillo tried to call Somers, he was put straight through to voice mail.

"Deakin must be avoiding the major routes," Alex said, tracing a line down her map and trying to estimate distances and travel times. "If all he's doing is heading south, he should've gotten to New Hampshire hours ago."

"He's probably sticking to the smaller roads. Less traffic means he's less likely to be seen." Castillo pushed his parking ticket into the machine at the barrier and tapped the wheel impatiently as the barrier lifted. "He takes the I-95 and he risks hitting the Turnpike as well."

"True." The Turnpike was a toll road with regular cameras monitoring the busiest sections.

"He hasn't had time to plan anything," Castillo said. "Tobin must have contacted him on the spur of the moment when Sarah's transfer paperwork came through. They take a chance and strike, but that's left Deakin operating on his wits now."

"And on his own."

"Most likely. At least until he manages to hook up with another contact. We still don't know what his endgame is; he hasn't tried to call you or the authorities. It's been, what?" His lips moved silently as he counted. "Almost ten hours. There's no driver's license registered in Leah's name, so she can't share the load, and Deakin will have to sleep at some point or he's going to start making mistakes. All we need is an idea of where he is, one positive sighting, something that gives us a chance to get organized and tighten the net." He hunched over the wheel, gazing up at another clear sky as it gradually lightened. "Perfect beach weather. Let's hope folks have watched the news before they head out there."

The streetlights began to flicker off one by one as the sun rose, and there were more and more commuters hurrying out of the way of Castillo's uncompromising emergency driving. Alex glimpsed people applying lip gloss in their rearview mirrors or balancing hot coffee against the wheel as they attempted to shake off fatigue with a jolt of caffeine. She envied their normality, their everyday routine undisturbed by the headlines about a murdered police officer and the violent kidnapping of a young woman. They weren't checking every car as it went past or struggling to suppress the images of Sarah slamming onto the ground with a bullet in her leg.

"Alex, you okay?"

She shook her head. "Not really."

"Do you want me to lie to you?"

"No." She glanced at him and saw the sorrow in his eyes. She knew what he was thinking: that Sarah was more trouble to Deakin alive and that if he came to value his own freedom above his craving for revenge he would probably kill her and dump her body, if he hadn't already done so.

Castillo didn't say anything. He turned back to the road, his chest falling in an exaggerated movement as he let out his breath.

"You don't have to lie to me," Alex said into the quiet. She rubbed at her tired eyes with her knuckles. "But please don't tell me the truth."

The rasp of the trunk opening prompted Sarah to try to push herself into its furthest recesses. Even when she dug in with her uninjured leg, nothing really moved, and she had barely rocked back an inch before warm sunlight washed over her. She shut her eyes against the glare and the person shielding her from the worst of it. There was a rustle of cloth, and then slim, cool fingers touched the tape on her lips.

"Don't scream," a woman's voice warned her, more a plea than a threat. "There's no one to hear you and you'll just make Caleb mad."

Sarah nodded and opened her eyes a little, giving them time to adjust to the daylight after so many hours in the dark. The woman was leaning close, so close that Sarah could distinguish only a slight build and thin wisps of hair coming loose from its tie. A breeze carried fresh air tinged with salt and seaweed down into the trunk, and as Sarah listened she picked up the familiar give-and-take of waves lapping at a nearby shore. A sudden longing to see the water was so powerful it made her feel half-crazed.

The sensation of the tape peeling away in slow increments provided a welcome diversion. It finally came free as the woman gave a reluctant tug. Sarah poked out her tongue to touch her cracked, oozing lips, but there was no moisture in her mouth to relieve the dryness.

"Here."

A hand cupped her head as a plastic bottle was held to her lips. She smelled something sweet and fruity, and then tasted a cold liquid that she gulped at too fast and had to force herself not to bring straight back up. Breathing through her nose in quick snatches, she waited for the nausea to pass. As it eased and the woman murmured encouragement, Sarah took another series of cautious sips.

"Can you swallow these?" Two pills were maneuvered awkwardly into her mouth. "It's okay. They're just Advil."

She took them with more of the juice. There was something almost comical about managing the pain of a bullet wound with ibuprofen, but she hoped they would take the edge off her headache if nothing else.

"You cracked the light." The woman's voice dropped to a whisper as she examined the damage to the brake light.

Sarah made a non-committal noise. She vaguely remembered waiting for a noisy stretch of road and then kicking at the light array, hoping to damage it badly enough that a vigilant police officer might find it reason for a traffic stop. It came as a surprise to learn that she had succeeded in smashing something; the pain from her leg had been so severe that it had caused her to pass out again. She had no idea how long she had remained unconscious on that occasion.

"Sorry," she said, grimacing at the hoarseness of her voice; it sounded as if she smoked fifty cigarettes a day and chased them along with whiskey. She wasn't sorry, not at all, but the woman looked so mortified that she thought it in her best interest to show remorse. The woman glanced over her shoulder; somewhere off to the left, Sarah heard a man speaking urgently, his conversation one-sided. It took her a long time to deduce that it was Deakin using his cell phone, and she wondered at how very punch-drunk she felt.

The woman must have sensed there was a problem too, because she rested her hand on Sarah's forehead and then checked the dressing for fresh bleeding. "You don't look too good," she said.

"Don't feel it," Sarah admitted, her teeth rattling as she spoke. "Think I'm in shock." It was difficult to form the words and almost impossible to remember her training on the pathophysiology and management of hypovolemia. With medical aid out of the question for the foreseeable future, oral fluids and keeping warm were the only options that seemed attainable. When she asked for more juice, the woman obliged, supporting Sarah's head and helping her to drink from the bottle until Sarah indicated that she was finished. The woman moved away, but she returned within minutes carrying a rough blanket that she tucked around Sarah.

"What's your name?" Sarah asked, trying to keep the conversation going, though her head was nodding and her eyes were heavy.

"Leah." The woman had lowered her voice to a cautious whisper and Sarah realized that Deakin had finished his call. "He told me to gag you again. I'll have to do that now." Leah's eyes flickered from side to side as if certain that at some point he would sneak up on her.

"It's all right." Sarah meant to sound reassuring but merely sounded resigned.

It took Leah three attempts to cut off a strip of tape, and she whispered an apology as she smoothed it into place. Her lips were bloodless, her face wan and pinched as if she hadn't slept or eaten properly in weeks, and nothing about the way she acted said she wanted to be a part of this. Even with a brain addled by trauma, Sarah recognized that Leah was her best hope of survival. Pushing aside her anger and revulsion at the extent of Leah's involvement with Deakin, she made herself meet Leah's eyes. The contact held for a few seconds, before a man's hand shoved Leah away and banged the lid of the trunk shut. The engine started and the car's steady acceleration folded Sarah forward onto her broken leg. Pain ripped through her. She tucked her face into the blanket and screamed.

❖

Almost a full half-hour had elapsed, and Caleb had yet to say anything. Aware of the warning signs, Leah had already braced herself for whatever was to come. She hunched away from him, watching the rocky coastline pass by in a blur of turquoise and choppy white foam, and envying the families wandering down to the beaches, children clutching inflatables running ahead of parents laden with picnic gear. The day-trippers were out early, taking advantage of another gloriously clear morning to photograph the lighthouses on the promontories or wave at the colorful fishing boats chugging out of the harbors. Not knowing whether she would ever be able to come back, Leah pressed her hands to the soft swell of her abdomen and tried to commit as many of the details to memory as she could.

Minutes later—as a flush began to creep upward from Caleb's neck—a news bulletin broadcast the make and model of his car, its color, and its full license plate. If Leah hadn't been so certain he would shoot her in spite of the number of witnesses, she would have taken her chances and flung herself onto the road. He stabbed a finger at the radio to silence it, turned off the main street, and hit the wheel with both hands.

"Fuck!" he yelled. "Fuck them all!"

Leah wasn't sure to whom he was referring, but there was nothing she could say to appease him, so she waited for the inevitable fist in her gut or open-palmed slap.

It never came. Instead, he turned to her, his expression eerily composed. "They said no. Every fucking one of them."

She nodded as if in sympathy, but she was shocked by the revelation. He had always led her to believe that his people, his father's people, would follow him to damnation. It seemed that those willing to assist anonymously and from a distance were less eager to get their hands dirty now that he was headline news.

A siren wailed behind them, approaching at speed, and he drew the pistol from the holster on his belt. He held it out of sight, his eyes glued to the rearview mirror, his breathing rapid and short. They both saw the ambulance at the same time, and she sagged back into her seat. He pulled aside to let it pass, and then set off again behind it as if to prove he wasn't fazed, shaking his head in derision at the cars he overtook. Nevertheless, he kept his gun on his lap within easy reach. From the corner of her eye, she studied the position of the weapon, but concluded that there was no way she would be able to grab it before he figured out her intent.

As he made the turn to rejoin the main road, he seemed calmer, as if he had come to a decision. "Nothing else for it, baby. Time to rattle that cage," he said, and dug a hand into his pocket for his cell. "Got an uncle on my daddy's side. Used to work the docks in Charlestown. Figure he might know a good place."

"Does he still live there?"

He was too preoccupied with dialing to answer her, so she took the opportunity to turn her face to the window. The only person to show any interest in her was a kid who crossed his eyes and flipped her the bird.

Caleb didn't notice the exchange; he already had the phone to his ear. "Hey, Aunt Ida, it's Caleb. Yeah, yeah, been a long time. No, everything's fine. I just wondered if Uncle Landon could help me out some. That'd be great, thanks."

Leah listened to him pouring on the charm, chattering to his aunt as she went to fetch his uncle and then explaining that he was in a bit of a "tight spot" and needed somewhere he could go to ground. He seemed confident that neither relative would have tuned in to the news that morning.

"No, not a motel, somewhere vacant," he said. "Lockup or warehouse. Yes, sir, that sounds ideal." His brow furrowed with concentration as he listened to his uncle's directions. As soon as he ended the call, he switched lanes and began to scan the road signs in earnest.

"He and my aunt moved back down to Raleigh ten years ago," he said, surprising Leah by returning to her earlier question. "While he'd been working twelve-hour shifts at the docks, my aunt had been fucking their neighbor." When he grinned at her, his teeth were stained pink by his soda. "Don't know why he bothered to move. Would've been easier just to kill the worthless whore."

A man in a suit, his hand already outstretched in greeting, made a beeline for Alex and Castillo as they entered the police station.

"I'm Agent Somers. I was told to assume the lead on the case until you arrived. I'm sure you can appreciate it's difficult to keep things coordinated when the investigation is moving so fast." He pumped Castillo's hand with enthusiasm and a certain amount of awe. "Sorry I missed you at the hospital, but we caught a break that was definitely worth chasing down."

Despite having worked through the night, he showed no signs of fatigue. His eyes were bright, his hair kempt, and his suit barely creased. He smiled, displaying pristine white teeth, which ruled out excess coffee as the cause of his perkiness. He made Alex feel older than her years; she wondered whether his mom knew he had been out so late.

"What break?" she asked as he shook her hand. She had to raise her voice above the bustle of police officers and clerical workers passing through on their way to start their shifts. Somers gestured for her and Castillo to follow him into a quieter corridor, counting down the offices until he came to the one he was using. He held the door open for them.

"Caleb and Leah Deakin were recognized by a gas station clerk in Hampton Falls at 5:02 a.m. We have the video from the security camera." The screen of a laptop came back to life when he hit a random key. "Sarah isn't on the tape," he told Alex gently. "But we have reason to believe she's still alive."

"What reason?"

He pulled out a seat for her and she sat gratefully, hunched forward, too weary to hold herself upright. The office was stuffy and smelled like it had recently been crowded with tired, unwashed people. She watched him open a file on the computer and skip through a grainy video recording. At last, he stepped aside, inviting Castillo to take his place. When the video resumed, it was at normal speed.

"Just watch what Leah Deakin does here," Somers said.

Wearing a dirty cap that kept his face shadowed, Caleb Deakin was already at the counter as Leah approached. She hesitated but then set a first aid kit, two packs of pain pills, and a bottle of Gatorade beside his pile of junk food. Deakin paid for everything with obvious resentment and strode out of the store. In contrast, Leah took the time to smile at the cashier, either unconcerned by the camera or deliberately giving it an excellent view of her. The video ended seconds later.

"Do you think she's trying to send us a message?" Alex asked. Sitting up properly now, she scrolled through the footage again. A first aid kit and a box of Advil would be completely inadequate to treat a wound as serious as Sarah's had looked, but neither Leah nor Deakin seemed to be injured, and Deakin's reaction to the purchases spoke volumes.

Alex looked up to meet Castillo's gaze and saw him nod once in confirmation. She let her breath out slowly, daring to allow herself to hope.

❖

A sharp slap to the side of her head brought Leah out of a restless sleep. She had drifted off as Caleb zigzagged his way across Massachusetts, following a route she had plotted to keep them away from toll roads and freeways.

"I'm sorry," she said. She pushed up in the seat, bewildered by how long she must have slept; the sun had disappeared and dusk seemed to have fallen. "Where..." Her question trailed into nothing as she dispelled the lingering drowsy haze and focused properly on her surroundings. It was still daylight, midafternoon according to the clock on the dash, and the misleading gloom had been created by the rows of tall brick buildings through which Caleb was negotiating a path. Rubble and glass strewn across the road forced him to drive at a low speed, weaving around the worst of it, trying to keep the tires intact.

Holyoke. She remembered the name of the city now; close to the Connecticut River and apparently once home to a thriving industry of some sort.

"Paper mills," Caleb told her. "Whole town's gone to shit since the spics moved in."

She wished she had the courage to challenge him, to argue against his hatred and prejudice, to ask when he had ever held down an honest job and contributed to the country he claimed to love so fervently. But then she wished for a lot of things she was never going to have, and in any case, he was too intent on driving to continue his diatribe. He turned a corner and braked hard, cursing at the unexpected expanse of murky water that carved a straight line alongside the empty road.

"There are three canals," she said, peering at the map, trying to be useful. "I think they all connect."

He tore the map from her hands and tossed it into the rear seat. "Don't need a fucking geography lecture," he said, angling the car away from the canal and easing it into a gap between two of the broken-down mills. "Perfect." He grabbed his flashlight from his duffel bag, clicked it on, and directed it at her face. "Stay here."

She nodded, jumping as his door slammed. She was already feeling hemmed in and claustrophobic, and the thought of Sarah, trapped in the trunk for more than twelve hours now, made her shudder. Craning her neck, she peered out her window, her eyes adjusting to the dim light. Tall redbrick walls loomed on either side of the car, their windows opaque with grease, their fire escapes poised to disintegrate the second anyone attempted to use them. How long would it be before anyone thought to look for her and Caleb here?

Within minutes, he returned, almost bouncing with enthusiasm as he dragged his bags from the rear seat. "Bring the food," he ordered, but he was in a good enough humor to wait and light her path for her.

She followed him through a shattered section of wooden hoarding into a dilapidated building and stopped beside him just over the threshold. A sudden flutter and clash made her step back in alarm, and he chuckled, tracking the panicked flight of a bird with his flashlight as it fled from their intrusion. It ventured as far as one of the smashed windows and settled on the sill, apparently unwilling to relinquish its home.

"Here." Caleb thrust a spare flashlight into her hand. "See that?" He shone his own beam on a door to the rear of the cavernous space. "Go through there and wait for me."

"Okay. Sure." She didn't move, though, until he shoved her in the back. As she stepped forward, she could hear his footsteps retreating rapidly. Using her light, she picked her way over and around the detritus left behind by years of neglect and misuse: garbage, syringes, excrement, and machines long since rusted. It was a relief when her fingers closed around the handle of the door. She gingerly pushed it open and entered a smaller room, subdivided by a wall with a single jagged hole leading into the second office-sized space. One unreachable, partially boarded-up window provided the sole source of light, and the rooms were cold despite the warmth outside. Folding her arms across her chest, she turned in a full circle and tried to imagine what it would be like to die there.

CHAPTER TWENTY-ONE

Deakin had opened the trunk and pulled Sarah into a sitting position before she managed to focus her eyes. The pain, coupled with the abrupt movement, made everything even more blurred, and she heard Deakin laugh as she swayed backward in his grip.

"What?" he said, using the collar of her jumpsuit to keep her upright. "You not gonna try and run?"

A wave of nausea stole her breath. She swallowed, and then shook her head, panicked, as she began to gag uncontrollably, bile pouring into her mouth.

"Oh, you fucking—" Deakin lifted her from the trunk and carried her into a building a short distance away, where he dumped her in a heap just across the threshold and ripped the tape from her lips. She retched, forcing him to step back while she vomited what little remained in her stomach onto the floor. The exertion was too much for her; she leaned her cheek on the cool concrete, aware of little else but the resurgence of agony in her leg and the sour taste in her mouth. As she calmed, more details began to filter in: vast brick walls stretching up toward metal rafters, the intermittent cooing of pigeons high overhead, and a pervasive stench of mold and excrement.

Deakin's boots splintered glass as he circled her. He stopped, and she felt him wrap the material of her jumpsuit in his fists and start to drag her across the floor as if she weighed nothing at all. Her leg jarred repeatedly as he hauled her, but she didn't have the strength to plead for respite and she wouldn't have given him the satisfaction anyway.

He took her into the farther of two rooms at the rear of the building and propped her up against a wall. Kneeling beside her, so close that she could smell a sweetness on his breath, he uncuffed her left wrist, threaded the chain behind a metal pipe, and recuffed her. The links rattled on the pipe as her arms sagged; she had spent so long bound in one position that she could barely feel them yet, let alone keep them raised. An insidious needling sensation had just begun to spread through her shoulders when Deakin yanked her hair, wrenching her head back.

"What's her phone number?"

She stared at him, the question taking a long time to sink in, and she continued to stare at him even when it had, because there was no way she was giving him an answer.

Despite the awkward angle, his punch connected forcefully enough to slam her into the wall.

"One more time," he said, holding up his fist to watch her blood drip from his knuckles. "I'm only gonna ask you one more time."

She lowered her head and let the blood trickle from her mouth. "Fuck you," she whispered; she didn't know if she was making a sound or not. Everything around her was turning gray at the edges. "Fuck you, fuck you…"

Alex used her fork to nudge her slice of meatloaf alongside her uneaten mashed potato. It made her plate look neater, but it didn't make the food seem any less unwanted. Abandoning her attempts to salve the feelings of the chef, she reached for her coffee.

"You should eat something," Castillo said, even though his own meal was barely touched.

"I know that." Coffee splashed over the rim of her mug as she slammed it down. "I should eat, I should sleep, I should think positive thoughts, but mostly, I should sit on my ass and do nothing but wait for someone to tell me they've found a lead that doesn't actually *lead* anywhere."

"You finished?"

She glared at him. "Yes."

"No," he said, indicating her meal, "you finished with that? It looks better than mine."

His non-reaction to her outburst had the desired effect: she laughed and pushed her plate toward him. "What did you get?"

"Lasagna. You want to do a swap?"

She shrugged but picked up her fork again to taste a small piece of his meal. The tiny cafeteria at the Concord PD definitely made a better lasagna than it did meatloaf, but Castillo seemed happy enough with the new arrangement. Having spent the last four hours staring at a telephone, Alex was just glad to have a change of scenery.

"Do you really think he'll call?" she asked.

Castillo chewed and swallowed thoughtfully. "I don't know," he said. "No one seems to know what the hell he'll do, or when he'll do it."

The frustration evident in Castillo's tone was beginning to spread through the team working the case. There had been no verifiable sightings of Deakin's car since a tip on the hotline had placed it in Massachusetts. Meanwhile, the FBI's psychological profiler was vacillating between the two most obvious scenarios: Deakin cutting his losses and killing Sarah, or him using her to lure Alex into a standoff. With nothing more concrete to go on, Alex had been instructed to sit with an agent and wait for a hypothetical phone call. It had been late afternoon by the time Castillo persuaded her to take a half-hour break. His pager would alert them to any developments meanwhile.

"They can't stop me from going, can they?" She looked at Castillo, who raised an eyebrow in confusion. "If he does call, and if he wants me to go to him, can the FBI or SWAT or whoever stop me?"

"They could try," he said.

"Yeah." She stabbed a final piece of pasta with her fork, making her own feelings perfectly clear. "Yeah, they could *try*."

Sarah didn't know at what point Deakin had left her alone. She felt better for having slept, and she was on the verge of closing her eyes again when Leah stepped through the gap in the wall, a bag in one hand and a flashlight in the other. A flickering orange glow outlined her shape; as Sarah listened, she could hear the faint crackle of a fire, together with a deeper, guttural noise.

"Caleb's asleep," Leah said.

Sarah nodded. It was obvious—now that she had been told—that the sound was snoring. "Can you get help?" she whispered. She didn't have anything to lose by asking, and this was as good an opportunity as she was going to get to see where Leah's allegiances really lay.

Leah walked closer, placing the bag down before answering in a low tone. "He's done something to the door. There are wires all around it. I don't dare try to open it."

"No." With mounting anger, Sarah watched her unzip the duffel bag. "You haven't dared to do anything for weeks, have you? How does it work? You just follow him wherever he goes, do whatever he tells you, and turn a blind eye to the shit he's involved in?"

Leah froze, as if terrified that Sarah might somehow be able to get free and turn the hatred of her words into physical violence.

"How could you do that?" Sarah felt tears slide down her cheeks. "How could you stay with him after what he's done? Why haven't you told someone?" Her rage vanished as suddenly as it had flared, replaced by a yearning to understand, to have something about this make sense.

Leah unscrewed the cap from a bottle of water and tentatively crouched by Sarah's side. "We've been married for three years now. He made sure we never had a phone, just his cell," she said, holding the bottle so Sarah could drink. "He locked me in if he needed to go out. About four months after we married, he caught me trying to pick the lock on the front door. He broke my leg. It was four days before he took me to the hospital. Four days of me promising not to tell. I guess I learned my lesson after that."

When she offered the water again, Sarah shook her head, feeling sick to her stomach. She remembered how easily she had been controlled and intimidated by the police officer in the cells following her arrest, how it had been safer to do whatever he told her, and how she had lied to Bridie to try to protect herself from further punishment. He had completely degraded her in a matter of hours. Caleb Deakin had had years to work on Leah.

"Did you ever love him?" she asked.

"No," Leah said simply. "My father pushed me into marrying him. The Deakins were a powerful family and my father had never been anything. My mom knows, she knows what Caleb does to me, but she can't even leave my father, so what can she do to help?" She tilted Sarah's chin. "You need to drink some."

Sarah swallowed another mouthful but started to retch. Leah lowered the bottle, and a pack rustled as she opened it.

"Here, try this. They're good for sickness."

The cracker was dry and crusted with salt, but nibbling at it helped alleviate Sarah's nausea. She studied Leah in the half-light, noting the careful way she sat and moved, and gradually forming a connection with what Leah had just said.

"How far along are you?"

Leah clearly understood the allusion; she drew her knees to her chest as if to protect her baby. "About fifteen, maybe sixteen weeks."

"Does he know?"

"Yes." The admission dropped like a stone, both of them silent for a moment as they contemplated a man who would involve the mother of his child in such violence. "You delivered a baby, didn't you?" Leah said, her voice wistful. She dampened a piece of gauze from a cheap first aid kit and used it to clean the blood from Sarah's face.

"Yes, a girl."

"What was it like?"

"Terrifying." Sarah smiled at the memory, even though Leah had inadvertently confirmed that it had led Deakin to their door. "Terrifying for a little while and then just lovely." She winced as Leah pressed too hard on a sore spot.

"Sorry." Leah had to pause to dry her own eyes with her sleeve. "I don't think I'm going to make it that far," she said, and there was nothing but hopelessness behind her words.

The chain binding Sarah's wrist clinked as she held out her hand. Leah stiffened and glanced toward the firelit space beyond the wall, listening intently for any sign that Deakin was awake. Her posture relaxed as he snored loudly. She dropped the gauze onto the floor and closed her hand around Sarah's.

❖

The back room was cold. Caleb had built a small fire in one corner of the outer room, but very little of its heat was reaching them. Leah considered going to look for a blanket but didn't want to leave Sarah, who had been quiet for so long that Leah thought she had fallen asleep. It was difficult to tell whether her eyes were open; one of them was swollen almost shut anyway and the poor light cast the other into shadow.

When she spoke, her voice unexpectedly strong, she startled Leah. "What happened to Lyssa?" she asked. "You saw what he did to her, didn't you?"

"Yes, I did." Leah pushed herself a little distance away, uncertain how Sarah would react. Since that night, the murder had replayed a thousand times in her head and in her nightmares, but nothing she did ever changed the outcome. "She tried to fight him, she ran, but he had the knife and he was too strong."

Sarah nodded in sharp little jerks. She took several labored breaths, as if building up her courage, before speaking again. "Did she suffer?"

"No." Leah answered automatically, though she knew that a lie would be of little comfort. "I think she must have been scared at first, but it happened so quickly. She can't have been aware of much."

Sarah appeared to accept that; her expression relaxed somewhat and she rested her head against the wall. "He's going to try to bring Alex here, isn't he?" she said.

"Yes." Leah had no doubt as to what Caleb's plan entailed. For the last two years, he had taken pleasure in describing in detail what he would do to Sarah and her girlfriend when he found them. The finer points of his fantasies would vary depending on his mood, but there was one constant: they were always together at the end.

"She'll be okay, though," Leah said. "The police will be able to protect her."

Sarah's laugh made Leah feel like ants were scurrying across her skin. "A man did the same thing to me, back when Alex and I first met," Sarah told her. "Well, similar. He took me hostage and left a trail for her to follow. She could've run the other way, she bloody should have, but she tracked us down armed with nothing but a stick."

She didn't seem to know whether to smile or weep. Leah touched her gently on her cheek. "What happened?"

"She killed him and saved my life." Sarah's voice weakened as her composure finally left her. "And I know she'll come running straight in here as soon as Caleb tells her to."

"She'll really do that?" Leah found that strength of bond hard to comprehend, but Sarah answered without a hint of doubt.

"Yes, she will. She's a bloody idiot." She smiled. "But then, I'd do it for her."

❖

There were hundreds of photos stored on Alex's cell phone, all of them taken in the last two years, and she knew that the worst thing she could do right now was scroll through the gallery. She was right; she didn't even make it past the first image. Framed by a perfect blue sky, Sarah waved at the camera. Sea salt had made her hair stick out in all directions, her cheeks were pink from running along the beach, and she was dressed haphazardly in tattered shorts and a tank top co-opted from Alex because she liked the color.

"Damn," Alex whispered. She stared at the photograph until her phone timed out and clicked to black. Aware that the image would still be there, she dared not reactivate the screen; she couldn't face seeing it a second time.

The agent sitting opposite her shuffled in his chair, obviously conscious of her distress but not knowing what to say for the best. He eventually resorted to offering her a cup of coffee. Only seconds after he left the room, Castillo rushed in.

"Deakin contacted the hotline," he said without preamble.

"Jesus." Alex tried to stand but abandoned the attempt. "What did he say?"

"He demanded the number for your cell, said he had something to send to you. That was enough to make Emerson twitchy. He managed to run interference, told Deakin we needed proof of his identity and bargained him into accepting my number instead."

That Castillo was so sure it had been Deakin on the line made Alex's next question obsolete, but she asked it anyway. "He sent you proof?"

A muscle jumped at the corner of Castillo's jaw but otherwise he gave nothing away. She hadn't noticed that his cell was already in his hand; when he set it in front of her, he left damp fingerprints around its casing.

"It's not pretty," he warned her.

"Okay."

It wasn't okay, *she* certainly wasn't okay, but with his hand firm on her shoulder, she was able to look at the message he opened.

Five words: *Your bitch is a screamer*.

Underneath the text was a photograph of Sarah that made Alex recoil.

"Oh God."

Deakin had had to hold Sarah's head up to take the shot. She seemed barely conscious, unaware of what he was doing.

"Alex, shut it down."

The only color in Sarah's face came from the blood and the bruising, purple and red around her right eye, her cheek swollen with it. Sweat plastered her hair to her forehead.

"I'm going to fucking kill him," Alex said. She calmly passed the phone back to Castillo. "If you don't give him my number, I will."

Even though every touch felt like someone was taking a jackhammer to Sarah's leg, she managed not to make a sound as Leah tightened the bandage below her knee.

"Should I stop?" Leah asked.

"No, no, keep going. One more near my ankle should do it."

At her suggestion, Leah had found two flat pieces of wood and fashioned a splint to stabilize the fracture. It was possible that Deakin would tear the thing off as soon as he saw it, but Leah had been willing to try, and the support from the wood reduced the near-constant grating as the bones moved.

"That feels better. Thank you." Sarah kept her voice to a whisper; this was the first time she had had any relief from the pain and she didn't want Deakin to come in and spoil it. "Should you be getting back?"

Leah shook her head, retaking her place by Sarah's side. "He'll come for me when he needs me."

Deakin had been checking on Leah at intervals, but he hadn't interfered so far, and she had continued to sit with Sarah. Sarah was unsure whether his confidence stemmed from an assumption of Leah's loyalty or from the fact that neither woman could escape. Having gotten to know Leah a little over the last few hours, she suspected it was more a case of the latter. As Leah was effectively imprisoned, it was of no consequence to Deakin which room she chose to wait in. In any case, Sarah was glad of her company.

In a hushed, hurried monologue, Leah had explained that he wouldn't let her go near the bag containing the weapons, and that he kept the key to the handcuffs in his jacket. Although she hadn't seen what he'd wired the door with, she knew he'd kept plastic explosives in their garage at home.

"Did these help any?" she asked Sarah, fishing the box of Advil from her pocket.

Sarah shrugged. "They got rid of my headache. Not sure they do an awful lot for broken bones, though."

"No, they don't." Leah sounded like she spoke from experience. She gave Sarah two of the pills and waited, her expression pensive, as Sarah swallowed them. "I was never one of those women, you know," she said quietly.

"What women?"

"Like my mom. She thought she could change my father. For years, even when she was hurting so bad she couldn't stand up straight, she thought she could change him. And then she started making excuses for him."

"A lot of abused women fall into that trap."

"Sometimes I wish I had," Leah murmured. "At least that explains why she stayed. I don't even have that as a reason."

The chain snapped taut as Sarah grasped Leah's arm. "He would have killed you if you'd left him. That's reason enough."

"No, it's not really. I've just never been brave." The admission obviously cost her. She kept her head bowed as she continued. "I read a little about what you did in the mountains. I can't imagine fighting like that or surviving out there on my own."

"I wasn't on my own." Sarah smiled in spite of herself. "I had Alex to help me."

"You love her very much, don't you?" There was a simple curiosity underlying Leah's question. When Sarah looked at her, a faint blush colored her cheeks.

"Yes, I do. I'm guessing Caleb does not approve."

The blush deepened and spread as Leah shook her head. She opened her mouth to say something but then seemed to think better of it. Her reticence made Sarah take pity on her.

"You surprised I don't have horns and a tail?"

Leah's hand flew to her lips, and it was only belatedly that Sarah realized she was trying to cover a smile.

"Proves how little he knows, huh?" Sarah said.

Leah's eyes widened, but she was starting to nod hesitantly when a sudden call from the next room made her startle.

"I have to go." She scrambled to her feet, then leaned low and spoke into Sarah's ear. "Try and snap the bracket," she said, and moved Sarah's hand onto the pipe.

Alex's chair was more comfortable, the technology was of a higher spec, and the coffee didn't taste quite so much like it had been sitting in the pot for the last week, but otherwise nothing except the location had changed.

Following Deakin's initial contact, the signal on his cell phone had been triangulated, placing it in Holyoke, Massachusetts. Even as technicians worked to pinpoint the location, agents and police officers were searching the city, combing through the streets in a grid pattern. Alex and Castillo had relocated to the FBI's Boston field office, to find a team of agents invigorated by an influx of new information and leads. Upon their arrival—and despite Castillo's obvious misgivings—he had forwarded her number to Deakin. Forty-four minutes ago, she had received a message stating that he would call her within the hour. She was under strict instructions to facilitate a trace by keeping him on the line for as long as possible, but she suspected that he would save them the trouble; if he was ready to speak to her, he was almost certainly ready to be found.

The technician sitting at her side stopped drumming his fingers on the desk as she turned away from the bustling office. She smiled nervously, her teeth working on the skin at the side of her thumbnail. When her phone rang, she bit down so hard she drew blood. She recognized the number as Deakin's, and the technician raised his hand, his eyes fixed on his computer as he used his fingers to count down. After a few seconds, he nodded and gave her a thumbs-up. She sensed movement to her left and heard Castillo's murmur of encouragement prompting her to answer the call.

"Hello?" The standard greeting seemed completely inappropriate, but she didn't know what else to say.

There was a low rumble on the line as Deakin laughed at her. "Guess you must be Alex," he said with a slow, soft intonation that reminded her of his father.

"Yes." Her throat felt dry, her tongue thick, and she took a sip of the water that Castillo nudged toward her. She couldn't remember what she was supposed to ask Deakin, her thoughts filling instead with variations on a single question: Can I talk to Sarah?

As she stalled, the technician made an impatient rolling gesture with his hand, urging her to keep Deakin engaged. She ignored him, fixing her eyes on a blank section of wall.

"What do you want?" she said.

Deakin chuckled again. "Cutting right to the chase, huh? The feds not looking to fix a trace on this?"

"You know they are. But I think you're probably done hiding."

"You know what I want then." His voice had changed, hardened, the amusement vanished from it in an instant.

"Yes." She tried to keep the tremor from her reply but didn't quite manage it. "You want me."

"On your own. Unarmed, no tricks. Remember, I know what you look like." He took a breath and the air shuddered from him when he released it. Not fear, she realized, but excitement.

"Where do I go?" she said. "I need to know where you are."

"Second level canal, Holyoke," he replied without hesitation, and she heard a flurry of activity in the next room as the details were passed through. "In this case, X does not mark the spot."

"What the hell does that mean?"

"You'll, *they'll* figure it out. I'll give you three hours."

She could visualize him checking his watch, marking the time as if he were arranging a first date. She wanted to scream at him. Instead she agreed to the deadline and then closed her eyes. "Let me talk to Sarah," she said. "I'm not going anywhere unless I know she's alive."

"Didn't you see the photo?"

"I saw it." She had to work hard to unclench her jaw. "That proved she was alive *then*. I want to know she's alive *now*."

"Fair's fair," he said affably. She heard something crunch as if beneath footsteps, and then his voice again, but faint, the words indistinguishable. Crackles sounded over the line, and a rub of friction as the phone was shifted.

"Alex?" Sarah's voice, shaky and weak but unmistakably hers.

"Hey, sweetheart," Alex whispered.

"Don't come here," Sarah said. "Please don't come here." She gasped and then groaned, the noises becoming quieter as the phone was taken from her.

"Three hours, Alex," Deakin reminded her in a singsong tone, and the line went dead.

CHAPTER TWENTY-TWO

Sarah had been left on her own since the phone call. A hint of something savory drifted in from the next room, and every so often metal rang against metal as if someone there was eating or stirring a meal. Her stomach churned in response, torn between hunger and nausea. She drew her good leg toward her, bracing herself for what she was about to do. On a silent count of three, she grabbed hold of the pipe around which she was cuffed, and wrenched it as hard as she could.

Just as it had on her last four attempts, the pipe wobbled in its brackets but remained attached to the wall. She hadn't noticed until Leah pointed it out, but the bottom end of the pipe wasn't connected to anything. All she needed to do to slip her hands free was detach the lowermost bracket.

"Fuck."

Forgetting that she needed to be quiet, she kicked at the floor, which made her dizzy and achieved nothing. Each time she hauled at the pipe, it was taking longer for her to recover, and every delay brought Deakin's deadline closer. Her fingernails were ragged from using them as improvised screwdrivers; it was only when that tactic failed that she had switched to brute force. She had no plan for what she would do were she successful, but anything was better than sitting chained to a wall and waiting for Alex to surrender.

She bowed her head to wipe the cold sweat from her face onto her sleeve. Then she took hold of the pipe and tried again.

❖

"No."

The man standing in front of Alex was almost as tall as Castillo, and his biceps bulged when he folded his arms. It was a posture meant to intimidate, but she was too frantic to back down. As he turned in dismissal, she grabbed hold of his arm, not caring that he was the leader of the SWAT team, only that he was wasting time by arguing with her.

"What the fuck do you mean, 'no'?"

"I mean I'm not going to allow an unarmed civilian to walk straight into the middle of a hostage situation," he said. "You do that, and you double the number of people my team has to worry about."

"I'm a *cop*." She spat out the last word. "And if we don't stop fucking around here, you're not going to have *any* hostages to worry about."

The first hour before Deakin's deadline had elapsed. Every spare agent and officer in the area was out scouring the buildings around the second level canal, while the SWAT team was poised to leave for a rendezvous point.

Their leader relaxed his stance slightly, his expression losing some of its rigidity. "It's too dangerous," he said.

"So, what? Do I need to sign a waiver or something?"

His lips twitched upward, almost a smile. "Well, that would be a start."

Castillo stepped forward, as if sensing that the man was beginning to relent. "Alex, think about this for a minute."

She gave him an incredulous look; did he really believe she had spent the last eighteen hours thinking about anything else?

He ignored her expression and lowered his voice as if to exclude the SWAT leader from the conversation. "What you're suggesting is tantamount to suicide."

"I know," she said, glancing away, "but I can't..." She shook her head, struggling to voice something she had long since come to terms with. "If he kills her, I don't think I want to be here anyway."

"Jesus, Alex. You think she'd want you talking like that?"

She looked back up at him. "I just need to be with her, one way or another," she said, pointedly ignoring his question. "If I go, he might at least take his time with us, giving you guys a chance to get us out of there. I don't go and he'll probably kill her outright."

"He might have killed her already."

She nodded. "It's possible, but I think he'll have something bigger planned, don't you?"

Castillo didn't answer, but his lack of denial conceded the point. A phone rang and they all reached automatically for their pockets, but only the SWAT leader pulled his cell out.

"Anderson." He listened without interrupting and hung up with a curt, "Wilco, ten minutes."

"They've found him, haven't they?" Alex asked. She could see the gleam in Anderson's eyes, the eagerness to get his team in place and do his job.

"Yes," he said, and nodded toward the door. "You're coming with me."

The tail end of Holyoke's rush hour did not combine well with a convoy of emergency vehicles. Weary, heat-frazzled commuters darted out of the way at the last minute or, stunned by the cacophony of sirens and flashing lights, stopped dead in the worst possible position and forced the police drivers to waste time swerving around them.

Sitting between Castillo and Anderson in one of the lead vans, Alex caught glimpses of curious or angry faces, their eyes often the only feature visible in the gathering dusk.

"Deakin's car was spotted parked between a couple of the derelict mills fronting onto the canal," Anderson told her as he tapped off his radio mike. He had spent much of the journey barking orders into his cell or over the radio, but now seemed satisfied enough with his team's preparations to fill in some of the blanks for her. "A number of the mills are marked with a red cross to warn the fire department that the structures are unsafe. Of the three mills closest to his car, only one is unmarked."

"X doesn't mark the spot," she muttered.

He nodded. "Initial surveillance found no sign of activity in the main part of the building, but heat signatures have been detected in two of the rear rooms."

"Any visuals?" Castillo asked.

"Not yet. The only access is via a metal door, got a small glass panel in it, but he's blacked it out with something. The walls are structurally intact. We're working on a window, but it's high and boarded and we don't want to spook him."

The convoy slowed, all the beacons and sirens abruptly shutting off as if an invisible signal had been given. Beyond the van window, Alex could see the wide, straight line of the canal, overlooked by hulking, darkened buildings.

"City is working on a regeneration project." Anderson craned his neck, taking stock of the area. "Guess they haven't gotten this far."

Perspiration made Alex's skin slick and cold. In less than thirty minutes, she would walk into one of these mills, and she would probably never walk out again. Castillo had stopped trying to argue against her involvement, while Anderson seemed to have fixed on a strategy he found acceptable. However scared she felt, she could not begin to imagine what Sarah was going through, and that alone made her determined to play her part.

"We're about ten minutes out," Anderson said. "Well within time."

Alex nodded, kept her eyes fixed on the water, and tried to remember to breathe.

❖

There was no shame in giving up. Sarah drew solace from that fact. A bullet had fractured her leg and she was undoubtedly concussed. Also, she was cold and exhausted and she really needed to pee. That she couldn't force a simple metal bracket from the wall should, she decided, in no way reflect badly upon her.

When she shook the pipe in one final burst of exasperation, a screw promptly fell away with a tiny, musical clink.

"Oh, you little git."

She picked it up and twirled it, marveling at how something so small could have put up such resistance for so long. The bracket was now swinging at an angle, making it easy for her to manipulate the pipe out of it and slip the handcuff chain free. Her arms protested at the movement, unaccustomed as they were to anything but the twin options of either outstretched or bent double. An intense tingling sensation shot down from her neck as she attempted to warm up muscles rendered immobile for hours. As she did so, she scanned the ground for anything she might be able to use as a weapon. A few feet behind her, a hefty, solid-looking piece of material—wood or metal, she thought—stood out as a black lump against the concrete floor. In the next room, Deakin was speaking rapidly, his footsteps pacing back and forth but showing no sign of heading in her direction. She wasn't going to get a perfect opportunity, and this was as good as any. Clamping her mouth shut, she pulled herself over to the object, grabbed hold of it, and carried it back to the wall.

For a few seconds, all she could do was lean on the bricks and watch the sparks dance in her eyes. They faded one by one, leaving her with another pounding headache and hands that were shaking uncontrollably. The bar of metal she had retrieved felt cool and weighty as she pushed it into the shadows behind her, out of sight. She arranged her hands back into position, looping the chain beneath the pipe and hoping Deakin would not spot what she had done.

She had barely managed to settle her breathing when the beam of a flashlight cut across the room and he strode in. There was no time for her to reach for the metal before he was kneeling by her side, grinning at the way she cowered when he raised his fist. Instead of striking her, he took a thick strip of cloth and secured it over her eyes.

"Your dyke bitch should be knocking on the door any minute," he said, tightening the knot. "Figured it might be more fun if you have to guess what I'm doing to her. For a little while, anyways. Then I'll let you watch."

"You're a fucking arsehole," she muttered, and heard the swish of air a split second before his hand hit her cheek.

She was still trying to recover from the blow when a ripping noise made her jump; she realized it was duct tape just as he sealed a piece over her lips.

"Time to shut your filthy mouth," he said, his spittle dashing warm and wet on her cheek. "Take either of those off and I'll break your fingers."

He walked away from her then, leaving her blind. She was already struggling to remember exactly how far away the doorway was, how best to maneuver her hands from the pipe, and where she had hidden her slab of metal. Despite his warning, she tried to pull the material down, but it was cutting into her eyes, leaving her no slack with which to work. Forcing herself not to panic, she felt methodically down the pipe and threaded the chain loose. With more freedom to move, she was able to find her makeshift weapon and draw it onto her lap. Neither of those small achievements made her feel any better. Tears began to soak the cloth. How could she help Alex when she couldn't see a damn thing?

Using both hands, she tore at the blindfold, wrenching and stretching it until she glimpsed a hint of light below her left eye. It should have encouraged her to continue, but she was too worn out. Instead, she let her hands and shoulders drop and began to count: one-Mississippi, two-Mississippi, giving herself three minutes to rest before she started again, all the time straining to listen for a knock on the door.

Metal glinted in the glow of the fire. Vicious-looking blades, carefully lined up on a cloth, easily outshone the dull black of Caleb's three handguns. With a surgeon's precision, he had arranged them all on an old metal crate beside the roll of duct tape, a pack of cable ties, and his Taser. He had ordered Leah into a corner near the door, away from Sarah and the weapons. Leah wondered whether he had caught her staring at them, trying to figure out how the Taser worked or which of the guns she knew how to fire.

Feeling at peace for the first time in years, she tucked her knees up to her chest and wrapped her arms around them. In the end, it had been remarkably easy for her to reach a decision. There were no shades of gray in her mind, just stark absolutes of black and white that had brought her to one immutable fact: if she and her child lived through this, she wanted to be able to look her child in the eye.

"You knock, you step back. Try to angle toward here." Anderson pointed to a red square on his sketch of the mill's layout. "This piece of machinery is pretty solid, should give you decent cover."

Studying the schematic, Alex nodded and made a noise she hoped sounded suitably compliant. The Kevlar vest they had given her to wear felt heavier than usual and the earpiece linking her through to the comms seemed to have been designed for a much larger person. She was aching and scared, and there were only seven minutes left on the clock, but Anderson still wouldn't leave her alone. The mill, fifty yards away from where they stood, looked like a haunted house, all sinister angles and shadows, the tattered wooden boards that had covered its entrance now propped open and waiting for her.

"One shot," Anderson said, as if it was the first time he had told her. "My guys are perfectly placed and they only need one shot. You—"

"I knock, bring Deakin to the door, step as far out of the line of fire as I can, and leave the snipers to do their job." By now she could recite his instructions word for word, but the plan was bullshit. She knew it was bullshit, and from the look on Castillo's face, she knew she wasn't alone in drawing that conclusion. The only one who didn't seem to perceive the limitations of Anderson's plan was Anderson himself, and she certainly wasn't going to point them out to him. If he began to consider the countless ways in which things could go awry, he might pull her out of participating. Time constraints or simple arrogance meant he had fallen into the trap of assuming Deakin was a redneck simpleton and no match for his team. She guessed he was only willing to accept her involvement because he was confident it would amount to nothing more than acting as a lure.

He patted her on the shoulder and marched across to confer with the remaining members of his team, leaving her alone with Castillo.

"I know he's not had long to get this together, but you think he might be underestimating Deakin slightly?" she said, as soon as Anderson was out of earshot and she had worked out how to mute her mike.

"I think his cardinal error is underestimating *you*." Castillo was clearly apprehensive, but he hadn't said anything to alert Anderson, and for that she was eternally grateful.

She smiled sadly at him. "There's no way Deakin's stupid enough to make himself a target."

"I know. So where does that leave us?"

"Out of options." She caught sight of Anderson beckoning her over. "I think I have to go." She held out her hand to Castillo, then changed her mind and pulled him into a fierce hug. "If I don't…" She swallowed and started again. "I just want you to know that I appreciate all you've ever done for us."

He laughed, but it was a tight, mournful sound. "Been nothing but pains in my ass, the pair of you." He kissed the top of her head. "Do your best in there. Hang on for as long as you can, okay?"

"Okay."

He released his hold on her and she reluctantly stepped away.

"I'll see you on the flipside," he said.

"Yeah."

She turned from him then and went over to Anderson, who handed her a small Maglite and escorted her toward the mill. Ten feet from its entrance, he halted. "Straight ahead," he told her. "You're gonna go past three sniper positions. Do not look at them or otherwise acknowledge them." The deep timbre of his voice echoed in her earpiece on a split-second delay, as if to emphasize his commands. "Under no circumstances do you go into that room with Deakin, understand?"

Somehow, she managed to look him in the eye as she answered. "I understand."

"Good luck."

"Thanks."

She stepped through the doorway and waited as the sound of his footsteps faded, her eyes struggling to adjust to the loss of his more powerful flashlight. Playing her Maglite across the floor, she picked out the pockets of garbage that gave the large space its pungent smell. Night had fallen, giving excellent cover to the men whose hiding places she slowly approached. Concealed behind long-abandoned machinery or torn-down dividing walls, far enough from the inner door that Deakin wouldn't have seen them enter the building, they remained invisible until the edges of the beam picked them out as she walked past. She drew little comfort from their proximity or their weapons; unless Deakin was waiting with a target painted on his chest, they were unlikely to play a significant role in what was about to happen.

Ahead of her, a glint of light flickered and then disappeared. For a moment, she paused in confusion before realizing that Deakin had removed some of the masking from the door panel and that it was his light she had seen. He must be gauging her approach, having sent instructions that she stand a short distance away while he verified her identity. Her hand trembled as she came within reach of the door, her first attempt at a knock a tinny, timid sound against the metal. She turned the Maglite and used its handle to knock again with more purpose.

"Step back," Anderson reminded her, his voice unexpected and startlingly loud in her ear. "Three steps, aim to your right."

She did as he told her, and saw another flicker of yellow at the window, followed by a shadow passing across the filthy glass. She heard Anderson instruct everyone to "hold," and then the scraping noise of the door opening drowned out everything else.

"Shit," she whispered.

Anderson reacted first, seconds before pandemonium broke out across the comms. He yelled at Alex to move, to stick to the plan, to get the fuck out of there, even as she raised her hands and made eye contact with Leah.

"He'll shoot her," Alex said, her voice cutting through the chaos and reducing it to a series of threats from Anderson that were easy to ignore. She could see a dark figure standing behind Leah, using her as a shield while pointing a gun at the back of her head.

"You're to come in," Leah told Alex. Then she mouthed the words, "Sarah's alive."

Relief hit Alex like a Mack Truck; she had to widen her stance to stop herself from rocking backward. As Anderson continued to rail at her from some remote, ineffectual point, she interlaced her fingers on the back of her head and stepped across the threshold.

Without the full use of her sight, Sarah's other senses seemed to have sharpened. She easily caught the first faint knock on the door; by the time the second and third rang out, she had the metal bar ready in her hand. No one had checked on her, so no one had noticed that her gag was on the floor and her blindfold was twisted enough to allow her a sliver of vision. It was by no means ideal, but it was better than nothing.

A high-pitched scrape as the door opened gave her the impetus to move. Inch by laborious inch, with the metal balanced in her lap, she used her good leg to push herself across the floor. The effort made her head swim, and her chest ached as it forced out breath after breath in dangerously fast succession. Her progress was clumsy, staggering, and almost certainly audible, but she was past caring about the noise she made. She *wanted* Deakin to come and see what she was doing. Maybe that way he would leave Alex alone.

❖

Keeping her hands behind her head, Alex cast her eyes around the room. She saw guns and knives set out strategically on a crate, next to a fire housed in a tin drum, with its smoke drifting up toward a single window. Deakin stood by the crate, stooping to keep himself from the sights of the snipers, and Leah was stock-still in front of her. The one thing Alex couldn't see was Sarah, just a gap in a wall, leading through into darkness.

"Shut the door."

Deakin didn't specify who was to perform the task but—keen not to antagonize him—Alex turned to comply. The door was heavy, taking both hands to shift it, and as she did so, her fingers brushed against a length of electrical cord: clean, blue-and-white striped, and obviously a recent addition.

"Fuck, the door's been wired," she hissed into her mike. Anderson's response was drowned out by a sudden burst of pain as Deakin used the butt of his pistol to smack her across the face. She lost her balance, reaching for the wall as he snarled like an animal and hit her again. When she dropped to the floor, he bent over her, snatched the earpiece and the mike away, and crushed them beneath his foot.

"You armed as well, huh? You carrying?"

"No." She started to shake her head, but the motion made her want to throw up. Blood dripped onto the concrete as she spoke. "No."

With one hand pushing the gun against her cheek, he used his other to flip her onto her front and search her. "Gonna be losing that fucking vest in a minute. You think I wouldn't see that?"

It seemed safer not to answer, until he slapped her.

"No, I knew you'd see it," she said.

"How the fuck did someone as pathetic as you manage to kill my father?" He punctuated his question with another slap.

"I didn't." She tensed, expecting to suffer for the denial, but he merely leaned back a little and waited for her to explain. "We both went into the river," she said. "I got out."

"You got out." His voice was dangerously quiet.

"Yes."

"And you left him in there."

She closed her eyes, knowing there was nothing she could say to make this better. *Like father, like son.* Nicholas Deakin had also held a gun to her head. Forcing him into the river with her had been an impetuous gambit to try to spare Sarah's life; she had never expected Sarah to haul her out of there alive.

"You left him in there," Deakin whispered, his mouth brushing her ear. He shifted, and she felt him press something against her thigh, heard a click and a crackle of electricity an instant before her entire body snapped rigid, every muscle seeming to lock and seize. She smelled her own flesh burning and lost consciousness to the raucous sound of his laughter.

CHAPTER TWENTY-THREE

Caleb had used the Taser on Leah once. It had been a weapon new to his repertoire and he had decided that she would be his guinea pig. She had woken in a puddle of her own urine, utterly disoriented and whimpering at the residual spasms that coursed through her body.

Having endured a more prolonged shock, Alex now lay insensible, her limbs twitching intermittently. Caleb had left her to it and turned his attention to the wiring on the door.

"Get me the screwdriver," he snapped.

Leah edged over to his bag to retrieve the tool. The bag was closer to the weapons than her corner had been, so she lingered there as if waiting to assist him further. From her new vantage point, she could hear Sarah doing something in the next room: a faint, repetitive brush of movement accompanied by tiny pained gasps. As she continued to listen, she noticed Alex curl soundlessly into a fetal position. Caleb didn't react, and Leah took advantage of his distractedness to take another two steps toward the metal crate. She thought she saw Alex's eyes tracking her, but she couldn't be sure.

Sarah opened her eyes to find her forehead flush against the concrete floor. Several long moments passed as she tried to work out where she was and why she hurt so much. It came back to her in disjointed fragments, her brain refusing to arrange the parts in any semblance of order. She must have fainted, somehow managing to prevent the metal from falling to the floor but bending her injured leg awkwardly beneath her in the process.

"Alex," she whispered, remembering at last why she was doing this. "Shit. *Shit*."

She had no idea how much time she had lost. The other room was quiet, bar the odd curse from Deakin, mere abstract mutterings that did not seem to be directed at anyone in particular. Beneath the edge of the blindfold, she could see only orange and black, the colors rapidly swapping places. It made her dizzy, but when she closed her eyes, she was still dizzy and she knew she couldn't go any farther.

A whoop from Deakin brought her head up again. His footsteps approached, then halted, and the pause was swiftly followed by a yelp in a voice that Sarah would recognize anywhere, even when it was so distorted by pain. She closed her eyes and tightened her fingers around the metal.

Now or never.

Alex could feel Deakin tugging at her shirt, trying to unfasten the buttons to get at the Kevlar, so she tucked her arms tighter together to make things difficult for him. He broke off to punch her twice, once in the face and once in the abdomen, driving his fist low under the vest. She gulped for air, instantly forgetting everything other than trying to breathe. It gave him the opportunity to tear her shirt open, buttons pinging across the floor as he started to rip at the Velcro fastenings. He leaned over her, working on the shoulder straps, his face inches from hers. The barrel of his gun nudged her ear, a constant reminder to lie still and behave.

A long piece of metal suddenly careered through from the next room, crashing across the floor. It startled him badly enough that he swung his gun toward it. Sparks flew where the bar connected with the concrete. Leah dodged out of its path, and Alex reared up to head-butt Deakin with all the force she could muster.

Already wrong-footed, he went down hard, only just managing to turn in time to prevent his head from hitting the ground. He cried out, shock and anger bringing him back to his feet far sooner than she expected.

"Fucking bitch!" he screamed, his fingers pawing at the wound she had opened up on his forehead.

Blood streamed down his face as she barreled into him and drove him backward. He slammed against the wall, knocking over a metal crate as he did so. She heard the breath whoosh from his lungs, felt his fist pounding against her even as she ground his cheek into the bricks. Then a sharp, familiar sound that should have been a warning, and a blast that sent her staggering away from him.

Then nothing.

❖

"Stop!"

Leah put everything she had into the command, but she still needed to repeat it.

"Caleb. *Stop.* Don't move. I mean it."

He turned to look at her, his expression incredulous, and actually started to laugh. "You stupid fucking whore," he said. "You even know how to fire that?" His arm was still by his side, his gun aimed benignly at the floor. It was clear that he didn't consider her a serious threat.

"Yes."

The certainty of her response seemed to give him pause. When the falling crate had scattered the weapons, she had picked the one most familiar to her. Her finger touched its trigger in an unsubtle warning.

Lying halfway across the room, Alex coughed and then moaned, a terrible, agonized sound. Next door, Leah could hear Sarah sobbing inconsolably.

"Put the gun down, Caleb," she said. "Please, put it down. No one else needs to get hurt."

He scoffed, his eyes flitting to the side, to where he had left the detonator for the door.

"Don't." She stepped forward.

"Gonna stop me?"

She nodded, her mouth too dry to speak.

His lips curved into a cocksure grin. "Don't think you're gonna stop me," he said, and brought his gun up an instant before she fired hers.

❖

Already half-deafened by the first gunshot, Alex barely heard the second. She saw Caleb drop to his knees, blood beginning to seep between his fingers as he pressed them to the hole the bullet had just punched in his guts.

"I'll fucking…" He sagged back against the wall. "I'll kill you, you Godless…"

The threat tapered off into nothing, his mouth working soundlessly. When he coughed, flecks of claret sprayed out to stain his shirt.

Leah's chest heaved as she stared at him, her body shaking so violently that the gun in her hand was little more than a blur.

"Leah." Unable to draw a deep breath, Alex could only wheeze out the name, but she saw Leah nod. "Leah, keep it steady, honey. Okay?"

"Okay." Leah's teeth chattered as she answered. She shifted her grip on the gun and widened her stance, her gaze never leaving Deakin, who lay slumped and motionless in front of her.

"Good, you're doing real good." Alex clawed at the straps on her vest, the heavy padding suddenly too constrictive. She let it fall to the floor. "Oh shit," she muttered, sweat breaking out on her forehead. The bullet had hit her in the chest. It had gone no further than the Kevlar, but it still felt like it had snapped a few of her ribs. She didn't bother to look at the injury. She supported the fractures with her hand and pushed herself to her feet, trying to order her thoughts when all she wanted to do was run to Sarah.

"I need his cell," she said, approaching Leah tentatively.

That the gunshots hadn't prompted the SWAT team to launch an assault suggested someone had heeded her warning about the door. The sooner the FBI were given the all-clear, the sooner they could get an explosives expert into the building to defuse whatever Deakin had rigged, and get them all out of there.

"It's in his pocket." Leah pointed to Caleb's jacket but didn't attempt to retrieve the phone.

"Right."

Alex crouched by him, acutely aware that she was placing herself in the line of fire. She jumped as something skittered toward her and stopped at her leg.

"Tie him up," Leah whispered. "Please tie him up."

The anguish in her voice set Alex on edge, even though it was clear that Deakin no longer posed a threat. He was unconscious, his abdomen distended with internal bleeding, and he didn't react as Alex picked up the length of rope Leah had thrown, bound him with it, and then patted him down for concealed weapons.

"Where's Sarah?" she snapped, dialing Castillo's number.

"In the other room." Without needing to be told, Leah threw down her gun and retreated to huddle against the far wall. Alex tucked the weapon into her belt; she trusted Leah enough not to restrain her, but it felt better to be armed.

"Mike, it's me," she said, as soon as Castillo answered. She grabbed a flashlight and ran toward the gap in the wall.

"Alex? Jesus, fuck. Are you all right?"

"Fine, I'm fine." The temperature dropped noticeably when Alex stepped through into the next room, but it was fear, not cold that made her shiver as she moved the flashlight beam in a wide arc. She tried unsuccessfully to control the tremor in her voice. "Leah shot Deakin and he's bleeding out. He wired the door, so SWAT will have to use the window."

A metal chain glittered in the light. At first, she couldn't really work out what she was looking at. When she did, she almost lost her grip on the phone.

"Oh God."

"Alex?"

"Get the medics in here." She could hardly speak, but still it felt like she was screaming. "Please, Mike, we need them in here." Ignoring his attempt to keep her on the line, she disconnected the call. "Sarah?" she said, too scared to move any closer. "*Sarah?*"

The metal chain lifted slightly, as Sarah raised and then waggled the fingers on her right hand.

"Fucking hell." Alex gave a short laugh of disbelief; Sarah had just waved at her.

"Hey." Sarah hardly made a sound, but it was enough to bring Alex to her side.

"Hey, yourself," Alex said, her resolute facade shattering as Sarah began to cry. "You're okay, sweetheart. You're okay, you're okay."

Maybe if she said it enough times it would be true.

Her fingers fumbled with the knot holding the blindfold in place. She rocked back on her heels, unable to loosen the tie. "God damn it," she whispered. The smell of blood hung heavy in the air, Sarah was so pale her face looked ghastly in the light, and Alex couldn't get a simple fucking knot unfastened.

"Use this."

The quiet instruction made Alex's head snap up. She hadn't heard Leah enter the room. She took the knife and nodded her thanks as Leah placed a first aid kit and blanket within easy reach.

"I'll get her some water," Leah said, leaving them alone again.

Alex stroked a finger down Sarah's cheek, murmuring softly to calm her. What Sarah had survived during the last twenty-four hours must have been traumatic enough, but for Deakin to have bound her eyes seemed beyond cruel. She would have had no way of knowing who had survived the gunshots until Alex spoke to her. Now, as if still uncertain, her hand reached out, fumbling for Alex's and then holding it clumsily.

"Are you..." She had to stop to take a breath, obviously distressed by her own weakness. "You hurt?"

"No," Alex said, and smiled at Sarah's immediate frown. "Not much," she allowed. She touched the blindfold, drawing Sarah's attention to it. "I need to cut this. Stay real still for me."

"Okay."

The knife made quick work of the cloth. Alex shielded Sarah's eyes as it came away. "Keep them closed for now. You can check me for bruises in a few minutes."

Despite everything, Sarah managed to arch an eyebrow.

Alex chuckled. "I know you too well."

"I know you tell fibs," Sarah countered, but her attempt at levity was ruined as she began to shiver violently.

Alex had never felt so useless. There was no way she could lift Sarah off the cold concrete without hurting her; she could only tuck the blanket around her and hope that would make her more comfortable. Desperate to keep doing something, she picked up the first aid kit, whose lid jammed as she tried to remove it. Snarling beneath her breath, she wrestled it off, to find two small bandages, gauze, scissors, and half a pack of Advil. The sheer inadequacy of the contents made her want to launch the box across the room, but she hesitated as Leah ran back in.

"They're coming through the window: medics and bomb disposal. They said to tell you five minutes." Relief seemed to have taken years off Leah's face; she moved purposefully, unwrapping a piece of gauze and soaking it in water. "Her mouth is so dry, but this helps," she said. She put the gauze in Alex's hand and nodded encouragement as Alex carefully bathed Sarah's lips.

"That better?" Alex asked Sarah. She used more water, squeezing a few drops onto Sarah's tongue, making her smile and open her eyes. It took a moment for her to focus on Alex's face, but when she did, her smile broadened.

"Perfect," she whispered.

For two minutes, Sarah had done little else but study Alex. She had relearned the curve of her lips and the color of her eyes and the way the splash of freckles fell across her nose. Cuts and bruises stood out brutally against her pale skin and stress had left her face haggard, but Sarah couldn't take her eyes off her.

High above the next room, voices were calling urgently to one another, the commotion rising and falling amid a series of bangs and cracks, but no one seemed to have made it to ground level yet. Sarah simply held Alex's hand while she had the chance and let everything else fade into the background.

"I guess that was you who threw the javelin, then?" Alex's voice seemed to come from a long way away. Her fingers stroked through the sticky strands of Sarah's hair.

"Mmhm." Sarah had to force her eyes open. Judging by Alex's expression, Sarah had just scared the wits out of her by drifting off. "Sorry," she mumbled. "Tired."

"I know you are," Alex said. "Just try to talk to me or something."

"'Bout what?"

"Anything. Tell me about your day."

It was a suggestion ridiculous enough to make Sarah smile. "Bit crap, if I'm being honest with you," she said. Alex's laugh gave her the impetus to continue; she tried to concentrate on the original question. "Thought I could get up." She gestured vaguely toward the dividing wall. "Bash Deakin with the metal. Didn't make it very far."

"Why, where were you?" Alex shone the flashlight around as Sarah pointed to the pipe. "Jesus, you got far enough."

"Just had to chuck the bloody thing in the end." Sarah shook her head, thinking of that last, somewhat delirious decision. "Half expected it to bounce back off the wall and clock me on the nose."

Alex bent to kiss her forehead. "You saved the day."

"I did?"

"Made sparks fly and everything. You were brilliant."

"Don't feel too brilliant," Sarah muttered. Her vision seemed to be failing, even though she was sure her eyes were still open.

"Sarah, stay awake. Please stay awake." There was sudden panic in Alex's entreaty. Sarah felt her shift as if turning away, and seconds later heard her start yelling for someone to come and help them.

Strangers shouted back, then Leah's voice, tense and insistent. "In here, they're in here."

Heavy footsteps were followed by the slam of equipment hitting the concrete.

"Can you give me some space here, ma'am?" a man's voice said.

Sarah didn't catch Alex's response, but the grip around her hand tightened and Alex didn't move an inch.

CHAPTER TWENTY-FOUR

The sounds and sensations were disturbingly familiar to Sarah: pain breaking through despite the drugs, a thin supply of oxygen that made her nose cold, footsteps and the murmur of voices behind a closed door. An unnatural flushed feeling in her cheeks told her she was running a fever, and every time she breathed she could feel the answering vibration of something cumbersome affixed to her broken leg.

In the ICU after her car accident, she had often woken up alone, terrified and hurting, her buzzer summoning an ever-changing parade of strangers. She wasn't alone now; a warm hand was wrapped around hers, its fingers tightening in response to the first signs of her regaining consciousness.

"Sarah?" Alex kept her voice low. "You awake in there?"

Sarah worked her tongue around her mouth, searching in vain for moisture. Instead of a coherent answer, she managed only a pathetic-sounding moan. She sensed Alex move, then seconds later the touch of chilled metal and liquid against her lips. The skin there, abraded by the gag Deakin had used, tore and bled as she opened her mouth, but the relief from the ice was more than worth that irritation.

"You gonna open your eyes for me?" Alex asked. Her breath whispered across Sarah's cheek and her lips touched just below Sarah's left eye. "This one, at least. I'm not sure the other side will cooperate."

It didn't. The swelling kept it firmly closed, but by tilting her head, Sarah was able to see the smile that brightened Alex's face.

"Hi." Afraid to make anything worse by moving, she lay still and took advantage of the improved lighting to check Alex for injuries. She lifted a cautious hand to trace the sutures closing a gash through Alex's eyebrow. "Ouch," she said. "Think you're going to have a new scar there."

"Yeah." Alex guided her hand back to the bed. "Will it look rakish? I don't mind if it'll look rakish."

Even though Sarah felt sick and too hot and uncomfortable just about everywhere, the silly grin Alex gave her was enough to make her smile. "Very dashing," she confirmed. "It'll go beautifully with the one on your forehead."

Alex's expression sobered at that reminder. They would both bear the scars from two generations of the Deakin family. "I think yours might outdo mine," she said.

"Mm, probably." With both arms snared up by IV tubing, Sarah couldn't do much for herself, and her attempts to investigate her own wounds were largely unsuccessful. Frustrated, she forgot all about keeping still and thumped her head back on the pillow. "What the hell have they got clamped onto my leg?"

Alex lifted the sheets, despite her obvious reluctance, and Sarah squinted at the convoluted contraption.

"Damn, those were two of the only bones I didn't have metal in," she said. Bracing herself, she wiggled her toes, just to be sure that she could. In all honesty, she was surprised to find she still had toes there to wiggle, and the look on Alex's face suggested she had shared the same fears. It would be a long time before Sarah could start jogging again, but the outcome could certainly have been worse.

She closed her good eye as a chill ran through her. Then she snapped it open again, acutely afraid of the dark. "Is he dead?" she said.

"No. He coded in the warehouse, but they brought him here for surgery and transferred him out to UMass Memorial for specialist care as soon as he was stable enough."

Sarah couldn't cope with thinking through the ramifications of that right then. "Leah?" she asked instead.

"She's fine. The baby's fine. Castillo left to interview her a few hours ago."

"Oh, thank goodness." She bit nervously at the tattered skin on her bottom lip. "And you're really okay, aren't you? I heard shots and I didn't know…I couldn't see anything." Her words tumbled over each other, out of synch with her efforts to breathe.

"I know, sweetheart. I really am okay, honest." Alex cast a glance at the monitor as its figures flashed red.

"I heard two shots," Sarah insisted. Two shots that had set her ears ringing, and then Leah's voice, not Alex's. "What happened?"

Alex sighed. "I was wearing a vest. The bullet broke three of my ribs."

"Jesus bloody Christ."

"Yeah." Alex left her chair and sat carefully on the side of the bed. She placed her hand over Sarah's heart, her firm touch reassuring them both. "Jesus bloody Christ." Her brow furrowed as she closed her eyes.

It took Sarah a moment to figure out what she was doing. "Are you counting?"

"Might be." Alex used the monitor to confirm her calculation. "Your pulse is a bit quick. I think you're due a shot of morphine."

Sarah shook her head vehemently. "I don't want to go back to sleep," she said, and then, knowing Alex would understand better than anyone, "I've been having nightmares."

"What if I wake you as soon as you get twitchy?"

A yawn caught Sarah unawares. "You never told me I get twitchy," she mumbled.

"Where'd you think all those bruises on my legs come from?"

"Thought you were just a clumsy bugger." She heard Alex chuckle and she covered the hand still resting on her chest with her own fingers.

"That's good," Alex told her, apparently back to counting. "Much slower."

For a minute, it was so quiet in the room that Sarah could hear drops of blood falling into her transfusion. She closed her eyes but still couldn't rest.

"Alex?"

"What?"

"Will you leave the lights on?"

"Of course I will, and I'm staying right here," Alex said, the absolute certainty of her reply giving Sarah the assurance she craved. "I promise I won't let you wake up in the dark."

❖

The peppermint tea was sweet, with an unusual taste that lingered after every sip. Honey, Leah realized belatedly; someone had put a spoonful of honey in it for her. She cradled the mug with both hands, the heat turning her fingers pink and plump, healthy-looking. The doctor who had examined her the previous night had warned her that she was too thin, that her baby was small for sixteen weeks. She had made polite noises of acquiescence, but it had been hard to listen to his dietary advice as she gazed at the tiny but perfect form on the ultrasound screen. The FBI agent at her side had obviously paid attention, though, because breakfast that morning had been the best meal she had eaten in months. Earlier, that same agent had come down to her cell and woken her from a deep, dreamless sleep, and when he told her the time she had been astounded by how late it was; she had expected them to come for her after only an hour or two, but instead they had allowed her to sleep through the night.

At the sound of voices outside the interview room, she smoothed her fingers nervously through her hair. The agent who had brought her the tea came in first, nodded at her, and then stood to one side so another man could enter the room. Leah remembered seeing this second man at the mill. He had been one of the first to come through the door, and had left his colleagues and the medics to arrange Caleb's extrication while he headed straight into the next room, to Alex and Sarah.

"I'm Agent Castillo," he said, sinking into a chair. His eyes were red-rimmed and there was a tatty growth of stubble covering his chin. She guessed he had come directly from the hospital.

"Is Sarah okay?" she asked.

The smile he gave her was tired but genuine. "She came through the surgery and Alex is with her. The doctors are hopeful."

"Thank God," she whispered, a small spark of her faith rekindling for an instant.

"Leah?" He said her name quietly and ensured she made eye contact before he continued. "Caleb came through his surgery as well."

She licked her lips, certain that she should say something but unable to speak. Caleb had stopped breathing; she had heard the medics shouting that, had seen them performing CPR. He should have died. Why hadn't they just let him die?

Castillo's face became unfocused around the edges as tears blurred her vision, and she raised a hand to dash them from her eyes. She had woken up feeling safe, contented. Now she felt as if someone were wrapping their fingers around her neck and choking the life from her. She pulled at the top buttons on her shirt to loosen it, her nails scratching at the skin on her throat, but still she couldn't breathe.

"Leah, look at me." Castillo didn't raise his voice, but pitched his request to cut neatly through her panic. "We can protect you," he told her. "We can keep you and your baby safe."

She stared at him, incredulous. "I'm going to prison. You think he won't be able to get to me there?"

"I think there are options we should discuss. Your lawyer called to let me know he's caught up in traffic. I'm going to grab a coffee. Can I get you more tea?"

"What options?" She spoke quickly to stop him from leaving. It didn't matter to her whether she had a lawyer present; she knew there was no defense for what she had done.

Castillo looked at the other agent, who shrugged in implicit consent.

"You can tell us everything that happened and agree to testify against Caleb," Castillo said.

She nodded, thinking it over. She had thought Caleb was dead, so the prospect of testifying had never entered her head. No one else had been there when he murdered the paramedic. She was the only witness, the only one who could piece everything together for the FBI. No matter how irrefutable the evidence, Caleb wouldn't plead guilty to that murder; he would expect her to provide him with an alibi, and he could afford to hire the best legal advice.

"If I testify, will that help Sarah?"

Clearly startled by her question, Castillo stared at her as if trying to work out what her angle might be. "Yes, I think that'll help Sarah a great deal."

She smiled and drew in a huge breath. She had told Sarah that she had never been brave. Now seemed as good a time as any to rectify that.

Always quite adept at multitasking, Alex was fielding texts from Ash and Tess while keeping a close eye on what the nurse was doing to Sarah. The beep of the thermometer made Sarah's nose furrow, but she showed no other signs of waking, which was hardly surprising given the amount of morphine being pumped into her. The nurse flashed Alex a quick okay sign as he recorded Sarah's vitals on her chart. Then he gathered an empty IV and headed to the door, but as he was about to push it open, he paused and turned back.

"Think you might have visitors. Lady with a sour face, and a handsome-looking cop. They were talking to the officers outside. I asked them to wait there. Should I send them in?"

"If Agent Somers has approved them, then yes, go ahead." Alex had a good idea who the visitors might be.

"That woman a friend of yours?"

"Not even close."

He left the door and crouched by her side, lowering his voice in exaggerated confidentiality. "She gives you any shit, press the call button. I'll accidentally empty Sarah's drain all over her nasty Louboutin slingbacks."

Alex could barely reply for laughing. "I would pay to see you do that."

He shook the hand she held out. "Deal. I love my job, but the money's terrible."

As soon as he opened the door, Linda Kryger strode into view.

"Remember, press the buzzer," he hissed to Alex over his shoulder, and then stepped aside to allow the ADA to enter the room.

Alex tried to stand, certain that Kryger was there to enforce the official protocol for hospitalized prisoners and determined to keep her away from Sarah. The murder charge against Sarah hadn't yet been dismissed and, up until now, only Castillo's intervention had prevented the prison officers on sentry duty outside the room from handcuffing Sarah to the bed.

Alex made it to the edge of the chair before the pain in her ribs bent her double. "Fuck."

The clack of heels on the tiles stopped abruptly, but a softer tread continued to approach.

"Easy, Alex. You okay there?" Scott Emerson rested his hand on her shoulder and she sagged back, relief draining all the fight from her.

"Yeah, I am now." She looked up at him and shook her head. "It's good to see you."

"Likewise." He smiled, oblivious to Kryger's peevish expression. "How's Sarah doing?"

"Good. Well, better. They have her on some heavy-duty pain meds, so she's mostly sleeping."

"Best thing for her. You should probably try it yourself. No offense, but you look like crap."

Slightly self-conscious in a pair of purloined scrubs, Alex ran her hands through her hair. The gesture didn't seem to achieve much; she could still feel the wayward tufts sticking out, just in a different permutation. She sighed and gave up.

"What can I say? It's been a crappy week."

Emerson opened his mouth to respond, but Kryger cut him off by clearing her throat pointedly. The brusque interruption made Alex place a protective hand on Sarah's wrist. She ran a finger over the bandages swathed around it.

Catching her stricken expression, Emerson seemed to realize what she was anticipating. "No, damn it, Alex, that's not why we're here." He motioned to Kryger, urging her to speak.

Taking her time, she came just close enough to pass Alex a sheaf of paperwork from the file in her hand. "Late this afternoon, we received the forensic results from the samples collected at the cottage," she said. "The blood on the knife handle and on the items of clothing retrieved from the fire belonged to Lyssa Mardell. Hair and semen samples from the cottage interior were matched to Caleb Deakin, and a partial thumbprint on the knife handle was also identified as his." With a contemptuous flick of her hand, she indicated the paperwork. "Leah Deakin has provided a witness statement that accuses Caleb Deakin of Mardell's murder, and she is willing to testify to that fact, should the case go to trial. Accordingly, the charges against Sarah have been dismissed."

Alex blinked. She looked at the carefully tabulated mass of information in front of her, and then back at Kryger. "What am I supposed to do? *Thank* you?"

Her voice was barely raised above a whisper, but the derision in it made Kryger retreat a couple of steps. She snapped the file closed and straightened her shoulders. "You'll both be subpoenaed to testify against Deakin," she said, as if determined to have the last word.

"You think we don't know that?" This time Alex did raise her voice. "We'll worry about the trial once we find out whether Sarah will be able to walk again." She turned to Emerson. "Get her the fuck out of here."

Kryger raised a hand to ward off any potential action by Emerson. "I was doing my job," she said. "I'm not going to apologize for that."

"No," Alex said. "I wouldn't expect you to."

Kryger opened her mouth to reply, but then seemed to reconsider, and left the room without another word.

Emerson caught the door as it began to close. "Agent Castillo wanted to speak to you as well," he said. "I'll go find him."

Alex nodded and waited for him to leave before she laid the report flat on the bedside table, intent only on resuming her vigil and trying to calm down. Closing her eyes, she made an effort to breathe through her nose.

"You done yelling?"

Peeking through one eye, she saw Sarah smiling at her. "Yeah, think so. How much of that did you hear?"

Sarah tried to shuffle up a little but stopped almost immediately, wincing. "Something about us both having supper, and then you said 'fuck.'"

"Subpoenaed, not supper."

"Oh. Supper sounded much nicer."

Using the remote control, Alex raised the head of the bed. "How's that?"

"Lovely. So who were you swearing at?"

"ADA Kryger. She just dropped by to let you know you were a free woman."

Sarah's good eye widened. "Bloody hell."

"They waited for the DNA results and Leah's statement."

"Well, I suppose being kidnapped and tortured doesn't automatically make me innocent." Sarah sounded so reasonable that it made Alex wonder exactly how much morphine she was being given. "Surprised they didn't cuff me to the bed," she continued.

"They would've, had Kryger gotten her way."

"Oh. Castillo?"

"Yeah, I think we owe him. Again."

"No time like the present." Sarah pointed to the large shadow lurking outside the door. Castillo knocked, and she called out for him to come in.

"Well, look at you." He grinned at Sarah from the doorway before coming over to give her a hug. Emerson stood on the threshold, and Alex beckoned him forward as well.

"I'd offer you guys a beer, but we're all out, and Sarah's keeping all the really good drugs for herself," she said. "But I'm guessing this isn't a social visit."

"No, it's not." Castillo pulled up a chair. "I just wanted to let you both know that Leah Deakin has been taken into protective custody. After the trial—assuming that there is one, that Deakin doesn't plead guilty or die in the meantime—she'll be given a new identity and relocated."

"Is she being charged with anything?" Sarah asked.

"No. That was the crux of her deal. Are you okay with that?"

She nodded vigorously. "Yes, definitely."

"We'll need statements from both of you as soon as you're feeling up to it," Emerson said. "And Kryger was right about needing you to testify."

Alex waited for Sarah's response, but all she did was nod, the news apparently not coming as a bombshell.

"She won't be involved in your interviews," he assured them. "I've asked the DA's office for a different representative and they've agreed to assign one."

Something in his tone and his phrasing provided Alex with the clue she had been missing. "What happened to Quinn?" she asked.

"He resigned this morning," Emerson said. "I'm assuming his role, temporarily."

The revelation took her aback, but she found it difficult to feel any real emotion—neither guilt nor sadness, elation nor satisfaction. Quinn hadn't acted maliciously, just with poor judgment, and he had gotten off lightly compared to Sarah.

"Chief Emerson," she said, and smiled as he blushed to the tips of his ears. "I think that has a real nice ring to it."

For Sarah, it was easy to divide her time in the hospital into good days and bad days. On the good days, the pain was manageable and she made progress in physical therapy. Alex might sneak burgers and shakes into the ward, or take her outside for a walk with Tilly. On the bad days, she saw Caleb Deakin in the face of everyone she met, her room felt so claustrophobic that she had to prop the door open, and nothing made the pain stop.

It was only six a.m., but today was already shaping up to be a bad day.

She had woken when she attempted to throw herself out of bed. Running: she was always running in her nightmares, and it was always pitch-black, and she could never scream. Her leg, now in a fiberglass cast, had worked as an anchor of sorts, keeping her on the bed, but the abrupt movement and the resultant bolt of pain had torn her from sleep.

Moving carefully so as not to disturb Alex, who as usual had stayed too late and crashed out on a foldaway bed, she managed to get into her wheelchair and roll it over to the window. Rain was splattering against the glass, the sky outside alive with storm clouds. It was warm in the room, but fear had left her T-shirt soaked and her teeth were beginning to chatter. She tried to pull one of the thin blankets from her bed, and the swish of material broke the stillness; she held her breath as she heard Alex turn over. There was silence for a minute, then another creak of the bed's flimsy frame.

"You're going to get cold." Still gravelly with sleep, Alex's voice rose out of the darkness.

"I'm fine. Stay put."

"Bad dream?"

Sarah used her finger to track the passage of a raindrop down the pane. "Is there any other sort?" She rolled her eyes, annoyed by her own self-pity, but she hated constantly feeling either hunted or trapped. She didn't know which was worse: the nightmares where she tried to flee, or the memories of what had happened to her after she was caught. When Alex got out of bed and wrapped the blanket around Sarah's shoulders, Sarah used it to hide her face away.

"You want to tell me about it?" Alex asked, perching back on the bed. She never pushed, but little by little, over the past six weeks she had learned just about everything that had happened to Sarah after Tobin took her from the jail. The doctors had urged Sarah to speak to a therapist, unaware that most of her "therapy" was taking place in the witching hours while the rest of the hospital slept.

"Woke myself up trying to get out of bed again," she said. "I was running; I never remember the cast. If I feel any pain, I just think it's from the bullet."

She saw Alex's throat work as she swallowed. Knowing that Alex had watched the entire scene play out on the recording added another layer of horror. Some nights, the sound of Alex crying woke Sarah before the nightmares could take hold.

Alex dropped down from the bed, collected a pile of clothing, and came to kneel at the side of the chair. "Want to get some fresh air?"

Sarah tapped the window, drawing Alex's attention to the grim weather. "It's pouring down."

"So we'll get wet. Here, stick your foot in your sneaker."

"We're in our pajamas."

"So we'll get wet pajamas." Alex held out Sarah's jacket. "It'll be good for you. Come on."

"The Storm Troopers will not be impressed," Sarah said, wrestling into her jacket. The protective detail camped in the corridor were duty-bound to accompany them if they left the room.

"They won't mind. They're used to us keeping some pretty odd hours." From behind the chair, Alex leaned over and kissed the top of her head. "Let's go wake them up."

Outside, the rain had softened into a fine drizzle, the temperature mild beneath it. Sarah turned her face toward the sky and let the mist bathe her skin, sluicing away the clammy residue she could still feel clinging to her. The roads they walked beside were quiet, with few cars passing them as they approached Van Horn Park.

"Is it the weekend?" she asked. She found it hard to keep track of the days when there was little in the hospital to distinguish them.

"You really don't know what day it is?" Alex chuckled. "It's Sunday. Hang on while I get you over this bump." She tilted the chair, easing it down onto the rough path that curved toward the park's two ponds. The rain tapered off before stopping completely, and hazy fingers of sunlight broke through the clouds as she steered the chair toward a bench at the side of the water.

"You'll get your bum wet if you sit on that," Sarah said, and then laughed as Alex produced two plastic bags from the carryall strapped to the back of the chair. "Think of everything, don't you?"

"Come and sit with me." Alex held her arms out.

Sarah carefully transferred herself across to the bench, tucked her face into Alex's neck, and kissed the damp skin there.

"Happy birthday." Alex spoke so softly that Sarah thought she had misheard. The gift that Alex pulled out of the carryall quickly disabused her of that notion.

"Oh." She pushed away a little. "Really? Today?"

"Definitely, today. I thought about baking you a cake, but…well, baking just wouldn't be as much fun without you there," Alex said. She smirked and dodged Sarah's attempt to smack her on the arm. "Ash sent about three tons of Cadbury's chocolate to the hospital for you, and this is from me." She set the gift in Sarah's hands.

When Sarah pulled at the ribbon, the wrappings fell away to reveal a hardback book. Its bold red cover was edged with beautiful gold filigree, the letters *JA* inscribed in the center in a flowing script. That gave her a good clue, but it was only when she turned to the spine that she found the title: *Pride and Prejudice*.

"I wasn't sure if you'd gotten a chance to read it properly," Alex said as Sarah ran her fingers over the embossed lettering. "And I wasn't sure if you'd even like it, or whether it'd bring back bad—"

"I *love* it," Sarah assured her. "And no, I never got to read it properly." She pushed as close to Alex as she could and kissed her.

"Tell me what I can do to help," Alex said. "What do you want to do?"

"Now?"

"No, after you get out of the hospital, after the trial, after all this…" She floundered, clearly searching for the right words. "After it's all finished."

"Finished" was exactly the right word but for all the wrong reasons. "I feel like he stole everything from us," Sarah whispered. It was something she had never voiced aloud: the unfairness of it, the enormity of what Caleb Deakin had cost them. "Lyssa lost her life. We lost our home, and all that time while I was in jail. You've lost your career. We were so fucking happy, Alex, and he took it all."

Alex tilted Sarah's chin, ensuring that their eyes met. "So we start again," she said. "We make sure that bastard gets locked away for the rest of his life, and we start ours over."

Sarah nodded, drawing courage from Alex's calm confidence. "Where?"

"Wherever you want to go."

She rested her forehead against Alex's. "I think I want to go back to England," she said.

❖

A strange blue-white flash woke Sarah. For a second, the bedroom was illuminated, its unfamiliar layout puzzling until she remembered where she was. The light vanished as quickly as it had appeared, leaving a yellow diode blinking as her cell phone notified her of an incoming text. Before going to bed, she had turned the phone onto silent, but forgotten to leave the damn thing next door. Instead it was sitting on the dresser, where she couldn't reach it without getting up.

Oblivious to the disturbance, Alex slept on, too jetlagged to respond even to Sarah's fidgeting. The trip to England had taken three months to finalize: three months of organizing and arguing, the calling in of several favors, and some serious pulling of strings. They had been granted permission to rent a cottage in the Derbyshire Peak District for three weeks while they tried to figure out where they might want to buy a property and what their job prospects were. To placate Kryger, Castillo had sent a detailed itinerary through to the local Criminal Investigations Department, arranging for them to monitor Alex's and Sarah's safety during their stay, and—more pertinently as far as Kryger was concerned—ensure that they returned to America to testify.

Wide-awake now, Sarah was beginning to worry why someone was contacting her at such a stupid hour. She fretted for another five minutes, and then crept out of bed, collected the phone, and took it into the living room. Already regretting leaving the warmth of the duvet, she wrapped a blanket around her shoulders and huddled on the sofa. Her hands were numb, her fingers repeatedly fumbling the numbers on her passcode, but she eventually managed to enter it and open the new message.

It was from Castillo, who started by apologizing for the early morning shout. The remainder of his text was brief and short on detail, but it brought a smile to Sarah's face. She set the phone on the arm of the sofa, gathered up the blanket, and headed for the kitchen.

Alex couldn't be sure at what point she had noticed that Sarah was no longer in bed. She vaguely recalled some odd sounds infiltrating her dream: soft footsteps, the click of a door, the turning of a key. Then she had rolled over onto a cold patch of sheet and woken to find Sarah missing. The bedside clock told her it was still early, the pattern on the drapes just becoming visible as dawn lightened the sky. She pulled on a thick sweater and socks, and decided to start her search in the living room.

The cottage was tiny, and it didn't take her long to establish that Sarah wasn't in it. Growing concerned, she opened the front door to find their rental car still parked in the driveway, and a black cat that yowled optimistically at her.

"Hey, big guy." Alex bent to stroke him. "Have you seen a lovely young lady, bit shorter than me, slight limp, pretty eyes?"

The cat purred, wrapping himself around her legs and pointedly not being helpful, but from somewhere around the back of the cottage, she heard Sarah laugh.

"You need to go out of the kitchen door," Sarah shouted.

Alex followed her instructions, shadowed by the cat, who trotted through the building as if he owned it. He seemed just as familiar with the garden, leading her down a set of stone steps to a bench where she found Sarah tucked beneath a tartan blanket.

"Morning." Sarah opened the blanket and rewrapped it around them both as Alex sat down.

"Wow," Alex said, taking her first chance to get a proper look at where they were.

Sarah nudged her. "Gorgeous, isn't it?"

All around them, the hills of the Dark Peak rose from undulating valleys. Dry-stone walls crisscrossed the lower sections where the land was cultivated, but the farthest reaches were given up to a wild tangle of heather, bilberry, and sedge. The sun was creeping above the horizon, picking out pink and lilac hues on the moors and prompting the sheep in the nearby fields to bleat to their neighbors. The cat halfheartedly stalked a magpie, then seemed to think better of it and rolled over in the grass at Sarah's feet.

She wiggled a toe into his belly. "Look at the size of him. He'd have Bandit for breakfast."

"He'd have Tilly for breakfast, never mind Bandit. What do they feed cats over here?"

"It's the fresh air," Sarah said. "Builds character."

Alex arched an eyebrow. "I don't think Bandit needs any more character. We could just leave him in the States, you know. He's perfectly happy there." She laughed when Sarah slapped the back of her hand.

"You don't mean that, and his sister would never forgive us. Besides, it'll be funny watching him get his arse spanked by the hill sheep. They have a reputation for being feisty." Sarah kissed Alex's cheek. "Sorry I woke you."

"Nightmare?" Alex asked. It was the most obvious explanation, but to her relief Sarah shook her head.

"Text from Castillo." She took a breath, and when she spoke again there were tears in her eyes. "Leah had the baby late last night. A little girl. Well, a tiny girl, actually. She was a few weeks early. She's in the NICU, but Castillo thinks she'll be all right."

"And Leah?"

"She's fine." Sarah smiled. "And her daughter is called Grace."

"Huh. Seems appropriate."

"It does, doesn't it?" She sighed deeply, as if letting go of months of turmoil. "I love you," she whispered.

It was a simple sentiment, but it told Alex that, given time, everything would heal.

"I love you too." She encircled Sarah's cold fingers with her own, then raised them to her lips and kissed them one by one. "Come on," she said, nodding toward the cottage. "Let's go get a cup of tea."

End

About the Author

Cari Hunter lives in the northwest of England with her partner, two cats, and a pond full of frogs. She works as a paramedic and dreams up stories in her spare time.

Cari enjoys long, wind-swept, muddy walks in her beloved Peak District and forces herself to go jogging regularly. In the summer she can usually be found sitting in the garden with her feet up, scribbling in her writing pad. She also loves hiking in the Swiss Alps and playing around online. Although she doesn't like to boast, she will admit that she makes a very fine Bakewell Tart. She can be contacted at: carihunter@rocketmail.com.

Books Available from Bold Strokes Books

Wingspan by Karis Walsh. Wildlife biologist Bailey Chase is content to live at the wild bird sanctuary she has created on Washington's Olympic Peninsula until she is lured beyond the safety of isolation by architect Kendall Pearson. (978-1-60282-983-1)

Night Bound by Winter Pennington. Kass struggles to keep her head, her heart, and her relationships in order. She's still having a difficult time accepting being an Alpha female. But her wolf is certain of what she wants and she's intent on securing her power. (978-1-60282-984-8)

Slash and Burn by Valerie Bronwyn. The murder of a roundly despised author at an LGBT writer's conference in New Orleans turns Winter Lovelace's relaxing weekend hobnobbing with her peers into a nightmare of suspense—especially when her ex turns up. (978-1-60282-986-2)

The Blush Factor by Gun Brooke. Ice-cold business tycoon Eleanor Ashcroft only cares about the three P's—Power, Profit, and Prosperity—until young Addison Garr makes her doubt both that and the state of her frostbitten heart. (978-1-60282-985-5)

The Quickening: A Sisters of Spirits Novel by Yvonne Heidt. Ghosts, visions, and demons are all in a day's work for Tiffany. But when Kat asks for help on a serial killer case, life takes on another dimension altogether. (978-1-60282-975-6)

Windigo Thrall by Cate Culpepper. Six women trapped in a mountain cabin by a blizzard, stalked by an ancient cannibal demon bent on stealing their sanity—and their lives. (978-1-60282-950-3)

Smoke and Fire by Julie Cannon. Oil and water, passion and desire, a combustible combination. Can two women fight the fire that draws them together and threatens to keep them apart? (978-1-60282-977-0)

Asher's Fault by Elizabeth Wheeler. Fourteen-year-old Asher Price sees the world in black and white, much like the photos he takes, but when his little brother drowns at the same moment Asher experiences his first same-sex kiss, he can no longer hide behind the lens of his camera and eventually discovers he isn't the only one with a secret. (978-1-60282-982-4)

Love and Devotion by Jove Belle. KC Hall trips her way through life, stumbling into an affair with a married bombshell twice her age. Thankfully, her best friend, Emma Reynolds, is there to show her the true meaning of Love and Devotion. (978-1-60282-965-7)

Rush by Carsen Taite. Murder, secrets, and romance combine to create the ultimate rush. (978-1-60282-966-4)

The Shoal of Time by J.M. Redmann. It sounded too easy. Micky Knight is reluctant to take the case because the easy ones often turn into the hard ones, and the hard ones turn into the dangerous ones. In this one, easy turns hard without warning. (978-1-60282-967-1)

In Between by Jane Hoppen. At the age of 14, Sophie Schmidt discovers that she was born an intersexual baby and sets off on a journey to find her place in a world that denies her true existence. (978-1-60282-968-8)

Secret Lies by Amy Dunne. While fleeing from her abuser, Nicola Jackson bumps into Jenny O'Connor, and their unlikely friendship quickly develops into a blossoming romance—but when it comes down to a matter of life or death, are they both willing to face their fears? (978-1-60282-970-1)

Under Her Spell by Maggie Morton. The magic of love brought Terra and Athene together, but now a magical quest stands between them—a quest for Athene's hand in marriage. Will their passion keep them together, or will stronger magic tear them apart? (978-1-60282-973-2)

Homestead by Radclyffe. R. Clayton Sutter figures getting NorthAm Fuel's newest refinery operational on a rolling tract of land in Upstate New York should take a month or two, but then, she hadn't counted on local resistance in the form of vandalism, petitions, and one furious farmer named Tess Rogers. (978-1-60282-956-5)

Battle of Forces: Sera Toujours by Ali Vali. Kendal and Piper return to New Orleans to start the rest of eternity together, but the return of an old enemy makes their peaceful reunion short-lived, especially when they join forces with the new queen of the vampires. (978-1-60282-957-2)

How Sweet It Is by Melissa Brayden. Some things are better than chocolate. Molly O'Brien enjoys her quiet life running the bakeshop in a small town. When the beautiful Jordan Tuscana returns home, Molly can't deny the attraction—or the stirrings of something more. (978-1-60282-958-9)

The Missing Juliet: A Fisher Key Adventure by Sam Cameron. A teenage detective and her friends search for a kidnapped Hollywood star in the Florida Keys. (978-1-60282-959-6)

Amor and More: Love Everafter edited by Radclyffe and Stacia Seaman. Rediscover favorite couples as Bold Strokes Books authors reveal glimpses of life and love beyond the honeymoon in short stories featuring main characters from favorite BSB novels. (978-1-60282-963-3)

First Love by CJ Harte. Finding true love is hard enough, but for Jordan Thompson, daughter of a conservative president, it's challenging, especially when that love is a female rodeo cowgirl. (978-1-60282-949-7)

Pale Wings Protecting by Lesley Davis. Posing as a couple to investigate the abduction of infants, Special Agent Blythe Kent and Detective Daryl Chandler find themselves drawn into a battle over the innocents, with demons on one side and the unlikeliest of protectors on the other. (978-1-60282-964-0)

Mounting Danger by Karis Walsh. Sergeant Rachel Bryce, an outcast on the police force, is put in charge of the department's newly formed mounted division. Can she and polo champion Callan Lanford resist their growing attraction as they struggle to safeguard the disaster-prone unit? (978-1-60282-951-0)

Meeting Chance by Jennifer Lavoie. When man's best friend turns on Aaron Cassidy, the teen keeps his distance until fate puts Chance in his hands. (978-1-60282-952-7)

At Her Feet by Rebekah Weatherspoon. Digital marketing producer Suzanne Kim knows she has found the perfect love in her new mistress Pilar, but before they can make the ultimate commitment, Suzanne's professional life threatens to disrupt their perfectly balanced bliss. (978-1-60282-948-0)

Show of Force by AJ Quinn. A chance meeting between navy pilot Evan Kane and correspondent Tate McKenna takes them on a roller-coaster ride where the stakes are high, but the reward is higher: a chance at love. (978-1-60282-942-8)

Clean Slate by Andrea Bramhall. Can Erin and Morgan work through their individual demons to rediscover their love for each other, or are the unexplainable wounds too deep to heal? (978-1-60282-943-5)

Hold Me Forever by D. Jackson Leigh. An investigation into illegal cloning in the quarter horse racing industry threatens to destroy the growing attraction between Georgia debutante Mae St. John and Louisiana horse trainer Whit Casey. (978-1-60282-944-2)

Trusting Tomorrow by PJ Trebelhorn. Funeral director Logan Swift thinks she's perfectly happy with her solitary life devoted to helping others cope with loss until Brooke Collier moves in next door to care for her elderly grandparents. (978-1-60282-891-9)

Forsaking All Others by Kathleen Knowles. What if what you think you want is the opposite of what makes you happy? (978-1-60282-892-6)

Exit Wounds by VK Powell. When Officer Loane Landry falls in love with ATF informant Abigail Mancuso, she realizes that nothing is as it seems—not the case, not her lover, not even the dead. (978-1-60282-893-3)

Dirty Power by Ashley Bartlett. Cooper's been through hell and back, and she's still broke and on the run. But at least she found the twins. They'll keep her alive. Right? (978-1-60282-896-4)

The Rarest Rose by I. Beacham. After a decade of living in her beloved house, Ele disturbs its past and finds her life being haunted by the presence of a ghost who will show her that true love never dies. (978-1-60282-884-1)

Code of Honor by Radclyffe. The face of terror is hard to recognize—especially when it's homegrown. The next book in the Honor series. (978-1-60282-885-8)

Does She Love You? by Rachel Spangler. When Annabelle and Davis find out they are both in a relationship with the same woman, it leaves them facing life-altering questions about trust, redemption, and the possibility of finding love in the wake of betrayal. (978-1-60282-886-5)

The Road to Her by KE Payne. Sparks fly when actress Holly Croft, star of UK soap Portobello Road, meets her new on-screen love interest, the enigmatic and sexy Elise Manford. (978-1-60282-887-2)

Shadows of Something Real by Sophia Kell Hagin. Trying to escape flashbacks and nightmares, ex-POW Jamie Gwynmorgan stumbles into the heart of former Red Cross worker Adele Sabellius and uncovers a deadly conspiracy against everything and everyone she loves. (978-1-60282-889-6)

Date with Destiny by Mason Dixon. When sophisticated bank executive Rashida Ivey meets unemployed blue collar worker Destiny Jackson, will her life ever be the same? (978-1-60282-878-0)

The Devil's Orchard by Ali Vali. Cain and Emma plan a wedding before the birth of their third child while Juan Luis is still lurking, and as Cain plans for his death, an unexpected visitor arrives and challenges her belief in her father, Dalton Casey. (978-1-60282-879-7)